D1107184

OMNI SOCIETY

THE BEST OF OMNI SCIENCE FICTION

Cover painting by Pierre Lacombe

CONTENTS	PAGE
FOUND! fiction by Isaac Asimov, illustration by H. R. Giger	4
ROBOTS pictorial by Harry Harrison	10
COUNT THE CLOCK THAT TELLS THE TIME fiction by Harlan Ellison, illustration by Mati Klarwein	20
INNER DOMAINS pictorial by Frank Armitage and Paul Peck, text by Kathleen Stein	28
BODY GAME fiction by Robert Sheckley, illustration by Samuel Bak	34
UNACCOMPANIED SONATA fiction by Orson Scott Card, illustration by Evelyn Taylor	38
MAGNIFICATIONS pictorial by David Scharf, text by Scot Morris	46
ICEBACK INVASION fiction by Hayford Peirce, illustration by Evelyn Taylor	52
VISIONS OF THE COSMOS pictorial by Andrei Sokolov, text by F. C. Durant III	60
NO FUTURE IN IT fiction by Joe Haldeman, illustration by Gottfried Helnwein	68
GALATEA GALANTE fiction by Alfred Bester, illustration by H. R. Giger	72
ALIEN LANDSCAPES pictorial by Les Edwards, John Harris, Terry Oakes, and Tony Roberts	87
KINSMAN fiction by Ben Bova, illustration by John Schoenherr	94
SPACE CITIES pictorial by Harry Harrison	102
HALFJACK fiction by Roger Zelazny, illustration by Michel Henricot	110
SANDKINGS fiction by George R. R. Martin, illustration by Ernst Fuchs	114
PLANET STORY pictorial by Jim Burns and Harry Harrison	130
ARTHUR C. CLARKE interview and illustration by Malcolm S. Kirk	138

 From *Omni* magazine (Bob Guccione, editor, publisher, and design director; Kathy Keeton, associate publisher), 909 Third Avenue, New York, N.Y. 10022. Published simultaneously in the United States of America and in Canada.

THE GREAT EXPERIMENT. It is difficult to understand, now that *Omni* magazine is such an obvious success, how great a risk Bob Guccione took when he decided to launch "the magazine of the future."

No one had ever dared to produce a magazine that blended factual science, science fiction, fantasy, and sophisticated graphics into a single handsome package of extremely high quality—and high cost.

Publishing "experts" predicted that the magazine would never get off the ground. It would contain *science fiction*! Who would read that stuff? The only people who read science fiction then were tiny groups of fanatics who never lifted their noses up from their digest-sized magazines and paperback books. They preferred this literary isolation.

Even within the science-fiction community itself, considerable doubt was expressed about an "outsider" bringing out such a magazine, someone who wasn't intimately connected with science fiction from childhood.

I had a deeper worry. *Omni* immediately captured the attention of millions of readers. Science fiction was no longer confined to digest-sized magazines and a relatively small and "in group" readership. As *Omni*'s fiction editor, I wondered whether the science-fiction writers would come through for *Omni*. Could they write stories that would entertain those readers who had never read science fiction before?

Take a look!

In just the first twelve issues of *Omni*, science-fiction writers from Asimov to Zelazny came through with memorable, exciting stories. This anthology presents the cream of the first years crop: ten fine new stories by such Old Pros as Harlan Ellison and Robert Sheckley as well as such newer stars as George R. R. Martin and Orson Scott Card.

And in keeping with *Omni*'s breadth of subject material, we include in this volume some of the pictorials that, for the first time, opened up the visual side of science fiction to your future-seeking eyes. We offer an interview with Arthur C. Clarke, perhaps the best-known and most respected science-fiction writer in the world.

The great experiment that is *Omni* has proved to be a stunning success. Turn the page and learn why.

—BEN BOVA

FOUND!

Thousands of lives were jeopardized by Computer-Two's malfunction . . . so we had to go aloft and set things straight

BY ISAAC ASIMOV

Computer - Two, like the other three that chased each other's tails in orbit round the Earth, was much larger than it had to be.

It might have been one-tenth its diameter and still contained all the volume it needed to store the accumulated and accumulating data to control all space flight.

They [illegible]eeded the extra space, however, so tha[illegible]oe and I could get inside, if we had to. And we had to.

Computer-Two was perfectly capable of taking care of itself. Ordinarily, that is. It was redundant. It worked everything out three times in parallel and all three programs had to mesh perfectly; all three answers had to match. If they did not, the answer was delayed for nano-seconds while Computer-Two checked itself, found the malfunctioning part and replaced it.

There was no sure way in which ordinary people would know how many times it ca[illegible] itself. Perhaps never. Perhaps twice a day. Only Computer-Central could measure the time-delay induced by error and only Computer-Central knew how many of the component spares had been used as replacements. And Computer-Central never talked about it. The only good public image is perfection.

And it's *been* perfection. Until now, there was never any call for Joe and me.

We're the troubleshooters. We go up there when something really goes wrong; when Computer-Two or one of the others can't correct itself. It's never happened in the five years we've been on the job. It did happen now and again in the early days, but that was before our time.

We keep in practice. Don't get me wrong. There isn't a computer made that Joe and I can't diagnose. Show us the error and we'll s[illegible] the malfunction. Or Joe will, anyw[illegible]ot the kind who sings one's own [illegible] record speaks for itself.

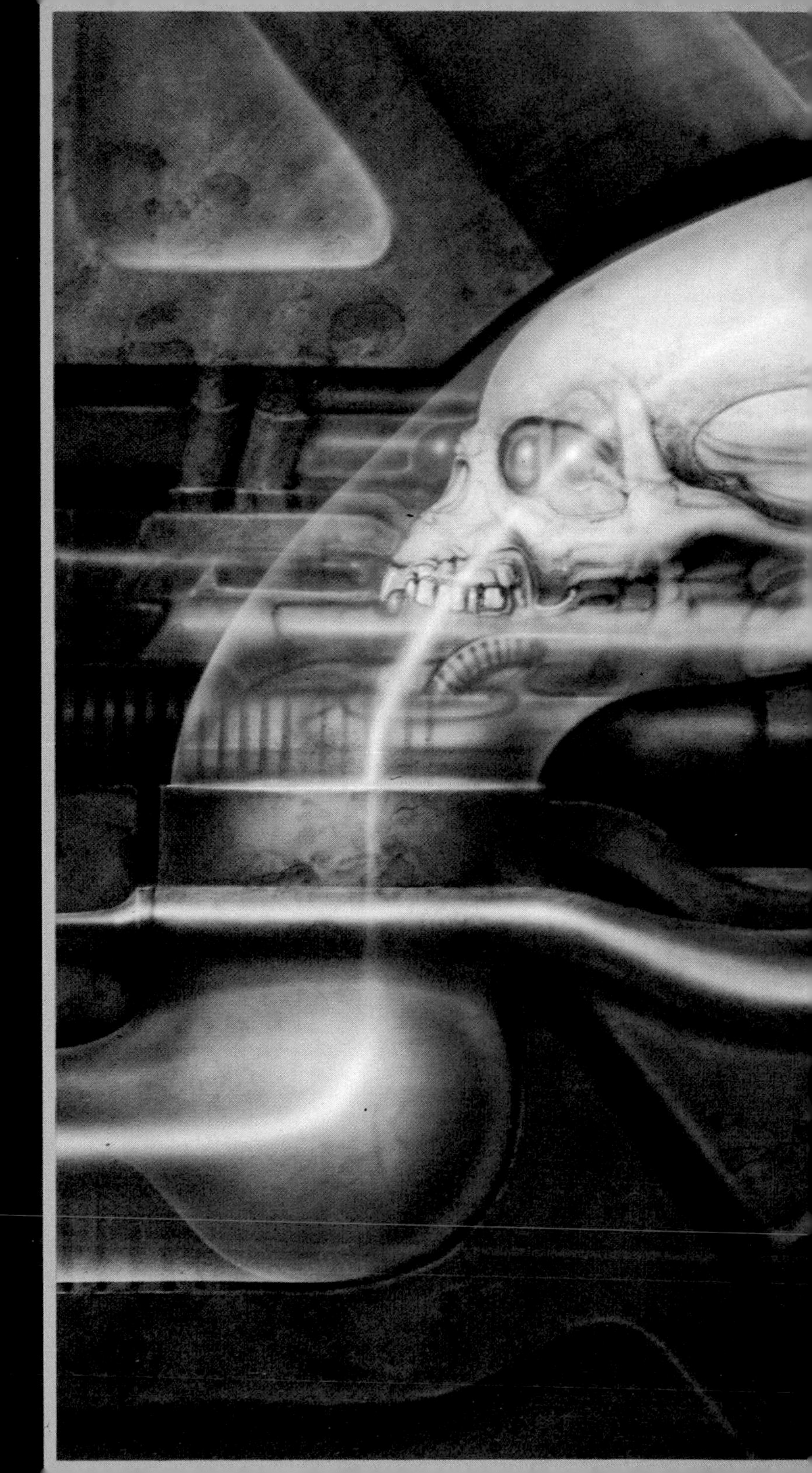

Painting By H.R. Giger

Anyway, this time, neither of us could make the diagnosis.

The first thing that happened was that Computer-Two lost internal pressure. That's not unprecedented, and it's certainly not fatal. Computer-Two can work in a vacuum after all. An internal atmosphere was established in the old days when it was expected there would be a steady flow of repairmen fiddling with it. And it's been kept up out of tradition. Who told you scientists aren't chained by tradition? In their spare time from being scientists, they're human, too.

From the rate of pressure loss, it was deduced that a gravel-sized meteoroid had hit Computer-Two. Its exact radius, mass, and energy were reported by Computer-Two itself, using that rate of pressure loss, and a few other irregularities, as data.

The second thing that happened was the break was not sealed and the atmosphere was not regenerated. After that came errors, and they called us in.

It made no sense. Joe let a look of pain cross his homely face and said, "There must be a dozen things out of whack."

Someone at Computer-Central said, "The hunk of gravel ricocheted very likely."

Joe said, "With that energy of entry, it would have passed right through the other side. No ricochets. Besides even with ricochets, I figure it would have had to take some very unlikely strikes."

"Well, then, what do we do?"

Joe looked uncomfortable. I think it was at this point he realized what was coming. He had made it sound peculiar enough to require the troubleshooters on the spot—and Joe had never been up in space. If he had told me once that his chief reason for taking the job was because it meant he would never have to go up in space, he had told it to me 2^x times, with x a pretty high number.

So I said it for him. "We'll have to go up."

Joe's only way out would have been to say he didn't think he could handle the job, and I watched his pride slowly come out ahead of his cowardice. Not by much, you understand—by a nose, let's say.

To those of you who haven't been on a spaceship in the last fifteen years—and I suppose Joe can't be the only one—let me emphasize that initial acceleration is the only troublesome thing. You can't get away from it, of course.

After that it's nothing, unless you want to count possible boredom. You're just a spectator. The whole thing is automated and computerized. The old romantic days of space pilots are gone totally. I imagine they'll return briefly when our space settlements make the shift to the asteroid belt as they constantly threaten to do—but then only until additional computers are placed in orbit to set up the necessary additional capacity.

Joe held his breath through acceleration, or at least he seemed to. (I must admit, I wasn't very comfortable myself. It was only my third trip. I've taken a couple of vacations on Settlement-Rho with my husband, but I'm not exactly a seasoned hand.) After that he was relieved for a while, but only for a while. He got despondent.

"I hope this thing knows where it's going," he said, pettishly.

I extended my arms forward, palms up, and felt the rest of me sway backward a bit in the zero-gravity field. "You," I said, "are a computer specialist. Don't you *know* it knows?"

"Sure, but Computer-Two is off."

"We're not hooked into Computer-Two," I said. "There are three others. And even if only one were left functional, it could handle all the spaceflights undertaken on an average day."

"All four might go off. If Computer-Two is wrong, what's to stop the rest?"

"Then we'll run this thing manually."

"You'll do it, I suppose. You know how—I think not?"

"So they'll talk me in."

"For the love of Eniac," he groaned.

There was no problem, actually. We moved out to Computer-Two as smooth as vacuum, and less than two days after takeoff we were placed into a parking orbit not ten meters behind it.

What was not so smooth was that, about twenty hours out, we got the news from Earth that Computer-Three was losing internal pressure. Whatever had hit Computer-Two was going to get the rest, and when all four were out, spaceflight would grind to a halt. It could be reorganized on a manual basis, surely, but that would take months at a minimum, possibly years, and there would be serious economic dislocation on Earth. Worse yet, several thousand people now out in space would surely die.

It wouldn't bear thinking of, and neither Joe nor I talked about it, but it didn't make Joe's disposition sweeter and, let's face it, it didn't make me any happier.

Earth hung more than two hundred thousand kilometers below us, but Joe wasn't bothered by that. He was concentrating on his tether and checking the cartridge in his reaction gun. He wanted to make sure he could get to Computer-Two and back again.

You'd be surprised—if you've never tried it—how you can get your space legs if you absolutely have to. I wouldn't say there was nothing to it, and we did waste half the fuel we used, but we finally reached Computer-Two. We hardly made any bump at all when we struck Computer-Two. (You hear it, of course, even in vacuum, because the vibration travels through the metalloid fabric of your spacesuit—but there was hardly any bump, just a whisper.)

Of course, our contact and the addition of our momentum altered the orbit of Computer-Two slightly, but tiny expendi-

"Now don't say anything that will ruin my meal."

tures of fuel compensated for that, and we didn't have to worry about it. Computer-Two took care of it, for nothing had gone wrong with it, as far as we could tell, that affected any of its external workings.

We went over the outside first, naturally. The chances were pretty overwhelming that a small piece of gravel had whizzed through Computer-Two and left an unmistakable hole. Two of them, in all probability, one going in and one coming out.

The chances of that happening are one in two million on any given day—even money that it will happen at least once in six thousand years. It's not likely, but it can, you know. The chances are one in not more than ten billion that, on any one day, it will be struck by a meteoroid large enough to demolish it.

I didn't mention that because Joe might realize that we were exposed to similar odds ourselves. In fact, any given strike on us would do far more damage to our soft and tender bodies than to the stoical and much-enduring machinery of the computer, and I didn't want Joe more nervous than he was.

The thing is, though, it wasn't a meteoroid.

"What's this?" said Joe, finally.

It was a small cylinder stuck to the outer wall of Computer-Two, the first abnormality we had found in its outward appearance. It was about half a centimeter in diameter and perhaps six centimeters long. Just about cigarette-size for any of you who've been caught up in the antique fad of smoking.

We brought out our small flashlights.

I said, "That's not one of the external components."

"It sure isn't," muttered Joe.

There was a faint spiral marking running round the cylinder from one end to the other. Nothing else. For the rest, it was clearly metal, but of an odd, grainy texture—at least to the eye.

Joe said, "It's not tight."

He touched it gently with a fat and gauntleted finger, and it gave. Where it had made contact with the surface of Computer-Two it lifted, and our flashes shone down on a visible gap.

"There's the reason gas pressure inside declined to zero," I said.

Joe grunted. He pushed a little harder and the cylinder popped away and began to drift. We managed to snare it after a little trouble. Left behind was a perfectly round hole in the skin of Computer-Two, half a centimeter across.

Joe said, "This thing, whatever it is, isn't much more than foil."

It gave easily under his fingers, thin but springy. A little extra pressure and it dented. He put it inside his pouch, which he snapped shut, and said, "Go over the outside and see if there are any other items like that on it. I'll go inside."

It didn't take me very long. Then I went in. "It's clean," I said. "That's the only thing there is. The only hole."

"One is enough," said Joe, gloomily. He looked at the smooth aluminum of the wall, and, in the light of the flash, the perfect circle of black was beautifully evident.

It wasn't difficult to place a seal over the hole. It was a little more difficult to reconstitute the atmosphere. Computer-Two's reserve gas-forming supplies were low and the controls required manual adjustment. The solar generator was limping, but we managed to get the lights on.

Eventually we removed our gauntlets and helmet, but Joe carefully placed the gauntlets inside his helmet and secured them both to one of his suit loops.

"I want these handy if the air pressure begins to drop," he said, sourly.

So I did the same.

There was a mark on the wall just next to the hole. I had noted it in the light of my flash when I was adjusting the seal. When the lights came on, it was obvious.

"You notice that, Joe?" I said.

"I notice."

There was a slight, narrow depression in the wall, not very noticeable at all, but there beyond a doubt if you ran your finger over it. It could be noticed for nearly a meter. It was as if someone had scooped out a very shallow sampling of the metal so that the surface was distinctly less smooth than elsewhere.

I said, "We'd better call Computer-Central downstairs."

"If you mean back on Earth, say so," said Joe. "I hate the phony space-talk. In fact, I hate everything about space. That's why I took an Earthside job—I mean a job on Earth—or what was supposed to be one."

I said patiently, "We'd better call Computer-Central back on Earth."

"What for?"

"To tell them we've found the trouble."

"Oh? What did we find?"

"The hole. Remember?"

"Oddly enough, I do. And what caused the hole? It wasn't a meteoroid. I never saw one that would leave a perfectly circular hole with no signs of buckling or melting. And I never saw one that left a cylinder behind." He took the cylinder out of his suit pocket and smoothed the dent out of its thin metal, thoughtfully. "Well, what caused the hole?"

I didn't hesitate. I said, "I don't know."

"If we report to Computer-Central, they'll ask the question and we'll say we don't know, and what will we have gained? Except hassle?"

"They'll call us, Joe, if we don't call them."

"Sure. And we won't answer, will we?"

"They'll assume something killed us, Joe, and they'll send up a relief party."

"You know Computer-Central. It will take them two days to decide on that. We'll have something before then, and once we have something, we'll call them."

The internal structure of Computer-Two was not *really* designed for human occupancy. What was foreseen was the occasional and temporary presence of troubleshooters. That meant there needed to be room for maneuvering, and there were tools and supplies.

There weren't any armchairs, though. For that matter, there was no gravitational field, either, or any centrifugal imitation of one.

We both floated in midair, drifting slowly this way or that. Occasionally one of us touched the wall and gently rebounded. Or else part of one of us overlapped part of the other.

"Keep your foot out of my mouth," said Joe, and he pushed it away violently. It was a mistake because we both began to turn. Of course, that's not how it looked to us. To us, it was the interior of Computer-Two that was turning, which was most unpleasant, and it took us a while to get relatively motionless again.

We had the theory perfectly worked out in our planetside training, but we were short on practice. A lot short.

By the time we had steadied ourselves, I felt unpleasantly nauseated. You can call it nausea, or astronausea, or space sickness, but whatever you call it, it's the heaves, and it's worse in space than anywhere else, because there's nothing to pull the stuff down. It floats around in a cloud of globules, and you don't want to be floating around with it. So I held it back; so did Joe.

I said, "Joe, it's clearly the computer that's at fault. Let's get at its insides." Anything to get my mind off *my* insides and let them quiet down. Besides, things weren't moving fast enough. I kept thinking of Computer-Three on its way down the tube; maybe Computer-One and Four by now, too; and thousands of people in space with their lives hanging on what we did.

Joe looked a little greenish, too, but he said, "First I've got to think. Something got in. It wasn't a meteoroid, because whatever it was chewed a neat hole out of the hull. It wasn't cut out, because I didn't find a circle of metal anywhere inside. Did you?"

"No. But I hadn't thought to look."

"*I* looked, and it's nowhere in here."

"It may have fallen outside."

"With the cylinder covering the hole till I pulled it away? A likely thing. Did you see anything come flying out?"

"No."

Joe said, "We may still find it in here, of course, but I doubt it. It was somehow dissolved and something got in."

"What something? Whose is it?"

Joe's grin was remarkably ill-natured. "Why do you bother asking questions to which there are no answers? If this was last century, I'd say the Russians had somehow stuck that device onto the outside of Computer-Two—no offense. If it was last century, you'd say it was the Americans."

I decided to be offended. I said, coldly, "We're trying to say something that makes sense *this* century, Iosif," giving it an exaggerated Russian pronunciation.

"We'll have to assume some dissident group."

"If so," I said, "we'll have to assume one with a capacity for spaceflight and with the ability to come up with an unusual device."

Joe said, "Spaceflight presents no difficulties, if you can tap into the orbiting computers illegally—which has been done. As for the cylinder, that may make more sense when it is analyzed back on Earth—downstairs, as you space buffs would say."

"It doesn't make sense," I said. "Where's the point in trying to disable Computer-Two?"

"As part of a program to cripple space-flight."

"Then everyone suffers. The dissidents, too."

"But it get's everyone's attention, doesn't it, and suddenly the cause of whatever-it-is makes news. Or the plan is to just knock out Computer-Two and then threaten to knock out the three others. No real damage, but lots of potential, and lots of publicity."

He was studying all parts of the interior closely, edging over it square centimeter by square centimeter. "I *might* suppose the thing was of nonhuman origin."

"Don't be silly."

"You want me to make the case? The cylinder made contact, after which something inside ate away a circle of metal and entered Computer-Two. It crawled over the inside wall, eating away a thin layer of metal for some reason. Does that sound like anything of human construction?"

"Not that I know of, but I don't know everything. Even you don't know everything."

Joe ignored that. "So the question is, how did it—whatever it is—get into the computer, which is, after all, reasonably well sealed. It did so quickly, since it knocked out the resealing and air-regeneration capacities almost at once."

"Is *that* what you're looking for?" I said, pointing.

He tried to stop too quickly and somersaulted backward, crying, "That's it!"

In his excitement, he was thrashing his arms and legs, which got him nowhere, of course. I grabbed him, and for a while we were both trying to exert pushes in uncoordinated directions, which got us nowhere either. Joe called me a few names, but I called him some back and there I had the advantage. I understand English perfectly, better than he does in fact; but his knowledge of Russian is—well, *fragmentary* would be a kind way of putting it. Bad language in an ununderstood language always sounds very dramatic.

"Here it is," he said when we finally had sorted ourselves out.

Where the computer shielding met the wall, a small circular hole appeared when Joe brushed aside a small cylinder. It was just like the one on the outer hull, but it seemed even thinner. In fact, it seemed to disintegrate when Joe touched it.

"We'd better get into the computer," said Joe.

The computer was a shambles.

Not obviously. I don't mean to say it was like a beam of wood that had been riddled by termites.

In fact, if you looked at the computer casually, you might swear it was intact.

Look closely, though, and some of the chips would be gone. The more closely you looked, the more you realized were gone. Worse, the stores that Computer-Two used in self-repair had dwindled to almost nothing. We kept looking and would discover something else missing.

Joe took the cylinder out of his pouch again and turned it end for end. He said, "I suspect it's after high-grade silicon in particular. I can't say for sure, of course, but my guess is that the sides are mostly aluminum and the flat end is mostly silicon."

I said, "Do you mean the thing is a solar battery?"

"Part of it is. That's how it gets its energy in space—energy to get to Computer-Two, energy to eat a hole into it, energy to—to—I don't know how else to put it. Energy to stay alive."

"You call it alive?"

"Why not? Look, Computer-Two can repair itself. It can reject faulty bits of equipment and replace them with working ones, but it needs a supply of spares to work with. Given enough spares of all kinds, it could build a computer just like itself, when properly programmed, but it needs the supply; so we don't think of it as alive. This object that entered Computer-Two is apparently collecting its own supplies. That's suspiciously lifelike."

"What you're saying," I said, "is that we have here a microcomputer advanced enough to be considered alive."

"I don't honestly know what I'm saying."

"Who on Earth could make such a thing?"

"Who *on Earth*?"

I made the next discovery. It looked like a stubby pen drifting through the air. I just caught it out of the corner of my eye, and it registered as a pen.

In zero gravity, things will drift out of pockets and float off. There's no way of keeping anything in place unless it is physically confined. You expect pens and coins and anything else that finds an opening to drift wherever the air currents and inertia lead it.

So my mind registered "Pen," and I groped for it absently, and, of course, my fingers didn't close on it. Just reaching for something sets up an air current that pushes it away. You have to reach over and sneak behind it with one hand and then reach for it with the other. Picking up any small object in midair is a two-handed operation.

I turned to look at the object and pay a little more attention to retrieval, then realized that my pen was safely in its pouch. I felt for it, and it was there.

"Did you lose a pen, Joe?" I called out.

"No."

"Anything like that? Key? Cigarette?"

"I don't smoke. You know that."

A stupid answer. "Anything?" I said in exasperation. "I'm seeing things here."

"No one ever said you were stable."

"Look, Joe. Over there. Over there."

He lunged for it. I could have told him it would do no good.

By now, though, our poking around in the computer seemed to have stirred things up. We were seeing them wherever we looked. They were floating in the air currents.

I stopped one at last. Or, rather, it stopped itself, for it was on the elbow of Joe's suit. I snatched it off and shouted.

Joe jumped in terror and nearly knocked it out of my hand.

I said, "Look!"

There was a shiny circle on Joe's suit, where I had taken the thing off. It had begun to eat its way through.

"Give it to me," said Joe. He took it gingerly and put it against the wall to hold it steady. Then he shelled it, gently lifting the paper-thin metal.

There was something inside that looked like a line of cigarette ash. It caught the light and glinted, though, like lightly woven metal.

There was a moistness about it, too. It wriggled slowly, one end seeming to seek blindly.

The end made contact with the wall and stuck. Joe's finger pushed it away. It seemed to require a small effort to do so. Joe rubbed his finger and thumb and said, "Feels oily."

The metal worm—I don't know what else to call it—seemed limp now after Joe had touched it. It didn't move again.

I was twisting and turning, trying to look at myself.

"Joe," I said, "for Heaven's sake, have I got one of them on me anywhere?"

"I don't see one," he said.

"Well, *look* at me. You've got to watch me, Joe, and I'll watch you. If our suits are wrecked, we might not be able to get back to the ship."

Joe said, "Keep moving, then."

It was a grisly feeling, being surrounded by things hungry to dissolve your suit wherever they could touch it. When any showed up, we tried to catch them and stay out of their way at the same time, which made things almost impossible. A rather long one drifted close to my leg, and I kicked at it, which was stupid, for if I had hit it, it might have stuck. As it was, the air current I set up brought it against the wall, where it stayed.

Joe reached hastily for it—too hastily. The rest of his body rebounded as he somersaulted, one booted foot striking the wall near the cylinder lightly. When he finally righted himself, it was still there.

"I didn't smash it, did I?"

"No, you didn't," I said. "You missed it by a decimeter. It won't get away."

I had a hand on either side of it. It was twice as long as the other cylinder had been. In fact, it was like two cylinders stuck together longways, with a constriction at the point of joining.

"Act of reproducing," said Joe as he peeled away the metal. This time what was inside was a line of dust. Two lines. One on either side of the constriction.

"It doesn't take much to kill them," said Joe. He relaxed visibly. "I think we're safe."

"They do seem alive," I said reluctantly.

"I think they seem more than that. They're viruses—or the equivalent."

"What are you talking about?"

Joe said, "Granted I'm a computer technologist and not a virologist, but it's my understanding that viruses on Earth, or 'downstairs' as you would say, consist of a nucleic acid molecule coated in a protein shell.

"When a virus invades a cell, it manages to dissolve a hole in the cell wall or membrane by the use of some appropriate enzyme and the nucleic acid slips inside, leaving the protein coat outside. Inside the cell it finds the material to make a new protein coat for itself. In fact, it manages to form replicas of itself and produces a new protein coat for each replica. Once it has stripped the cell of all it has, the cell dissolves, and in place of the one invading virus there are several hundred daughter viruses. Sound familiar?"

"Yes. Very familiar. It's what's happening here. But where did it come from, Joe?"

"Not from Earth, obviously, or any Earth settlement. From somewhere else, I suppose. They drift through space till they find something appropriate in which they can multiply. They look for sizable objects ready-made of metal. I don't imagine they can smelt ores."

"But large metal objects with pure silicon components and a few other succulent matters like that are the products of intelligent life only," I said.

"Right," said Joe, "which means we have the best evidence yet that intelligent life is common in the universe, since objects like the one we're on must be quite common or it couldn't support these viruses. And it means that intelligent life is old, too, perhaps ten billion years old—long enough for a kind of metal evolution forming a metal/silicon/oil life as we have formed a nucleic/protein/water life. Time to evolve a parasite on space-age artifacts."

I said, "You make it sound that every time some intelligent life form develops a space culture, it is subjected before long to parasitic infestation."

"Right. And it must be controlled. Fortunately, these things are easy to kill, especially now when they're forming. Later on, when ready to burrow out of Computer-Two, I suppose they will grow, thicken their shells, stabilize their interior, and prepare, as the equivalent of spores, to drift a million years before they find another home. They might not be so easy to kill then."

"How are you going to kill them?"

"I already have. I just touched that first one when it instinctively sought out metal to begin manufacturing a new shell after I had broken open the first one, and that touch finished it. I didn't touch the second, but I kicked the wall near it, and the sound vibration in the metal shook its interior apart into metal dust. So they can't get us—or any more of the computer—if we just shake them apart, now!"

He didn't have to explain further—or as much. He put on his gauntlets slowly and banged at the wall with one. It pushed him away, and he kicked at the wall where he next approached it.

"You do the same!" he shouted.

I tried to, and for a while we both kept at it. You don't know how hard it is to hit a wall at zero gravity—at least on purpose—and do it hard enough to make it clang. We missed as often as not or just struck a glancing blow that sent us whirling but made virtually no sound. We were panting with effort and aggravation in no time.

But we had acclimated ourselves. We kept it up and eventually gathered up more of the viruses. There was nothing inside but dust in every case. They were clearly adapted to empty, automated space objects, which, like modern computers, were vibration-free. That's what made it possible, I suppose, to build up the exceedingly rickety-complex metallic structures that possessed sufficient instability to produce the properties of simple life.

I said, "Do you think we got them all?"

"How can I say? If there's one left, it will cannibalize the others for metal supplies and start all over. Let's bang around some more."

We did until we were sufficiently worn out not to care whether one was still left alive.

"Of course," I said, panting, "the Planetary Association for the Advancement of Science isn't going to be pleased with our killing them all."

Joe's suggestion as to what the PAAS could do with itself was forceful, but impractical. He said, "Look, our mission is to save Computer-Two, a few thousand lives, and, as it turns out, our own lives, too. Now they can decide whether to renovate this computer or rebuild it from scratch. It's their baby.

"The PAAS can get what they can out of these dead objects, and that should be something. If they want live ones, I suspect they'll find them floating about in these regions."

I said, "All right. My suggestion is we tell Computer-Central we're going to jerry-rig this computer and get it doing some work anyway, and we'll stay till a relief is sent up for main repairs or whatever in order to prevent any reinfestation. Meanwhile they'd better get to each of the other computers and set up a system that can set it to vibrating strongly as soon as the internal atmosphere shows a pressure drop."

"Simple enough," said Joe, sardonically.

"It's lucky we found them when we did."

"Wait a while," said Joe, and the look in his eye was one of deep trouble. We didn't find them. *They* found *us*. If metal life has developed, do you suppose it's likely that this is the only form it takes?

"What if such life forms communicate somehow and, across the vastness of space, others are now converging on us for the picking. Other species, too—all of them after the lush new fodder of an as-yet-untouched space culture. *Other* species! Some that are sturdy enough to withstand vibration. Some that are large enough to be more versatile in their reactions to danger. Some that are equipped to invade our settlements in orbit. Some, for the sake of Univac, that may be able to invade the earth for the metals of its cities.

"What I'm going to report, what I must report, is that we've been *found*!" ∞

One danger that haunts science fiction is the looming form of threatening robots: The earliest of these were constructed of flesh and bone and would now be called androids: Frankenstein's monster (1817); and Capek's R.U.R. (1923), Rossum's Universal Robots, the source of the term. The idea that if you built it it couldn't be good carries on through C.C. Campbell's *The Avatar* (1935), in which the perfect artificial man becomes dictator of the world and has to be destroyed.

It was only with the construction of metal robots—obedient machines—that mechanical men began operating on the side of justice. In the early pulp magazine, Frank Reade's Steam Man fought the Indians for the good guys, and Eando Binder's robot, built for peace to prove its worth to mankind, was smart enough to choose sides against the Nazis in *Adam Link Fights a War*. Edmond Hamilton's Captain Future could count upon the faithful robot Krag, as well as the faithful but not so nice

Excerpted from the book *Mechanismo* by Harry Harrison. By permission of Reed Books, a subsidiary of Addison House Publishers.

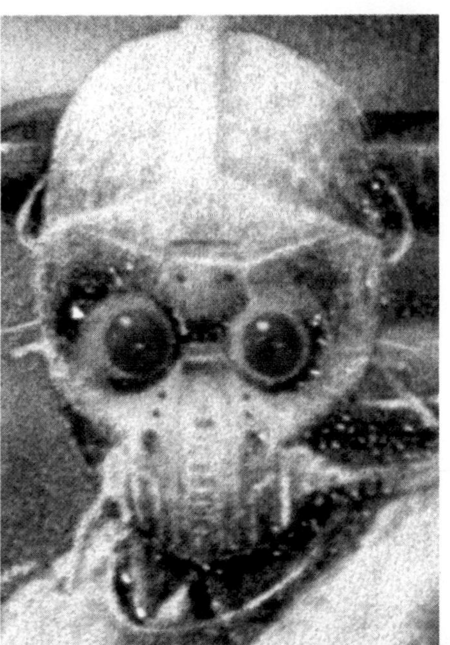

ROBOTS

BY HARRY HARRISON

A glittering gallery to celebrate those timeless workhorses of science fiction

android Lothar, to aid him at all times. A later development is the part man, part metal (or plastic) creature. This theme and the psychological effects of bionic engineering have been explored successfully in Budry's *Who* (1958) and more recently in the preposterous bionic man, woman, dog, hamster, etc., tv series. The authors of these stories never seem to realize that all mechani-

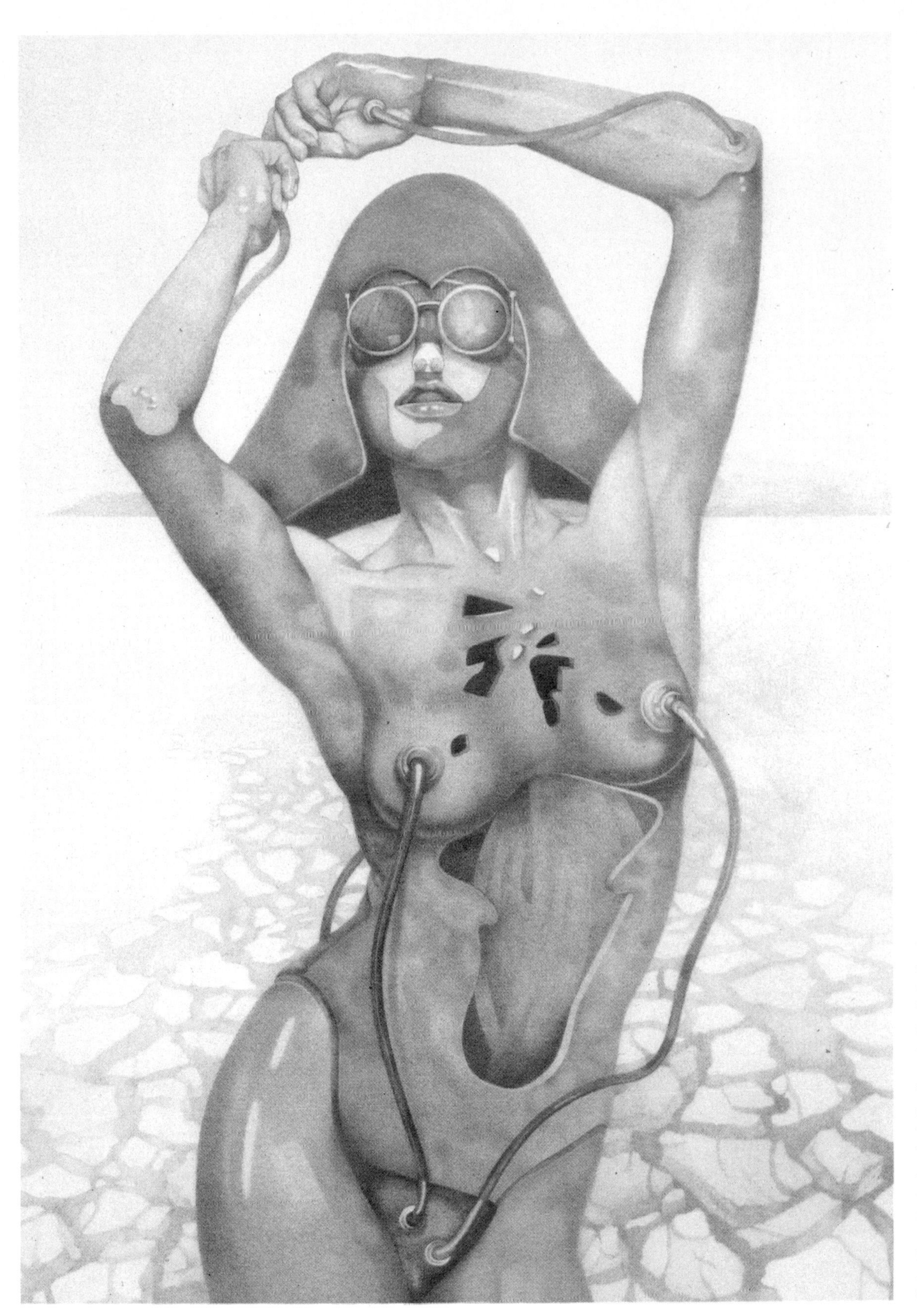

cal substitutes for human parts are far weaker than the originals; the bionic man needs a wheelchair—not a springboard to leap over buildings. We must slip far into the future to rationalize a superior technology that makes the creature work well, as in Saul Dunn's Mandroid, who is only 10 percent human, the rest being manufactured parts.
A touch of order entered robotic cir-

cles in 1940 with Asimov's *Robby* and *Liar*. The mechanical men now began to clank about radiating security, since they had the Laws of Robotics stamped into their positronic brains. Asimov gets full credit for these laws, and countless are the writers who have utilized them:

1. A robot may not injure a human being, or, through inaction, allow a human to come to harm.
2. A robot must obey the orders given it by human beings except where such orders

would conflict with the First Law.

3. A robot must protect its own existence as long as such protection does not conflict with the First or Second Law.

Once the robotic threat had been removed, the infinitely varied relationships of robot with man could be explored. Clifford Simak, in his *City* series, shows mankind evolving and leaving the earth to the robots

and highly evolved dogs. Jack Williamson's *With Folded Hands . . .* (1947) does discover a danger in robot control, but a benevolent one. To prevent men from being hurt, the robots are stunting all development of the human race. With all the robotic goodness around it was a pleasure to see Alfred Bester's *Fondly Fahrenheit*, about a slightly insane robot.

Having once assigned man's attribute to a machine, we must consider the relationship of this intelligent machine with man's mystical nature. Boucher's *The Quest for Saint Aquin* asked if it is possible to have a robot saint. Silverberg answered the question years later with *Good News from the Vatican*. If you can have a robot pope—then why not a saint?

Of course these are just the human-appearing robots, although there is no good reason at all to shape a robot in this manner, other than it looks nice and it is handy to have around the house. Real robots, the ones actually in use in industry today, look nothing at all like the classic clanker. The commonest are just collections of machine tools and mechanical manipulators.

SF also has nonhumanoid robots of this kind. The computer-controlled, fully automated spaceship has been with us for quite a while. Fully automated cities, usually so well designed that they keep operating after their inhabitants are gone, have had their day, and fully automated trains ran first in the pages of science fiction. At sea we have Bass's Godwhale, a sentient giant robot designed for harvesting plankton for undersea food processing plants. In Space—and at war again—are Saberhagen's Berserkers, super war machines, launched by alien nutters, whose job it is to zip about the galaxy destroying all forms of life. ∞

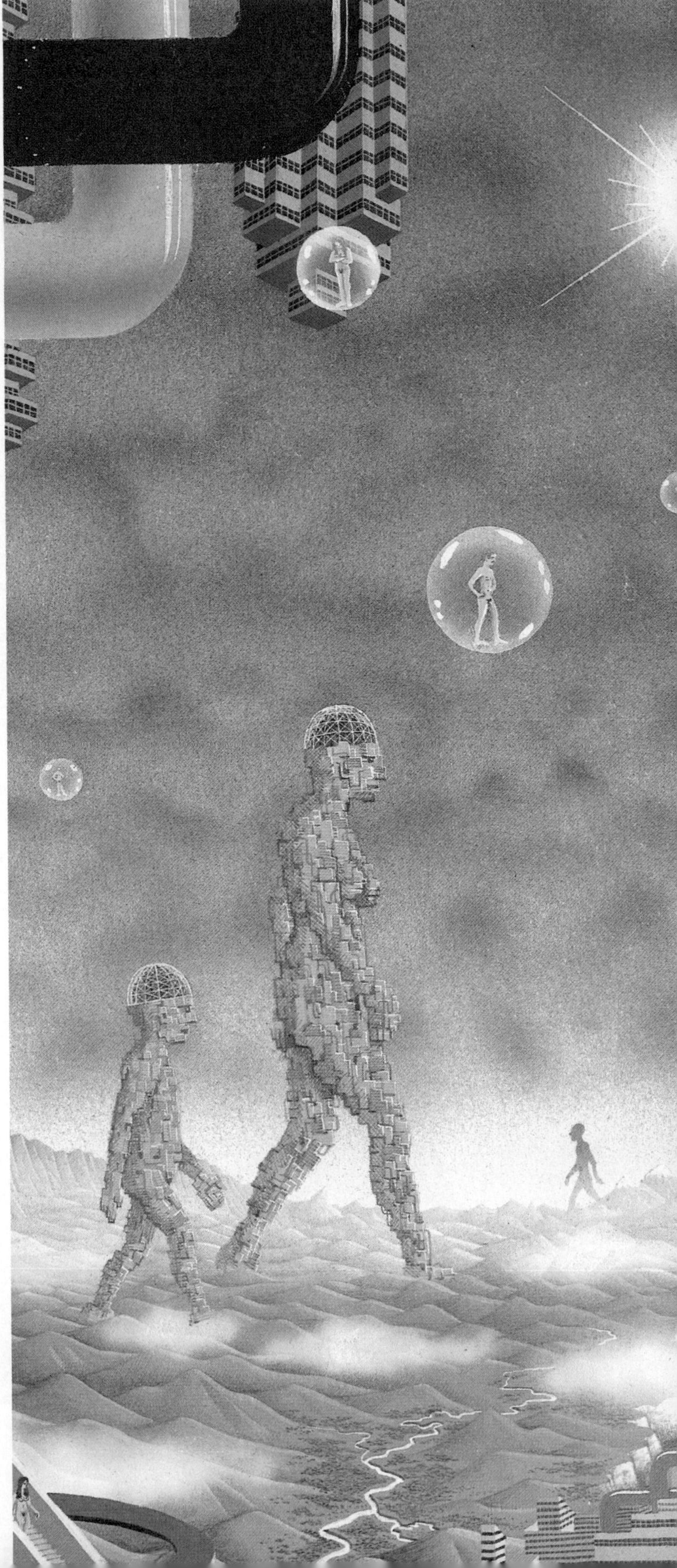

MW78

COUNT THE CLOCK THAT TELLS THE TIME

BY HARLAN ELLISON

When I do count the clock that tells the time,
And see the brave day sunk in hideous night;
When I behold the violet past prime,
And sable curls all silver'd o'er with white;
When lofty trees I see barren of leaves
Which erst from heat did canopy the herd,
And summer's green all girded up in sheaves
Borne on the bier with white and bristly beard;
Then of thy beauty do I question make,
That thou among the wastes of time must go . . .

William Shakespeare,
The XIIth Sonnet

Waking in the cool and cloudy absolute dead middle of a Saturday afternoon one day, Ian Ross felt lost and vaguely frightened. Lying there in his bed, he was disoriented, and it took him a moment to remember when it was and where he was. Where he was: in the bed where he had awakened every day of his 35-year-old life. When it was: the Saturday he had resolved to spend *doing* something. But as he lay there he realized he had come to life in the early hours just after dawn, it had looked as though it would rain, the sky seen through the high French windows, and he had turned over and gone back to sleep. Now the clock-radio on the bedside table told him it was the absolute dead middle of the afternoon; and the world outside his windows was cool and cloudy. "Where does the time go?" he said.

He was alone, as always: there was no one to hear him or to answer. So he continued lying there, wasting time, feeling vaguely frightened. As though something important were passing him by.

PAINTING BY MATI KLARWEIN

A fly buzzed him, circled, buzzed him again. It had been annoying him for some time. He tried to ignore the intruder and stared off across Loch Tummel to the amazing flesh tones of the October trees, preparing themselves for Winter's disingenuous attentions and the utter absence of tourism. The silver birches were already a blazing gold, the larches and ash trees still blending off from green to rust; in a few weeks the Norway spruces and the other conifers would darken until they seemed mere shadows against the slate sky.

Perthshire was most beautiful at this time of year. He had taken the time to learn to pronounce the names—Schiehallion, Killiecrankie, Pitlochry, Aberfeldy—and had come here to sit. The dream. The one he had always held: silent, close to him, unspoken, in his idle thoughts. The dream of going to Scotland. For what reason he could not say. But this was the place that had always called, and he had come.

For the first time in his life, Ian Ross had *done* something. Thirty-seven years old, rooted to a tiny apartment in Chicago, virtually friendless, working five days a week at a drafting table in a firm of industrial designers, watching television till sign-off, tidying the two and a half rooms till every picture hung from the walls in perfect true with the junctures of walls and ceiling, entering each checkbook notation in the little ledger with a fine-point ink pen, unable to remember what had happened last Thursday that made it different from last Wednesday, seeing himself reflected in the window of the cafeteria slowly eating the $2.95 Christmas Dinner Special, a solitary man, somehow never marking the change of the seasons save to understand only by his skin that it was warmer or colder, never tasting joy because he could never remember having been told what it was, reading books about *things* and *subject matter*, topics not people, because he knew so few people and *knew* none of them, drawing straight lines, feeling deserted but never knowing where to put his hands to relieve that feeling; a transient man, passing down the same streets every day and perceiving only dimly that there were streets *beyond* those streets, drinking water, and apple juice, and water, replying when he was addressed directly, looking around sometimes when he was addressed to see if it was, in fact, himself to whom the speaker was speaking, buying gray socks and white undershorts, staring out the windows of his apartment at the Chicago snow, staring for hours at the invisible sky, feeling the demon wind off Lake Michigan rattling the window glass in its frame and thinking this year he would reputty and this year failing to reputty, combing his hair as he always had, cooking his own meals, alone with the memories of his mother and father who had died within a year of each other and both from cancer, never having been able to speak more than a few awkward sentences to any woman but his mother . . . Ian Ross had lived his life like the dust that lay in a film across the unseen top of the tall wardrobe cabinet in his bedroom: colorless, unnoticed, inarticulate, neither giving nor taking.

Until one day he had said, "Where does the time go?" And in the months following those words he had come to realize he had not, in any remotely valuable manner, *lived* his life. He had wasted it. Months after the first words came, unbidden and tremulous, he admitted to himself that he had wasted his life.

He resolved to actualize at least the one dream. To go to Scotland. Perhaps to live. To rent or even buy a crofter's cottage on the edge of a moor or overlooking one of the lochs he had dreamed about. He had all the insurance money still put by; he hadn't touched a cent of it. And there, in that far, chill place in the north he would live . . . walking the hills with a dog by his side, smoking a pipe that trailed a fragrant pennant of blue-white smoke, hands thrust deep into the pockets of a fleece-lined jacket. He would *live* there. That was the dream.

And from King's Cross Station he had taken the 2130 sleeper to Edinburgh, and he had walked the Royal Mile and gazed in wonder at Edinburgh Castle high on the bluff overlooking that bountiful city, and finally he had rented a car and had driven north out the Queensferry Road, across the bridge that spanned the Firth of Forth, on up the A-90 till he reached Pitlochry. Then a left, a random left, but not so random that he did not know it would come out overlooking the Queens View, said to be the most beautiful view in the world, certainly in Scotland; and he had driven the twisting, narrow road till he was deep in the hills of Perth.

And there he had pulled off the road, gotten out of the car, leaving the door open, and walked away down the October hills to finally sit staring at the Loch, green and blue and silent as the mirror of his memory.

Where only the buzzing fly reminded him of the past.

He had been 35 when he said, "Where does the time go?" And he was 37 as he sat on the hill.

And it was there that the dream died.

He stared at the hills, at the valley that ran off to left and right, at the sparkling water of the Loch, and knew he had wasted his time again. He had resolved to *do* something; but he had done nothing. Again.

There was no place for him here.

He was out of phase with all around him. He was an alien object. A beer can thrown into the grass. A broken wall untended and falling back into the earth from which it had been wrenched stone by stone.

He felt lonely, starved, incapable of clenching his hands or clearing his throat. A ruin from another world, set down in foreign soil, drinking air that was not his to drink. There were no tears, no pains in his body, no deep and trembling sighs. In a moment, with a fly buzzing, the dream died for him. He had not been saved; had, in fact, come in an instant to understand that he had been a child to think it could ever change. What do you want to be when you grow up? Nothing. As I have always been nothing.

The sky began to bleach out.

The achingly beautiful golds and oranges and yellows began to drift toward sepia. The blue of the loch slid softly toward chalkiness, like an ineptly prepared painting left too long in direct sunlight. The sounds of birds and forest creatures and insects faded, the gain turned down slowly. The sun gradually cooled for Ian Ross. The sky began to bleach out toward a gray-white newsprint colorlessness. The fly was gone. It was cold now; very cold now.

Shadows began to superimpose themselves over the dusty mezzotint of the bloodless day:

A city of towers and minarets, as seen through shallow, disturbed water; a mountain range of glaciers with snow untracked and endless as an ocean; an ocean, with massive, serpent-necked creatures gliding through the jade deeps; a parade of ragged children bearing crosses hewn from tree branches; a great walled fortress in the middle of a parched wasteland, the yellow earth split like strokes of lightning all around the structure; a motorway with hundreds of cars speeding past so quickly they seemed to be stroboscopic lines of colored light; a battlefield with men in flowing robes and riding great-chested stallions, the sunlight dancing off curved swords and helmets; a tornado careening through a small town of slatback stores and houses, lifting entire buildings from their foundations and flinging them into the sky; a river of lava burst through a fissure in the ground and boiled toward a shadowy indication of an amusement park, with throngs of holiday tourists moving in clots from one attraction to another.

Ian Ross sat, frozen, on the hillside. The world was dying around him. No . . . it was vanishing, fading out, dematerializing. As if all the sand had run out of the hourglass around him; as if he were the only permanent, fixed, and immutable object in a metamorphosing universe suddenly cut loose from its time-anchor.

The world faded out around Ian Ross: the shadows boiled and seethed and slithered past him, caught in a cyclonic wind-tunnel and swept away past him, leaving him in darkness.

He sat now, still, quiet, too isolated to be frightened.

He thought perhaps clouds had covered the sun.

There was no sun.

He thought perhaps it had been an eclipse, that his deep concentration of his hopeless state had kept him from noticing.

There was no sun.

No sky. The ground beneath him was gone. He sat, merely sat, but on nothing, surrounded by nothing, seeing and feeling nothing save a vague chill. It was cold now, very cold now.

After a long time he decided to stand and *did* stand: there was nothing beneath or above him. He stood in darkness.

He could remember everything that had ever happened to him in his life. Every moment of it, with absolute clarity. It was something he had never experienced before. His memory had been no better or worse than anyone else's, but he had forgotten all the details, many years in which nothing had happened, during which he had wasted time—almost as a mute witness at the dull rendition of his life.

> *"He was out of phase with all around him . . . an alien object. A ruin from another world . . . drinking air that was not his to drink. . . . In a moment, with a fly buzzing, the dream died for him."*

But now, as he walked through the limbo that was all he had been left of the world, he recalled everything perfectly. The look of terror on his mother's face when he had sliced through the tendons of his left hand with the lid from the tin can of pink lemonade: he had been four years old. The feel of his new Thom McAn shoes that had always been too tight from the moment they had been bought but that he had been forced to wear to school every day, even though they rubbed him raw at the back of his heels: he had been seven years old. The Four Freshmen standing and singing for the graduation dance. He had been alone. He had bought one ticket to support the school event. He had been 16. The taste of egg roll at Choy's, the first time. He had been 24. The woman he had met at the library, in the section where they kept the books on animals. She had used a white lace handkerchief to dry her temples. It had smelled of perfume. He had been 30. He remembered all the sharp edges of every moment from his past. It was remarkable. In this nowhere.

And he walked through gray spaces, with the shadows of other times and other places swirling past. The sound of rushing wind, as though the emptiness through which he moved was being constantly filled and emptied, endlessly, without measure or substance.

Had he known what emotions to call on for release, he would have done so. But he was numb in his skin. Not merely chilled, as this empty place was chilled, but somehow inured to feeling from the edge of his perceptions to the center of his soul. Sharp, clear, drawn back from the absolute past, he remembered a day when he had been 11, when his mother had suggested that for his birthday they make a small party to which he would invite a few friends. And so (he remembered with diamond-bright perfection), he had invited six boys and girls. They had never come. He sat alone in the house that Saturday, all his comic books laid out in case the cake and party favors and pin-the-tail-on-the-donkey did not hold their attention sufficiently. Never came. It grew dark. He sat alone, with his mother occasionally walking through the living room to make some consoling remark. But he was alone, and he knew there was only one reason for it: they had all forgotten. It was simply that he was a waste of time for those actually living their lives. Invisible, by token of being unimportant. A thing unnoticed: on a street, who notices the mailbox, the fire hydrant, the crosswalk lines? He was an invisible, useless thing.

He had never permitted another party to be thrown for him.

He remembered that Saturday now. And found the emotion, 26 years late, to react to this terrible vanishment of the world. He began to tremble uncontrollably, and he sat down where there was nothing to sit down on, and he rubbed his hands together, feeling the tremors in his knuckles and the ends of his fingers. Then he felt the constriction in his throat, he turned his head this way and that, looking for a nameless exit from self-pity and loneliness; and then he cried. Lightly, softly, because he had no experience at it.

A crippled old woman came out of the gray mist of nowhere and stood watching him. His eyes were closed, or he would have seen her coming.

After a while, he snuffled, opened his eyes, and saw her standing in front of him. He stared at her. She was standing. At a level somewhat below him, as though the invisible ground of this nonexistant place was on a lower plane than that on which he sat.

"That won't help much," she said. She wasn't surly, but neither was there much succor in her tone.

He looked at her and immediately stopped crying.

"Probably just got sucked in here," she said. It was not quite a question, though it had something of query in it. She knew and was going carefully.

He continued to look at her, hoping she

could tell him what had happened to him. And to her? She was here, too.

"Could be worse," she said, crossing her arms and shifting her weight off her twisted left leg. "I could've been a Saracen or a ribbon clerk or even one of those hairy pre-humans." He didn't respond. He didn't know what she was talking about. She smiled wryly, remembering. "First person I met was some kind of a retard, little boy about 15 or so. Must have spent what there'd been of his life in some padded cell or a hospital bed, something like that. He just sat there and stared at me, drooled a little, couldn't tell me a thing. I was scared out of my mind, ran around like a chicken with its head cut off. Wasn't till a long time after that before I met someone who spoke English."

He tried to speak and found his throat was dry. His voice came out in a croak. He swallowed and wet his lips. "Are there many other, uh, other people . . . we're not all alone . . . ?"

"Lots of others. Hundreds, thousands. God only knows; maybe whole countries full of people here. No animals, though. They don't waste it the way we do."

"Waste it? What?"

"Time, son. Precious, lovely time. That's all there is, just time. Sweet, flowing time. Animals don't know about time."

As she spoke, a slipping shadow of some wild scene whirled past and through them. It was a great city in flames. It seemed more substantial than the vagrant wisps of countryside or sea scenes that had been ribboning past them as they spoke. The wooden buildings and city towers seemed almost solid enough to crush anything in their path. Flames leaped toward the gray, dead-skin sky; enormous tongues of crackling flame that ate the city's gut and chewed the phantom image, leaving ash. (But even the dead ashes had more life than the grayness through which the vision swirled.)

Ian Ross ducked, frightened. Then it was gone.

"Don't worry about it, son," the old woman said. "Looked a lot like London during the Big Fire. First the Plague, then the Fire. I've seen its like before. Can't hurt you. None of it can hurt you."

He tried to stand, found himself still weak. "But what *is* it?"

She shrugged. "No one's ever been able to tell me for sure. Bet there's some around in here who can, though. One day I'll run into one of them. If I find out and we ever meet again I'll be sure to let you know. Bound to happen." But her face grew infinitely sad and there was desolation in her expression. "Maybe. Maybe we'll meet again. Never happens, but it might. Never saw that retarded boy again. But it might happen."

She started to walk away, hobbling awkwardly. Ian got to his feet with difficulty, but as quickly as he could. "Hey, wait! Where are you going? Please, lady, don't leave me here all alone. I'm scared to be here by myself."

She stopped and turned, tilting oddly on her bad leg. "Got to keep moving. Keep going, you know? If you stay in one place you don't get anywhere; there's a way out . . . you've just got to keep moving till you find it." She started again, saying, over her shoulder, "I guess I won't be seeing you again; I don't think it's likely."

He ran after her and grabbed her arm. She seemed very startled. As if no one had ever touched her in this place during all the time she had been here.

"Listen, you've got to tell me some things, whatever you know. I'm awfully scared, don't you understand? You have to have some understanding."

She looked at him carefully. "All right, as much as I can, then you'll let me go?"

He nodded.

"I don't know what happened to me . . . or to you. Did it all fade away and just disappear, and everything that was left was this, just this gray nothing?"

He nodded.

She sighed. "How old are you, son?"

"I'm 37. My name is Ian—"

She waved his name away with an impatient gesture. "That doesn't matter. I can see you don't know any better than I do. So I don't have the time to waste on you. You'll learn that, too. Just keep walking, just keep looking for a way out."

He made fists. "That doesn't tell me *anything*! What was that burning city, what are these shadows that go past all the time?" As if to mark his question a vagrant filmy phantom caravan of cassowary-like animals drifted through them.

She shrugged and sighed. "I think it's history. I'm not sure . . . I'm guessing, you understand. But I *think* it's all the bits and pieces of the past, going through on its way somewhere."

He waited. She shrugged again, and her silence indicated—with a kind of helpless appeal to be let go—that she could tell him nothing further.

He nodded resignedly. "All right. Thank you."

She turned with her bad leg trembling; she had stood with her weight on it for too long. And she started to walk off into the gray limbo. When she was almost out of sight, he found himself able to speak again, and he said . . . too softly to reach her . . . "Good-bye, lady. Thank you."

He wondered how old she was. How long she had been here. If he would one time far from now be like her. If it was all over and if he would wander in shadows forever.

He wondered if people died here.

Before he met Catherine, a long time before he met her, he met the lunatic who told him where he was, what had happened to him, and why it had happened.

They saw each other standing on opposite sides of a particularly vivid phantom of the Battle of Waterloo. The battle raged past them, and through the clash and slaughter of Napoleon's and Wellington's forces they waved to each other.

When the sliding vision had rushed by, leaving emptiness between them, the lunatic rushed forward, clapping his hands as if preparing himself for a long, arduous, but pleasurable chore. He was of indeterminate age but clearly past his middle years. His hair was long and wild, he wore a pair of rimless antique spectacles, and his suit was turn-of-the-eighteenth-century. "Well, well, well," he called, across the narrowing space between them, "so good to see you, sir!"

Ian Ross was startled. In the timeless time he had wandered through this limbo, he had encountered coolies and Berbers and Thracian traders and silent Goths . . . an endless stream of hurrying humanity that would neither speak nor stop. This man was something different. Immediately, Ian knew he was insane. But he wanted to *talk*!

The older man reached Ian and extended his hand. "Cowper, sir. Justinian Cowper. Alchemist, metaphysician, consultant to the forces of time and space, ah yes, *time*! Do I perceive in you, sir, one only recently come to our little Valhalla, one in need of illumination? Certainly! Definitely, I can see that is the case."

Ian began to say something, almost anything, in response, but the wildly gesticulating old man pressed on without drawing a breath. "This most recent manifestation, the one we were both privileged to witness was, I'm certain you're aware, the pivotal moment at Waterloo in which the Little Corporal had his fat chewed good and proper. Fascinating piece of recent history, wouldn't you say?"

Recent history? Ian started to ask him how long he had been in this gray place, but the old man barely paused before a fresh torrent of words spilled out.

"Stunningly reminiscent of that marvelous scene in Stendahl's *Charterhouse of Parma* in which Fabrizio, young, innocent, fresh to that environ, found himself walking across a large meadow on which men were running in all directions, noise, shouts, confusion . . . and he knew not what was happening, and not till several chapters later do we learn—ah, marvelous!—that it was, in fact, the Battle of Waterloo through which he moved, totally unaware of history in the shaping all around him. He was there, while *not* there. Precisely *our* situation, wouldn't you say?"

He had run out of breath. He stopped, and Ian plunged into the gap. "That's what I'd like to know, Mr. Cowper: What's happened to me? I've lost *everything*, but I can *remember* everything, too. I know I should be going crazy or frightened, and I *am* scared, but not out of my mind with it . . . I seem to *accept* this, whatever it is. I-I don't know how to take it, but I know I'm not feeling it yet. And I've been here a long time!"

The old man slipped his arm around Ian's back and began walking with him, two gentlemen strolling in confidence on a summer afternoon by the edge of a cool park. "Quite correct, sir, quite correct. Dissociative behavior; mark of the man unable to accept his destiny. Accept it, sir. I urge you; and fascination follows. Perhaps even obsession, but we must run that risk, mustn't we?"

Ian wrenched away from him, turned to face him. "Look, mister, I don't want to hear all that craziness! I want to know where I am and how I get out of here. And if you can't tell me, then leave me alone!"

"Nothing easier, my good man. Explanation is the least of it. Observation of phenomena, ah, *that's* the key. You can follow? Well, then: we are victims of the law of conservation of time. Precisely and exactly linked to the law of the conservation of matter; matter, which can neither be created nor destroyed. Time exists without end. But there is an ineluctable entropic balance, absolutely necessary to maintain order in the universe. Keeps events discrete, you see. As matter approaches universal distribution, there is a counterbalancing, how shall I put it, a counterbalancing 'leaching out' of time. Unused time is not wasted in places where nothing happens. *It goes somewhere.* It goes here, to be precise. In measurable units—which I've decided, after considerable thought, to call 'chronons'."

He paused, perhaps hoping Ian would compliment him on his choice of nomenclature. Ian put a hand to his forehead; his brain was swimming.

"That's insane. It doesn't make sense."

"Makes perfectly *good* sense, I assure you. I was a top savant in my time; what I've told you is the only theory that fits the facts. Time unused is not wasted; it is leached out, drained through the normal space-time continuum and recycled. All this history you see shooting past us is that part of the time-flow that was wasted. Entropic balance, I assure you."

"But what am *I* doing here?"

"You force me to hurt your feelings, sir."

"What am I doing here?!"

"You wasted your life. Wasted time. All around you, throughout your life, unused chronons were being leached out, drawn away from the contiguous universe, until their pull on you was irresistible. Then you went on through, pulled loose like a piece of wood in a rushing torrent, a bit of chaff whirled away on the wind. Like Fabrizio, you were never really *there*. You wandered through, never seeing, never participating, and so there was nothing to moor you solidly in your own time."

"But how long will I stay here?"

The old man looked sad and spoke kindly for the first time: "Forever. You never used your time, so you have nothing to rely on as anchorage in normal space."

"But everyone here thinks there's a way out. I know it! They keep walking, trying to find an exit."

"Fools. There is no way back."

"But you don't seem to be the sort of person who wasted his life. Some of the others I've seen, yes, I can see that; but *you*?"

The old man's eyes grew misty. He spoke with difficulty. "Yes, I belong here . . ."

Then he turned and, like one in a dream, lost, wandered away. Lunatic, observing phenomena. And then gone in the grayness of time-gorged limbo. Part of a glacial period slid past Ian Ross and he resumed his walk without destination.

And after a long, long time that was timeless but filled with an abundance of time, he met Catherine.

He saw her as a spot of darkness against the gray limbo. She was quite a distance away, and he walked on for a while, watching the dark blotch against gray, and then decided to change direction. It didn't matter. Nothing mattered: he was alone with his memories, replaying again and again.

The sinking of the *Titanic* wafted through him.

She did not move, even though he was approaching on a direct line.

"The world was vanishing . . . as if all the sand had run out of the hourglass around him; as if he were the only fixed and immutable object in a universe suddenly cut loose from its time-anchor."

When he was quite close he could see that she was sitting cross-legged on nothingness; she was asleep. Her head was propped in one hand, the bracing arm supported by her knee. Asleep.

He came right up to her and stood there simply watching. He smiled. She was like a bird, he thought, with her head tucked under her wing. Not really, but that was how he saw her. Though her cupped hand covered half her face he could make out a sweet face, very pale skin, a mole on her throat; her hair was brown, cut quite short. Her eyes were closed: he decided they would be blue.

The Greek Senate, the Age of Pericles, men in a crowd—property owners—screaming at Lycurgus's exhortations in behalf of socialism. The shadow of it sailed past not very far away.

Ian stood staring, and after a while he sat down opposite her. He leaned back on his arms and watched. He hummed an old tune the name of which he did not know.

Finally, she opened her brown eyes and stared at him.

At first momentary terror, startlement, chagrin, curiosity. Then she took umbrage. "How long have *you* been there?"

"My name is Ian Ross," he said.

"I don't care what your name is!" she said angrily. "I asked you how long you've been sitting there watching me."

"I don't know. A while."

"I don't like being watched; you're being very rude."

He got to his feet without answering and began walking away. Oh well.

She ran after him. "Hey, wait!"

He kept walking. He didn't have to be bothered like that. She caught up with him and ran around to stand in front of him. "I suppose you just think you can walk off like that!"

"Yes, I can. I'm sorry I bothered you. Please get out of my way if you don't want me around."

"I didn't say that."

"You said I was being rude. I am *never* rude; I'm a very well-mannered person, and you were just being insulting."

He walked around her. She ran after him.

"All right, okay, maybe I was a little out of sorts. I *was* asleep, after all."

He stopped. She stood in front of him. Now it was her move. "My name is Catherine Molnar. How do you do?"

"Not too well, that's how."

"Have you been here long?"

"Longer than I wanted to be here, *that's* for sure."

"Can you explain what's happened to me?"

He thought about it. Walking *with* someone would be a nice change. "Let me ask you something," Ian Ross said, beginning to stroll off toward the phantom image of the Hanging Gardens of Babylon wafting past them. "Did you waste a lot of time, sitting around, not doing much, maybe watching television a lot?"

They were lying down side by side because they were tired. Nothing more than that. The Battle of the Ardennes, First World War, was all around them. Not a sound. Just movement. Mist, fog, turretless tanks, shattered trees all around them. Some corpses left lying in the middle of no-man's-land. They had been together for a space of time . . . it was three hours, it was six weeks, it was a month of Sundays, it was a year to remember, it was the best of times, it was the worst of times: who could measure it? There were no signposts, no town criers, no grandfather clocks, no change of seasons, who could measure it?

They had begun to talk freely. He told her again that his name was Ian Ross, and she said Catherine, Catherine Molnar again. She confirmed his guess that her life had been empty. "Plain," she said. "I was plain. I *am* plain. No, don't bother to say you think I have nice cheekbones or a trim figure; it won't change a thing. If you want plain, I've got it."

He didn't say she had nice cheekbones or a trim figure. But he didn't think she was plain.

The Battle of the Ardennes was swirling

away now.

She suggested they make love.

Ian Ross got to his feet quickly and walked away.

She watched him for a while, keeping him in sight. Then she got up, dusted off her hands though there was nothing on them, an act of memory, and followed him. Quite a long time later, after trailing him but not trying to catch up to him, she ran to match his pace and finally, gasping for breath, reached him.

"I'm sorry," she said.

"Nothing to be sorry about."

"I offended you."

"No, you didn't. I just felt like walking."

"Stop it, Ian. I did. I offended you."

He stopped and spun on her. "Do you think I'm a virgin? I'm not a virgin."

His vehemence pulled her back from the edge of boldness. "No, of course you're not. I never thought such a thing." Then she said, "Well . . . I am."

"Sorry," he said, because he didn't know the right thing to say, if there *was* a right thing.

"Not your fault," she said. Which *was* the right thing to say.

From nothing *to* nothing. Thirty-four years old, the properly desperate age for unmarried, unmotherhooded, unloved. Catherine Molnar, Janesville, Wisconsin. Straightening the trinkets in her jewelry box, ironing her clothes, removing and refolding the sweaters in her drawers, hanging the slacks with the slacks, skirts with the skirts, blouses with the blouses, coats with the coats, all in order in the closet, reading every word in *Time* and *Reader's Digest*, learning seven new words every day, never using seven new words every day, mopping the floors in the three-room apartment, putting aside one full evening to pay the bills and spelling out Wisconsin completely, never the WI abbreviation on the return envelopes, listening to talk-radio, calling for the correct time to set the clocks, spooning out the droppings from the kitty box, repasting photos in the album of scenes with round-faced people, pinching back the buds on the coleus, calling Aunt Beatrice every Tuesday at seven o'clock, talking brightly to the waitress in the orange-and-blue uniform at the chicken pie shoppe, repainting fingernails carefully so the moon on each nail is showing, heating morning water for herself alone for the cup of herbal tea, setting the table with a cloth napkin and a placemat, doing dishes, going to the office and straightening the bills of lading precisely. *From* nothing *to* nothing. Thirty-four.

They lay side by side but they were not tired. There was more to it than that.

"I hate men who can't think past the pillow," she said, touching his hair.

"What's that?"

"Oh, it's just something I practiced, to say after the first time I slept with a man. I always felt there should be something original to say, instead of all the things I read in novels."

"I think it's a very clever phrase." Even now, he found it hard to touch her. He lay with hands at his sides.

She changed the subject. "I was never able to get very far playing the piano. I have absolutely *no* give between the thumb and first finger. And that's essential, you know. You have to have a long reach, a good spread, I think they call it, to play Chopin. A tenth: that's two notes over an octave. A *full* octave, a *perfect* octave, those are just technical terms. Octave is good enough. I don't have that."

"I like piano playing," he said, realizing how silly and dull he must sound and frightened (very suddenly) that she would find him so, that she would leave him. Then he remembered where they were and he smiled. Where could she go? Where could *he* go?

"I always hated the fellows at parties who could play the piano . . . all the girls clustered around those people. Except these days it's not so much piano; not too many people have pianos in their homes anymore. The kids grow up and go away and nobody takes lessons and the kids don't buy pianos. They get those electric guitars."

"Acoustical guitars."

"Yes, those. I don't think it would be much better for fellows like me who don't play, even if it's acoustical guitars."

They got up and walked again.

Once they discussed how they had wasted their lives, how they had sat there with hands folded as time filled space around them, swept through, was drained off, and their own "chronons" (he had told her about the lunatic; she said it sounded like Benjamin Franklin; he said the man hadn't looked like Benjamin Franklin, but maybe, it might have been) had been leached of all potency.

Once they discussed the guillotine executions in the Paris of the Revolution, because it was keeping pace with them. Once they chased the Devonian and almost caught it. Once they were privileged to enjoy themselves in the center of an Arctic snowstorm that held around them for a measure of measureless time. Once they saw nothing for an eternity but were truly chilled—unlike the Arctic snowstorm that had had no effect on them—by the winds that blew past them. And once he turned to her and said, "I love you, Catherine."

But when she looked at him with a gentle smile, he noticed for the first time that her eyes seemed to be getting gray and pale.

Then, not too soon after, she said she loved him, too.

But she could see mist through the flesh of his hands when he reached out to touch her face.

They walked with their arms around each other, having found each other. They said many times, and agreed it was so, that they were in love and being together was the most important thing in that endless world of gray spaces, even if they never found their way back.

And they began to *use* their time together, setting small goals for each "day" upon awakening. We will walk *that* far; we will play word games in which *you* have to begin the name of a female movie star from the last letter of a male movie star's name that *I* have to begin off the last letter of a female movie star; we will exchange shirt and blouse and see how it feels for a while; we will sing every camp song we can remember. They began to *enjoy* their time together. They began to live.

And sometimes his voice faded out, and she could see him moving his lips but there was no sound.

And sometimes when the mist cleared she was invisible from the ankles down and her body moved as through thick soup.

And as they used their time, they became alien in that place where wasted time had gone to rest.

And they began to fade. As the world had leached out for Ian Ross in Scotland, and for Catherine Molnar in Wisconsin, *they* began to vanish from limbo. Matter could neither be created nor destroyed, but it could be disassembled and sent where it was needed for entropic balance.

He saw her pale skin become transparent.

She saw his hands as clear as glass.

And they thought: *too late. It comes too late.*

Invisible motes of their selves were drawn off and were sent away from that gray place. Were sent where needed to maintain balance. One and one and one, separated on the wind and blown to the farthest corners of the tapestry that was time and space. And could never be recalled. And could never be rejoined.

So they touched, there in that vast limbo of wasted time, for the last time, and shadows existed for an instant, and then were gone; he first, leaving her behind for the merest instant of terrible loneliness and loss, and then she, without shadow, pulled apart and scattered, followed. Separation without hope of return.

There was the faintest keening whine of matter fleeing.

There was the soundless echo of a diminishing moan.

The universe was poised to accept restored order.

And then balance was regained; as if they had never been.

Great events hushed in mist swirled past. Ptolemy crowned King of Egypt, the Battle of the Teutoburger Forest, Jesus crucified, the founding of Constantinople, the Vandals plundering Rome, the massacre of the Omayyad family, the Court of the Fujiwaras in Japan, Jerusalem falling to Saladin . . . and on and on . . . great events . . . empty time . . . and the timeless population trudged past endlessly . . . endlessly . . . unaware that finally, at last, hopelessly and too late . . . two of their nameless order had found the way out. ∞

"I'll never forget you, Xeena; I'll see your face in every omelet, I'll never again touch another dish of 'coq au vin,' . . ."

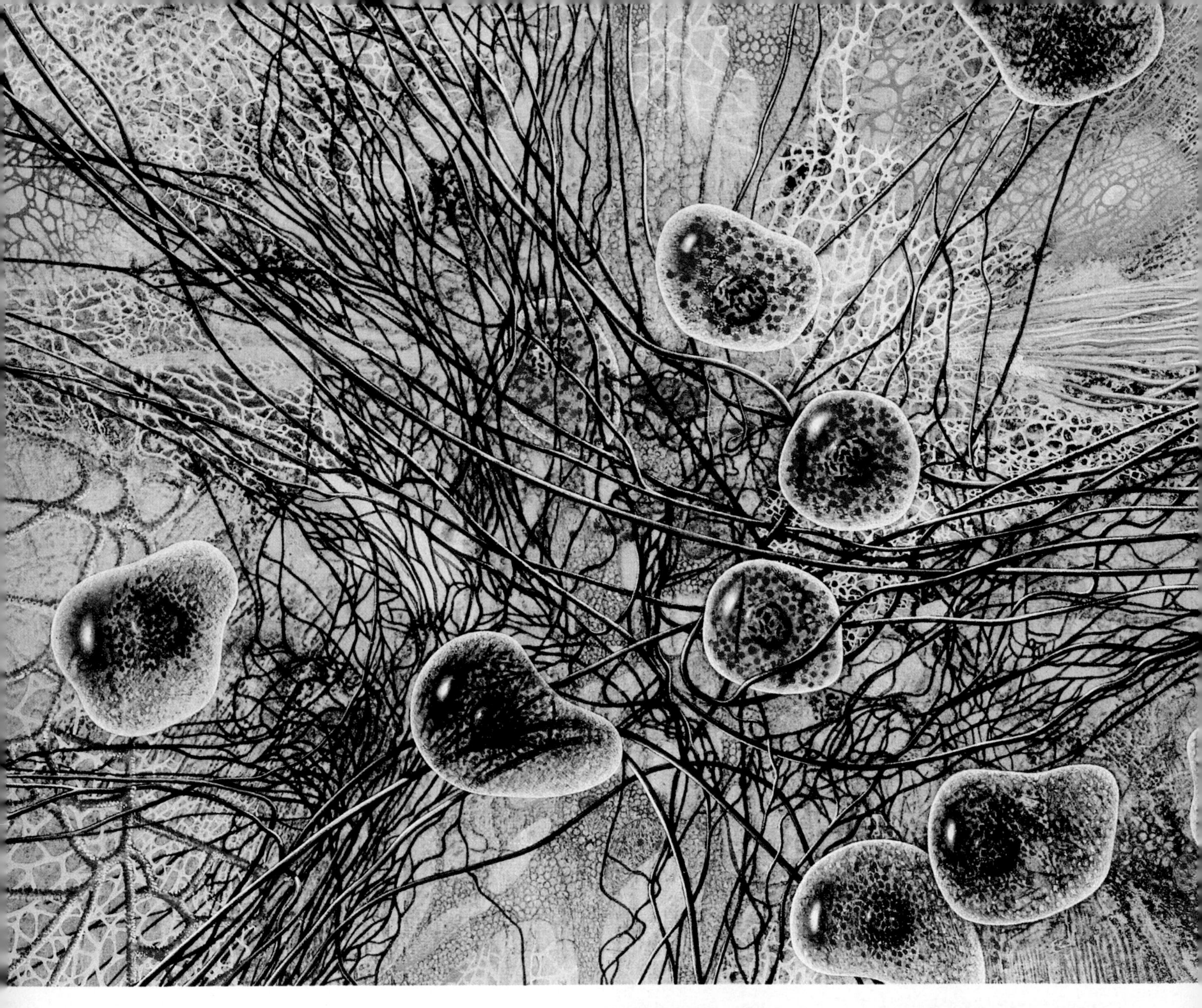

INNER DOMAINS

Uncharted regions of bone and sinew become fantastic art in the service of science

BY KATHLEEN STEIN

Early in my study of vertebrate structure, I became entranced by the aesthetic pleasure I derived from contemplating the organic form," says the renowned medical artist Paul Peck. Like his predecessors from Da Vinci to Andrew Wyeth, Peck contradicts the myth that the artist is at continual odds with the stringent discipline and accountability of the scientific method. To the contrary, the instant the artist records an observation—a leaf, sunlight falling on a pool of water, the complexities of a human face—he is participating in a scien-

Peck's three-dimensional rendering of the various fibrous and netlike components of connective tissue (top). Inner structure of the kidney (top right) depicts thousands of glomeruli and tubules; neurons (below).

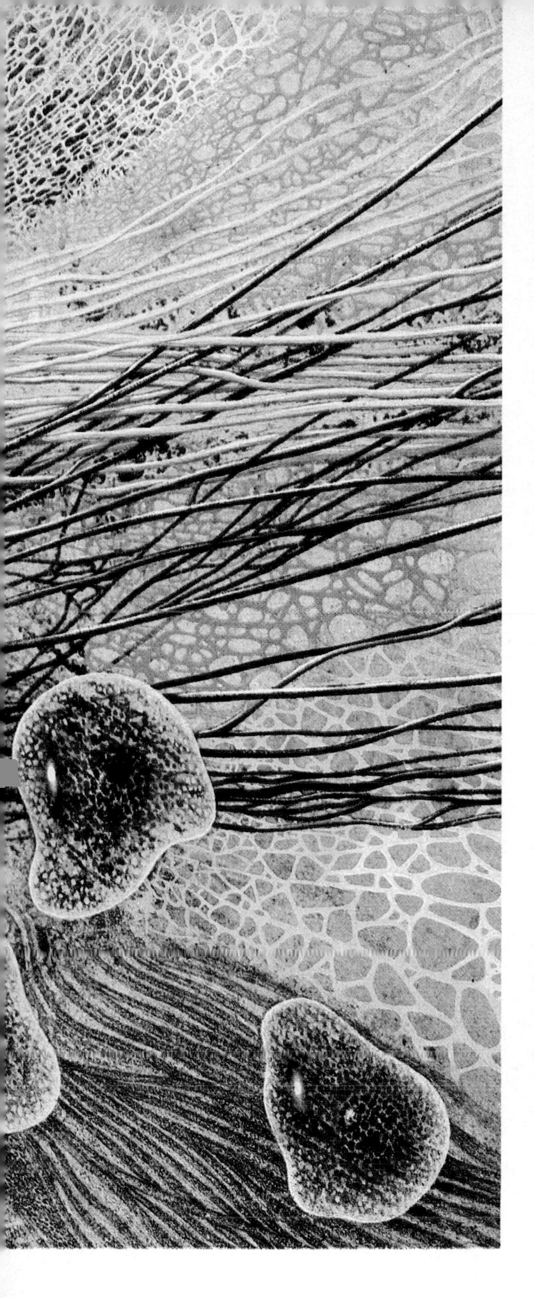

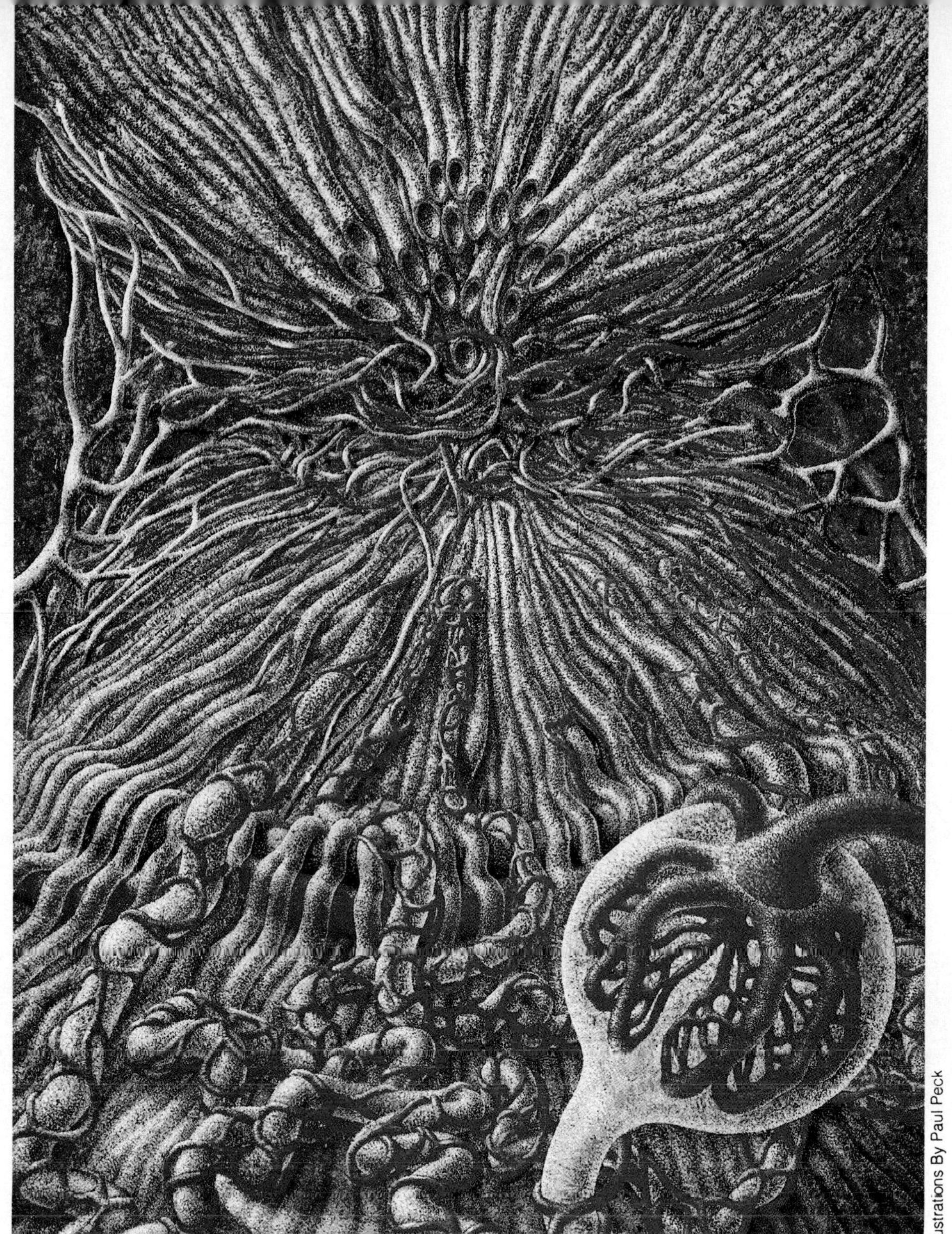

Illustrations By Paul Peck

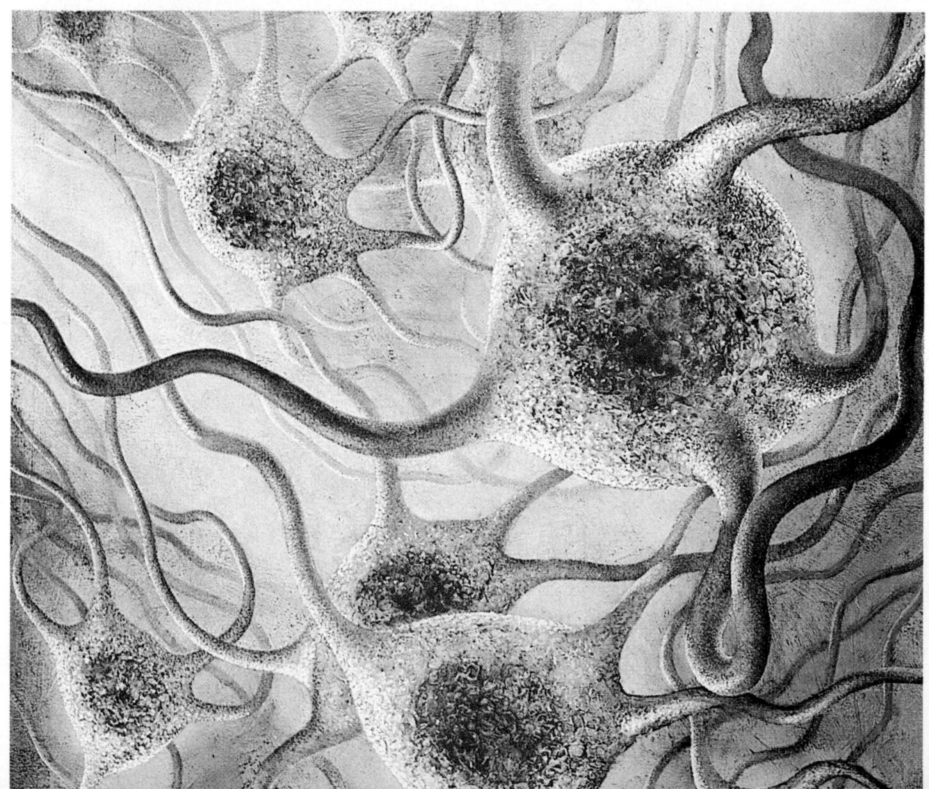

"I was determined," says Peck, "to create art that would reveal the harmony in living organisms."

tific event. Before the invention of the camera, medical illustration was the only means—other than dissecting corpses—of learning anatomy. Although photography has now replaced the illustrator's function in recording the appearance of objects, the camera is not able to dramatize important elements or simplify and clarify relationships. That is the work of art. In the case of anatomy, the arrangements of organs and their vessels and nerves are so intricate, the relationships so hidden by overlying tissue, that a photograph tends to confuse rather than clarify. Medical art captures the essence of life, a more subtle task. In fact, advancing photographic technology has done art a favor in

The structure of bone (above left). Right ventricle of the heart (above right) looking toward the bicuspid valve. Gallstones (below right). Lung section (below) painted by Frank Armitage for a pharmaceuticals house.

Frank Armitage

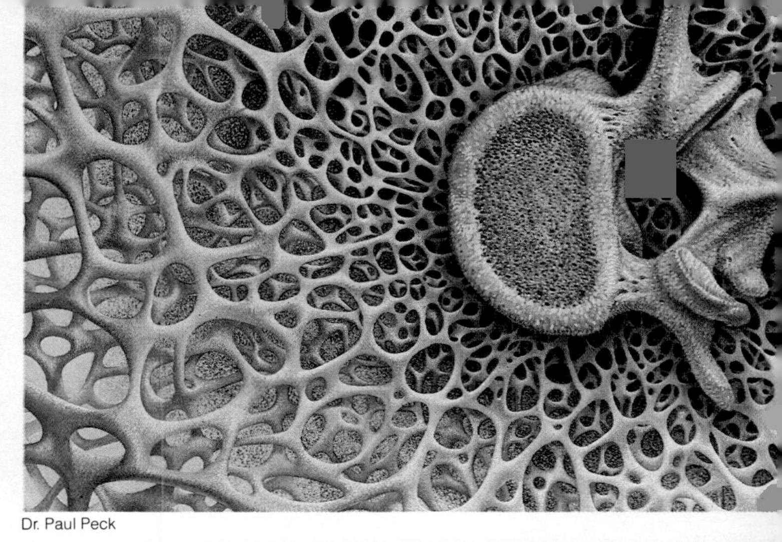

Dr. Paul Peck

Dr. Paul Peck

Frank Armitage

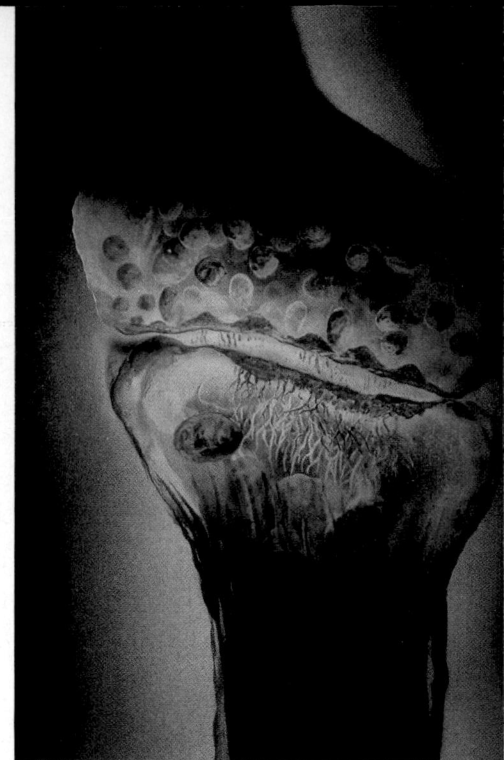

Illustrations By Frank Armitage

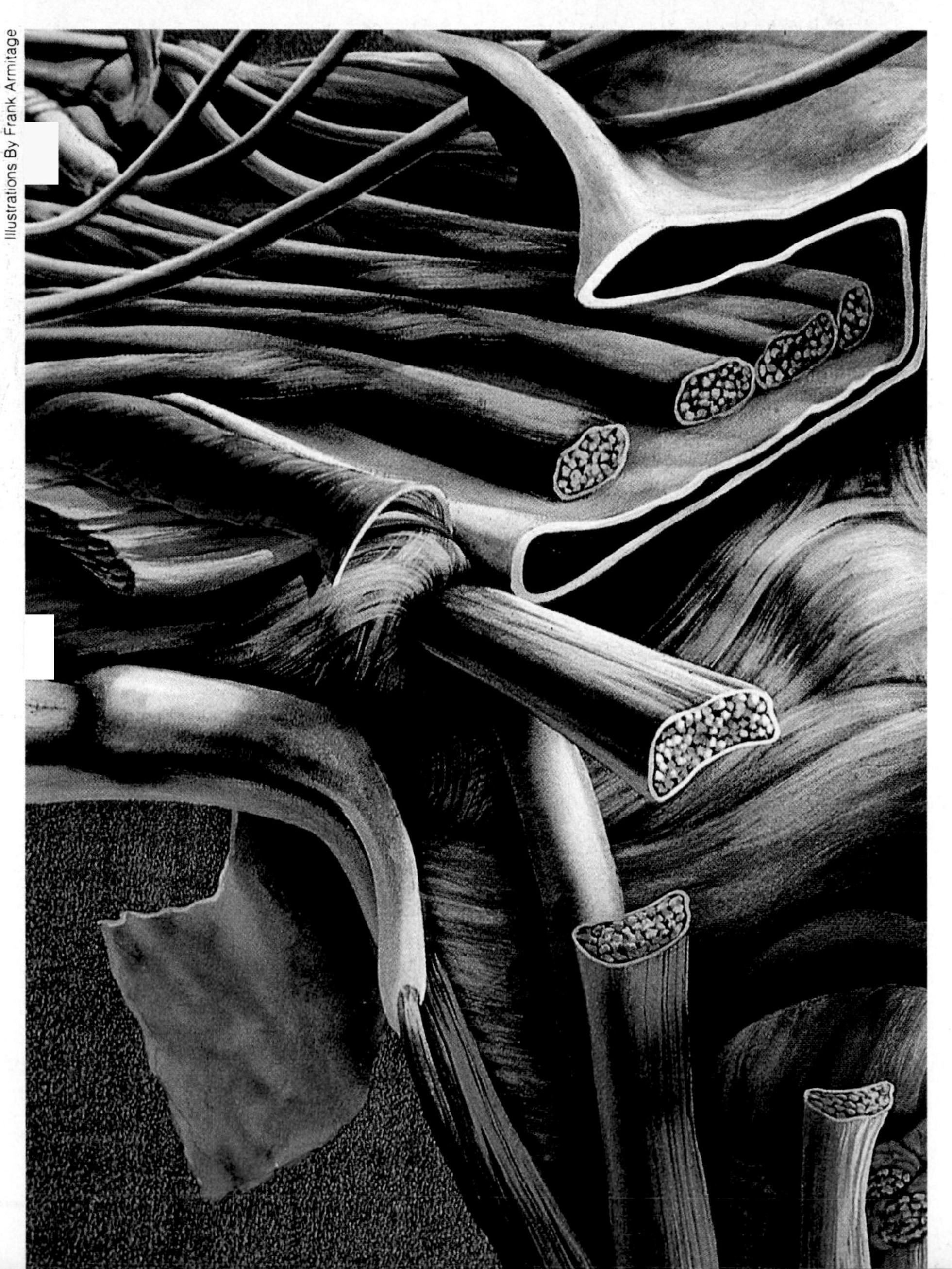

I would reveal especially those microscopic structures —in a manner to fire the imagination.

liberating the artist to create more exciting conceptual visions. "Artists must realize the creative potential inherent in the intricacies of science," comments Frank Armitage, who, as an art student, had to cajole his way into the dissecting rooms of medical schools. Once inside, the space-age Michelangelo made sketches and mental notes that would later become epic visions of the interior body. Armitage's inner landscapes have become the bases of numerous medical films. The SF movie *Fantastic Voyage* is an Armitage odyssey. So, in giving "the inward parts" a local habitation and a name, science has enlarged the artist's vocabulary: science in service to art. ∞

Armitage's conceptualization of the brain's optic system (above left). Nerve synapse (right). The exposed tendon sheaths of the hand, palm-side facing up (below left), dorsal view (right). Acrylic on mat board.

It was a prime corpus, complete with reconditioned heart, lungs, and enriched glands

BODY GAME

BY ROBERT SHECKLEY

Dear Senator, I'm writing to you because you are our senior Senator and because you said at election time last year that you were our servant and that we should write to you immediately if we had any grievances. You were very definite, and you even got a little huffy and said it was actually a citizen's duty to write to his Senator and let him know what was going on. Well, Senator, I thought about that a lot. Naturally, I didn't believe the part about you being our servant, what with you earning 50 times, or 100 times, or for all I know 1000 times what we do. But the thing about writing to you, which you were so insistent on, that part got to me.

Your words puzzled me at first when you said we should let you know what was going on here. I mean, you were raised in this city same as me, and a man would have to be blind, deaf, dumb, and stupid not to know what's happening here. But I decided that I was being unfair; you've got to spend a lot of

PAINTING BY SAMUEL BAK

your time in Washington, so maybe you are out of touch. Anyway, I'm taking you at your word and taking the liberty of writing to you. Specifically, I want to tell you about my grandfather's retread body, because it's a specific grievance, something you ought to know about and maybe even do something about.

At the time all this began, Grandfather was a healthy, sprightly 92 year old with all his own teeth still, a full head of white hair, and not an ounce of spare meat on his bones. He'd always taken care of himself, hadn't even had to wear glasses until he was 80-something. The old boy had worked for 50 years, until they retired him at age 65 with a pretty generous pension considering that he had been a second-grade comptometer operator. With the pension and social security and what he'd saved, Grandfather was able to pull his own weight and not be a burden to the rest of us, which was lucky since we were barely afloat, monetarily speaking.

The old boy just lay around the apartment for a while, sleeping late and watching television. He always made his own meals, and he always washed up afterwards. Afternoons he went down to the park and sat with some other old-timers. Then home to bed. He was very good with our kids; on Sundays he'd take them to Sheepshead Bay, and they'd walk along the shore and look for nose cones. He went fishing, too, just to pass the time; and once he caught a sand shark, though how it got close to shore through all the garbage and chemical junk is beyond me. We boiled it up for a couple of days and ate it, and it wasn't bad if you used enough ketchup.

But the old guy was getting bored. He'd worked for 50 years, and he simply didn't know how to retire gracefully. He moped around for a while, then made up his mind and went out looking for a job.

Well, of course, that was just plain silly, and we told him so. Man of 40 can't find anything these days, much less a man of 70, which was Grandfather's age at the time. But he went on trying. He'd wake up every morning and take his longevity serum prescribed by the Medicare people, wash and shave, and off he'd go.

He didn't find a thing, of course, and finally he had to swallow his pride and rent a job as a garbage sorter's assistant. It didn't cost him much, which was lucky because he didn't have much. But he could never get used to the idea of paying money every day in order to work when the government was willing to pay him to not work. "It's a useful job, and I do it damned well," he used to tell us. "Why in God's name must I *pay* in order to work a useful job I do well?" As if that had anything to do with it.

Well, he held that job or others like it for nearly 20 years. But then someone invented self-consuming garbage, and my grandfather and a lot of other men were out of work. Grandfather was about 90 now, and he still had a lot of ideas about useful jobs. But he wasn't feeling well. This was the first time in his life he hadn't felt well. We took him to Doc Saunders at the U Thant Memorial Socio-Medical Center on East 103rd Street. It took us the better part of a day to hike up there. Those moving sidewalks cost five bucks a ride, and that's too much just to get around.

Doc Saunders had an office filled with one hell of a batch of instruments. He ran a three-day checkout on Grandfather. At the end of it he said, "There's nothing wrong with you except old age. Your heart's just about used up, and your arteries can't stand up to pressure. There's more, but that's the most important part."

"Can you replace anything, Doc?" Grandfather wanted to know.

Doc Saunders shook his head. "Put in a new heart, and it'd blow out your arteries. Patch and mend your arteries, and your lungs couldn't oxygenate the blood flow. Do something about that, and your kidneys would declare a holiday. Fact is, your whole internal system is just plain worn out."

Grandfather nodded. He read the *Daily News* every morning. He knew about this stuff.

"What should I do?" he asked.

"Get a new body," Saunders said.

Grandfather thought it over. "Well, by God," he said, "maybe a man my age ought to be ready to die; but I'm not. Still too many things to look at, you know what I mean? Sure, I'm ready to put on a new body. But the money. . . ."

"That's the problem," Saunders said. "Medicare doesn't handle corpus replacement, you know."

"I know," Grandfather said sadly.

"Could you meet the price?"

"Don't see how," Grandfather said.

For the next couple of days Grandfather sat on the curb near our apartment and thought. It wasn't too nice for him there. The kids would come by after school and shout at him, "Die, old man, why don't you die? Selfish old bastard using up air and food and water. Lousy old pervert, why can't you die decent like old men are supposed to do? Die, die, greedy son-of-a-bitch, die!"

When I heard about that I swore I was going out there with a stick and raise some welts. But Grandfather wouldn't allow it. "They're just repeating what their parents say," he told me. "There's no harm in a child, no more than in a parrot. And besides, they're right; probably I should die."

"Now don't start that," I said.

"Die, die," Grandfather said. "Hell, I've been worthless for 30 years, and if I had an ounce of guts I damned well would die, and good riddance to me!"

"That's crazy talk," I'd tell him. "What do you think that longevity stuff is for if they meant for old men to die?"

"Maybe they made a mistake," he'd say.

"Like hell they did," I came back. "They taught me in school that people have been aiming for long-life for hundreds and hundreds of years. You've heard of Dr. Faustus, haven't you?"

"Famous Austrian doctor, wasn't he?" Grandfather asked.

"German," I told him. "A friend of Freud and Einstein and smarter than both of them. He put longevity on the map. You wouldn't argue with a brainy guy like that, would you?"

Maybe I didn't have all my facts straight, but I had to say something. And I didn't want the old man to die. I don't know why because it didn't make any sense to have an old man in the house with things getting tougher every year. But I wanted him to live. He was never any trouble, and the kids liked him, and even May, my wife, said he was nice to talk to.

Well, he didn't pay any attention to my Faustus talk, which I guess was about what it was worth. He sat with his chin on his fist and thought. He must have thought for ten full minutes. And then he looked up and blinked, like he was a little surprised I was still there.

"Sonny," he asked, "how old is Arthur Rockefeller?"

"One hundred and thirty or so," I said. "He's in his third body."

"And how old is Eustis Morgan Hunt?"

"Must be about the same age."

"And Blaise Eisenhower?"

"Must be a good 175. He's gone through four bodies."

"And Morris Mellon?"

"Around 210, 220. But what's that got to do with anything?"

He gave me a pitying look. "The poor are like children. It takes them nearly a hundred years just to grow up, and then they still can't do anything because they're dying. But the rich can try to live forever."

He didn't say anything for a while. Then he spit into the street, got up, and went inside to the apartment. It was time for his favorite afternoon show.

I don't know how or where he got the money. Maybe he had savings tucked away, or maybe he went to New Jersey and held up a candy store. Your guess is as good as mine. All I know is three days later he came up to me and said, "Johnny, let's go body shopping."

"Body dreaming, you mean," I said.

"Shopping," he said again and showed me 380 dollars in his fist. And he wouldn't tell me where he got it, either—me, his own grandson who's going to need a new body one of these days.

So we went body shopping.

Senator, I guess you know how it is with the poor. Everything costs more and is not as good. When you are poor like us you don't want to go downtown to Saks's Body Shop, for example, or Lord & Taylor's Relife Center. You figure they'll laugh at you or arrest you for loitering. You simply don't shop there. You shop in your neighborhood.

In our case, that means that we bring our business to Dapper Dan's Living Models store, which is located at 103rd Street and Broadway. I'm not trying to get that company into trouble. It just happens to be where we went.

Maybe you've read what those places are like. Plenty of neon, three or four good-looking bodies in the window, junk inside. Always a couple of salesmen in sharp suits telling jokes on the videophone. These salesmen must sell to each other, because I never see anyone else in there.

We walked in and started looking over the goods. One of the salesmen came drifting over, nice and easy, smiling while he was still 50 feet away.

"Looking for a nice body?" he asked.

"No, just looking for a fourth for bridge," told him.

He laughed. I was a very witty fellow. "Take your time," he said. "But if there is anything specific—"

"How much is that one?" Grandfather asked.

"I see that you're a man of taste," the salesman said. "That is our Eton model—part of General Dynamics's new spring line. The Eton is six feet tall, 170 pounds, reflexes rated AA. All its organs have received the Good Housekeeping seal of approval. General Clay Baxter occupies a modified Eton, did you know that? The brain and nervous system are by Dynaco and have been rated a 'best buy' by Consumer Queries. Sculpturewise, this particular model came out very nicely—notice the facial flesh tones and the crinkly laugh lines around the eyes. You don't always get that sort of detail."

"How much is it?" Grandfather asked.

"I forgot to mention, it comes with a ten-year guarantee on parts and labor backed by a Good Housekeeping seal of approval."

"How much?"

"Well, sir, this week we're having our annual clearance sale. Solely because of that, I can let you have this number for eighteen thousand nine hundred dollars, twelve percent off list."

Grandfather shook his head. "Do you actually expect to sell that thing up here?"

"You'd be surprised," the salesman told him. "Sometimes a man hits it on the numbers or comes into an inheritance—"

"For eighteen grand it'd pay me to die," my grandfather said. "You got anything cheaper?"

The salesman had plenty of cheaper models. There was a Renault-Bofors 'Hombre' for $10,000 and a Socony-GM 'Everyman' for $6500. There was a Union Carbide-Chrysler 'Go-Man' with plastic hair and glass eyes for $2200 and a Texas Instrument 'Veracruzano' without voicebox, gyrocenter, or protein conversion unit for $1695.

"Hell, I wasn't interested in a new synthetic, anyhow," Grandfather said. "You got a used-body department?"

"Yes, sir, we do."

"Then show me some good retreads."

He took us into a back room where the bodies were stacked against the wall like cordwood. It was like one of those old-time chamber of horror things. I mean, honestly, you wouldn't have worn one of those bodies to a dog-fight. There really ought to be a law against selling that sort of thing—lopsided bodies with chewed ears, bodies still bloody, with a new heart sewed in quick, lab bodies that hadn't worked out, bodies assembled out of parts found at wrecks and other disasters, suicides' bodies with the wrists taped and a couple of quarts of new blood pumped in, lepers' bodies with flesh-tone plastic sprayed over the sores.

We hadn't been expecting the retreads to be pretty, but we hadn't expected anything like this, either. I thought Grandfather was going to turn around and march out of that store. But he didn't. Shaking his head a little, he picked out a pretty good-looking synthetic with an extruded arm and a leg missing. God knows it was no beauty, but at least it didn't look as if it had just been pulled out of a train wreck.

"I might be interested in something like this," Grandfather said cautiously.

"You have a good eye for merchandise," the salesman told him. "It just so happens that this little number will outperform a lot of the high-price new jobs."

"It looks sickly," Grandfather said.

"Not a chance! This is a prime corpus, my dear sir, and it comes complete with reconditioned heart, extractor-type lungs, heavy-duty liver, and enriched glands. This model comes with four kidneys as standard equipment, a double-insulated stomach, and two hundred feet of Armour's finest intestine. What do you think of that, sir?"

"Well, I don't know," Grandfather said.

But the salesman knew. It took about fifteen minutes for him to sell the lopsided body to my grandfather.

You get a one-month guarantee on retreads. My grandfather got into it the following day, and it lasted him three weeks. Then the heart began to race and flutter, one kidney shut down completely, and the other three only worked part-time. A lung patch blew out, the intestines started leaking, and the liver began to shrink.

Grandfather is in bed now, and Doc Saunders says it's a day-to-day thing. The company won't make good on the body. They got some pretty nifty clauses in that contract of theirs, and our block legal advisor says we could fight it in the courts for ten years and not be sure of the outcome. And in the meantime, Grandfather would be dead.

So I'm writing to you first and primarily, Senator, to ask you to do something about this quick, while there's still time. My grandfather says that all I'll get from you is a form letter or maybe even a real letter from your secretary expressing regret at your inability to rectify this grievous wrong and that you'll probably mention how you've introduced or sponsored a bill before Congress that'll do something about it if it ever gets passed. And all that crap. So I and Grandfather expect he'll die because he hadn't the price of a decent body, and nobody will do anything about it. That's business as usual, right? Isn't that what always happens to the little people?

But that brings me to the second reason I've written you. I've been talking it over with my buddies, Senator, and we all agree that my grandfather and all the rest of the poor have been conned long enough. This Golden Age is not so nice for people like us. It's not that we want anything so much; we just can't go on knowing that other people have privileges—like long-life—that we don't have. We figure that that stuff has gone on long enough.

We've decided that if you and the other people in power don't do something about it, then we're going to. The time has come to take a stand.

We're going to declare war.

You may think this is sort of sudden, Senator. But it isn't, really. You'd be surprised how many people have been thinking about this sort of thing. But each of us has thought we were alone and that everyone else was satisfied. And now we learn that a hell of a lot of us have been thinking the same thoughts as Grandfather and doing a slow burn about it.

Before this, we didn't know what to do. Now we do know.

We are simple men, Senator, and we don't have any big thinkers among us. We figure that all men ought to be roughly equal. And we understand that no laws are going to do that.

So our program is to kill rich guys. Do away with them entirely.

That may not sound very *constructive*, as the tv says. But to us it looks simple, straightforward, and we think it'll be effective.

We're going to kill the rich when and how we can. And we're not going to discriminate, either. We don't care how the money was made, nor what he uses it for. We'll kill labor leaders as well as bankers, high-class criminals as well as big-deal oil men. We'll kill anyone and everyone who has a lot more than we do. We'll kill until the rich are like us, or we're like them, or until we all meet in the middle. We'll kill our own people if they profit off of this thing, too. And we'll sure as hell kill senators and congressmen, too.

So there it is, Senator. I hope you help my grandfather. If you do, it'll mean that maybe you see things our way, and we'll be glad to put you on the deferred list and give you three weeks to get rid of the wealth you've been able to accumulate.

You know where to reach my grandfather. Me, you can't reach at all. However this thing goes, I'm dropping out of sight. Don't bother looking for me.

Remember—there's a hell of a lot more of us than there are of you. We've never been able to bring this thing off before, my grandfather tells me—never in the history of the world. But what the hell, there's got to be a first time for everything. Maybe we'll even make it this time; pull down your Golden Age and build our own.

I don't expect you'll see it our way. So here's looking at you, Senator—right down the sights of a gun. ∞

UNACCOMPANIED SONATA

He was an artist, so he had to be kept under close control

BY ORSON SCOTT CARD

When Christian Haroldsen was six months old, preliminary tests showed a predisposition toward rhythm and a keen awareness of pitch. There were other tests, of course, and many possible routes still open to him. But rhythm and pitch were the governing signs of his own private zodiac, and already the reinforcement began. Mr. and Mrs. Haroldsen were provided with tapes of many kinds of sound and instructed to play them constantly, whether Christian was awake or asleep.

When Christian Haroldsen was two years old, his seventh battery of tests pinpointed the path he would inevitably follow. His creativity was exceptional; his curiosity, insatiable; his understanding of music, so intense that on top of all the tests was written "Prodigy."

Prodigy was the word that took him from his parents' home to a house in deep deciduous forest where winter was savage and violent and summer, a brief, desperate eruption of green. He grew up, cared for by unsinging servants, and the only music he was allowed to hear was bird song and wind song and the crackling of winter wood; thunder and the faint cry of golden leaves as they broke free and tumbled to the earth; rain on the roof and the drip of water from icicles; the chatter of squirrels and the deep silence of snow falling on a moonless night.

These sounds were Christian's only conscious music. He grew up with the symphonies of his early years only distant and impossible-to-retrieve memories. And so he learned to hear music in unmusical things—for he had to find music, even when there was none to find.

He found that colors made sounds in his mind: Sunlight in summer was a blaring chord; moonlight in winter, a thin, mournful wail; new green in spring, a low murmur in almost (but not quite) random rhythms; the flash of a red fox in the leaves, a gasp of sudden startlement.

PAINTING BY EVELYN TAYLOR

And he learned to play all those sounds on his Instrument. In the world were violins, trumpets, and clarinets, as there had been for centuries. Christian knew nothing of that. Only his Instrument was available. It was enough.

Christian lived in one room in his house, which he had to himself most of the time. He had a bed (not too soft), a chair and table, a silent machine that cleaned him and his clothing, and an electric light.

The other room contained only his Instrument. It was a console with many keys and strips and levers and bars, and when he touched any part of it, a sound came out. Every key made a different sound; every point on the strips made a different pitch; every lever modified the tone; every bar altered the structure of the sound.

When he first came to the house, Christian played (as children will) with the Instrument, making strange and funny noises. It was his only playmate; he learned it well, could produce any sound he wanted to. At first he delighted in loud, blaring tones. Later he began to learn the pleasure of silences and rhythms. And soon he began to play with soft and loud and to play two sounds at once and to change those two sounds together to make a new sound and to play again a sequence of sounds he had played before.

Gradually, the sounds of the forest outside his house found their way into the music he played. He learned to make winds sing through his Instrument; he learned to make summer one of the songs he could play at will. Green with its infinite variations was his most subtle harmony; the birds cried out from his Instrument with all the passion of Christian's loneliness.

And the word spread to the licensed Listeners:

"There's a new sound north of here, east of here: Christian Haroldsen, and he'll tear out your heart with his songs."

The Listeners came, a few to whom variety was everything first, then those to whom novelty and vogue mattered most, and at last those who valued beauty and passion above everything else. They came and stayed out in Christian's woods and listened as his music was played through perfect speakers on the roof of his house. When the music stopped and Christian came out of his house, he could see the Listeners moving away. He asked and was told why they came; he marveled that the things he did for love on his Instrument could be of interest to other people.

He felt, strangely, even more lonely to know that he could sing to the Listeners and yet never be able to hear their songs.

"But they have no songs," said the woman who came to bring him food every day. "They are Listeners. You are a Maker. You have songs, and they listen."

"Why?" asked Christian, innocently.

The woman looked puzzled. "Because that's what they want most to do. They've been tested, and they are happiest as Listeners. You are happiest as a Maker. Aren't you happy?"

"Yes," Christian answered, and he was telling the truth. His life was perfect, and he wouldn't change anything, not even the sweet sadness of the backs of the Listeners as they walked away at the end of his songs.

Christian was seven years old.

FIRST MOVEMENT

For the third time the short man with glasses and a strangely inappropriate mustache dared to wait in the underbrush for Christian to come out. For the third time he was overcome by the beauty of the song that had just ended, a mournful symphony that made the short man with glasses feel the pressure of the leaves above him, even though it was summer and they had months left before they would fall. The fall was still inevitable, said Christian's song; through all their life the leaves hold within them the power to die, and that must color their life. The short man with glasses wept—but when the song ended and the other Listeners moved away, he hid in the brush and waited.

"You have broken the law. You were put here because you were a genius, creating new things with only nature for your inspiration. Now . . . you're derivative. . . . You'll have to leave."

This time his wait was rewarded. Christian came out of his house, walked among the trees, and came toward where the short man with glasses waited. The man admired the easy, unpostured way that Christian walked. The composer looked to be about thirty, yet there was something childish in the way he looked around him, the way his walk was aimless and prone to stop so he would just touch (and not break) a fallen twig with his bare toes.

"Christian," said the short man with glasses.

Christian turned, startled. In all these years, no Listener had ever spoken to him. It was forbidden. Christian knew the law.

"It's forbidden," Christian said.

"Here," the short man with glasses said, holding out a small black object.

"What is it?"

The short man grimaced. "Just take it. Push the button and it plays."

"Plays?"

"Music."

Christian's eyes opened wide. "But that's forbidden. I can't have my creativity polluted by hearing other musicians' work. That would make me imitative and derivative, instead of original."

"Reciting," the man said. "You're just reciting that. This is Bach's music." There was reverence in his voice.

"I can't," Christian said.

And then the short man shook his head. "You don't know. You don't know what you're missing. But I heard it in your song when I came here years ago, Christian. You want this."

"It's forbidden," Christian answered, for to him the very fact that a man who knew an act was forbidden still wanted to perform it was astounding, and he couldn't get past the novelty of it to realize that some action was expected of him.

There were footsteps, and words being spoken in the distance, and the short man's face became frightened. He ran at Christian, forced the recorder into his hands, then took off toward the gate of the preserve.

Christian took the recorder and held it in a spot of sunlight coming through the leaves. It gleamed dully. "Bach," Christian said. Then, "Who the hell is Bach?"

But he didn't throw the recorder down. Nor did he give the recorder to the woman who came to ask him what the short man with glasses had stayed for. "He stayed for at least ten minutes."

"I only saw him for thirty seconds," Christian answered.

"And?"

"He wanted me to hear some other music. He had a recorder."

"Did he give it to you?"

"No," Christian said. "Doesn't he still have it?"

"He must have dropped it in the woods."

"He said it was Bach."

"It's forbidden. That's all you need to know. If you should find the recorder, Christian, you know the law."

"I'll give it to you."

She looked at him carefully. "You know what would happen if you listened to such a thing."

Christian nodded.

"Very well. We'll be looking for it, too. I'll see you tomorrow, Christian. And next time somebody stays after, don't talk to him. Just come back in and lock the doors."

"I'll do that," Christian said.

There was a summer rainstorm that night, wind and rain and thunder, and Christian found that he could not sleep. Not because of the music of the weather—he'd slept through a thousand such storms. It was the recorder that lay against the wall behind the Instrument. Christian had lived for nearly thirty years surrounded only by this wild, beautiful place and the music he himself made. But now . . .

Now he could not stop wondering. Who was Bach? Who *is* Bach? What is his music? How is it different from mine? Has he discovered things that I don't know?

What is his music? What is his music?

What is his music?

Wondering. Until dawn, when the storm was abating and the wind had died. Christian got out of his bed, where he had not slept but only tossed back and forth all night, and took the recorder from its hiding place and played it.

At first it sounded strange, like noise; odd sounds that had nothing to do with the sounds of Christian's life. But the patterns were clear, and by the end of the recording, which was not even a half-hour long, Christian had mastered the idea of fugue, and the sound of the harpsichord preyed on his mind.

Yet he knew that if he let these things show up in his music, he would be discovered. So he did not try a fugue. He did not attempt to imitate the harpsichord's sound.

And every night he listened to the recording, learning more and more until finally the Watcher came.

The Watcher was blind, and a dog led him. He came to the door, and because he was a Watcher, the door opened for him without his even knocking.

"Christian Haroldsen, where is the recorder?" the Watcher asked.

"Recorder?" Christian asked, then knew it was hopeless. So he took the machine and gave it to the Watcher.

"Oh, Christian," said the Watcher, and his voice was mild and sorrowful. "Why didn't you turn it in without listening to it?"

"I meant to," Christian said. "But how did you know?"

"Because suddenly there are no fugues in your work. Suddenly your songs have lost the only Bach-like thing about them. And you've stopped experimenting with new sounds. What were you trying to avoid?"

"This," Christian said, and he sat down and on his first try duplicated the sound of the harpsichord.

"Yet you've never tried to do that until now, have you?"

"I thought you'd notice."

"Fugues and harpischord, the two things you noticed first—and the only things you didn't absorb into your music. All your other songs for these last weeks have been tinted and colored and influenced by Bach. Except that there was no fugue, and there was no harpsichord. You have broken the law. You were put here because you were a genius, creating new things with only nature for your inspiration. Now, of course, you're derivative, and truly new creation is impossible for you. You'll have to leave."

"I know," Christian said, afraid, yet not really understanding what life outside his house would be like.

"We'll train you for the kinds of jobs you can pursue now. You won't starve. You won't die of boredom. But because you broke the law, one thing is forbidden to you now."

"Music."

"Not all music. There is music of a sort, Christian, that the common people, the ones who aren't Listeners, can have. Radio and television and record music. But live music and new music—those are forbidden to you. You may not sing. You may not play an instrument. You may not tap out a rhythm."

"Why not?"

The Watcher shook his head. "The world is too perfect, too at peace, too happy, for us to permit a misfit who broke the law to go about spreading discontent. And if you make more music, Christian, you will be punished drastically. Drastically."

Christian nodded, and when the Watcher told him to come, he came, leaving behind the house and the woods and his Instrument. At first he took it calmly, as the inevitable punishment for his infraction; but he had little concept of punishment, or of what exile from his Instrument would mean.

Within five hours he was shouting and striking out at anyone who came near him, because his fingers craved the touch of the Instrument's keys and levers and strips and bars, and he could not have them, and now he knew that he had never been lonely before.

"Once, Joe went to the piano and lifted the lid and played every key on the piano. And when he had done that he put his head down on the piano and cried. . . . It was like . . . losing his bar."

It took six months before he was ready for normal life. And when he left the Retraining Center (a small building, because it was so rarely used), he looked tired and years older, and he didn't smile at anyone. He became a delivery-truck driver, because the tests said that this was a job that would least grieve him and least remind him of his loss and most engage his few remaining aptitudes and interests.

He delivered doughnuts to grocery stores.

And at night he discovered the mysteries of alcohol; and the alcohol and the doughnuts and the truck and his dreams were enough that he was, in his way, content. He had no anger in him. He could live the rest of his life, without bitterness.

He delivered fresh doughnuts and took the stale ones away with him.

SECOND MOVEMENT

"With a name like Joe," Joe always said, "I had to open a bar and grill, just so I could put up a sign saying 'Joe's Bar and Grill.'" And he laughed and laughed, because, after all, Joe's Bar and Grill was a funny name these days.

But Joe was a good bartender, and the Watchers had put him in the right kind of place. Not in a big city but in a small town; a town just off the freeway, where truck drivers often came; a town not far from a large city, so that interesting things were nearby to be talked about and worried about and bitched about and loved.

Joe's Bar and Grill was, therefore, a nice place to come, and many people came there. Not fashionable people, and not drunks, but lonely people and friendly people in just the right mixture. "My clients are like a good drink. Just enough of this and that to make a new flavor that tastes better than any of the ingredients." Oh, Joe was a poet; he was a poet of alcohol, and like many another person these days, he often said, "My father was a lawyer, and in the old days I would have probably ended up a lawyer, too. And I never would have known what I was missing."

Joe was right. And he was a damn good bartender, and he didn't wish he were anything else, so he was happy.

One night, however, a new man came in, a man with a doughnut delivery truck and a doughnut brand name on his uniform. Joe noticed him because silence clung to the man like a smell—wherever he walked, people sensed it, and though they scarcely looked at him, they lowered their voices or stopped talking at all, and they got reflective and looked at the walls and the mirror behind the bar. The doughnut deliveryman sat in a corner and had a watered-down drink that meant he intended to stay a long time and didn't want his alcohol intake to be so rapid that he was forced to leave early.

Joe noticed things about people, and he noticed that this man kept looking off in the dark corner where the piano stood. It was an old, out-of-tune monstrosity from the old days (for this had been a bar for a long time), and Joe wondered why the man was fascinated by it. True, a lot of Joe's customers had been interested, but they had always walked over and plunked on the keys, trying to find a melody, failing with the out-of-tune keys, and finally giving up. This man, however, seemed almost afraid of the piano, and didn't go near it.

At closing time, the man was still there, and, on a whim, instead of making the man leave, Joe turned off the piped-in music, turned off most of the lights, and went over and lifted the lid and exposed the gray keys.

The deliveryman came over to the piano. *Chris*, his name tag said. He sat and touched a single key. The sound was not pretty. But the man touched all the keys one by one and then touched them in different orders, and all the time Joe watched, wondering why the man was so intense about it.

"Chris," Joe said.

Chris looked up at him.

"Do you know any songs?"

Chris's face went funny.

"I mean, some of those old-time songs, not those fancy ass-twitchers on the radio, but *songs*. 'In a Little Spanish Town.' My mother sang that one to me." And Joe began to sing, "In a little Spanish town, 'twas on a night like this. Stars were peek-a-booing down, 'twas on a night like this."

Chris began to play as Joe's weak and toneless baritone went on with the song. But his playing wasn't an accompaniment, not anything Joe could call an accompaniment. It was, instead, an opponent to his melody, an enemy to it, and the sounds coming out of the piano were strange and unharmonious and, by God, beautiful. Joe stopped singing and listened. For two hours he listened, and when it was over he soberly poured the man a drink and poured one for himself and clinked glasses with Chris the doughnut deliveryman who could take that rotten old piano and make the damn thing sing.

Three nights later, Chris came back, looking harried and afraid. But this time Joe knew what would happen (had to happen), and instead of waiting until closing time, Joe turned off the piped-in music ten minutes early. Chris looked up at him pleadingly. Joe misunderstood—he went over and lifted the lid to the keyboard and smiled. Chris walked stiffly, perhaps reluctantly, to the stool and sat.

"Hey, Joe," one of the last five customers shouted, "closing early?"

Joe didn't answer. Just watched as Chris began to play. No preliminaries this time; no scales and wanderings over the keys. Just power, and the piano was played as pianos aren't meant to be played; the bad notes, the out-of-tune notes, were fit into the music so that they sounded right, and Chris's fingers, ignoring the strictures of the twelve-tone scale, played, it seemed to Joe, in the cracks.

None of the customers left until Chris finished an hour and a half later. They all shared that final drink and went home, shaken by the experience.

The next night Chris came again, and the next, and the next. Whatever private battle had kept him away for the first few days after his first night of playing, he had apparently won it or lost it. None of Joe's business. What Joe cared about was the fact that when Chris played the piano, it did things to him that music had never done, and he wanted it.

The customers apparently wanted it, too. Near closing time people began showing up, apparently just to hear Chris play. Joe began starting the piano music earlier and earlier, and he had to discontinue the free drinks after the playing, because there were so many people it would have put him out of business.

It went on for two long, strange months. The delivery van pulled up outside, and people stood aside for Chris to enter. No one said anything to him. No one said anything at all, but everyone waited until he began to play the piano. He drank nothing at all. Just played. And between songs the hundreds of people in Joe's Bar and Grill ate and drank.

But the merriment was gone. The laughter and the chatter and the camaraderie were missing, and after a while Joe grew tired of the music and wanted to have his bar back the way it was. He toyed with the idea of getting rid of the piano, but the customers would have been angry at him. He thought of asking Chris not to come any more, but he could not bring himself to speak to the strange, silent man.

And so finally he did what he knew he should have done in the first place. He called the Watchers.

They came in the middle of a performance, a blind Watcher with a dog on a leash, and an earless Watcher who walked unsteadily, holding on to things for balance. They came in the middle of a song and did not wait for it to end. They walked to the piano and closed the lid gently, and Chris withdrew his fingers and looked at the closed lid.

"Oh, Christian," said the man with the seeing-eye dog.

"I'm sorry," Christian answered. "I tried not to."

"Oh, Christian, how can I bear doing to you what must be done?"

"Do it," Christian said.

And so the man with no ears took a laser knife from his coat pocket and cut off Christian's fingers and thumbs, right where they rooted into his hands. The laser cauterized and sterilized the wound even as it cut, but still some blood spattered on Christian's uniform. And, his hands now meaningless palms and useless knuckles, Christian stood and walked out of Joe's Bar and Grill. The people made way for him again, and they listened intently as the blind Watcher said, "That was a man who broke the law and was forbidden to be a Maker. He broke the law a second time, and the law insists that he be stopped from breaking down the system that makes all of you so happy."

The people understood. It grieved them; it made them uncomfortable for a few hours, but once they had returned home to their exactly right homes and got back to their exactly right jobs, the sheer contentment of their lives overwhelmed their momentary sorrow for Chris. After all, Chris had broken the law. And it was the law that kept them all safe and happy.

Even Joe. Even Joe soon forgot Chris and his music. He knew he had done the right thing. He couldn't figure out, though, why a man like Chris would have broken the law in the first place, or what law he would have broken. There wasn't a law in the world that wasn't designed to make people happy—and there wasn't a law Joe could think of that he was even mildly interested in breaking.

Yet. Once, Joe went to the piano and lifted the lid and played every key on the piano. And when he had done that he put his head down on the piano and cried, because he knew that when Chris lost that piano, lost even his fingers so he could never play again—it was like Joe's losing his bar. And if Joe ever lost his bar, his life wouldn't be worth living.

As for Chris, someone else began coming to the bar driving the same doughnut delivery van, and no one ever saw Chris again in that part of the world.

"Oh, what a beautiful mornin'!" sang the road-crew man who had seen *Oklahoma!* four times in his home town.

"Rock my soul in the bosom of Abraham!" sang the road-crew man who had learned to sing when his family got together with guitars.

"Lead, kindly light, amid the encircling gloom!" sang the road-crew man who believed.

But the road-crew man without hands, who held the signs telling the traffic to Stop or Go Slow, listened but never sang.

"Whyn't you never sing?" asked the man who liked Rogers and Hammerstein; asked all of them, at one time or another.

And the man they called Sugar just shrugged. "Don't feel like singin'," he'd say, when he said anything at all.

"Why they call him Sugar?" a new guy once asked. "He don't look sweet to me."

And the man who believed said, "His initials are *CH*. Like the sugar. C & H, you know." And the new guy laughed. A stupid joke, but the kind of gag that makes life easier on the road building crew.

Not that life was that hard. For these men, too, had been tested, and they were in the job that made them happiest. They took pride in the pain of sunburn and pulled muscles, and the road growing long and thin behind them was the most beautiful thing in the world. And so they sang all day at their work, knowing that they could not possibly be happier than they were this day.

Except Sugar.

Then Guillermo came. A short Mexican who spoke with an accent, Guillermo told everyone who asked, "I may come from Sonora, but my heart belongs in Milano!" And when anyone asked why (and often when no one asked anything), he'd explain: "I'm an Italian tenor in a Mexican body," and he proved it by singing every note that Puccini and Verdi ever wrote. "Caruso was nothing," Guillermo boasted. "Listen to this!"

Guillermo had records, and he sang along with them, and at work on the road crew he'd join in with any man's song and harmonize with it or sing an obbligato high above the melody, a soaring tenor that took the roof off his head and filled the clouds. "I can sing," Guillermo would say, and soon the other road-crew men answered, "Damn right, Guillermo! Sing it again!"

But one night Guillermo was honest and told the truth. "Ah, my friends, I'm no singer."

"What do you mean? Of course you are!" came the unanimous answer.

"Nonsense!" Guillermo cried, his voice theatrical. "If I am this great singer, why do you never see me going off to record songs? Hey? This is a great singer? Nonsense! Great singers they raise to be great singers. I'm just a man who loves to sing but has no talent! I'm a man who loves to work on the road crew with men like you and sing his guts out, but in the opera I could never be! Never!"

He did not say it sadly. He said it fervently, confidently. "Here is where I belong! I can sing to you who like to hear me sing! I can harmonize with you when I feel a harmony in my heart. But don't be thinking that Guillermo is a great singer, because he's not!"

It was an evening of honesty, and every man there explained why it was he was happy on the road crew and didn't wish to be anywhere else. Everyone, that is, except Sugar.

"Come on, Sugar. Aren't you happy here?"

Sugar smiled. "I'm happy. I like it here. This is good work for me. And I love to hear you sing."

"Then why don't you sing with us?"

Sugar shook his head. "I'm not a singer."

But Guillermo looked at him knowingly. "Not a singer, ha! Not a singer. A man without hands who refuses to sing is not a man who is not a singer. Hey?"

"What the hell did that mean?" asked the man who sang folk songs.

"It means that this man you call Sugar, he's a fraud. Not a singer! Look at his hands. All his fingers gone! Who is it who cuts off men's fingers?"

The road crew didn't try to guess. There were many ways a man could lose fingers, and none of them were anyone's business.

"He loses his fingers because he breaks the law and the Watchers cut them off! That's how a man loses fingers. What was he doing with his fingers that the Watchers wanted him to stop? He was breaking the law, wasn't he?"

"Stop," Sugar said.

"If you want," Guillermo said, but the others would not respect Sugar's privacy.

"Tell us," they said.

Sugar left the room.

"Tell us," and Guillermo told them. That Sugar must have been a Maker who broke the law and was forbidden to make music any more. The very thought that a Maker—even a lawbreaker—was working on the road crew with them filled the men with awe. Makers were rare, and they were the most esteemed of men and women.

"But why his fingers?"

"Because," Guillermo said, "he must have tried to make music again afterward. And when you break the law a second time, the power to break it a third time is taken away from you." Guillermo spoke seriously, and so to the road-crew men Sugar's story sounded as majestic and terrible as an opera. They crowded into Sugar's room and found the man staring at the wall.

"Sugar, is it true?" asked the man who loved Rogers and Hammerstein.

"Were you a Maker?" asked the man who believed.

"Yes," Sugar said.

"But Sugar," the man who believed said, "God can't mean for a man to stop making music, even if he broke the law."

Sugar smiled. "No one asked God."

"Sugar," Guillermo finally said, "There are nine of us on the crew, nine of us, and we're miles from any other human beings. You know us, Sugar. We swear on our mother's graves, every one of us, that we'll never tell a soul. Why should we? You're one of us. But sing, dammit man, sing!"

"I can't," Sugar said.

"It isn't what God intended," said the man who believed. "We're all doing what we love best, and here you are, loving music and not able to sing a note. Sing for us! Sing with us! And only you and us and God will know!"

They all promised. They all pleaded.

And the next day as the man who loved Rogers and Hammerstein sang "Love, Look Away," Sugar began to hum. As the man who believed sang "God of Our Fathers," Sugar sang softly along. And as the man who loved folk songs sang, "Swing Low, Sweet Chariot," Sugar joined in with a strange, piping voice, and all the men laughed and cheered and welcomed Sugar's voice to the songs.

Inevitably Sugar began inventing. First harmonies, of course, strange harmonies that made Guillermo frown and then, after a while, grin as he joined in, sensing as best he could what Sugar was doing to the music.

And after harmonies, Sugar began singing his own melodies, with his own words. He made them repetitive, the words simple and the melodies simpler still. And yet he shaped them into odd shapes and built them into songs that had never been heard of before, that sounded wrong and yet were absolutely right. It was not long before the man who loved Rogers and Hammerstein and the man who sang folk songs and the man who believed were learning Sugar's songs and singing them joyously or mournfully or angrily or gaily as they worked along the road.

Even Guillermo learned the songs, and his strong tenor was changed by them until his voice, which had, after all, been ordinary, became something unusual and fine. Guillermo finally said to Sugar one day, "Hey, Sugar, your music is all wrong, man. But I like the way it feels in my nose! Hey, you know? I like the way it feels in my mouth!"

Some of the songs were hymns: "Keep me hungry, Lord," Sugar sang, and the road crew sang it too.

Some of the songs were love songs: "Put your hands in someone else's pockets," Sugar sang angrily; "I hear your voice in the morning," Sugar sang tenderly; "Is it summer yet?" Sugar sang sadly; and the road crew sang them, too.

Over the months, the road crew changed, one man leaving on Wednesday and a new man taking his place on Thursday, as different skills were needed in different places. Sugar was silent when each newcomer arrived, until the man had given his word and the secret was sure to be kept.

What finally destroyed Sugar was the fact that his songs were so unforgettable. The men who left would sing the songs with their new crews, and those crews would learn them and teach them to others. Crew men taught the songs in bars and on the road; people learned them quickly and loved them; and one day a blind Watcher heard the songs and knew, instantly, who had first sung them. They were Christian Haroldsen's music, because in those melodies, simple as they were, the wind of the north woods still whistled and the fall of leaves still hung oppressively over every note and—and the Watcher sighed. He took a specialized tool from his file of tools and boarded an airplane and flew to the city closest to where a certain road crew worked. And the blind Watcher took a company car with a company driver up the road, and at the end of it, where the road was just beginning to swallow a strip of wilderness, he got out of the car and heard singing. Heard a piping voice singing a song that made even an eyeless man weep.

"Christian," the Watcher said, and the song stopped.

"You," said Christian.

"Christian, even after you lost your fingers?"

The other men didn't understand—all the other men, that is, except Guillermo.

"Watcher," said Guillermo. "Watcher, he done no harm."

The Watcher smiled wryly. "No one said he did. But he broke the law. You, Guillermo, how would you like to work as a servant in a rich man's house? How would you like to be a bank teller?"

"Don't take me from the road crew, man," Guillermo said.

"It's the law that finds where people will be happy. But Christian Haroldsen broke the law. And he's gone around ever since, making people hear music they were never meant to hear."

Guillermo knew he had lost the battle before it began, but he couldn't stop himself. "Don't hurt him, man. I was meant to hear his music. Swear to God, it's made me happier."

The Watcher shook his head sadly. "Be honest, Guillermo. You're an honest man. His music's made you miserable, hasn't it? You've got everything you could want in life, and yet his music makes you sad. All the time, sad."

Guillermo tried to argue, but he was honest, and he looked into his own heart. And he knew that the music was full of grief. Even the happy songs mourned for something; even the angry songs wept; even the love songs seemed to say that everything dies and contentment is the most fleeting of things. Guillermo looked in his own heart, and all Sugar's music stared back up at him; and Guillermo wept.

"Just don't hurt him, please," Guillermo murmured as he cried.

"I won't," the blind Watcher said. Then he walked to Christian, who stood passively waiting, and he held the special tool up to Christian's throat. Christian gasped.

"No," Christian said, but the word only formed with his lips and tongue. No sound came out. Just a hiss of air. "No."

"Yes," the Watcher said.

The road crew watched silently as the Watcher led Christian away. They did not sing for days. But then Guillermo forgot his grief one day and sang an aria from *La Bohème*, and the songs went on from there. Now and then they sang one of Sugar's songs, because the songs could not be forgotten.

In the city, the blind Watcher furnished Christian with a pad of paper and a pen. Christian immediately gripped the pencil in the crease of his palm and wrote: "What do I do now?"

The blind Watcher laughed. "Have we got a job for you! Oh, Christian, have we got a job for you!"

APPLAUSE

In all the world there were only two dozen Watchers. They were secretive men who supervised a system that needed little supervision because it actually made nearly everybody happy. It was a good system, but like even the most perfect of machines, here and there it broke down. Here and there someone acted madly and damaged himself, and to protect everyone and the person himself, a Watcher had to notice the madness and go to fix it.

For many years the best of the Watchers was a man with no fingers, a man with no voice. He would come silently, wearing the uniform that named him with the only name he needed—Authority. And he would find the kindest, easiest, yet most thorough way of solving the problem and curing the madness and preserving the system that made the world, for the first time in history, a very good place to live. For practically everyone.

For there were still a few people—one or two each year—who were caught in a circle of their own devising, who could neither adjust to the system nor bear to harm it, people who kept breaking the law despite their knowledge that it would destroy them.

Eventually, when the gentle maimings and deprivations did not cure their madness and set them back into the system, they were given uniforms, and they, too, went out. Watching.

The keys of power were placed in the hands of those who had most cause to hate the system they had to preserve. Were they sorrowful?

"I am," Christian answered in the moments when he dared to ask himself that question.

In sorrow he did his duty. In sorrow he grew old. And finally the other Watchers, who reverenced the silent man (for they knew he had once sung magnificent songs), told him he was free. "You've served your time," said the Watcher with no legs, and he smiled.

Christian raised an eyebrow, as if to say, "And?"

"So wander."

Christian wandered. He took off his uniform, but lacking neither money nor time he found few doors closed to him. He wandered where in his former lives he had once lived. A road in the mountains. A city where he had once known the loading entrance of every restaurant and coffee shop and grocery store. And, at last, a place in the woods where a house was falling apart in the weather because it had not been used in forty years.

Christian was old. The thunder roared, and it only made him realize that it was about to rain. All the old songs. All the old songs, he mourned inside himself, more because he couldn't remember them than because he thought his life had been particularly sad.

As he sat in a coffee shop in a nearby town to stay out of the rain, he heard four teenagers who played the guitar very badly singing a song that he knew. It was a song he had invented while the asphalt poured on a hot summer day. The teenagers were not musicians and certainly were not Makers. But they sang the song from their hearts, and even though the words were happy, the song made everyone who heard it cry.

Christian wrote on the pad he always carried, and showed his question to the boys. "Where did that song come from?"

"It's a Sugar song," the leader of the group answered. "It's a song by Sugar."

Christian raised an eyebrow, making a shrugging motion.

"Sugar was a guy who worked on a road crew and made up songs. He's dead now, though," the boy answered.

Christian smiled. Then he wrote (and the boys waited impatiently for this speechless old man to go away): "Aren't you happy? Why sing sad songs?"

The boys were at a loss for an answer. The leader spoke up, though, and said, "Sure, I'm happy. I've got a good job, a girl I like, and man, I couldn't ask for more. I got my guitar. I got my songs. And my friends."

And another boy said, "These songs aren't sad, mister. Sure, they make people cry, but they aren't sad."

"Yeah," said another. "It's just that they were written by a man who knows."

Christian scribbled on his paper. "Knows what?"

"He just knows. Just knows, that's all."

And then the teenagers turned back to their clumsy guitars and their young, untrained voices, and Christian walked to the door to leave because the rain had stopped and because he knew when to leave the stage. He turned and bowed just a little toward the singers. They didn't notice him, but their voices were all the applause he needed. He left the ovation and went outside where the leaves were just turning color and would soon, with a slight inaudible sound, break free and fall to the earth.

For a moment he thought he heard himself singing. But it was just the last of the wind, coasting madly through the wires over the street. It was a frenzied song, and Christian thought he had recognized his voice. ∞

"Four points to you, Fenwick."

M GNIFICATION

Mysteries of the miniscule seen through the eye of a scanning electron microscope. Science fact looking like science fiction

BY SCOT MORRIS

A tree ant becomes a futuristic alien; marijuana-resin sacs ripe with hashish become Disneyesque mushrooms; typing paper looks like a nightmare road map.

This is the miniature world of David Scharf, whom *Time* called "the Ansel Adams of inner space" and whose photos Adams has described as "absolutely wonderful." Scharf's peephole is the

Counterclockwise from below: Mite on the neck of a termite; front view of crane fly; hairlike antennae, mouth parts, and proboscis, or feeding tube, of young male mosquito; close encounter with the vicious biting black fly.

PHOTOGRAPHS BY DAVID SCHARF

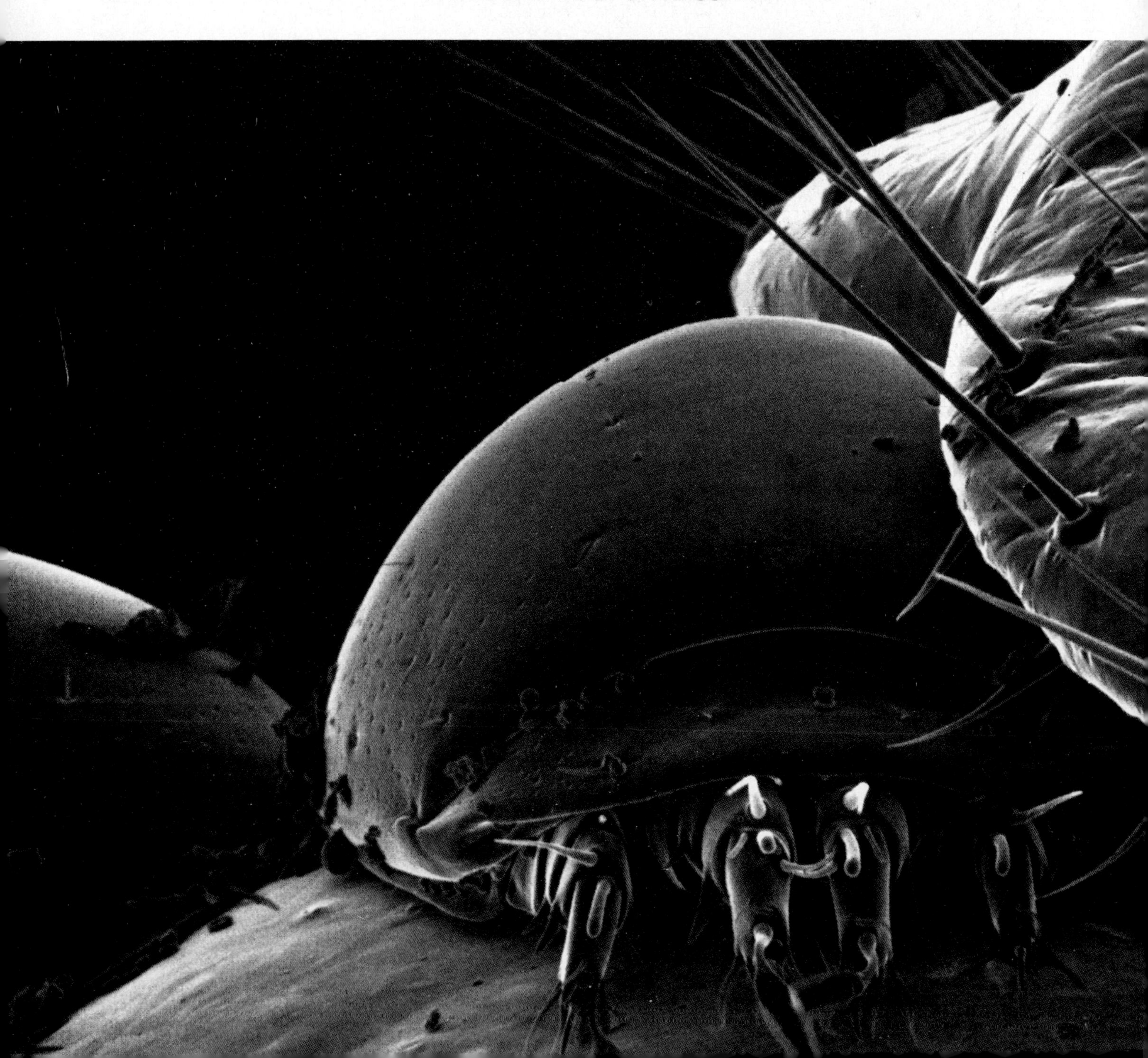

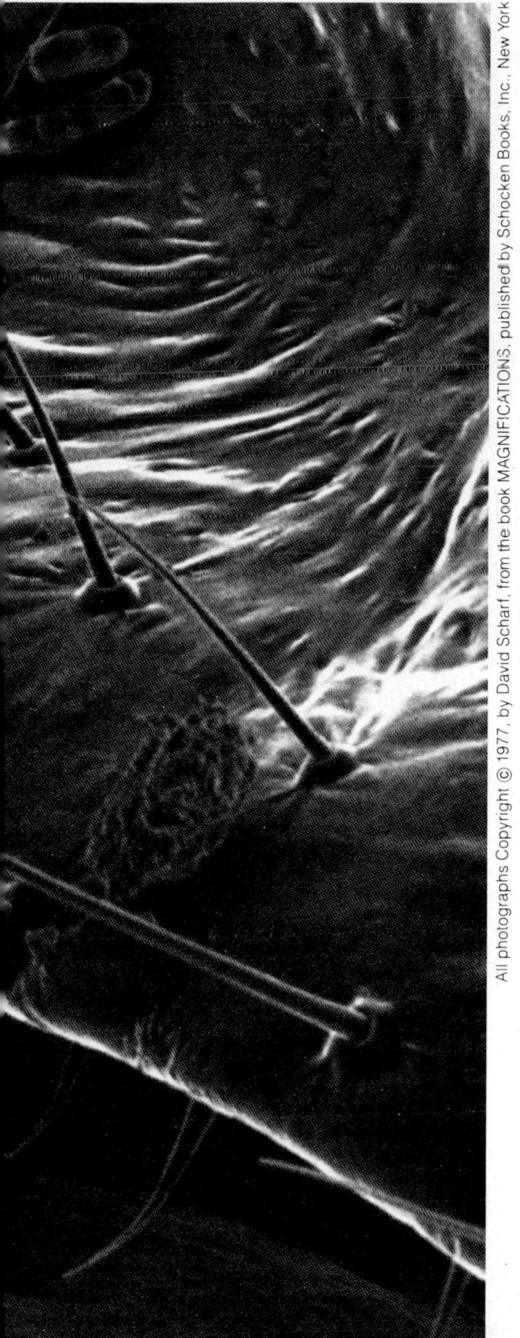

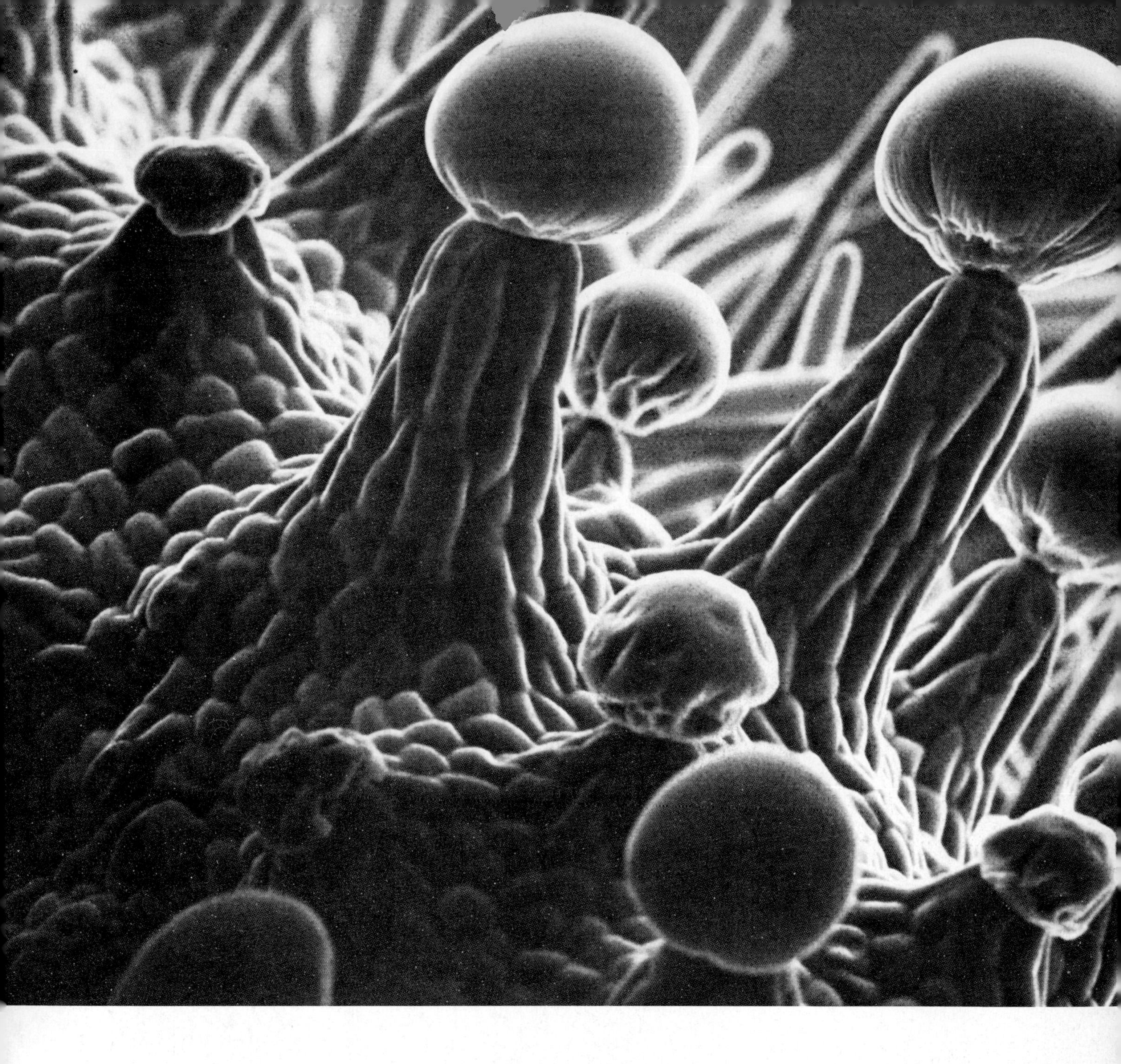

scanning electron microscope (SEM). An electron beam replaces visible light (hence, there is no color involved) and scans every contour to produce a 3-D image entirely in focus and incredibly lifelike. In part that's because Scharf's subjects *are* alive. Previously, most SEM photography was of subjects that were dead, dried, and coated with gold alloy. But Scharf has perfected ways of shooting living subjects temporarily immobilized in a vacuum. "I want my pictures to be an accurate representation of life," he says. "I take great care to keep my specimens uninjured. Some are returned to my garden alive."

Clockwise from above: drug-secreting resin nodules of a female marijuana flower; paper; helxine budding flower and leaves; fiberglass fabric; a curved protuberance from the style of a hibiscus flower.

"The heartbeat of a small animal can cause enough vibration to make photographing impossible."

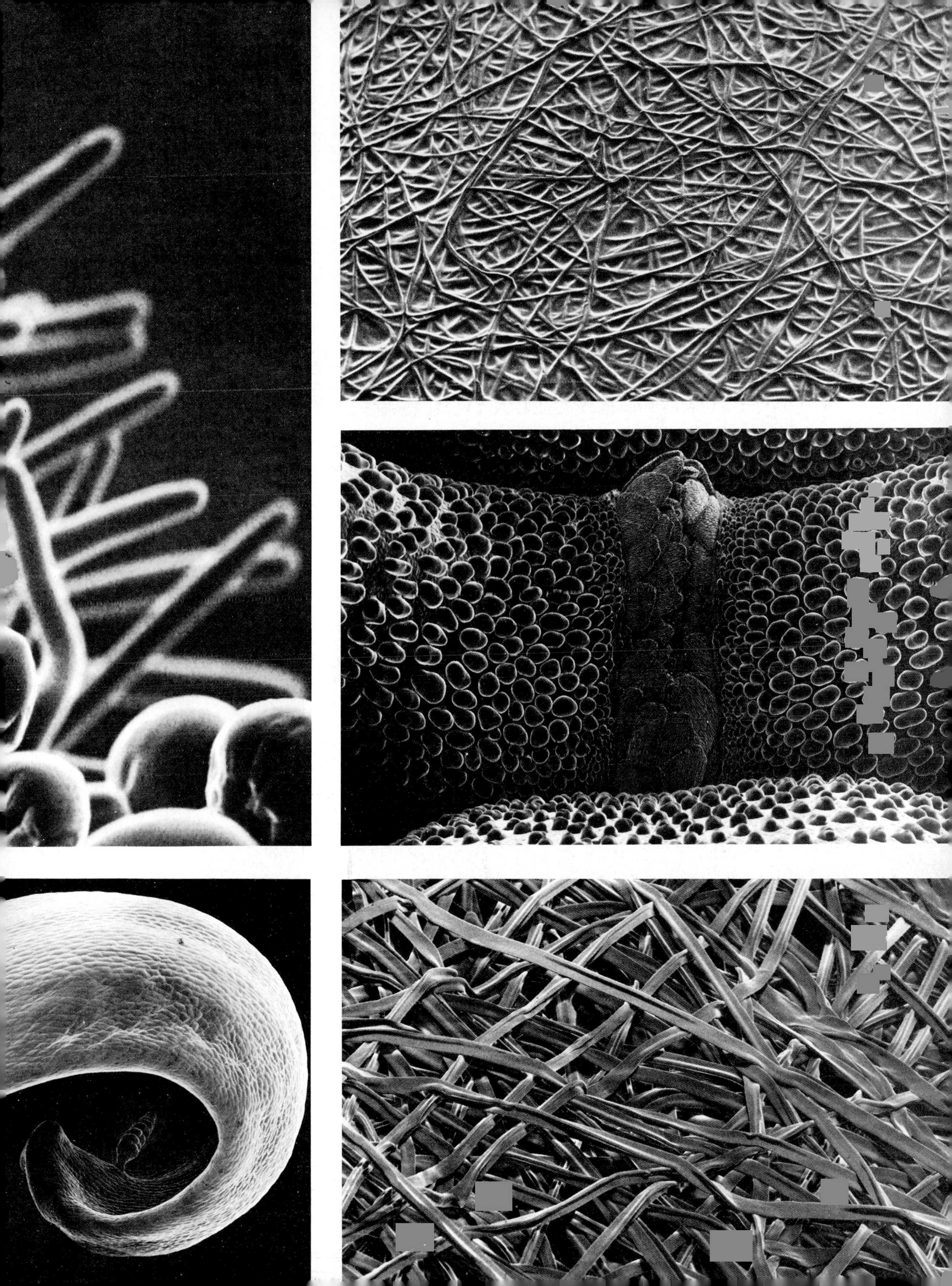

I'm extremely careful to keep my specimens uninjured; some are returned to my garden alive.

How does he get an insect to hold still while scanning him for seventy seconds per portrait? "The truth is, they don't all hold still. They tend to freeze in their tracks when the air is removed from the chamber, but many photos have been ruined by unpredicted movement. The mere heartbeat of a small animal can cause enough vibration of a limb to make photographing impossible."

Though Scharf's pictures contain impressive information, they are intended primarily as visual studies. Composition, balance, detail, and beauty are what he looks for. His photos are scientific records second, works of art first. ∞

Clockwise beginning below: Hairs and resin nodules of marijuana leaf; gladiolus pistil; oval seedlike fruits on strawberry surface with projecting stigmas and styles; multiple disc flowers in center of African daisy.

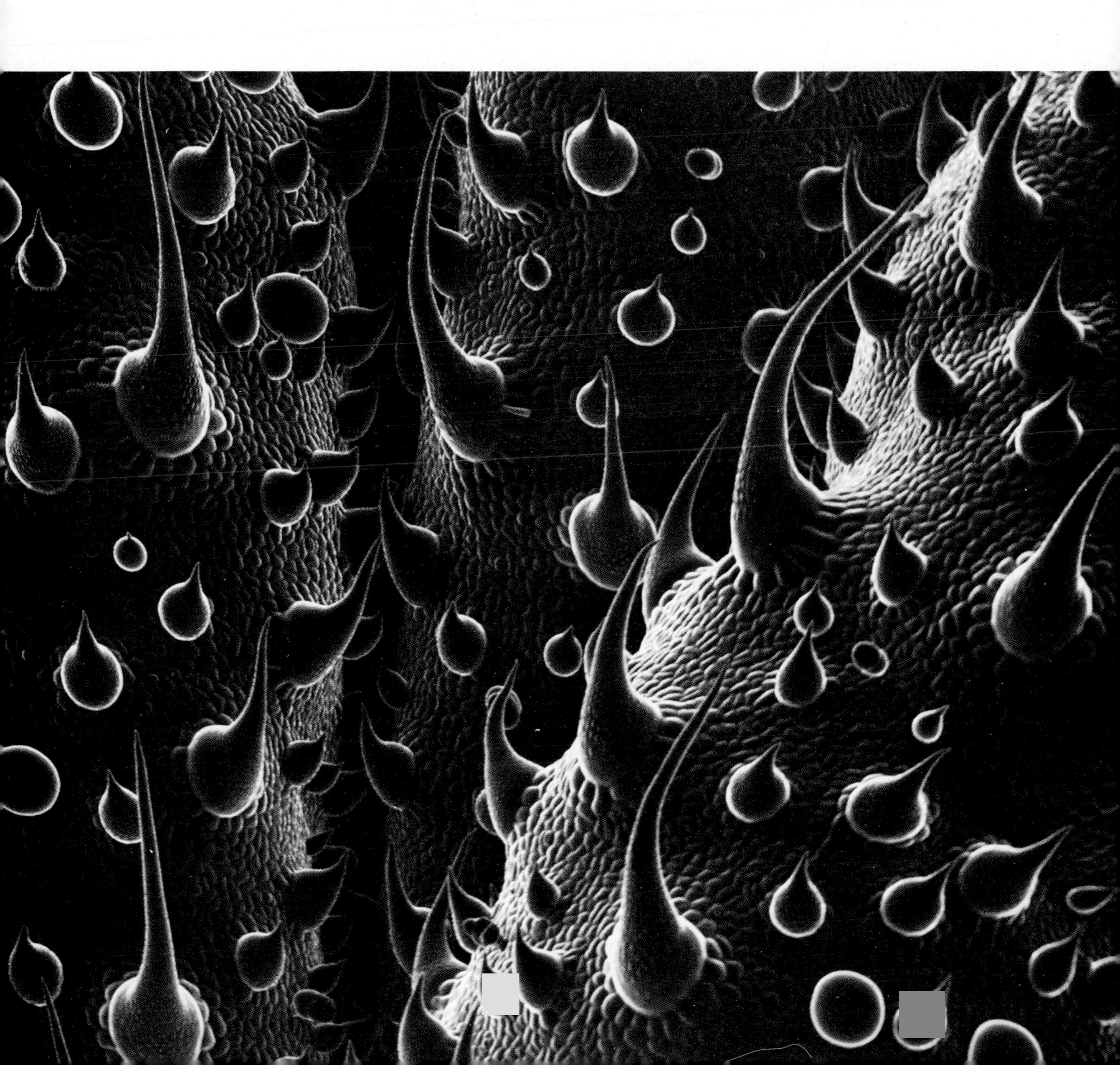

ICEBACK INVASION

BY HAYFORD PEIRCE

"Give me your tired, your poor . . ." Russians?

PAINTING BY EVELYN TAYLOR

There was a minor incident at the polling station in St. Tropez that year, nothing serious, merely another case of an inebriated American, good for a laugh at the discos that evening after the votes had been counted, but a nuisance nevertheless to those authorities who had to deal with it along with all the other problems of Election Day.

"*Numero 2871, Monsieur Goodman, Alexandre*," yelled the registrar, sitting behind the long table on which rested the voting list, the piles of unused ballots, and the ballot box itself.

"*Monsieur Goodman, Alexandre, numero 2871*," cried the second official, making a note in a register and handing a ballot to the red-faced, semi-dazed gentleman who stood before him dressed in bedraggled white linen.

"Listen, you, *écoutez*," enunciated Mr. Goodman with some difficulty (lunch aboard the dear Aga's yacht was always so tipsy making), "I wanna ballot in English, ya hear?"

"*Comment, Monsieur*?"

"I said I want, aw, the hell with it, *je veux voter en anglais, comprenez*?"

"*Mais, Monsieur, on n'est pas en Angleterre, on est en France*," replied the baffled registrar with a polite smile.

"*Non, non*, I mean *oui, oui, je sais, je veux mon* vote," here Mr. Goodman waved his ballot vigorously before the noses of the officials, "*en anglais, pas francais, vous comprenez? C'est mon* right."

An impatient murmur arose from those standing in line behind Mr. Goodman as the two officials conferred hastily.

"*Qu'est-ce qu'il dit? Son accent . . .*"

"*Si je comprends bien, il veut qu'on lui donne un bulletin de vote traduit en américain*!"

"*Mais tu rigoles*!"

"*Mais non, c'est lui qui rigole! Attends, on va voir.*" Turning to Mr. Goodman, he said in that fluent Oxford-accented English that so many Frenchmen possess and yet are so loath to use, "You are indeed a French citizen, sir?"

"Course I am," replied Mr. Goodman stoutly. "Ten years now."

"And you wish to cast a ballot paper *en américain*?"

"*Oui, oui*, now you *comprenez*!"

The mayor, two *agents de police*, and a gendarme had been attracted by the noise.

"*Mais c'est impossible*," pointed out the mayor, who prided himself on his grasp of Cartesian logic. "*Vous êtes en France, n'est-ce pas? Par définition, quoi, on vote en français, vous voyez ce que je veux dire*?"

"*Mais non*!" cried Mr. Goodman passionately. "In New York they got Spanish ballot, in California they got Spanish ballot, *espagnol*, savvy? It's their right, *savez, espagnol*. I jus' wan' my rights, tha's all. *Américain*!"

"*Il est fou*," explained the mayor to the others.

"*Votez, espèce de salaud*!" shouted the gendarme, less tolerant of folly.

"*Non*," replied Mr. Goodman, folding his arms with dignity.

"*Il est fou*," agreed the gendarme. A whistle was blown; brown khaki surged into the room; truncheons rose and fell; and presently Mr. Goodman's inert form was carried to the rear of a small jeep, which roared away in a cloud of dust. He awoke some time later in the *maison de fous* of Nice, tightly swathed in a wet sheet, from which three years later his lawyer would succeed in getting him released for a probationary weekend. . . .

The two border-patrol agents of the Immigration and Naturalization Service stared at each other glumly.

"Going to lose that arm, Padillo?"

"Naw, only us wops know how to really use knives. The doc says it'll take a couple months' therapy to get it working again and it'll always be a little stiff, but, what the hell, that oughta be okay for a desk job, right?"

"A nice desk job sounds pretty good to me right about now," said O'Hara, who lay immobilized in the hospital bed, connected to a collection of tubes, drains, and monitoring devices. "So what happened to those mothering wetbacks that jumped us? After that shotgun started blasting . . ."

Padillo scowled outlandishly. "Did you say *wetback*, you dumb mick?"

O'Hara grinned weakly. "Excuse *me*, commissioner. Illegal alien is what I meant to say."

"*Illegal alien!*"

"Well, pardon me all to hell, your honor. Undocumented worker."

"Worker?"

"Okay. Okay. I've got it. Probationary citizen. Undocumented probationary citizen. Or have they come up with a new one while I been in a coma?"

"Nope, undocumented probationary citizens is what carved me up and gunned you down. Don't hurt as much that way, does it, O'Hara?"

"Only when I laugh, pal, only when I laugh."

"Well, hold on to your sides then. This is really going to break you up. The six guys what did the carving have been released in custody of their new citizen-sponsors, the United Brotherhood of Sanitation Workers of Los Angeles. Their complaint sworn against us mentions little things like assault, battery, illegal use of force, unwarranted and unjustified stop and search, and there's about a dozen other charges pending before the court. The district director is trying to get them quashed, but he doesn't know how good the chances are. The UB swings a lotta weight, and there's a lotta garbage cans up in LA needing to be emptied."

"So it's our asses that swing, huh?"

"It sure is, O'Hara, it sure is."

"It is the end," announced President Martinez with gloomy foreboding, "of the Republic as we know it."

"Oh yeah?" said Secretary of State Richard XYZ, a study in ebony skepticism. "Our reparations to Black Africa is bein' paid on time, ain't they?"

"Humph!" snorted Attorney General Ahmed El-Ali. "Under my, our, *your* administration, all political prisoners detained because of race, color, creed, or revolutionary belief have been released."

"How exciting," drawled Labor Secretary Antonelli languidly. "Without having to refer the question to my, er, 'family,' I feel certain that no *union* problems are about to arise."

"Ugh," concurred Interior Secretary Chief Running Clubfoot, first and last a presidential supporter. "White man takem land belong Indian, *n'est-ce pas*?" and reverted to his customary lethargy.

"Gentlemen, *please*," implored the President.

"Gentle*men*? *Men*?" cried Secretary of Enforcement of Women's Constitutionally Guaranteed Equality Eliza Heliogabalus, founder and national chaircreature of the minority but powerful Le's Begin Party.

"Gentle*persons*."

"Touchy, touchy," muttered Rafael laPine, HEW, *sotto voce*, to Ms. Heliogabalus. "Rejected another ball transplant, dear?"

"Dat still leave her wit' two more dan you, ya fuckin' transvestite," explained Jeremy "Rocky Knucks" Kawolski, director of penal sequestration and rehabilitation, "so let's shut ya mout' an' listen to what da man has to say, huh?"

"Beast," muttered Mr. laPine, turning for sympathy to, and groping for the leg of, Commerce Secretary Codfish Saltonstall Winthrop—tall, dim, pinstriped, the token WASP of President Martinez's Cabinet.

> *"This is the most egalitarian army ever created. It consists of 51 percent females, 47 percent males, 1 percent transsexuals, 1 percent transvestites, 4 percent lesbians, 6 percent gays, 7 percent criminals."*

"The end of the Republic?" repeated Welfare Payments Secretary Morgan Phipps DuPont. "As we know it, of course. In what way?"

"The army," snapped President Martinez, glaring at Defense Secretary Mildred Haggleman.

"But surely," interjected Budget Director Cyrus Openhand, "next year's defense budget is some $950 billion?"

"Exactly," replied the President, "and do you realize that with a budget of nearly a trillion dollars a year, the entire armed forces personnel—Army, Navy, Air Force, Marines, National Guard, and what have you—is currently 348,000 effectives? Total! *This* in a country of 300 million?"

"On the other hand," pointed out Ms. Heliogabalus, "it is an exceptionally well-*equalized* army."

"*Extremely* important," concurred Richard XYZ.

"Overriding consideration, even," suggested Ahmed El-Ali.

"Figures, Ms. Secretary Haggleman?"

"Certainly," she replied proudly. "It is the most egalitarian armed force ever created. As of today it consists of 51 percent females, 47 percent males, 1 percent transsexuals, and 1 percent transvestites. It is, furthermore, 8 percent black, 26 percent Hispanic, 1 percent Amerind, 28 percent Catholic, 2 percent Jewish, 1 percent Muslim, 4 percent lesbian, 6 percent gay, 11 percent bisexual, 14 percent handicapped and mentally retarded, 7 percent criminal, 9 percent pacifist, 21 percent illiterate, and 100 percent unionized!"

"Bravo," applauded Mr. laPine.

"An' how many of dese bums is combat ready?" inquired "Rocky Knucks" Kawolski with professional interest.

"An *extremely* favorable ratio. Aside from the 6,200 men in the missile submarines at all times, I sincerely believe that upon seventy-two hours' notice, the armed forces of the United States of America could field some 27,000 battle-ready combat troops!" Ms. Haggleman blushed modestly. "And in six weeks we could *double* that figure!"

Mr. Kawolski nodded thoughtfully but remained a man who demanded absolute certitude. His massive jaw swung majestically around to confront President Martinez. "You mean like dere ain't enough guys in da army to defend da country, and dat's da end of da Republic?" he asked.

President Martinez gaped. "Why, whatever gave you *that* idea? I was referring, of course, to the potential dangers of a military *coup*!"

Charlie "The Fighting Eskimo" Rubenstein, circuit judge for the Twenty-seventh District, pouted dolefully. "It's all over," he moaned, "the election is down the tubes. Me, an ex-judge at forty-two. And by a lousy two hundred votes. That's what hurts, Maxie, two hundred votes, just—"

"Pipe *down*, Charlie, I gotta tell ya again to stop your worrying? Your two hundred votes will be coming in any moment now." The campaign manager pulled his rumpled jacket together, straightened his collar, and began to slick down his hair. "Get presentable, Charlie boy, your victory speech will be coming up any moment now."

"But, Maxie," enunciated Charlie ponderously, "where are the votes going to *come* from? We already counted the gay vote, the graveyard vote, the anti-pot vote, the Aaron Burr Society vote, the vegetarian vote, the men's-liberation vote, and we're *still* behind!"

"Charlie," said Maxie gently, "I'm gonna tell ya somepin: A lotta people don't like ya. But it don't matter, because that ballot box which they is carrying in and dumping on the registrar's table over there and which they are now opening up and counting the ballots thereof, that ballot box is gonna give you a landslide margin of a matter of thirty or maybe even forty votes. Believe me, baby, the electorate of the Twenty-seventh District has declared its will, and Charlie Rubenstein is the one they willed."

Charlie shook his head in baffled awe. "But Maxie, we've courted every nut group from here to the funny farm and—"

"Ah *hah*!" crowed Maxie. "I knew ya'd forget!"

"Forget? Forget what?"

"The funny farm."

"The *funny* farm?"

"Of course the funny farm."

"*Maxie*. Listen to me. *What are you saying? Do you take me for some kind of a NUT?*"

"Ssshhh."

"—certify 367 votes from the Sixteenth Ward, Sub-Division E, Polling Station Four. Seventeen votes for Sitka, three hundred fifty votes for Rubenstein. The winner in the Twenty-seventh District is—"

"You, ya dummy. Now—"

"Polling Station Four is the *funny farm*?"

"Woodchopper State Hospital for the Mentally Retarded," said Maxie smugly. "That's it."

Charlie inhaled slowly and profoundly, his eyes glazed. Suddenly he exhaled with a whoosh. He broke into a maniacal grin. "Maxie," he cried, staggering Maxie with a gleeful thump between the shoulder blades, "now I get it. *Now* I get it. You mean like you had the fix in, and like the doctors and the nurses and the orderlies and the gardeners and the guards and all of the others that take care of the nuts—"

"—mentally retarded, Charlie—"

"—and like, *they're* the ones that voted for me. Right, Maxie, isn't that right, Maxie?"

"Wrong, Charlie. *They* all vote in their own precincts, where they live, just like everyone else. I mean like the mentally retarded nuts in the funny farm is who has just reelected you the distinguished circuit judge for the glorious Twenty-seventh—"

The distinguished Judge could only sputter.

"Ya sound like a motorboat," said Maxie sourly. "Fa chrissake, they been doing it down in LA since '76 or '78, somepin like that, ten, fifteen years now."

"They *have*?"

"Sure they have. They get the hospital staffs to run voter-education plans, and the League of Women Voters comes in and conducts workshops, and they got judges and shrinks to certify that this one and that one suchlike moderately or mildly retarded patient is now deemed able to form, if ya see what I mean, an appropriate opinion." A didactic finger jabbed the Judge's breastbone painfully. "An' that's all it takes."

"And this is *legal*? Not like getting out the graveyard vote?"

"Of *course* it's legal. Ain't they got their own constitutional rights just like you and me and all the rest of the distinguished voters of this great district?"

The Judge fell into deep and somber thought. At last he uttered uncertainly, "Yeah, I suppose now that I think of it, they're no dumber than anyone *else* that's voting these days." Charlie's tone of voice did not carry absolute conviction. Another long moment's anguished thought and he was able to articulate that profound disquiet which had been nibbling like a fox at his bosom for some minutes now. "But, Maxie, doesn't that mean . . . like, these retarded guys, couldn't they . . . you know, have voted for the *other* guy?"

"For chris*sake*, Charlie," snarled Maxie, "who *else* would be dumb enough to vote for a schmuck like you? Now straighten ya tie, here comes the TV camera."

"Enough!" shouted the party secretary balefully. "You will support me on this measure or—"

"You will have us shot, Dimitri Andreyevich?" smirked the director of state security. "No, comrade, I think I speak on behalf of the entire Politburo when I say that your heroic labors in aid of the glorious peoples of the Soviet Union have earned you that so richly rewarding retirement from the cares of the anti-imperialist struggle in the quiet calm of your beloved dacha on the distant side of the Ural Mountains."

"The minister of consumer planning was suave, eager to expunge memories of the trifling matter of 54 million left shoes produced throughout the Soviet Union, excluding any right shoes whatsoever."

Somewhat later, after the former party secretary had been conveyed discreetly from the room and was snugly ensconced en route to his cozy one-roomed birchwood cabin deep in the trackless evergreen forests to the east of Lake Baykal, the foreign minister cleared his throat authoritatively:

"Actually, comrades, a certain, er, former person's project might well be construed to contain certain elements of interest. Let us be blunt," he snapped sharply. "The Soviet Union has not been so poorly off in relation to the rest of the world since the years before the Great Patriotic War.

"Consider: The European Common Market is now the single most powerful economic force in the world: Our Warsaw Pact allies are being drawn inexorably into its orbit. Our eastern flank is threatened militarily by the revisionist traitors and capitalists of the Sino-Nipponese conspiracy. Our policy in black Africa is a shambles, good ruble after bad is poured into a bottomless cesspool. The Arabs have squandered their oil and are bankrupt; the Moslem irredentists have declared holy war against the Communist infidel, a million of our agents and comrades lie [illegible] a dozen countries." [illegible] pounded the table.

"And finally, the United [illegible] us with submarines, with cru[illegible] with laser-armed satellites. Its [illegible] weakens, its economy groans, its moral[illegible] decay, its will to survive atrophies, its army is nearly nonexistent, it is clearly in the last days of degeneracy. *But*," he thumped the table anew, "still it survives. Clearly it is as comparatively dangerous to the Soviet Union as it was twenty years ago. Therefore, I submit that the tactics of fifty years of struggle have been to no avail, and that we implement—"

"That goat-befouled Resolution Six?" cried the minister of agriculture incredulously.

"Ah," said the minister of consumer planning suavely, eager to expunge memories of a trifling matter, recently discussed, of some 54 million left shoes produced throughout the Soviet Union to the exclusion of any right shoes whatsoever, "but ask yourself this, dear Ivan Mikhailovich: By adopting and implementing Resolution Six, what have we actually to lose?"

"And of equal importance," concluded the director of state security decisively, "even if anything *does* go wrong, what, short of nuclear war, can they *do* to us?"

"Fifteen years ago," said O'Hara, still attached to his plumbing, "I got called to testify in *Orinda*, the one that pulled the plug on the border patrol and let every greaser south of the border into the country and onto the payroll as easy as kiss my Irish ass."

"You were? In *Orinda*?" marveled Padillo, who settled back to listen to the story for the dozenth time.

"Sure was. Doin' a sweep through the garment-factory section. Pulled in these six guys couldn't speak a word of English. No ID, so off they go. Next thing we know, the sweatshop employer and all the rest of the clothing manufacturers, the ACLU, the League of Mexican Voters—and get this, the *unions*, 'cause they're losing membership all over the place and the union bosses figure they won't have no one to boss around much longer—*all* of these characters decide to make this a test case. So there I am in court listening to their million-dollar shyster defending these six scared Mexes what don't even understand what's going on."

"Laid it on pretty thick, I hear," prompted Padillo.

O'Hara snorted. "With a trowel, pal. 'What right,' says he, 'by what *right* does this uniformed and brutal Gestapo seize and humiliate these poor innocent honest hard-working migrants? Possibly, it isn't proven, they crossed the border unknowingly, certainly not in any intentionally illegal fashion. Does this deny them the right to work, the right to live peacefully among their families, the right to be free from attack by jackbooted authority?'" O'Hara's lips

…ed bitterly at the memory.

"And then?"

"And then *our* guy, *he* says, 'But, Your Honor, all these fine INS boys is doing is trying to uphold the law of the land, what says that illegal immigrants is just that, i.e., *illegal*, doncha know? And viz. by definition therefore aren't supposed to come into this country and work, and bring their children and wives, and establish residences, and go to schools, and a million other things, and all these overworked upstanding noblelike officers is doing is asking these guys who are plainly illegal is if they have any ID to identify themselves. Not a passport with an entry visa, mind you, and not even a green card, Your Honor, and maybe not even something in English, but just plain *anything* for chrissakes!' "

"Hey! Easy, pal, easy! You'll pull all your plumbing out."

"Yeah, so after a bit more of this, the judge, who knows which side his bread is buttered on, comes to his decision—namely, that 'since by the appearance of things, the defendants were doing nothing illegal or suspicious or immoral or fattening, nobody on God's green earth, except maybe outside this court's jurisdiction, has any right whatsoever to ask them for any identification whatsoever, merely because they happen to look like Mexicans and not like this big dumb Irishman what is sitting here, since it still isn't illegal in this here glorious state of California or even in these here glorious *United* States to look like Mexicans, a little light background music, maestro, and the case is hereby dismissed.' Pah!"

The first elements of the invasion force crossed the Bering Strait in mid-afternoon of August 17 in three dilapidated unmarked ground-effect machines. Leaving behind the choppy gray waters that form the fifty-four-mile gap between the eastern point of the Union of Soviet Socialist Republics and Cape Prince of Wales, the western tip of the continental United States, the six men and women in each craft heaved a sigh of relief as the ear-splitting whine of the turbines changed pitch and the GEMs moved sluggishly up the spume-tossed shingle and into the heartland of the Seward Peninsula.

Bypassing the tiny settlements of Wales and Lost River a few miles to the south, the three specially equipped long-range Arctic GEMs were off on the seven hundred-mile haul to the capital of the North Slope oil fields, Prudhoe Bay. One would disappear forever with all hands aboard into the depths of a snow crevasse, but the other two would successfully navigate the myriad hazards of overland travel within the Arctic Circle to reach their goal. . . .

"And that was *Orinda*, huh?"

"Yup, and that was O'Hara himself in the full flower of his youth up there on the witness stand what got that son-of-a-bitching million-dollar shyster so mad he could hardly decide whether to poop or blind. The Judge strikes the whole thing off the record," he added sadly, "my one chance for fame.

"See, here I am up on the stand and this lawyer is going at me pretty good, 'gestapoing' here and 'jackbooting' there and all that, and finally he says, 'So let me ask you, Officer, just what it is when you see these here innocent brown faces that makes you *think*, Officer, that you have the *right*, Officer, to make these outrageous and unconstitutional demands, *that's* what the Court would like to know, Officer.'

"And he draws himself up and cocks an ear at me and his snoot at the judge, who's eating this up, and gets ready for his next speech, since obviously this isn't a question wants any answering by some dumb INS officer, and a mick to boot.

"So just as he gets his yap open again ready to start shooting another line, I holds up my hand and says, 'Just a minute here,' and this Beverly Hills shyster is so surprised since no one in thirty years has ever told him to do *that*, he actually *does* hold it a minute. And everyone in the courtroom is looking at me now, I mean *really* looking, even the Mexes, like they're just seeing me for the first time.

"And I reach behind me and pull out my wallet and I start to leaf through it, all those credit card holders and photo holders, you know, and after a while I pull out these two pieces of paper, and I sort of squint at them like I never seen them before, and everyone in the courtroom is craning forward so that *they* can see what the hell it is I'm waving around, and I says real puzzled like:

"'Well, Counselor,' I says, 'I'm just a poor country boy and not much education, and I'm just a plain ol' US citizen, nothing special or fancy-like like these gentlemen over here,' and I wave a hand in the direction of the Mexes, 'and right here I've got these two pieces of paper, and the first one, which is called—lemme see, yes, it's written right up on top here—*Selective Service System Notice of Classification*, it says right here on the back: "You are required to have this notice, in addition to your registration certificate, on your person at all times." And here on this *other* piece of paper (you might have guessed, Counselor, this one says *Selective Service System Registration Certificate*), *it* says: "The law requires you to have this certificate in your personal possession at all times for identification and to notify your local board of any change of address."

"Now by this time the shyster is jumpin' up and jumpin' down and hootin' and hollerin' and rantin' and ravin', and the Judge is pounding his gavel and I'm ignoring the low-born bastards like I can't hear any of this hoohah at all and I'm saying: 'And it seems to me, Counselor, that if a native-born US citizen, who's got all his parents native-born US citizens, and all his *grand*-parents native-born US citizens, and this here US citizen is peaceful and law-abiding and pays his taxes and ups in the army when they tell him to and goes off to get his

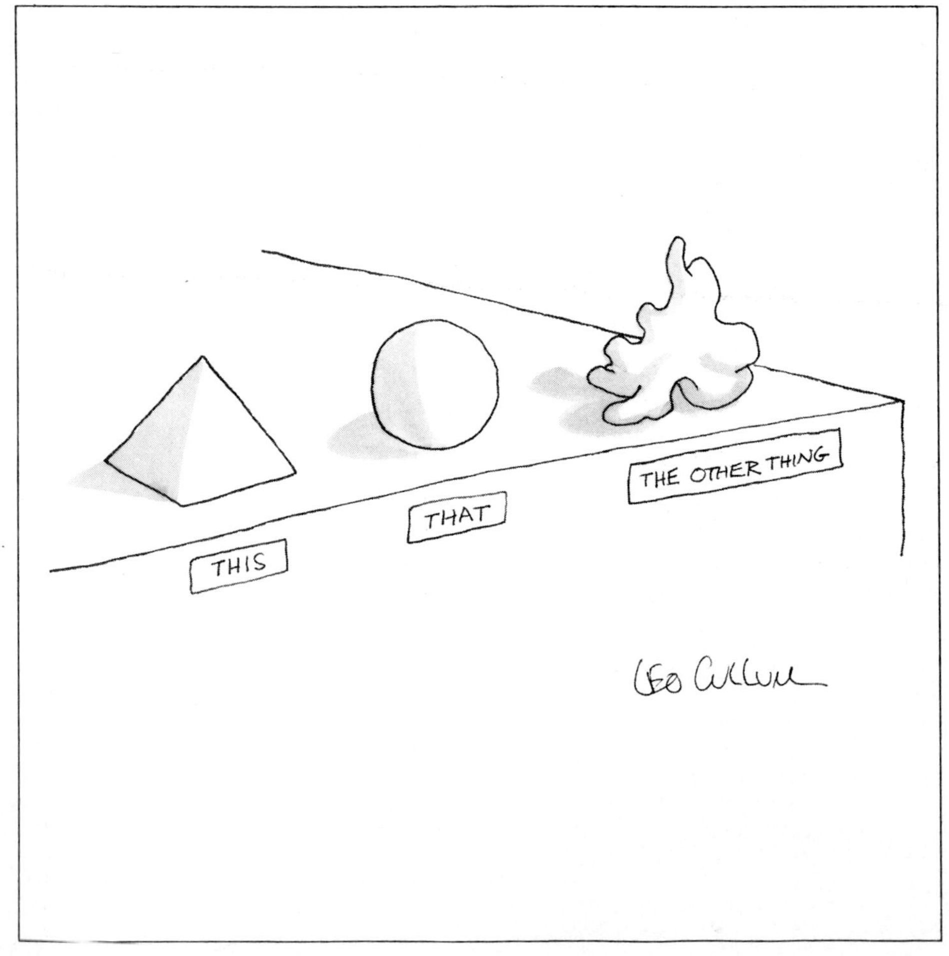

ass shot off in some stinking hole like Vietnam and maybe gets shipped home in a box, and this here guy is required by law, by *law*, Counselor,' I shout, 'to carry this ID around by *law*, and if he don't the federal marshals can come and take this guy and throw his ass into a federal *jail*, Counselor, then it seems to me that the United States Immigration and Naturalization Service has a right to ask for a little ID from a bunch of guys what can't even speak English and are about two hundred yards from the Mexican border and there's a great big hole under the fence and—'

"By now the judge has broken his gavel he's banging so hard, and he's yelling, 'Bailiff! Bailiff! Bailiff!!' and the lawyer is just sort of pop-eyed and muttering, 'Objection, objection, objection,' and about half the courtroom has burst into applause, and the other half is looking around for rocks to throw at me, and, and, and . . . and I guess that was it."

"Jeez. So *then* what happened?"

"So then the judge chewed my ass and threatened to send me to jail for contempt but didn't, and the supervisor chewed my ass, and the district director chewed my ass, and the commissioner, he flew out from Washington, and *he* chewed my ass, and that's why I'm forty-six years old and been in the same field grade for fifteen years now and am lying in a hospital with a belly full of buckshot instead of sitting behind some desk and calling in the reporters to tell them things like: 'We must stop picking on undocumented workers and start working harder to help them get settled in this country.'

"So that's what happened, Padillo. Nothing much at all."

"Send them *back*?" exclaimed the foreman. "Listen, Bailey, you try to send them broads back and there'll be a *mutiny*."

"But they're *Russians*, you idiot," cried the production manager, North Slope Division, of Octopus Oil Organization.

"But they're Russian *broads*, you dried-up old dodo, and they also happen to be Russian *whore*-type broads, and the boys have got them set up in a couple of trailers down in the living quarters and there's a three-day waiting list already."

"In the trailers?" gasped the production manager.

"Well, where else? It's twenty-nine degrees and snowing, or hadn't you noticed? Now look, Bailey, let's be reasonable, shall we? Just because there hasn't been any women up here in the fifteen years you little old ladies been running things doesn't mean there'd *never* be no broads, does it?"

"But they could be *spies*," said Bailey dubiously.

"Spies! All you have to do is—er, shake hands with one of them to know they ain't no spies. Hell, man, you never *saw* such a bunch of broads who know more about supply and demand and cash and carry and all the rest of the capitalist system." MacKensie leaned forward and winked knowingly. "For chrissakes, Mr. Bailey, they even take Visa and Master Charge. Now tell me, what have we got to hide from a couple of cute little ol' capitalists like that, huh?"

"Well . . . what about those trailers where they're staying? We can't have any guys living there who might be susceptible to charges of—"

"Forget it! How many guys do you think are breaking their contracts and scramming out of this hell-hole every week? There's at least twenty vacant trailers at any given time."

"Humph! I feel certain that this gross irregularity should be reported to the proper—"

"Authorities?" sneered MacKensie. "The government, huh? All this talk about how the government should leave the oil companies alone, and now just because an oil company wants to hire a couple of Diversified Entertainment Engineers we've gotta ask permission from Uncle Saphead? That's the spirit that made John D. Rockefeller rich, is it?"

"Okay, okay! But what about these six *men*? That's *another* kettle of borscht. Or are there enough roughnecks of, ah, refined appetites to propose—"

"Come *on*, be serious, will ya? Four of these guys are roughnecks themselves, one's a cold-weather engineer, and the other's a petroleum geologist. And they all speak English, a little funny, sure, but still English."

"You're suggesting . . . "

"I'll tell you one thing, Boss, you won't have to pay them no union wages or union benefits. They'll work any*where* for any*thing*, just so long as it ain't Siberia where they *been* working."

"But *you're* a union—"

"So screw the union," said MacKensie expansively. "We're gettin' a bonus based on production, ain't we? And we're so undermanned up here I'll go the rest of my hitch without gettin' any of that bonus money. Anyone who can . . ."

"Yes, I take your point." Running his hands through his thinning hair, Bailey gazed through the triple-glazed window at the flurries of snowflakes whirling about outside and made his decision. "So how can it hurt things? And if you think it'll help morale and production. . ."

"You just *watch* that oil start to pump, Mr. Bailey!"

"Humph." Bailey leaned forward. "Off the record, MacKensie. You don't think there's something just a *leetle* funny about the way these characters just *happen* to turn up *here*? A trillion miles from nowhere?"

"So where else would they go—join an Eskimo village to help them chew whale blubber?"

"Humph." Bailey stood up. "All right, MacKensie, all right." As the foreman began to bundle himself up, he added, "Did you say three-*day* waiting list?"

"Hey, Padillo, still got your arm attached, I see. Next time you come by, these tubes'll be out and I'll be outta bed. So what's new?"

"What's new? Jesus, *I'll* tell you what's new. You ain't gonna believe it, I mean like you just not gonna *believe* it."

"For chrissake, we're at war? No? Well, what is it?"

"Like we already got like forty million illegal Mexicans and Latin Americans and Hispanics in this country, *at least*, right?"

"Hey, Padillo! I *work* for the INS, remember? I said: What's *new*?"

"And I'm *telling* you, O'Hara. I'm telling you the reason we only got forty million illegal aliens or undocumented workers or unsomethinged citizens whatever they are, instead of maybe one hundred million, is that the *other* sixty million has been made citizens by executive order some seven, eight years ago, am I right?"

"Well, does a bear poop in the woods, for chrissake?"

"And it doesn't really make much difference whether the other *forty* million are citizens or not, since they can live here and work here and not get kicked out of here, right?"

"Right," echoed O'Hara wearily.

"And since that last Supreme Court ruling they can now also *vote* here, even though they're not citizens, 'the burden of absolute proof of nonnationality being the onus of the registering official, rather than positive proof of nationality being the responsibility of the voter.' Remember *that*, O'Hara?"

"Why do you think I stopped voting? Why do you think we got two Mexican senators and twenty-seven Mexican congressmen from this state alone, six of which can't speak English, but that don't matter no more neither, since the *Congressional Record* is printed up in two languages so they tell me, so's that President Martinez and Chief Justice Guerrero don't have to get out their dictionaries to find out what the braceros are up to over on The Hill. Yeah, I remember all right, Padillo. But like I said, ya dumb wop, what's *new*?"

"If you'd shut up for a minute, I'd tell ya! It's not *wet*backs we're chasing now, but *ice*backs!"

"Icepacks?" echoed O'Hara blankly.

"Ice*backs*, dummy. Illegal *Russian* icebacks."

"Did you say—?" O'Hara stopped as Padillo rocked back and began to shake with laughter. Finally, he wiped his eyes, leaned forward, and tapped O'Hara on the shoulder.

"What I'm looking forward to," said Padillo, "is seeing just how these hundreds of millions of *Hispanic*-Americans is gonna deal with all these new *Russian*-Americans."

"But *where*, for chrissake? It don't make sense."

"In Alaska, of course, where else? The Bering Sea, it's just like the Rio Grande, ain't it, only a little wider and a little colder. They're wading across on ground-effect machines and snowmobiles and dogsleds and on snowshoes and skis, and they even drove a couple of army-truck loads across now it's winter."

"But, but, but—"

"An' if they get caught, they say two things: One, they're fleeing the oppression of communist tyranny; and two, in any case, they're just returning to their ancestral lands where their old grandpappies made time with the papooses before the wicked czar gave it away illegally to the imperialists."

"But—"

"And get *this*, O'Hara, every one of these clowns is big, brawny, and just dying to go to work for the oil companies and the logging companies and the mining companies and the fishing companies, and all the broads are young and beautiful and descended from White Russian princesses and either they're trying to screw every red-blooded Alaskan male to death or they're trying to find work as housemaids for room and board and a dollar a week."

"But that's an *invasion*, for chrissake!"

"Of *course* it's an invasion, but if nobody *cares*, then it ain't an invasion no more, is it?"

O'Hara shook his head numbly. "Well, how many *are* there?"

Padillo shrugged. "Maybe a thousand, maybe *twenty* thousand. How can you tell? You noticed many border patrols up in Alaska to keep Canadian Eskimos from sneaking across the border?"

"So what *are* the politicians doing about it?"

Padillo grinned broadly. "Well now, Agent O'Hara," he said, punctuating his reply with taps on the other's shoulder, "That kinda depends on the politician, don't it?"

"It's election time *already*?" wailed Judge Charlie "The Fighting Eskimo" Rubenstein. "Jeez, it seems like only yesterday we were counting up the retard vote and—"

"We're gonna have to be doing more than just counting the 'tard vote," said Maxie. "That's a gimmick that only works once: Those guys have gotten *smart*—they could vote for *any*one."

"Oof. So what are the chances, old Maxie?"

"Lousy, Charlie, just plain lousy. It's like I tol' ya a couple years ago: A lotta people *still* don't like ya."

The Judge lowered his ample chins against his pouter-pigeon breast in token of profound thought, but was interrupted by a tap on the chamber door and the court recorder calling, "Two o'clock, Judge, they're waiting on you."

"Sure, sure, be right there." Judge Rubenstein climbed ponderously to his feet. "Think on it, Maxie, think on it."

"Jeez, Charlie," complained Maxie, "we got important stuff to talk about, you gotta go out there and try some jaywalking ticket or somepin?"

"Yeah, I know what you mean, Maxie, but there's lots of reporters and like that out there. That Russian iceback case."

"Iceback case?"

"Sure. The feds are asking for a court order allowing them to round up those Russkies that are working all over the place. That's what they're asking for at any rate, but I think they'd settle for just the right to ID them."

"Well, I should hope *not*!" exclaimed Maxie. "You let them bastards 'round up' those two Russkie maids we got working at home and the old lady'll kill ya! And so will I, though not for the same reason," he added with a leer.

"Well, gee, Maxie, I know, they're awfully *use*ful and all that, but there's an awful *lot* of them around now, you know, like maybe a hundred, two hundred thousand, and—"

"Two hundred *thousand*?" echoed Maxie in wonderment.

"—and they say there's an awful lot of these big Russkies carrying guns, you know, not like hunting rif—"

"Charlie boy," said Maxie, eyes peering rapturously into the future, "isn't one of the duties of judges naturalizing immigrants? Yes? Tell me, Judge Rubenstein, how would you like to become a United States senator in one easy election?"

"Why do you think we got 27 Mexican congressmen from this state alone, six of whom can't speak English? It's so President Martinez don't have to get out his dictionary."

"Look, Commissioner, I don't care whether you think I been drinking or *not*. I'm telling ya there's fifty thousand Russkoffs staging a sit-in on—yeah, you guessed it, Commissioner, *Russian Hill*. So what are you gonna do?

"Well, where do ya *think* they're gonna sit, except in the street? Sure the traffic's jammed up, from the Civic Center to the Golden Gate. . . .

"Naw, they're peaceful all right, singin' and chantin' and wavin' banners. . . . Hold on, lemme look. . . . Yeah, they're all about how California and San Francisco useta belong to the Russkies, and Fair Play for Russo-Americans, and Give Us Back Russian Hill. . . . Hold it a minute, oh, it's himself the Mayor I'm talking to now is it? Hold it, Mr. Mayor, they're chanting something. . . . Yeah, listen, I'll repeat it:

'Hey, hey, vote our way.
Vote a bill, for our Hill.
Just beware, Mr. Mayor,
Be unfair, no more mayor.
If we vote, we'll change your coat.
Hey, hey . . .'

"You hear that, sir?"

"Er, yes, Inspector. Before I, er, call the National Guard, how many did you say were, er, demonstrating?"

"Oh, I'd say a good fifty thousand spread over a six-block area."

"And they all seem of, er, voting age?"

"Oh, yes, sir, all of voting age."

"I see, I see. Tell me, Inspector Houlihan, do you think that Russians can, er, *vote*, Houlihan?"

"Gee, sir," said Houlihan in what he hoped was a soothing tone, "I think these are maybe Alaskan-type *naturalized* Russians, but I guess you'd have to ask the city attorney about that. . . ."

"Has anyone noticed," inquired the chief operation officer of the walnut-paneled boardroom of Octopus Oil Organization, "that our entire Prudhoe Bay operation, indeed, the entire North Slope fields and Alaskan pipeline, are now, for all practical purposes, being manned and maintained by some twenty thousand Russian workers?"

"Huh?" said the chairman of the board, a retired general straight from the Joint Chiefs of Staff, awaking with a snort.

"Well, *really*," frowned the president of Triple O, wondering how soon he could decently ask the steward to fetch a martini.

"You don't think it might be possible to view such a situation as a knifeblade held at the jugular vein of Triple O, the rest of the oil industry, and by extension the United States of America?"

The chairman gaped blankly while the president reviewed the ancient olive-onion controversy.

"Well, leaving all these *emotional*-type issues to one side," interjected the vice-president for public relations, "what's the bottom line?"

"Production is up 26 percent," replied the VP for accounting (internal, confidential) instantly.

"Profits?"

"Up 32 percent on gross, 47 percent on net."

"*There's* your bottom line, gentlemen," said Public Relations with finality.

"Does that mean a bigger dividend?" inquired the chairman with that charming naïveté which had caused his election to the boards of forty-seven major industrial concerns.

"Yes, sir, a *much* larger dividend."

"Well, that's good, isn't it?" beamed the general, "and surely what's good for Triple O is good for the country. Isn't it?"

"Ya know, Charlie," mused Maxie, "I been thinkin'. Thinkin' about you bein' president, Charlie."

"*President*?" gasped the junior senator from Alaska, Charlie "The Fighting Eskimo" Rubenstein.

"So why not?" asked Maxie reasonably.

"Look, we already got some fifty, sixty million so-called undocumented probationary citizens, most of 'em Mexes, voting in the federal elections, right?"

"Right, Maxie."

"And you got yourself a natural constituency of maybe a million Russkie-Americans back home, and maybe another five million in California and the Northwest, right? They *oughta* vote for ya, you're the fighting judge what showed 'em the way to citizenship, aren't ya?"

"Sure, Maxie."

"So the next step, and it's only logical, Charlie, is to get the vote extended to all them *other* undocumented probationary Russkie-American citizens what ain't yet got the opportunity to visit this glorious country of theirs, and what has to vote by absentee ballot back there in the old Motherland! Like maybe three hundred million of them!"

"But, *Maxie*—"

"All they'd haveta do is mail in an absentee ballot, like millions of other overseas Americans, right? So all you gotta do, Charlie, is introduce a bill that . . . "

". . . is working perfectly," chortled the director of state security. "I *told* you my plan would work!"

"*My* plan, Vladimir Vasilyevich," growled the foreign minister.

"Please, comrades," interceded the minister of agriculture, "what, if you please, is the next step? I am so looking forward to voting in the next presidential elections."

"Ah hah!" crowed Vladimir Vasilyevich Ostrovsky. "Already the order has gone out, already the fraternal-aid contingent stands ready, all two million of them, already the doom of the capitalist-imperialist warmongers is pending, already—"

"So all right already," muttered the minister of hydroelectric power, who had attended an extremely amusing seminar in Brooklyn the year before, but not so loudly that the director might overhear him.

"Comrades! The moment we have been waiting for has arrived! The orders have come from Moscow! The workers' general oil-field strike will begin tomorrow at dawn, the pipeline will be seized at noon, the housemaids and clerical workers shall revolt in the afternoon, and by evening Alaska will be ours! Five million fellow citizens on the West Coast will rise in sympathy and immobilize half the country. Attacked by the running-dog gestapo lackeys of fascist capitalism, they shall appeal for fraternal aid to their brothers-in-arms across the waters, and within hours, millions of peacekeeping personnel of the glorious and fraternal Red Army shall—" He went on for some time.

"Jeez," whispered Mikhail Nikolayeyvich to his wife Natasha Petrovna, "whaddya think this'll do to the interest rate on the mortgage?"

"And that new washing machine I—"

"My new snowmobile," interjected Pietor Sergeyevich glumly.

"In just three days the World Series!" cried Daniel Danielovich.

"My bonus trip to Hawaii!" moaned Katrina Varvarana.

"Just when we'd found a school for the kids with none of those disgraceful Eskimos cluttering it up!" complained Alexsey Ivanovich.

"I think we had better think this over," whispered Mikhail Nikolayeyvich.

"*Very carefully*," grated his wife between clenched teeth. "Oh shut up, you blithering fathead!" she yelled at the speaker, KGB Colonel Yevgeny Fyodorovich Zhukovsky, who instantly fell silent from sheer astonishment.

"Oh dear, oh dear, oh dear," bleated President Martinez piteously.

"Capitalist tool," rejoined Defense Secretary Haggleman.

"*Pig*," hissed Ms. Heliogabalus.

"Knock it off, ya fuckin' broads," admonished Mr. Kowalski. "What's da problem now, Señor Jelly-Belly?"

❝The Bering Sea is just like the Rio Grande, only a little wider and a little colder. They're wading across it on ground-effect machines and snowmobiles, skies and trucks.❞

"The problem is all these wretched Russians ready to revolt all over the Northwest and West Coast. And once they've paralyzed the country they'll simply invite in the Red Army and *we* will all be put up against a wall!" President Martinez broke into sobs.

"Speak for yaself, Jelly-Belly," snarled Mr. Kowalski. "No Russkoff is sticking Mrs. Kowalski's little boy up against no wall. Da foist t'ing ya do," jabbing a thick finger deep into the quivering breast of Defense Secretary Haggleman, "is ta send in da army against dese strikers or revolters or whadever dey are, and den—"

"*What* army?" wailed President Martinez.

"Oh yeah, dat's right, I forgot." Mr. Kowalski nodded somberly. "What army?"

"—the issue is clear," read Chief Justice Esteban Guerrero. "With one dissenting vote," he paused to glare briefly and unjudiciously at Mr. Justice Rubenstein, recently appointed by President Martinez to preempt those strongly rumored presidential aspirations of The Fighting Eskimo from The Great Northwest, "with one dissenting vote, I say, this court holds that all so-called naturalizations of all so-called Russo-American so-called citizens performed at any time in the past three years have been, are now, and will continue to be, clearly illegal, unwarranted, unjust, discriminatory, lacking in due process, and flagrantly unconstitutional. All so-called naturalizations, therefore, are by order of this court declared null and void, and any so-called Russo-American so-called citizens will revert to their previous status of legality and being, i.e. that of being illegal aliens, illegally in this country. There are numerous precedents for this judgment, among them . . . "

"Comrades! It just came over the radio! We've been deprived of our citizenship!"

"My house!"

"My washing machine!"

"My bonus trip to Hawaii!"

"My bet on the Red Sox!"

"My snowmobile!"

"My insurance policy!"

"Oh, Andrei Pietorevich, what are we to do?" sobbed Anna Petrovna.

"At dawn tomorrow we will march fraternally—" declaimed Colonel Zhukovsky.

"There is only one thing to do," replied Pietorevich somberly. "Correction, two. First, we shut up that madman. Next . . . "

"Mr. President! Mr. President!" cried an aide as he burst into the emergency session of the National Security Council. "Oh please stop crying, sir. Please?"

"What now?" groaned that unhappy man. "Texas has seceded from Mexico?"

"No, sir. The flash just came in from the Pentagon—"

"Oh no . . . ."

"All over the West Coast, sir. Millions and millions of Russians, sir—"

"The invasion, it's all over. . . ."

"No, sir. It hasn't started yet, and maybe it never will. It's *our* Russians. They're all joining the army!"

"They're what? I seem to have misunderstood you."

"The army, sir. They're flooding every Army, Navy, Air Force, and Marine recruiting station west of the Rockies. The best estimate is three million men and women already sworn in, and another three million waiting their turn."

President Martinez looked peevishly at the director of the CIA. "But why? They're supposed to be invading the country, not *defending* it, they don't need to—"

"But, sir, don't you remember? If you're a foreign-type alien and you join the armed forces, at the end of your enlistment you become a United States citizen!"

"You do? How strange," mused President Martinez. "But why would anyone want to become a US citizen?" he inquired of the room at large.

"Beats me, sir," replied the aide. "But I think I heard someone mention something about a bonus trip to Hawaii. . . ." ∞

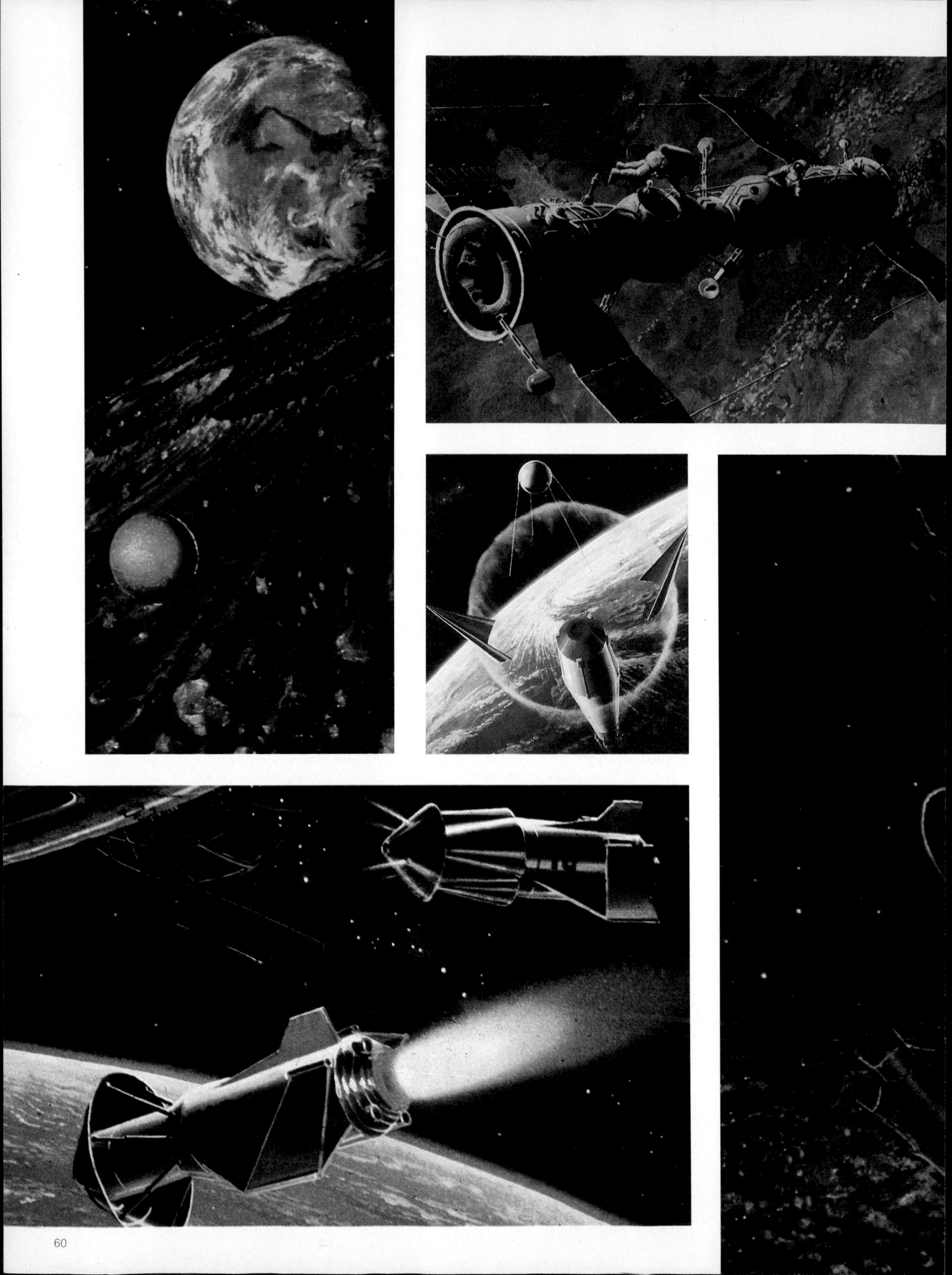

VISIONS OF THE COSMOS

An exclusive gallery of Soviet space art offers revealing glimpses of Russian fact and fantasy

BY F. C. DURANT III

Cosmonauts Romanenko and Grechko carried a special cargo with them into celestial orbit. Aboard *Soyuz XXVIII* were two paintings by Russia's foremost space artist, Andrei Sokolov. The paintings were gouache on nonfolding cardboard, measured 47 centimeters by 36 centimeters, and weighed 130 grams each. They were transferred to the orbiting space laboratory *Salyut*, there to become the first orbiting art exhibition in history.

The cosmic art of Andrei Sokolov, beginning clockwise from below: An early painting entitled Soft Landing on the Moon; Shuttles to Space Station in Orbit; Lunar Base; Transfer of Cosmonauts (*between* Soyuz *craft*); Launch of Sputnik I.

PAINTINGS BY ANDREI SOKOLOV

Sokolov's paintings later returned to earth aboard *Soyuz XXX* in July 1978. Thrilled that his paintings had been sent aloft, the artist presented one of them to Polish cosmonaut Miroslaw Hermazewski, command pilot of *Soyuz XXX*. Entitled *Cosmic Morning* (page 64), it is a fanciful representation of *Salyut VI* with two *Soyuz* craft docked at both ends, lit by the morning sun. Sokolov is currently reworking the other, *Over the Aral Sea*, making corrections in color tones and geographical features from notes provided by the crew.

Since *Sputnik I*, Andrei Sokolov has dedicated his professional life to artistic concepts of the cosmos. His art now numbers more than 150 works. These paintings vary; some are rough impressions, others are precise and meticulous. He illustrates contemporary space activities of the USSR and US, as well as future encounters with planets of far-off stellar systems. Sokolov is big physically, over six feet, a burly and pow-

‘My greatest challenge in life is to visualize and depict future cosmic voyages.’

Zond V (left) returns lunar sample to earth. Below: On the Planet of Boiling Lava. *Bottom:* Cosmodrome on Phobos; Silicon Crystal Life on Planet of Red Giant.

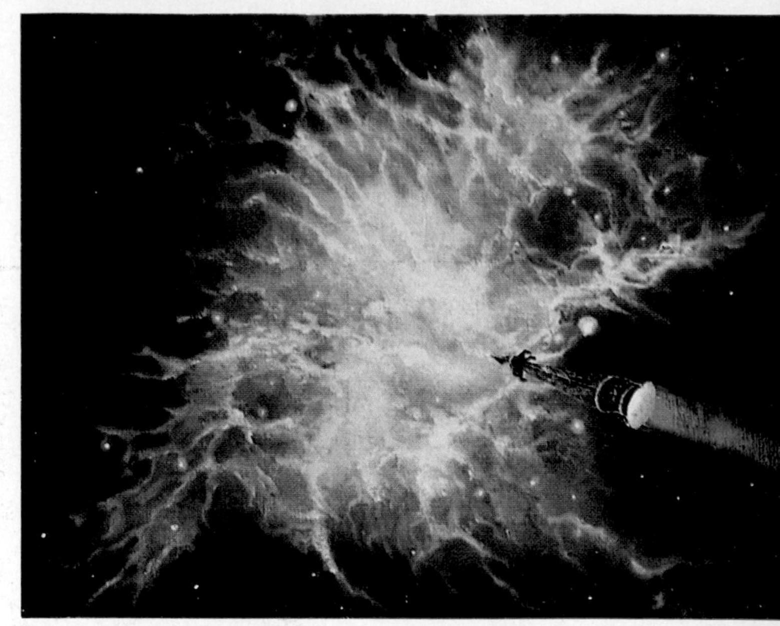

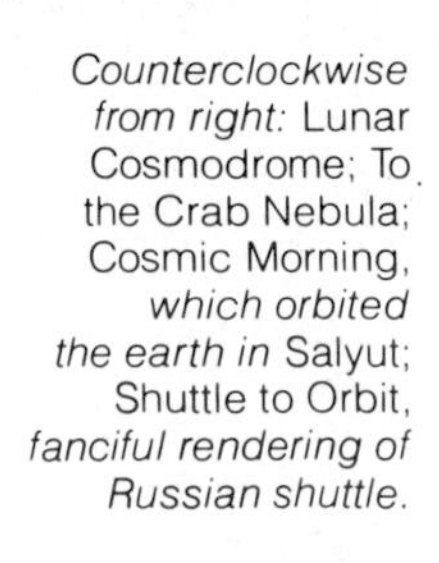

Counterclockwise from right: Lunar Cosmodrome; To the Crab Nebula; Cosmic Morning, *which orbited the earth in* Salyut; Shuttle to Orbit, *fanciful rendering of Russian shuttle.*

“Cosmic exploration,” opines Andrei Sokolov, “staggers the human imagination.”

erful former motorcycle racer whose boldness is reflected in his art.

Sokolov was born in Leningrad 48 years ago and grew up in Moscow. His father was a construction engineer prominent in building the Moscow metro in the 1930s. Trained as an architect, Sokolov was captivated by Ray Bradbury's *Fahrenheit 451* more than 20 years ago. Visualizing scenes from the book, he created a number of paintings, his first in this genre. The artist has presented one of these to Bradbury.

Since 1965, Sokolov has collaborated with cosmonaut Alexei Leonov. An amateur artist, Leonov sketched views of space while in orbit and upon return rendered them in watercolor and oils. Works of Sokolov and Leonov have been published in four art books in the Soviet Union; the most recent is *Man in the Universe* (1975). Moreover, collections of postcards and some 20 Soviet postage stamps carry their art. Through his close relationship with Leonov and other cosmonauts, Sokolov is

able to keep abreast of advances in space technology.

In 1975, the Soviet space artist married Nina F. Lapinowa. Today, they live and work in an attractive studio apartment in downtown Moscow.

Several years ago, the Soviet Artists Union sponsored a touring exhibit of US space art throughout Russia. In exchange, a Soviet space art show was displayed at the Smithsonian Institution's National Air and Space Museum in 1976. Included were 14 works by Sokolov and Leonov. Under the auspices of the Smithsonian, the show toured in the US for 18 months. Both artists have donated works to the National Air and Space Museum. ∞

Much of Sokolov's art has never been published in the US; counterclockwise from above: Apollo-Soyuz Rendezvous in Orbit; Launch of Soyuz XXVI; Entering the Atmosphere of Mars; *early vintage communications satellite* Molniya XIV.

“Sokolov describes the immensity of the cosmos as “awesomely unknowable.””

NO FUTURE IN IT

He could travel through time, but he could never return to the place where he started

BY JOE HALDEMAN

It's not easy to keep exactly one-eighth inch of beard on your face. For a writer, though, it's good protective coloration. With a suit and tie, you look like a gentleman who's decided to grow a beard. With rumpled old Salvation Army clothes, you look like a down-and-out rummy. It depends on the class of people you want to listen to, study.

I was in the rummy outfit when I met Bill Caddis and heard his incredible story. At first I thought Bill was on the same scam I was; he talked too well to be in the dreg business. He was for real, though.

There's this wonderful sleazy bar in downtown Tampa. No name, just a bunch of beer signs in the window. The one for Pearl has a busted laser that flutters stroboscopically. You don't want to sit too near the window. It's a good bar for private conversations because it's right under the twelve-laner that sweeps out over the bay, and there's a constant moan of traffic, all day and all night. There's a fine, gritty layer of plaster dust everywhere, and not too much light. The bartender is missing an eye and ten front teeth and smiles frequently. The booze is cheap; they make most of their money upstairs and like to have lots of customers in the bar, for camouflage.

I sat down at the bar, and the bartender polished glasses while one of the whores, a pretty boy-girl, sidled in for the kill. When I said no she pleaded mechanically, saying she was saving for a real pair of tits and The Operation. I hesitated—I string for the Bad News Wire Service sometimes, and they

PAINTING BY GOTTFRIED HELNWEIN

like sexy bathos—but turned her down more finally. Bad News doesn't pay that well.

When she left, the bartender came over and I ordered a Meyers with a beer chaser, a suitably hard-core combination. I'd taken two Flame-outs before I came, though, so I could drink a dozen or so without too much ill effect. Until morning.

"Little early in the day for that, isn't it?" The man next to me chuckled hoarsely. "Not to criticize." He was nursing a double bourbon or scotch, neat.

"Dusty," I said. The man was dressed a little more neatly than I, in faded work clothes. He looked too old to be a laborer, shock of white hair with a yellowish cast. But he did have the deep tan and permanent squint of one who's spent decades in the Florida sun. I tossed back the jigger of rum and sipped the beer. "Come here often?"

"Pretty often," he said. "When my check comes in I put a few bucks on a number. Otherwise . . ." He shrugged. "Cheap whiskey and pretty women. To look at."

"How many of them do you think are women?"

"Just looking, who cares?" He squinted even more, examining me. "Could I see your palms?"

Oh boy, I thought, a fortune-teller. Might be a story if he actually believes in it. I held out my hands.

He glanced at them and stared at my face. "Yeah, I could tell by the eyes," he said softly. "You're no alcoholic. You're not as old as you look, either. Cop?"

"No. Used to be a teacher." Which was true. "Every now and then I go on these binges."

He nodded slowly. "Used to be a teacher, too. Until '83. Then I worked the sponge boats twenty years." When he picked up his glass, his hand had the regular, slow shake of a confirmed alky. "It was good work."

I reached in my pocket and turned on the tape recorder. "What was it made you stop teaching? Booze?"

"No. Who drank in the eighties?" I didn't, but I wasn't old enough. "It's an interesting sort of pancake. You want to hear a story?"

"Sure." I signaled the bartender for two drinks.

"Now, you don't have to buy me anything. You won't believe the story, anyhow."

"Try me."

"You a social worker? Undercover social worker?" He smiled wryly.

"Is there such a thing?"

"Should be. I know—you're a writer."

"When I get work, yeah. How could you tell, Sherlock?"

"You've got two pens in your pocket, and you want to hear a story." He smiled. "Steal a story, maybe. But you'll never get it published. It's too fantastic."

"But true."

"It's true, all right. Thank you kindly." He touched his new drink to see whether it was real, then drained off the old one in one gulp and sighed.

"My name's Bill Caddis; Doctor William Caddis, it used to be."

"Medical doctor?"

"I detect a note of reproof. As if no medico ever—Well, no, I was an academic, newly tenured at Florida State. History department. Modern American history."

"Hard to get a job then as it is now?"

"Just about. I was a real whiz."

"But you got fired in '83."

"That's right. And it's not easy to fire a tenured professor."

"What, boffing the little girls?"

That was the only time he laughed that day, a kind of wheeze. "Undergraduates were made for boffing. No, I was dismissed on grounds of mental instability; with my wife's help, my then-wife, they almost had me institutionalized."

"Don't they teach you anything about relativity? If you get up from the bar, go to the john, and return in a couple of minutes, the bar's moved thousands of miles. But it's still here. You're on the same track, that's all."

"Strong stuff."

"Strong." He stared into his drink and swirled it around. "I never know how to start this. I've told dozens of people, and they all think I'm crazy before I get halfway into it. You'll think I'm crazy too."

"Just jump in feet-first. Like you say, I'm a writer. I can believe in six impossible things before my first drink in the morning."

"All right. I'm not from . . . here."

A loony, I thought; there goes the price of a double. "Another planet," I said, seriously.

"See? Now you want me to say something about UFOs and how I'm bringing the secret of eternal peace to mankind." He raised the glass to me. "Thanks for the drink."

I caught his arm before he could slug the drink down. "Wait. I'm sorry. Go on."

"Am I wrong?"

"You're right, but go on. You don't *act* crazy."

He set the drink down. "Layman's error. Some of the most reasonable people you meet are strictly Almond Joy."

"If you're not from 'here,' where are you from?"

"Miami." He smiled and took a sip. "I'm a time traveller. I'm from a future."

I just nodded.

"That usually takes some explaining. There's no *the* future. There's a myriad of futures radiating from every instant. If I were to drop this glass on the floor and it broke, we would shift into a future where this bar owned one less glass."

"And the futures where the glass wasn't broken . . ."

"They would be. And we would be in them; we are now."

"Doesn't it get sort of crowded up there? Billions of new futures every second?"

"You can't crowd infinity."

I was trying to think of an angle, a goofball feature. "How does this time travel work?"

"How the hell should I know? I'm just a tourist. It has something to do with chronons. Temporal uncertainty principle. Conservation of coincidence. I'm no engineer."

"Are there lots of these tourists?"

"Probably not here and now. You get quite a crowd clustered around historically important events. You can't see them, of course."

"I can see you."

He shrugged. "Something went wrong. Power failure or something; someone tripped over a cable. Happens."

"They didn't try to come back and rescue you?"

"How could they? There are lots of futures but only one past. Once I materialized *here*, I wasn't in my own past anymore. See?"

"So you can kill your own grandfather," I said.

"Why would I want to do that? He's a nice old bird."

"No, I mean, there's no paradox involved? If you killed him before you were born, you wouldn't cease to exist?"

"Of course not. I'd have to be there to kill him." He sipped. "For that matter, I could go back and kill myself, as a boy. If I could afford it. Travel gets more expensive the closer you get to the present. Like compressing an infinitely tough spring."

"Hold it." I had him. "I'll buy another round if you can talk your way out of this one. The earth is moving all the time, spinning around, going around the sun; the sun's moving through space. How the hell do you *aim* this time machine?"

He bleared at me. "Don't they teach you anything about relativity? Look, if you get up from the bar, go to the john, and come back in a couple of minutes, the bar's moved thousands of miles. But it's still here. You're on the same track, that's all."

"But I'm talking about time, and you're talking about *space*!"

"There a difference?" He drained his glass and slid it toward me with one finger.

I decided I'd stay long enough to find out what his con was. Maybe do a one-pager for a crime magazine. I ordered him another double. "You folks from the future can sure hold your liquor."

"Couple of centuries of medicine," he said. "I'm ninety-two years old." He looked about seventy.

Looked like I was going to have to push him for the gaff. "Seems to me you could be a millionaire. Knowing where to invest . . ."

"It's not that easy. I tried. I should have left well enough alone." His drink came, and he stuck his fingertip in it; flicked a drop away. "I'm sort of a Moslem," he said. "Not supposed to drink a drop of liquor.

"People try it all the time; there's no law against it. But put yourself in this position: You're going to deliberately strand yourself two hundred years in the past. What do you do for capital? Buy old money from collectors?"

"You could take gold and diamonds."

"Sure. But if you can afford that—and time travel isn't cheap either—why not invest it in your own present? Remember, once you materialize, you aren't in your own past anymore. You can never tell what might have changed. People do try it, though. Usually they take gadgets."

"Does it work?"

"Who knows? They can't come back to tell about it."

"Couldn't they build their own time machine; go back to the future?"

"Aren't you hearing me? There's no such thing as *the* future. Even if you could travel forward, there's no way you could find the right one."

Somebody came into the bar; I waited until the door eased shut, muting the traffic noise. "So what happened to you? You made some bad investments?"

"In spades. Seemed like a sure thing. Let me explain. Where I come from, almost nobody lives on Earth, just caretakers and the time-travel people. It's like a big park, a big museum. Most of us live in orbital settlements, some on other planets.

"I really was a history professor, specializing in the history of technology. I saved up my money to go back and see the first flight to the Moon."

"That was in '70?"

"No, '69. It was during the launch when the accident happened. Nobody noticed me materializing; I didn't even notice until I tried to walk through someone afterwards.

"Fortunately, that was a time when everybody dressed as they damn well pleased, so my clothes didn't look especially outrageous. I bummed my way down to Homestead and picked up some work sorting tomatoes, that kind of thing. Saved up enough to get fake IDs made up, eventually went back to school and wound up teaching again. Married along the way."

"The one who tried to put you in the peanut jar."

"That's right. Here's what happened. If there was one sure thing to invest in, it was space. My wife didn't agree, but there was no way I could tell her why I was so sure.

"I went ahead and invested heavily in space industries—really heavily, buying on the margin, wheeling, dealing—but my wife thought it was all going into a conservative portfolio of municipals. I even snitched some stationery from our accountant and wrote up annual reports to show her."

"I think I see what's coming." Not a bad story.

"Yeah. The Soviet-American Orbital Non-Proliferation Treaty, the goddamned Proxmire Bill."

"Well, killer satellites . . ."

"That's the kicker. That's really the kicker. In *my* future's past, it was the killer satellites that ended the possibility of nuclear war forever! They finally scrapped the missiles and began shouting across tables."

"Well, you can't think we're in any danger of nuclear war now. Not realistically."

"Yeah. I liked our way better. Anyway, the bottom dropped out. I had to tell my wife that we were broke and in debt; I had to tell her everything. I thought I knew her. I thought she would believe. The rest is pretty obvious."

"Sponge boats."

"Right." He took a long drink and stared moodily into the cloudy mirror behind the bar.

"That's it?" No scam?

"That's it. Write it up. You'll never sell it."

I checked my watch. Could just make the 1:35 to Atlanta, get in a half-day at the typewriter. "Well, I gotta run. Thanks for the story, Bill."

I stood up and put my hand on his shoulder. "Take it easy on the sauce, okay? You're no spring chicken anymore."

"Sure." He never looked at me.

On the way to the subway terminal it occurred to me that I shouldn't try to sell the thing as a human-interest feature. Just write it up as fiction, and I could hawk it to *Planet Stories* or one of those rags.

The ticket machine gave me an argument about changing a hundred-ruble note, and I had to go find a conductor. Then there were repairs going on, and it took us twenty minutes to get to Atlanta; I had to sprint to make my Seattle connection.

Space settlements. Time travel. Nobody would swallow that kind of bull in 1924. ∞

GALATEA GALANTE

He created the Perfect Woman,
with one little flaw designed into her

BY ALFRED BESTER

He was wearing a prefaded jump suit, beautifully tailored, the *dernier cri* in the nostalgic 2100s, but really too youthful for his thirty-odd years. Set square on his head was a vintage (circa 1950) English motoring cap with the peak leveled on a line with his brows, masking the light of lunacy in his eyes.

Dead on a slab, he might be called distinguished, even handsome, but alive and active? That would depend on how much demented dedication one could stomach. He was shouldering his way through the crowded aisles of

THE SATURN CIRCUS
50 PHANTASTIK PHREAKS 50
!!! ALL ALIENS !!!

He was carrying a mini sound-camera that looked like a chrome-and-ebony pepper mill, and he was filming the living, crawling, spasming, gibbering monstrosities exhibited in the large showcases and small vitrines, with a murmured running commentary. His voice was pleasant; his remarks were not.

"Ah, yes, the *Bellatrix basilisk*, so the sign assures us. Black-and-yellow bod of a serpent. Looks like a Gila-monster head attached. Work of that Tejas tailor who's so nitzy with surgical needle and thread. Peacock coronet on head. Good theater to blindfold its eyes. Conveys the conviction that its glance will kill. Hmmm. Ought to gag the mouth, too. According to myth the basilisk's breath also kills. . . .

"And the *Hyades hydra*. Like wow. Nine heads, as per revered tradition. Looks like a converted iguana. The Mexican again. That seamstress has access to every damn snake and lizard in Central America. She's done a nice join of necks to trunk—got to admit that—but her stitching shows to *my* eye. . . .

"*Canopus cerberus*. Three dog heads. Look like oversized Chihuahuas. Mastiff bod. Rattlesnake tail. Ring of rattlers around the waist. Authentic but clumsy. That Tejas woman ought to know you can't graft snake scales onto hound hide. They look like crud; but at least all three heads are barking. . . .

"Well, well, well, here's the maladroit who claims he's my rival; the Berlin butcher with his zoo castoffs. His latest spectacular, the *Rigel griffin*. Ta-daaa! Do him justice, it's classic. Eagle head and wings, but it's molting. Lion bod implanted with feathers. And he's used ostrich claws for the feet. *I* would have generated authentic dragon's feet. . . .

"Now *Martian monoceros*; horse bod, elephant legs, stag's tail. Yes, convincing, but why isn't it howling as it should, according to legend? *Mizar manticora*. Kosher. Kosher. Three rows of teeth. Look like implanted shark's. Lion bod. Scorpion tail. Wonder how they produced that red-eyed effect. The *Ares assida*. Dull. Dull. Dullsville. Just an ostrich with camel feet, and stumbling all over them, too. No creative imagination!

"Ah, but I call that poster over the *Sirius sphinx* brilliant theater. My compliments to the management. It's got to be recorded for posterity: THE PUBLIC IS RESPECTFULLY REQUESTED NOT TO GIVE THE CORRECT ANSWER TO THE ENIGMA POSED BY THE SPHINX.

"Because if you do give the correct answer, as Oedipus found out, she'll destroy herself out of chagrin. A sore loser. I ought to answer the riddle, just to see how they stage it, but no. Theater isn't my shtick; my business is strictly creative genesis. . . .

"The Berlin butcher again, *Castor chimera*. Lion head. Goat's bod. Looks like an anaconda tail. How the hell did he surgify to get it to vomit those flames? Some sort of catalytic gimmick in the throat, I suppose. It's only a cold corposant fire, quite harmless but very dramatic—and those fire extinguishers around the showcase are a lovely touch. Damn good theater. Again, my compliments to the management. . . .

"Aha! Beefcake on the hoof. *Zosma centaur*. Good-looking Greek joined to that Shetland pony. Blood must have been a problem. They probably drained both and substituted a neutral surrogate. The Greek looks happy enough; in fact, damn smug. Anyone wondering why has only to see how the pony's hung. . . .

PAINTING BY H.R. GIGER

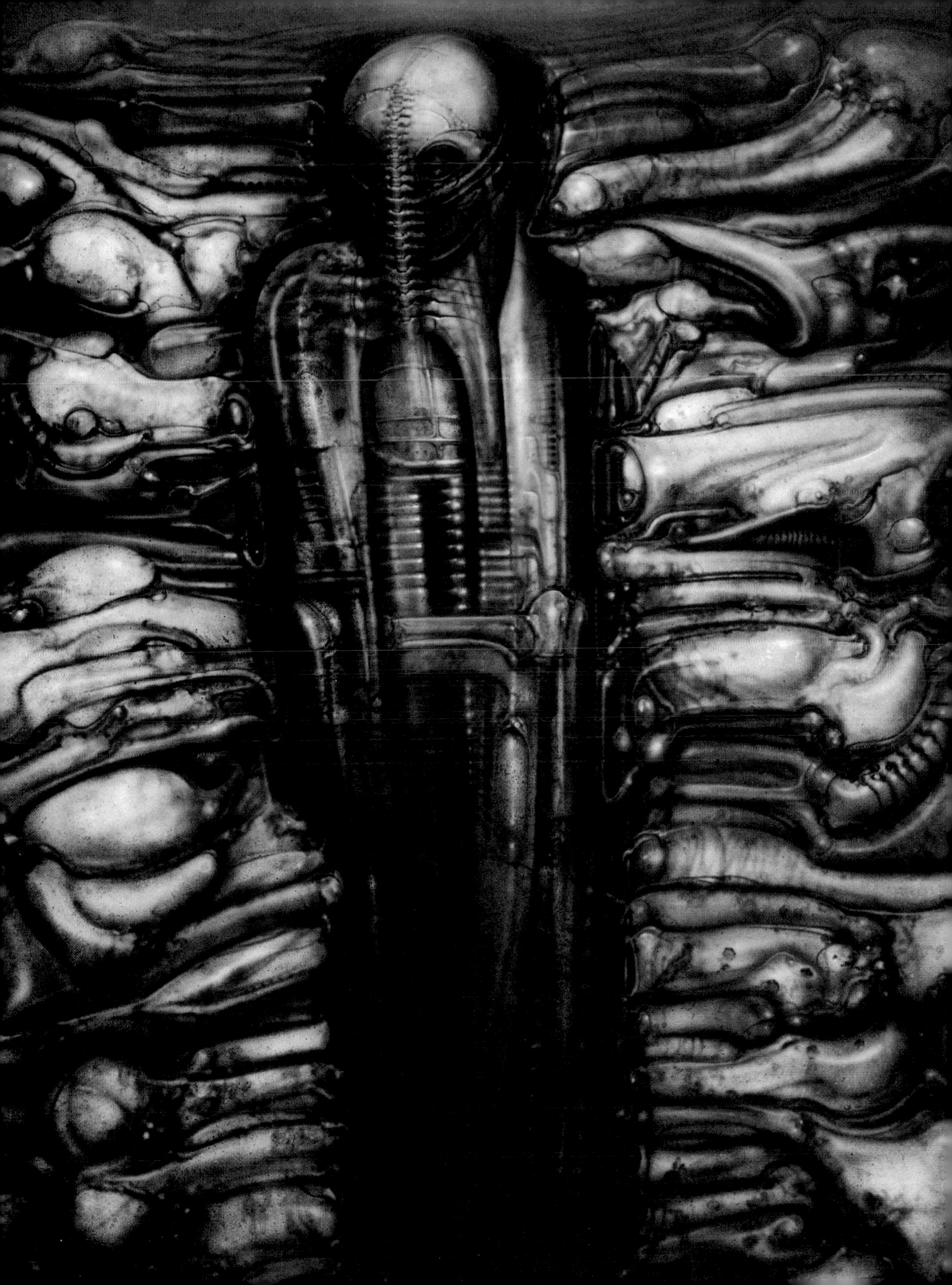

"What have we here? *Antares unicorn*, complete with grafted narwhal tusk but not with the virgin who captured it, virgin girls being the only types that can subdue unicorns, legend saith. I thought narwhals were extinct. They may have bought the tusk from a walking-stick maker. I know virgins are not extinct. *I* make 'em every month; purity guaranteed or your money back. . . .

"And a *Spica siren*. Lovely girl. Beautiful. She— But damn my eyes, she's no manufactured freak! That's Sandra, *my* Siren! I can recognize my genesis anywhere. What the hell is Sandy doing in this damn disgusting circus? Naked in a showcase! This is an outrage!"

He charged the showcase in his rage. He was given to flashes of fury that punctuated his habitual exasperated calm. (His deep conviction was that it was a damned intransigent world because it wasn't run *his* way, which was the *right* way.)

He beat and clawed at the supple walls, which gave but did not break. He cast around wildly for anything destructive, then darted to the *chimera* exhibit, grabbed a fire extinguisher, and dashed back to the Siren. Three demoniac blows cracked the plastic, and three more shattered an escape hatch. His fury outdrew the freaks, and a fascinated crowd gathered.

He reached in and seized the smiling Siren. "Sandy, get the hell out. What were you doing there in the first place?"

"♪"

"Where's your husband?"

"♪"

"For God's sake!" He pulled off his cap, revealing pale, streaky hair. "Here, cover yourself with this. No, no, girl, downstairs. Use an arm for upstairs, and hide your rear elevation against my back."

"♪"

"No, I am *not* prudish. I simply will not have my beautiful creation on public display. D'you think I—" He turned fiercely on three security guards closing in on him and brandished the heavy brass cylinder. "One more step, and I let you have it with this. In the eyes. Ever had frozen eyeballs?"

They halted. "Now look, mister, you got no—"

"I am *not* called 'mister.' My degree is Dominie, which means master professor. I am addressed as Dominie, Dominie Manwright, and I want to see the owner at once. Immediately. Here and now. *Sofort! Immediatamente!* Mr. Saturn or Mr. Phreak or whatever!

"Tell him that Dominie Regis Manwright wants him here now. He'll know my name, or he'd better, by God! Now be off with you. Split. Cut." Manwright glared around at the enthralled spectators. "You turkeys get lost, too. All of you. Go eyeball the other sights. The Siren show is *kaput*."

As the crowd shuffled back from Manwright's fury, an amused gentleman in highly unlikely twentieth-century evening dress stepped forward. "I see you understand Siren, sir. Most impressive." He slung the opera cape off his shoulders and offered it to Sandra. "You must be cold, madame. May I?"

"Thank you," Manwright growled. "Put it on, Sandy. Cover yourself. And thank the man."

"♪"

"I don't give a damn whether you're cold or not. Cover yourself. I won't have you parading that beautiful body I created. And give me back my cap."

"♪"

"Women!" Manwright grumbled. "This is the last time I ever generate one. You slave over them. You use all your expertise to create beauty and implant sense and sensibility, and they all turn out the same. Irrational! Women! A race apart! And where the hell's 50 Phantastik Phreaks 50?"

"At your service, Dominie," the gentleman smiled.

"What? You? The management?"

"Indeed yes."

"In that ridiculous white tie and tails?"

"So sorry, Dominie. The costume is traditional for the role. And by day I'm required to wear hunting dress. It *is* grotesque, but the public expects it of the ringmaster."

> *"He beat and clawed at the supple walls, which gave but did not break. He cast around wildly for anything destructive, then. . . grabbed a fire extinguisher and dashed back to the Siren."*

"Hmph! What's your name? I'd like to know the name of the man I skin alive."

"Corque."

"Cork? As in Ireland?"

"But with a *Q U E*."

"Corque? Cor-kew-ee?" Manwright's eyes kindled. "Would you by any chance be related to Charles Russell Corque, Syrtus professor of ETM biology? I'll hold that in your favor."

"Thank you, Dominie. I *am* Charles Russell Corque, professor of extraterrestrial and mutation biology at Syrtus University."

"What!"

"Yes."

"In that preposterous costume?"

"Alas, yes."

"Here? On Terra?"

"In person."

"What a crazy coincidence. D'you know, I was going to make that damned tedious trip to Mars just to rap with you."

"And I brought my circus to Terra hoping to meet and consult with you."

"How long have you been here?"

"Two days."

"Then why haven't you called?"

"Setting up a circus show takes time, Dominie. I haven't had a moment to spare."

"This monstrous fakery is really yours?"

"It is."

"You? The celebrated Corque? The greatest researcher into alien life forms that science has ever known? Revered by all your colleagues, including myself, and swindling the turkeys with a phony freak show? Incredible, Corque! Unbelievable!"

"But understandable, Manwright. Have you any idea of the cost of ETM research? And the reluctance of the grants committees to allocate an adequate amount of funds? No, I suppose not. You're in private practice and can charge gigantic fees to support your research, but I'm forced to moonlight and operate this circus to raise the money I need."

"Nonsense, Corque. You could have patented one of your brilliant discoveries— that fantastic Jupiter III methophyte, for instance. Gourmets call it 'The Ganymede Truffle.' D'you know what an ounce sells for?"

"I know, and there *are* discovery rights and royalties. Enormous. But you don't know university contracts, my dear Dominie. By contract, the royalties go to Syrtus, where"—Professor Corque's smile soured—"where they are spent on such studies as Remedial Table Tennis, Demonia Orientation, and The Light Verse of Leopold von Sacher-Masoch."

Manwright shook his head in exasperation. "Those damned faculty clowns! I've turned down a dozen university offers, and no wonder. It's an outrage that you should be forced to humiliate yourself and— Listen, Corque, I've been dying to get the details on how you discovered that Ganymede methophyte. When will you have some time? I thought— Where are you staying on Terra?"

"The Borealis."

"What? That fleabag?"

"I have to economize for my research."

"Well, you can economize by moving in with me. It won't cost you a cent. I've got plenty of room, and I'll put you up for the duration, with pleasure. I've generated a housekeeper who'll take good care of you—and rather startle you, I think. Now do say yes, Corque. We've got a hell of a lot of discussing to do and I've got a lot to learn from you."

"I think it will be the other way around, my dear Dominie."

"Don't argue! Just pack up, get the hell out of the Borealis, and—"

"♪"

"What, Sandy?"

"♪"

"Where?"

"♪"

"Oh, yes. I see the rat-fink."

"What now, Manwright?"

"Her husband. I'll trouble you to use restraint on me, or he'll become her *late* husband."

An epicene hove into view—tall, slender, elegant, in flesh-colored SkinAll—with chest, arms, and legs artfully padded to macho dimensions, as was the ornamented codpiece. Manwright juggled the extinguisher angrily, as though groping for the firing pin of a grenade. He was so intent on the encounter that Corque was able to slip the cylinder out of his hands as the epicene approached, surveyed them, and at last spoke.

"Ah, Manwright."

"Jessamy!" Manwright turned the name into a denunciation.

"Sandra."

"♪"

"And our impresario."

"Good evening, Mr. Jessamy."

"Manwright, I have a bone to pick with you."

"You? Pick? A bone? With me? Why, you damned pimp, putting your own wife, my magnificent creation, into a damned freak show!" He turned angrily on Professor Corque. "And you bought her, eh?"

"Not guilty, Dominie. I can't supervise everything. The Freak Foreman made the purchase."

"He did, did he?" Manwright returned to Jessamy. "And how much did you get for her?"

"That is not germane."

"♪"

"That little? Why, you padded procurer? Why? God knows, you don't need the money."

"Dr. Manwright—"

"Don't you 'Doctor' me. It's Dominie."

"Dominie—"

"Speak."

"You sold me a lemon."

"What!"

"You heard me. You sold me a lemon."

"How dare you!"

"I admit I'm a jillionaire."

"Admit it? You broadcast it."

"But nevertheless I resent a rip-off."

"Rip! I'll kill the man. Don't restrain me. I'll kill! Look, you damned minty macho, you came to me and contracted for the perfect wife. A Siren, you said. The kind that a man would have to lash himself to the mast to resist, à la Ulysses. Well? Didn't you?"

"Yes, I did."

"Yes, you did. And did I or did I not generate a biodroid miracle of beauty, enchantment, and mythological authenticity, guaranteed or your money back?"

"Yes, you did."

"And one week after delivery I discover my Pearl of Perfection sold to the distinguished Charles Russell Corque's obscene freak show and displayed naked in a bizarre showcase. My beautiful face and neck! My beautiful back and buttocks! My beautiful breasts! My beautiful mons veneris! My—"

"That's what she wanted."

"Did you, Sandy?"

"•"

"Shame on you, girl. I know you're vain—that was a glitch in my programming—but you don't have to flaunt it. You're a damned exhibitionist." Back to Jessamy: "But that doesn't excuse your selling her. Why, did you do it, dammit? Why?"

"She was tearing my sheets."

"What?"

"Your beautiful, enchanting Pearl of Perfection was tearing my monogrammed silk sheets, woven at incredible cost by brain-damaged nuns. She was tearing them with her mythologically authentic feet. Look at them."

There was no need to look. It was undeniable that the beautiful, enchanting Siren was feathered from the knees down and had delicate pheasant feet.

"So?" Manwright demanded impatiently.

"She was also scratching my ankles."

"Damn you!" Manwright burst out. "You asked for a Siren. You paid for a Siren. You received a Siren."

"With bird feet?"

"Of course with bird feet. Sirens are part bird. Haven't you read your Bulfinch? Aristotle? Sir Thomas Browne? Matter of fact, you're lucky Sandy didn't turn out bird from the waist down. Ha!"

"Very funny," Jessamy muttered.

"But it wasn't luck," Manwright went on. "No, it was genius. My biodroid genius for creative genesis, and my deep understanding of the sexual appetites."

"♪"

"Don't be impudent, girl. I have sexual appetites, too, but when I guarantee a virgin, I— No matter. Take her home, Jessamy. Don't argue, or I'll kill you, if I can find that damned brass thing I thought I had. Take Sandra home. I'll refund Professor Corque in full. Got to support his brilliant research. Sandy, trim your talons, for God's sake! Sense and sensibility, girl! Corque, go pack up and move in with me. Here's my card with the address. What the devil are you doing with that silly-looking fire extinguisher?"

"And that's the full shmeer, Charles. I'm sorry I haven't any work in progress to show you, but you can see I'm no tailor or seamstress, cutting up mature animals, human or otherwise, and piecing parts together, like you see with those show-biz monsters in your circus. No, I macrogenerate 'em, pure and whole, out of the basic DNA broth. Mine are all test-tube babies. Florence-flask babies, as a matter of fact, which is where I start 'em. Biodroids need womb space like any other animal."

"Fascinating, my dear Reg, and quite overwhelming. But what I can't fathom is your RNA process."

"Ah! The RNA messenger service, eh?"

"Exactly. Now we all know that DNA is the life reservoir—"

"All? We all know? Ha! Not bloody likely. Some time I'll show you the abuse I get from the Scripture freaks."

"And we know that RNA is the messenger service delivering commands to the developing tissues."

"Right on, Charles. That's where the control lies."

"But how do you control the controls? How do you direct the RNA to deliver specific commands from DNA to embryo? And how do you select the commands?"

"Penthouse."

"Wh-what?"

"Come up to the penthouse. I'll show you."

Manwright led Corque out of the enormous crimson-lit cellar laboratory which was softly glowing with ruby-colored glassware and liquids ("My babies *must* be insulated from light and noise") and up to the main floor of the house. It was decorated in the Dominie's demented style: a hodgepodge of Regency, classic Greek, African, and Renaissance. There was even a marble pool inhabited by iridescent manic fish, which gazed up at the two men eagerly.

"Hoping we'll fall in," Manwright laughed. "A cross between piranha and golden carp. One of my follies."

Thence to the second floor, twenty-five by a hundred, Manwright's library and study: four walls shelved and crammed with tapes, publications, and software; a rolling ladder leaning against each wall; a gigantic carpenter's workbench center, used as a desk and piled with clutter.

Third floor divided between dining room (front), kitchen and pantry (center), and servants' quarters (rear, overlooking garden).

Fourth floor, enjoying maximum sky and air, bedrooms. There were four, each with its own dressing room and bath, all rather severe and monastic: Manwright regarded sleep as a damned necessity which had to be endured but which should never be turned into a luxury.

"We all get enough sleep during our nine months in the womb," he had growled to Corque, "and we'll get more than we'll ever need after we die. But I'm working on regenerative immortality, off and on. Trouble is, tissues just don't want to play ball." He led the professor up a narrow stair to the penthouse.

It was a clear plastic dome, firmly anchored against wind and weather. In the center stood a glimmering Rube Goldberg, Heath-Robinson, Da Vinci mechanical construct. If it resembled anything it would be a giant collapsing robot waiting for a handyman to put it together again. Corque stared at the gallimaufry and then at Manwright.

"Neutrinoscope," the Dominie explained. "My extrapolation of the electron microscope."

"What? Neutrinos? The beta-decay process?"

Manwright nodded. "Combined with a cyclotron. I get particular particle selection that way and acceleration up to ten Mev. Selection's the crux, Charles. Each genetic molecule in the RNA coil has a specific response to a specific particle bombardment. That way I've been able to identify and isolate somewhere in the neighborhood of ten thousand messenger commands."

"But-but— My dear Reg, this is positively fantastic!"

Manwright nodded again, "Uh-huh. Took me ten years."

"But I had no idea that— Why haven't you published?"

"What?" Manwright snorted in disgust. "Publish? And have every damned quack and campus cretin clowning around with the most sacred and miraculous phenomenon ever generated on our universe? Pah! No way!"

"*You're* into it, Reg."

Manwright drew himself up with hauteur. "*I*, sir, do not clown."

"But Reg—"

"But me no buts, professor. By heaven, if Christ, in whom I've never believed, ever returned to Terra and this house, I'd keep it a secret. You know damn well the hell that would break loose if I published. It'd be Golgotha all over again."

While Corque was wondering whether Manwright meant his biodroid techniques, Christ's epiphany, or both, there was a sound of a large object slowly falling upstairs. Manwright's scowl was transformed into a grin. "My housekeeper," he chuckled. "You didn't get the chance to see him when you moved in last night. A treasure."

An imbecile face, attached to a pinhead, poked through the penthouse door. It was followed by a skewed hunchback body with gigantic hands and feet. The mouth, which seemed to wander at will around the face, opened and spoke in a hoarse voice.

"Mahth-ter . . . "

"Yes, Igor?"

"Should I thteal you a brain today, mahth-ter?"

"Thank you, Igor. Not today."

"Then breakfahtht ith therved, mahth-ter."

"Thank you, Igor. This is our distinguished guest, the celebrated Professor Charles Corque. You will make him comfortable and obey him in everything."

"Yeth, mahth-ter. At your thervithe, thelebrated Profethor Charlth Corque. Should I thteal you a brain today?"

"Not today, thank you."

Igor bobbed his head, turned, disappeared, and there was a sound of a large object rapidly falling downstairs. Corque's face was convulsed with suppressed laughter. "What in the world—?"

"A reject," Manwright grinned. "Only one in my career. No, the first of two, if we count Sandy, but I do think Jessamy will keep his Siren. Anyway," he continued, leading Corque downstairs, "this client was absolutely hypnotized by the Frankenstein legend. Came to me and contracted for a faithful servitor, like the Baron's accomplice. Returned five months later, paid like a gent, but said he'd changed his mind. He was now on a Robinson Crusoe kick and wanted a Friday. I made him his Friday, but I was stuck with Igor."

"Couldn't you have dissolved him back into the DNA broth?"

"Good God, Charles! No way. Never. I generate life; I don't destroy it. Anyway, Igor's an ideal housekeeper. He does have this brain-stealing hang-up—that was part of the original model—and I have to lock him in a closet when there's thunder and lightning, but he cooks like an absolute genius."

"I hadn't known that Baron Frankenstein's henchman was a chef."

"To be quite honest, Charles, he wasn't. That was an error in programming—I *do* glitch now and then—with a happy ending. When Igor's cooking, he thinks he's making monsters."

The card came in on the same tray with the Tomato-Onion Tart (ripe tomatoes, sliced onions, parsley, basil, Gruyère, bake in pastry shell forty minutes at 375°F), and Manwright snatched the embossed foil off the salver.

"What's this, Igor? 'Anthony Valera, Chairman, Vortex Syndicate, 69 Old Slip, CB: 0210–0012–036–216291'?"

"In the waiting room, mahth-ter."

"By God, Charles, a potential client. Now you may have your chance to watch my genesis from start to finish. Come on!"

"Oh, have a heart, Reg. Let the chairman wait. Igor's monster looks delicious."

"Thank you, thelebrated Profethor Charlth Corque."

"No, no, Igor. The thanks go from me to you."

"Pigs, both of you," Manwright snorted and dashed for the stairs. Corque rolled his eyes to heaven, grabbed a slice of tart, winked at Igor, and followed, chewing ecstatically.

One would expect the chairman of a syndicate with a seventeen-figure CB telephone number to look like Attila the Hun. Anthony Valera looked and dressed like a suave Spanish grandee; he was black and silver, including ribboned peruke. He was very much au courant, for as Corque entered he smiled, bowed, and murmured, "What a happy surprise, Professor Corque. Delighted. I had the pleasure of hearing you speak at the Trivium Charontis convention." And Mr. Valera considerately offered his left palm, Corque's right hand being busy with the tart.

"He wants an ideal executive secretary," Manwright refused to waste time on courtesies. "And I told him that my biodroid talents are damned expensive."

"To which I was about to respond when you most happily entered, Professor Corque, that Vortex is criminally solvent."

"Then it's to be a company contract?"

"No, Dominie, personal." Mr. Valera smiled. "I, also, am criminally solvent."

"Good. I hate doing business with committees. You must know the old saw about camels. Let's discuss the specs and see whether we understand each other. Sex?"

"Female, of course."

"Of course. Physical appearance?"

"You don't take notes?"

"Total recall."

"You *are* lucky. Well, then. Fair. Medium tall. Endowed with soft grace. Soft voice. Blue eyes. Clear skin. Slender hands. Slender neck. Auburn hair."

"Mmm. Got any particular example of the type in mind?"

"Yes. Botticelli's *Birth of Venus*."

"Ha! Venus on the Half-shell. Lovely model. Character?"

"What one would expect of a secretary: sterling, faithful, devoted . . . to my work, of course."

"To your work, of course."

"And clever."

"D'you mean clever or intelligent?"

"Aren't they the same?"

"No. Cleverness requires humor. Intelligence does not."

"Then clever. I'll provide the intelligence. She must be able to learn quickly and remember. She must be able to acquire any skill necessary for my work. She must be perceptive and understand the stresses and conflicts that make a chairman's life one constant battle."

"So far you could hire such a girl," Manwright objected. "Why come to me?"

"I haven't finished, Dominie. She must have no private life and be willing to drop everything and be instantly available at all times."

"Available for what?"

"Business luncheons, dinners, last-minute parties, client entertainment, and so forth. She must be chic and fashionable and able to dazzle men. You would not believe how many tough tycoons have been charmed into dubious deals by a seductive secretary."

"You've left out an important point. On what salary will she be seducting?"

"Oh, I'll provide the money for the wardrobe, the maquillage, and so forth. She must provide the taste, the charm, the wit, the entertaining conversation."

"Then you want a talker?"

"But only when I want her to talk. Otherwise, mum."

Corque whistled softly. "But you're describing a paragon, my dear sir."

"I would say a miracle, Professor Corque, but Dominie Manwright is celebrated for his miraculous creations."

"You married?" Manwright shot.

"Five times."

"Then you're a chaser."

"Dominie!"

"And easily landed."

"Really, you're extraordinarily blunt. A chaser? Well . . . let's say that I'm attracted, occasionally."

"Would you want your executive secretary to be responsive—occasionally? Is that to be programmed?"

"Only unilaterally. If I should happen to desire, I would want a beautiful response. But she is not to make demands. Nevertheless she will, of course, be faithful to me."

"These parameters are preposterous," Corque exclaimed indignantly.

"Not at all, Charles, not at all," Manwright soothed. "Mr. Valera is merely describing what all men desire in a woman: an Aspasia, the beautiful *femme galante* who

was the adoring mistress and adviser to Pericles of ancient Greece. It's wishful fantasy, but my business is turning fantasy into reality, and I welcome the challenge. This girl may be my magnum opus." Again he fired a shot at Valera. "And you'll become very bored."

"What?"

"Within six months this adoring, talented, dedicated slave will bore you to tears."

"But how? Why?"

"Because you've left out the crux of a kept woman's hold over a man. Don't protest, Valera. We know damn well you're ordering a mistress, and I make no moral judgment, but you've forgotten the drop of acid."

"Dominie, I do protest. I—"

"Just listen. You're contracting for an enchanting mistress, and it's my job to make sure that she remains enchanting, always. Now there are many sweet confections that require a drop of acid to bring out the full flavor and keep them enjoyable. Your Aspasia will need a drop of acid for the same reason. Otherwise, her perpetual perfection will cloy you in a matter of months."

"You know," Valera said slowly, "that's rather astute, Dominie. What would you advise? I'm all anticipation!"

"The acid in any woman who can hold a man: the unexpected, the quality that makes it impossible to live with them or without them."

"And what would that be in my ... my secretary?"

"How the devil can I tell you?" Manwright shouted. "If you knew in advance, it wouldn't be unexpected; and anyway *I* won't know. I can't guarantee surprise and adventure with a woman. All I can do is program a deliberate error into the genesis of your perfect Aspasia, and the discovery of that kink will be the charming drop of acid. Understood?"

"You make it sound like a gamble."

"The irrational is always a gamble."

After a pause Valera said. "Then you're challenging me, Dominie?"

"We're both being challenged. You want the ideal mistress created to your specs; I've got to meet them to your complete satisfaction."

"And your own, Reg?" Corque murmured.

"Certainly my own. I'm a professional. The job is the boss. Well, Valera? Agreed?"

After another thoughtful pause, Valera nodded. "Agreed, Dominie."

"Splendid. I'll need your Persona Profile from the syndicate."

"Out of the question, Dominie! Persona Profiles are Inviolable Secret. How can I ask Vortex to make an exception?"

"Damn it, can't you understand?" Manwright was infuriated by this intransigence but controlled himself and tried to speak reasonably. "My dear chairman, I'm shaping and conditioning this Aspasia for your exclusive use. She will be the cynosure of all men, so I must make sure that she'll be implanted with an attraction for your qualities and drawn to you alone."

"Surely not all, Dominie. I have no delusions of perfection."

"Then perhaps to your defects, and that will be *your* charming drop of acid. Come back in twenty-one weeks."

"Why twenty-one specifically?"

"She'll be of age. My biodroids average out at a week of genesis for every physical year of the creation's maturity. One week for a dog; twenty-one weeks for an Aspasia. Good day, Mr. Valera."

After the chairman had left, Manwright cocked an eye at Corque and grinned. "This is going to be a magnificent experiment, Charles. I've never generated a truly contemporary biodroid before. You'll pitch in and help, I hope?"

"I'll be honored, Reg." Suddenly, Corque returned the grin. "But there's one abstruse reference I can't understand."

"Fear not, you'll learn to decipher me as we go along. What don't you understand?"

"The old saw about the camel."

"The usual biodroid accommodations weren't good enough for Manwright's magnum opus. . . . The red infant was on the floor, flat on her belly, propped on a pillow, and deep in a book. She looked up and crawled."

Manwright burst out laughing. "What? Never heard it? Penalty of spending too much time on the outer planets. Question: What is a camel? Answer: A camel is a horse made by a committee." He sobered. "But by God, our gallant girl won't be any camel. She'll be devastating."

"Forgive the question, Reg: Too devastating for you to resist?"

"What? That? No way! Never! I've guaranteed and delivered too many virgin myths, deities, naiads, dryads, *und so weiter*. I'm seasoned, Charles; tough and hard and impervious to all their lures. But the breasts are going to be a problem," he added absently.

"My dear Reg! Please decipher."

"Her breasts, Charles. Botticelli made em too small in his Venus. I think I should program 'em fuller, but what size and shape? Like pears? Pomegranates? Melons? It's an aesthetic perplexity."

"Perhaps your deliberate error will solve it."

"Perhaps, but only the Good Lord, in whom I've never believed, can know what her mystery kink will turn out to be. *Selah!* Let's get to work on our perfect mistress, Charles, or, to use an antique expression that's just become a new vogue word, our perfect Popsy."

The Dominie's program for a devastating Popsy who was to be enchanting, trustworthy, loyal, helpful, friendly, courteous, kind, obedient, cheerful, clever, chic, soft-spoken, beautiful, busty, eloquent on demand, and always available to entertain, began as follows:

A	12-1	0	0	(scald)
B	12-2	1	1	
C	12-3	2	2	(V.S.O.P.)
D	12-4	3	3	
E	12-5	4	4	
F	12-6	5	5	(¼ dram)
G	12-7	6	6	
H	12-8	7	7	(crimped)
I	12-9	8	8	
J	11-1	9	9	(½ scruple)
K	11-2	(garni)		
L	11-3	#	8-3	
M	11-4	!	11-8-2	
N	11-5	@	8-4	(eau)
O	11-6	$	11-8-3	
P	11-7	%	0-8-4	(MSG)
Q	11-8	¢	12-8-2	
R	11-9	&	12	
S	0-2	*	11-8-4	(only a dash)
T	0-3	+	0-8-3	
U	0-4	:	12-8-3	

Und so weiter for 147 pages. *Und* good luck to the computer software for creative biogenesis, which couldn't possibly interest anyone.

"Anyway, there's no point in reading the program, Charles. Numbers can't paint the picture. I'll just describe the sources I've used for the generation of our Popsy. You may not recognize some of the names, but I assure you that most of them were very real and famous celebrities in their time."

"What was your lecture to Igor the other day, Reg? 'A chef is no better than his materials.'"

"Right on. And I'm using the best. Beauty—Botticelli's Venus of course, but with Egyptian breasts. I thought of using Pauline Borghese, but there's a queen in a limestone relief from the Ptolemaic period who's the ideal model. Callipygian rear elevation. Maidenhair frontispiece, delicate and fritillary. Did you say something, Charles?"

"Not I, Reg."

"I've decided not to use Aspasia for the virtues."

"But you said that was what Valera wanted."

"So I did, but I was wrong. The real Aspasia was a damned premature Women's

Rights activist. Too strong for the chairman's taste."

"And yours?"

"Any man's. So I'm using Egeria instead."

"Egeria? I haven't had an education in the classics, Reg."

"Egeria, the legendary fountain nymph who was the devoted adviser to King Numa of ancient Rome. She also possessed the gift of prophecy, which might come in handy for Valera. Let's see. Fashion and chic—a famous couturiere named Coco Chanel. Subtle perceptions—the one and only Jane Austen. Voice and theater sense—Sarah Bernhardt. And she'll add a soupçon of lovely Jew."

"What on earth for?"

"It's obvious you haven't met many on the outer planets or you wouldn't ask. Remarkable race, Jews; freethinking, original, creative, obstinate, impossible to live with or without."

"That's how you described the ideal mistress, wasn't it?"

"I did."

"But if your Popsy is obstinate, how can she respond to Valera's desires?"

"Oh, I'm using Lola Montez for that. Apparently, she was a tigress in the sex department. Hmmm. Next? Victoria Woodhull for business acumen. La Pasionaria for courage. Hester Bateman—she was the first woman silversmith—for skills. Dorothy Parker for wit. Florence Nightingale for sacrifice. Mata Hari for mystery. What else?"

"Conversation."

"Quite right. Oscar Wilde."

"Oscar Wilde!"

"Why not? He was a brilliant talker; held dinner parties spellbound. I'm giving her dancer's hands, neck, and legs, Dolly Madison hostessing, and—I've omitted something. . . ."

"Your deliberate mistake."

"Of course. The mystery kink which will catch us all by surprise." Manwright flipped through the software. "It's programmed somewhere around here. No, that's Valera's Persona Profile. Charles, you won't believe the damned intransigent, stubborn, know-it-all, conceited egomania concealed beneath that polished veneer. It's going to be hell imprinting our girl with an attraction engram for such an impossible man. Oh, here's the unexpected in black and white."

Manwright pointed to:

$R = L \times \sqrt{N}$

"Wait a minute," Corque said slowly. "That equation looks familiar."

"Aha."

"I think I remember it from one of my boyhood texts."

"Oh-ho."

"The . . . the most probable distance . . ." Corque was dredging up the words ". . . from the lamppost after a certain number of . . . of irregular turns is equal to the average length of each track that is—"

"Straight track, Charles."

"Right. Each straight track that is walked, times the square root of their number." Corque looked at Manwright with a mixture of wonder and amusement. "Confound you, Reg! That's the solution to the famous 'Drunkard's Walk' problem from *The Law of Disorder*. And this is the deliberate uncertainty that you're programming? You're either a madman or a genius."

"A little of both, Charles. A little of both. Our Popsy will walk straight lines within my parameters, but we'll never know when or how she'll hang a right or a left."

"Surely she'll be aiming for Valera?"

"Of course. He's the lamppost. But she'll do some unexpected staggering on the way." Manwright chuckled and sang in an odd, husky voice, "There's a lamp on a post, There's a lamp on a post, And it sets the night aglowin'. Boy girl boy girl, Boy boy girl girl, But best when flakes is snowin'."

Regis Manwright's laboratory notes provide a less-than-dramatic description (to put it politely) of the genesis and embryological development of Galatea Galante, the Perfect Popsy.

GERMINAL
Day 1: One hundred milliliter Florence flask.
Day 2: Five hundred milliliter Florence flask.
Day 3: One thousand milliliter Florence flask.
Day 4: Five thousand milliliter Florence flask.
Day 5: Decanted.

(E & A charging *too damn much* for flasks!!!)

(Baby nominal. Charles enchanted with her. Too red for my taste. Poured out of the amnion blowing bubbles and talking. Couldn't shut her up. Just another fresh kid with a damn big mouth.)

"Reg, Gally must have a nurse."

"For heaven's sake, Charles! She'll be a year old next week."

"She must have someone to look after her."

"All right. All right. Igor. She can sleep in his room."

"No, no, no. He's a dear creature, but hardly my idea of a nursemaid."

"I can convince him he made her. He'll be devoted."

"No good, Reg; he isn't child oriented."

"You want someone child oriented? Hmmm. Ah, yes. Got just the right number for you. I generated The Old Woman Who Lived in a Shoe for the Positively Peerless Imitation Plastic company to use in their genuine plastics sales promotion."

" 'She had so many children she didn't know what to do'?"

"The same." Manwright punched the CB keyboard. "Seanbhean? This is Regis."

The screen sparkled and cleared. A gypsy crone appeared with begging hand outstretched for alms.

"How's everything going, Seanbhean?"

"*Scanruil aduafar*, Regis."

"Why?"

"*Briseadh ina ghno e*."

"What! PPIP gone bankrupt? That's shocking. So you're out of a job?"

"*Deanfaidh sin*!"

"Well perhaps I have something for you, Seanbhean. I've just generated—"

"Cut off, Reg" Corque broke in sharply.

Manwright was so startled by Corque's tone that he obeyed and looked up perplexedly. "Don't think she'll do, Charles?"

"That old hag? Out of the question."

"She isn't old," Manwright protested. "She's under thirty. I made her look like that according to specs: Seventy-year-old Irish gypsy. They call 'em 'tinkers' in Ireland. Speaks Irish and can handle kid actors who are a pain in the ass. And I delivered, by God."

"As you always do; but still out of the question. Please try someone else."

"Charles, has that damn infant got you enthralled?"

"No."

"Her first conquest, and she's just out of the flask! Can you imagine what she'll do to men in another twenty weeks? Be at each other's throats. Fighting duels. Ha! I *am* a genius, and I don't deny it."

"We need a nurse for Gally, Reg."

"Nag, nag, nag."

"Someone warm and comforting after the child has endured a session with you."

"I can't think what the man is implying. All right, cradle-snatcher, all right. I'll call Claudia." Manwright punched the CB. "She's warm and maternal and protective. Wish she'd been *my* nanny. Hello? Claudia? It's Regis. Switch on, darling." The screen sparkled and cleared. The magnificent head and face of a black mountain gorilla appeared.

"!!" she grunted.

"I'm sorry, love. Been too busy to call. You're looking well. How's that no-good husband of yours?"

"!"

"And the kids?"

"!!!"

"Splendid. Now don't forget. You promised to send them to me so I can surgify them into understanding our kind of speech. Same like you, love, and no charge. And speaking of kids, I've got a new one, a girl, that I'd like you to—"

At this point the stunned Corque collected himself enough to press the cutoff stud. Claudia faded.

"Are you mad?" he demanded.

Manwright was bewildered. "What's wrong, Charles?"

"You suggest that terrifying beast for the child's nurse?"

"Beast! She's an angel of mother love. She'll have the kid climbing all over her, hugging and kissing her. It's interesting," he reflected, "I can manipulate the cognition centers, but I can't overcome muscular limitations. I gave Claudia college-level comprehension of spoken and written communications, but I couldn't give her human speech. She's still forced to use Mountain, which is hardly a language of ideas. Damn frustrating. For both of us."

"And you actually want her to mother Gally?"

"Of course. Why not?"

"Your Claudia will frighten the daylights out of the infant."

"Ridiculous."

"She's hideous."

"Are *you* mad? She's beautiful. Pure. Majestic. And a hell of a lot brighter than your Remedial Table Tennis bums at Syrtus University."

"But she can't talk. She only grunts."

"Talk? Talk? For God's sake, Charles! That damn red Popsy was poured out talking sixteen to the dozen. We can't shut her up. She's filling the house with enough of her jabber as it is. Be grateful for some silence."

So Claudia, the black mountain gorilla, moved into the Manwright ménage, and Igor was furiously jealous.

The first morning that Claudia joined Manwright and Corque at breakfast (while Igor glowered at his massive rival), she printed a message on a pad and handed it to the Dominie: R DD YU GV G TLT TRG IN YR PRGRM?

"Let's see if I remember your abbreviations, darling. Did you . . . that's me . . . give Galatea . . . yes, toilet training in your program? My God, Claudia! I gave her the best of 47 women. Surely at least one of them must have been toilet trained."

BY DPRS

"By what, Claudia?"

"Buy diapers, Reg."

"Oh. Ah. Of course. Thank you, Charles. Thank you, Claudia. More coffee, love? It's frustrating, Charles. Muscular dyspraxia again. Claudia can manage caps in her writing but she can't hack lower case. How many diapers, Claudia?"

1 DZ

"Right. One doz. *Zu Befehl*. Did you bring your kids to play with the baby?"

TO OD

"Too odd for what?"

TOO OLD

"Your kids?"

G

"What? Galatea? Too old for your boys? And still in diapers? I'd best see for myself."

One of the top-floor bedrooms had been converted into a nursery. The usual biodroid cellar accommodations weren't good enough for Manwright's magnum opus. When the Dominie entered with Claudia, the red infant was on the floor, flat on her belly, propped on a pillow, and deep in a book. She looked up and crawled enthusiastically to Claudia.

"Nanny dear, I've found the answer, the old linear shorthand. Just slashes, dots, and dashes, and you won't have to worry your hand and head over cursive abbreviations. It's a simple style, and we can practice together." She climbed up on Claudia and kissed her lovingly. "One would think this might have occurred to that egotistical know-it-all whose name escapes me." The infant turned her auburn head. "Why, good morning, Dominie Manwright. What an unpleasant surprise."

"You're right, Claudia," Manwright growled. "She's too damned old for your kids. Diaper her."

"My sphincter will be under control by tomorrow, Dominie," Galatea said sweetly. "Can you say the same for your tongue?"

"Guh!" And Manwright withdrew with what he hoped was impressive dignity.

Of course, she shot up like a young bamboo plant and filled the house with joy as she entertained them with her escapades. She taught herself to play Manwright's Regency harpsichord, which was sadly out of repair. She convinced Igor that it was a monster in the making, and together they refinished and tuned it. The sound of concert-A on the tuning fork droned through the house with agonizing penetration. The others were forced to eat out because she gave Igor no time for cooking.

She studied linear shorthand with Claudia and then translated it into finger language. They had glorious raps, silently talking to each other until Manwright banned the constant finger waggling, which he denounced as a damned invasion of vision. They simply held hands and talked into each other's palm in their secret code, and Manwright was too proud to ask what they were gossiping about.

"Corque took her to his Saturn Circus, where she mesmerized him into letting her try riding bareback and leaping through burning hoops. . .and thrusting her auburn head into a lion's mouth."

"As if I'd get an answer anyway," he growled to Corque.

"D'you think that's her mystery surprise, Reg?"

"Damned if I know. She's unexpected enough as it is. Rotten kid!"

She stole liquid licorice from Igor's sacred pantry and tarred herself; phosphorous from Manwright's sacred laboratory and irradiated herself. She burst into Corque's dark bedroom at three in the morning, howling, "ME METHOPHYTE MOTHER FROM GANNYMEEDY! YOU KILL ALL MY CHILDERS, ALIEN INVADER FROM OUTSIDE SPACE! NOW ME KILL YOU!"

Corque let out a yell and then couldn't stop laughing for the rest of the day. "The beautiful shock of the apparition, Reg!" Manwright didn't think it was funny.

"That damned child is giving me *real* nightmares," he complained. "I keep dreaming that I'm lost in the Grand Teton mountains and Red Indians are chasing me."

She sneaked up into the sacred penthouse and decorated the robotlike neutrinoscope with items stolen from Manwright's wardrobe. The construct assumed a ludicrous resemblance to the Dominie himself.

The innocent child fast-talked E & A Chemical delivery—"My Daddy forgot to order it. So absent-minded, you know"—into an extra gallon of ethyl alcohol which she poured into the marble pool and got the piranhas disgustingly drunk. Then she jumped in and was discovered floating with her plastered pals.

"Doesn't know the meaning of fear, Reg."

"Pah! Just the Pasionaria I programmed."

She stole two hundred meters of magnetic tape from the library and fashioned a scarecrow mobile. The gardener was enraptured. Manwright was infuriated, particularly because art-dealer friends offered huge amounts for the creation.

"But *that's* her charming unexpected, Reg. Gally's a born artist."

"Like hell she is. That's only the Hester Bateman I gave her. No $L \times \sqrt{N}$ yet. And the nightmares are continuing in sequence. Those damned Red Indians have cut me off at the pass."

Claudia took Galatea to her home, where the girl got on famously with Claudia's two sons and brought them to Manwright's house to demonstrate a new dance which she'd devised called: "The Anthro Hustle." It was performed to a song she'd composed entitled: "Who Put the Snatch on Gorilla Baby?" which she banged out fortissimously on the harpsichord.

"Bring back the tuning fork," Manwright muttered.

Corque was applauding enthusiastically. "Music's her surprise kink, Reg."

"Call that music?"

Corque took her to his Saturn Circus, where she mesmerized him into letting her try riding bareback and leaping through burning hoops, acting as target for a knife thrower, trapeze aerobatics, and thrusting her auburn head into a lion's mouth. He couldn't understand how she'd persuaded him to let her take such horrifying risks.

"Perhaps cajolery's her mystery quality," he suggested. "But she did miraculously well, Reg. My heart was in my mouth. Gally never turned a hair. Pure aplomb. She's a magnificent creation. You've generated a Super-Popsy for Valera."

"Guh."

"Could her unexpected kink be psychic?"

"The redskins have got me surrounded," Manwright fretted. He seemed strangely disoriented.

What disturbed him most were the daily tutoring sessions with the young lady. Invariably they degenerated into bickering and bitching, with the Dominie usually getting the worst of it.

"When our last session ended in another bitch we both steamed for the library door," he told Corque. "I said, 'Age before beauty, my dear,' which you must admit was gracious, and started out. That red Popsy snip said, 'Pearls before swine,' and swaggered past me like a gladiator who's wiped an entire arena."

"She's wonderful!" Corque laughed.

"Oh, you're insanely biased. She's been twisting you around her fingers since the moment she was poured."

"And Igor and Claudia and her two boys and the CB repair and the plumber and the electronics and the gardener and the laundry and E & A Chemical and half my circus? All insanely biased?"

"Evidently I'm the only sanity she can't snow. You know the simple psychological truth, Charles; we're always accusing others of our own faults. That saucebox has the impudence to call me intransigent, stubborn, know-it-all, conceited. Me! Out of her own mouth. QED."

"Mightn't it be the other way around, Reg?"

"Do try to make sense, Charles. And now that the Grand Teton breastworks are making her top-heavy (I think maybe I was a little too generous with my Egyptian programming) there'll be no living with her vanity. Women take the damned dumbest pride in the thrust of their boozalums."

"Now Reg, you exaggerate. Gally knows we'd all adore her even if she were flatchested."

"I know I'm doing a professional job, and I know she has too much ego in her cosmos. But next week we start *schlepping* her to parties, openings, talk-ins, routs, and such to train her for Valera. *That* ought to take her down a peg. The Red Indians have got me tied to a stake," he added.

"Canapés?"

"Ta evah so. Lahvely pahty, Ms. Galante."

"Thank you, Lady Agatha. Canapés?"

"Grazie, Signorina."

"Prego, Commendatore. Canapés?"

"A dank, meyd'l. Lang leb'n zolt ir."

"Nito far vus, General. Hot canapés, dear Professor Corque?"

"Thank you, adorable hostess. Igor's?"

"Mine."

"And perfection. Don't be afraid of the Martian counsul. He won't bite."

"Canapés, M'sieur Consul?"

"Ah! Mais oui! Merci, Mademoiselle Gallée. Que pensez-vous du lumineux Dominie Manwright?"

"C'est un type très compétent."

"Oui. Romanèsque, mais formidablement compétent."

"Quoi? Manwright? Romanèsque? Vous me gênez, mon cher consul."

"Ma foi, oui, romanèsque, Mademoiselle Gallée. C'est justement son côté romanesque qui lui cause du mal à se trouver une femme."

"These damn do's are a drag, Charles."

"But isn't she wonderful?"

"And they're making my nightmares worse. A sexy Indian squaw tore my clothes off last night."

"Mi interesso particolarmente ai libri di fantascienza, magia-orrore, umorismo, narrativa, attualità, filosofia, sociologia, e cattivo, putrido Regis Manwright."

"Charles, this is the last literary talk-in I ever attend."

"Did you see how Gally handled those Italian publishers?"

"Yes, gibes at my expense. She put iron claws on her hands."

"My dear Reg, Gally did no such thing."

"I was referring to that sexy squaw."

"Então agora sabes dançer?"

"Sim. Danço, falo miseravelmente muchas linguas, estudo ciência e filosofia, escrevo uma lamentával poesia, estoirome com experiências idiotas, egrimo como un louco, jogo so boxe como up palhaco. Em suma, son a celebra bioroid, Galatea Galante, de Dominie Manwright."

"She was magnificent dancing with that Portuguese prince, Reg."

"Portuguese ponce, you mean."

"Don't be jealous."

"She's heating the claws in a damned campfire, Charles."

"Didn't you ever fight back, Sandy?"

"Yes, I know, he's a bully. But all bullies are cowards at heart. You should have fought him to a standstill, like me. Did he ever make a pass at you?"

"Uh-huh. Me neither. He's an arrogant egomaniac, too much in love with himself to love anyone else."

"What. Sandy? Me? Give the come-on to that dreadful man? Never! Did you?

"Uh-huh. And he didn't even have to lash himself to the mast. Iceberg City. Ah, Mr. Jessamy. So sweet of you to give us your box for the concert. I've just been comparing notes with your adorable wife on our common enemy, whose name escapes me. He's the gentleman on my right, who slept through the Mozart."

"And dreamed that she's torturing me with her burning claws, Charles, all over my bod."

"Man nehme: zwei Teile Selbstgefälligkeit, zwei Teile Selbstsucht, einen Teil Eitelkeit, und einen Teil Esel, mische kräftig, füge etwas Geheimnis hinzu, und man erhält Dominie Regis Manwright."

"Especially my private parts."

"Dominie Manwright's biodroid está al dia en su manera de tratar los neologismos, palabras coloquiales, giro y modismos, clichés y terminos de argot, Señor. Yo soy Galatea Galante, la biodroid."

"Thank you, madame. I am not Spanish; I merely admire and respect the old Castilian style."

"Oh. Scuse me, chorley guy. You tollerday donsk?"

He burst out laughing. "I see you're very much with the classics, madame. Let me think. Yes. The proper response in that James Joyce litany is 'N.' "

"You talkatiff scowegian?"

"Nn."

"You spigotty anglease?"

"Nnn."

"You phonio saxo?"

"Nnnn."

"Clear all so. 'Tis a Jute. Let us swop hats and excheck a few strong verbs weak oach eather yapyazzard."

"Brava, madame! Bravissima!"

She tilted her auburn head and looked at him strangely. "Against my will," she said slowly, "I'm compelled to invite you to a dinner party tonight."

"More classics, madame? The Beatrice and Benedict scene from *Much Ado About Nothing*?"

"No, it's the Galatea and—I don't know your name."

"Valera. Antony Valera."

"It's the Galatea and Valera scene. Can you come?"

"With delight."

"When this bash is finished I'll give you the address."

"I know it. Galatea."

"My friends call me Gally. How do you know my address? We've never met."

"I contracted with—I'm acquainted with Dominie Manwright. Gally. Tonight? Eight o'clock?"

"Eight tonight."

"Dress party?"

"Optional." She shook her head dizzily. "I don't know what's got into me, Valera. The moment I saw you at this clambake I knew I had to see you again, intimately. I'm possessed!"

The rest of the household was dining in The Gastrologue, and their moods were not compatible.

"Thrown out," Corque kept repeating. "Thrown out without a moment's notice by that ungrateful tyrant!"

"Naturally. She wants to be alone with Valera, Charles. Instant, devoted attraction, as per my brilliant programming. I tell you, I'm a genius."

"She athed me to make month-terth for her to therve, mahth-ter."

"Quite right, Igor. We must all pitch in and

abet Valera's romance. He was so turned on meeting her at that bash this afternoon that he sent his check by messenger. Payment in full . . . to protect his claim on my Perfect Popsy, no doubt."

"Thrown out! Thrown out by that tyrant!"

"And good riddance to her very soon, Charles. The house will be back to normal."

"But she didn't order a brain, mahth-ter."

"Not to worry, Igor. Tell you what; *we'll* order *cervelles de veau au beurre noir*, and if Gastrologue doesn't have any calves' brains you can go out and steal some." He beamed and bobbed his pale, streaky head.

"Thank you, mahth-ter."

"Evicted!"

The silent Claudia printed: PLANTAINS FR ME PLS RENELLOS DE AMARILLO.

At one minute past eight Valera said, "It's fashionable to be a half-hour late, but I— Is it all right to come in?"

"Oh please! I've been biting my nails for a whole minute."

"Thank you. To tell the truth, I tried to be chic, but it didn't take as long as I thought it would to walk up from Old Slip."

"Old Slip? Isn't that where your office is? Were you working late, poor soul?"

"I live there too, Gally. A penthouse on top of the tower."

"Ah, à la Alexander Eiffel?"

"Somewhat, but the Syndicate complex is no *Tour Eiffel*. What a fantastic place this is. I've never done more than peep beyond the waiting room."

"D'you want the full tour?"

"I'd like nothing better."

"You've got it, but drink first. What would you like?"

"What are you serving?"

"My dear Valera, I—"

"Tony."

"Thank you. My dear Tony, I share this house with two and a half men and a mountain gorilla. We have everything in stock."

"Stolichnaya, please. Half?"

"Igor, our housekeeper," Galatea explained as she brought a tray with a bucket of ice, a bottle, and shot glasses. She opened the vodka deftly and began revolving the bottle in the ice. "A biodroid replica of Baron Frankenstein's accomplice."

"Oh yes, I've met him. The lisping hunchback."

"A dear, dear soul, but only half with it."

"And a gorilla?"

"That's Claudia, my beloved nanny. She's beautiful. This vodka really isn't chilled enough yet, but let's start anyway." She filled the glasses. "Russian style, eh? Knock it back, Tony. Death to the fascist, imperialist invaders from outer space."

"And their Conestoga star-wagons."

They knocked their shots back.

"Gally, what miracle are you wearing?"

"Là, sir!" She did a quick kick-turn. "Like it?"

"I'm dazzled."

"If I tell you, promise not to turn me in?"

"I promise."

"I copied it from a Magda."

"Who or what is a Magda? Oh, thank you."

"I'm afraid I filled it too high, but boys like big sandwiches and big drinks. She's *the* vogue designer of the year. Down with countertenors."

"May they be heard only in Siberia. Why must I keep it a secret about your copy?"

"Good Lord! They hang, draw, and quarter you if you pinch a designer original."

"How did you manage?"

"I fell in love with it at one of her openings and memorized it."

"And made it yourself? From memory? You're remarkable!"

"You're exaggerating. Don't you remember complicated stock manipulations?"

"Well, yes."

"So with me it's the same damn thing. Oops! That's the tag of a dirty joke. Apologies to the chairman."

"The chairman needs all the dirty jokes he can get for client entertainment. What's this one?"

"Maybe someday, if you coax me nicely."

"Where do you get them? Surely not from Dominie Manwright."

"From Claudia's naughty boys. Another shot to the damnation of Blue Laws, and then the guided tour."

Valera was bewildered and delighted by the madness of Manwright's house, and enchanted by the high style with which Galatea flowed through it with equally mad comments. An old song lyric haunted him:

Hey, diddle dee-dee,
I've found the girl for me.
With raunchy style
And virgin guile
She's just the girl for me.

"Never mind the polite compliments, Tony," she said, pulling him down on a couch beside her and refilling his glass. "I'll give you the acid test. Of all things in this house, which would you be most likely to steal?"

"You."

"I didn't say kidnap. Come on, man, steal something."

"I think I spilled my drink."

"It's my fault; I joggled your arm. Don't mop. So?"

"You're so sudden, Gally. Well . . . don't laugh. . . . The scarecrow mobile in the garden."

"Oh, I love you for that! *I* made it, when I was a little kid months ago." She gave him a smacking kiss on the cheek and jumped up. "Like some music?" She turned on the hi-fi and a soft murmuring drifted through the house.

Valera glanced at his watch. "Your guests must be frightfully chic."

"Oh?"

"You said eight. That was an hour ago. Where's everybody?"

"As a matter of fact, they came early."

"I'm the only one who was early."

"That's right."

"You mean I'm . . . ?"

"That's right."

"But you said a dinner party, Gally."

"It's ready any time you are."

"The party is us? Just us?"

"I can call some more people if you're bored with me."

"You know that's not what I meant."

"No? What did you mean?"

"I—" He stopped himself.

"Go ahead," she bullied. "Say it. I dare you."

He capitulated. For perhaps the first time in his suave life he was overpowered. In a low voice he said, "I was remembering a tune from twenty years ago. Hey, diddle-dee-dee/I've found the girl for me/With raunchy style/And virgin guile/She's just the girl for me."

She flushed and began to tremble. Then she took refuge in the hostess role. "Dinner," she said briskly. "Beef Stroganoff, potatoes baked with mushrooms, salad, lemon pie, and coffee. Mouton Rothschild. No, not upstairs, Tony; I've made special arrangements for you. Help me with the table."

Together, in a sort of domestic intimacy, they arranged a gaming table alongside the marble pool with two painted Venetian chairs. She had already set the table with Spode china and Danish silver, so it needed some careful balancing. Before she began serving, she drew the cork from the Bordeaux bottle and poured a few drops into Valera's goblet.

"Try it, Tony," she said. "I've never been able to decide whether the concept of 'letting a wine breathe' is fact or show-offey. I appeal to your sophistication. Give me your opinion."

He tasted and rolled his eyes to heaven. "Superb! You're magnificent with your compliments, Gally. Sit down and try it yourself. I insist." And he filled her glass.

"Wait," she laughed. "The floor show first. I snowed electronics into bootlegging ultralight into the pool. That's why I wanted our table here. Wait till you see 20 Performing Piranhas 20." She ran to a wall, extinguished the living room lights, and flipped a switch. The pool glowed like lava, and the excited fish became a ballet of darting embers. Galatea returned to the table, sat opposite Valera, and raised her goblet to him. He smiled back into her face.

"Hey, diddle-dee—" he began and then froze. He stared. Then he started to his feet so violently that he overturned the table.

"Tony!" She was appalled.

"You goddamn bitch," he shouted. His face was black. "Where's the CB?"

"Tony!"

"Where's the goddamn CB? Tell me before I break your goddamn neck!"

"Th-that table." She pointed. "B-but I don't understand. What's—"

"You'll understand soon enough." He punched buttons. "By God, you and this whole damn lying house will understand. Rip me? Play me for a patsy?" His rage was

"It's one goddam thing after another."

a terrifying echo of Manwright at his worst. "Hello. Larson? Valera. Don't waste time with visual. Crash mission. Call full Security and comb the city for a son of a bitch named Regis Manwright. Yes, that's the pig. I give you a half hour to find him and—"

"B-but I know where he is," Galatea faltered.

"Hold it, Larson. You do? Where?"

"The Gastrologue."

"The bastard's in The Gastrologue Club, Larson. Go get him and bring him to his house, which is where I am now. And if you want to get rough with him I'll pay all legals and add a bonus. I'm going to teach that lying pimp and his bitch a lesson they'll remember for the rest of their lives."

The four were herded into the main floor of Manwright's house at the point of a naked laser which Larson thought advisable in view of the threat of Claudia's mass. They saw a grotesque: Valera and Galatea silhouetted before the glowing pool in the dark room. Valera was holding the weeping girl by her hair, for all the world like a chattel in a slave market.

In this ominous *crise* Manwright displayed an aspect of his character which none had ever seen: a tone of quiet command that took obedience for granted, as if by divine right, and won it through its assurance.

"Mr. Larson, you may pocket that laser now. It was never needed. Valera, you will let Galatea go," he said softly. "No, dear, don't move. Stay alongside him. You belong to him, unless he's changed his mind. Have you, Valera?"

"You're goddamn right I have," the chairman stormed. "I want no part of this cheap secondhand trash. Larson, keep that gun handy and get on the CB. I want my check stopped."

"Don't bother, Mr. Larson. The check has not been deposited and will be returned. Why, Valera? Doesn't Galatea meet your exalted standards?"

"Of course she does," Corque burst out. "She's brilliant! She's beautiful! She's perfection! She—"

"I'm handling this, Charles. I repeat: Why, Valera?"

"I don't buy whores at your prices."

"You think Galatea's a whore?"

"Think? I know."

"You contracted for the perfect mistress who would be faithful and loving and devoted to you."

Galatea let out a moan.

"I'm sorry, my love, you never knew. I'd planned to tell you, but only after I was sure you were genuinely attracted to him. I never had any intention of forcing him on you."

"You wicked men!" she cried. "You're all hateful!"

"And now, Valera, you think of a mistress as a whore? Why this sudden eruption of archaic morality?"

"It isn't a question of morality, damn you. It's a question of secondhand goods. I want no part of a shopworn woman."

"Must I stay here with him? Does he own me? Am I bought and paid for?"

"No, love. Come to us."

She dashed away from Valera's side and then hesitated. Claudia held out her arms, but Galatea surprised everybody by going to Manwright, who took her gently.

"All right, Valera," he said. "Go now and take your army with you. Your check will be returned first thing in the morning."

"Not until I know who it was."

"Not until who what was?"

"The goddamn lover-boy who knocked her up."

"What?"

"She's pregnant, you goddamn pimp. The bitch has been sleeping around, and I want to know the stud who knocked her up. He's got plenty coming."

After a long pause, Manwright asked, "Are you under a psychiatrist's care?"

"Don't be ridiculous."

"No more ridiculous than your slander. Galatea pregnant? My lovely, tasteful young lady sleeping around with studs? You're obviously quite mad. Go."

"Mad, am I? Ridiculous? You can't see that she's pregnant? Turn her around and look at her face in this ultralight. Look at her!"

"I'll go through the motions only to get rid of you."

Manwright smiled at Galatea as he turned the girl around. "Just a gesture, love. You'll have your dignity back in a moment, and I swear you'll never lose it ag—"

His words were cut off, as if by a guillotine. In the ultralight from the glowing pool there was no mistaking the dark pregnancy band across Galatea's face, similar to the banded mask of a raccoon. He took a slow deep breath and answered the confusion in her eyes by placing a hand over her mouth.

"Go, Valera. This is now a family affair."

"I demand an answer. I won't leave until I know who it was. Your half-wit hunchback, Igor, probably. I can picture them in bed; the slobbering idiot and the—"

Manwright's interruption was an explosion. He hurled Galatea into Claudia's arms, drove a knee into Larson's groin, tore the laser away from the convulsed man, whipped Valera across the neck with the barrel, and held the staggering chairman over the edge of the pool.

"The piranhas are starving," he murmured. "Do you go in or get out?"

After the syndicate had left, not without dire promises, Manwright turned up the house lights and extinguished the pool ultralight and, with that, the pregnancy stigma banding Galatea's face. In a strange way they were all relieved.

"Not to play the district attorney," he said, "but I must know how it happened."

"How what happened?" Galatea demanded.

"Sweetheart, you *are* pregnant."

"No, no, no!"

"I know it can't be anyone in this house. Claudia, has she been at all promiscuous outside?

NO

"How can you ask such questions!"

"Has Galatea been alone with a man in a possibly intimate situation?"

"You're hateful!"

NO

"Reg, we all know that. We've chaperoned Gally every moment outside: you, me, Claudia."

"Not every moment, Charles. It could have happened with this innocent in five minutes."

"But nothing ever happened with a man! Nothing! Ever!"

"Dear love, you *are* pregnant."

"I can't be."

"You are, undeniably. Charles?"

"Gally, I adore you, no matter what, but Reg is right. The pregnancy band is undeniable."

"But I'm a virgin."

"Claudia?"

HR MNS HV STOPT

"Her what have stopped?"

Corque sighed. "Her menses, Reg."

"Ah so."

"I'm a virgin, you wicked, detestable men. A virgin!"

Manwright took her frantic face in his hands. "Sweetheart, no recriminations, no punishments, no Coventry, but I must know where I slipped up, how it happened. Who were you with, where and when?"

"I've never been with any man, anywhere or anywhen."

"Never?"

"Never . . . except in my dreams."

"Dreams?" Manwright smiled. "All girls have them. That's not what I mean, dear."

R MAB U SHD MN

"Maybe I should mean what, Claudia?"

LT HR TL U HR DRMS

"Let her tell me her dreams? Why?"

JST LSN

"All right, I'll listen. Tell me about your dreams, love."

"No. They're private property."

"Claudia wants me to hear them."

"She's the only one I've ever told. I'm ashamed of them."

Claudia fingerwagged, "Tell him, Gally. You don't know how important they are."

"No!"

"Galatea Galante, are you going to disobey your nanny? I am ordering you to tell your dreams."

"Please, nanny. No. They're erotic."

"I know, dear. That's why they're important. You must tell."

At length, Galatea whispered, "Put out the lights, please."

The fascinated Corque obliged.

In the darkness, she began, "They're erotic. They're disgusting. I'm so ashamed. They're always the same . . . and I'm always ashamed . . . but I can't stop. . . .

"There's a man, a pale man, a moonlight man, and I . . . I want him. I want him to . . . to handle me and ravish me into ecstasy, b-but he doesn't want me, so he runs, and I chase him. And I catch him. Th-there are some sort of friends who help me catch him and tie him up. And then they go away and leave me alone with the moonlight man, and I . . . and I do to him what I wanted him to do to me. . . ."

They could hear her trembling and rustling in her chair.

Very carefully, Manwright asked, "Who is this moonlight man, Galatea?"

"I don't know."

"But you're drawn to him?"

"Oh yes. Yes! I always want him."

"Just him alone, or are there other moonlight men?"

"Only him. He's all I ever want."

"But you don't know who he is. In the dreams do you know who you are?"

"Me. Just me."

"As you are in real life?"

"Yes, except that I'm dressed different."

"Different? How?"

"Beads and . . . and buckskin with fringe."

They all heard Manwright gasp.

"Perhaps like . . . like a Red Indian, Galatea?"

"I never thought of that. Yes. I'm an Indian, an Indian squaw up in the mountains, and I make love to the paleface every night."

"Oh. My. God." The words were squeezed out of Manwright. "They're no dreams." Suddenly he roared, "Light! Give me light, Charles! Igor! Light!"

The brilliant lights revealed him standing and shaking, moonlight pale in shock. "Oh my God, my God, my God!" He was almost incoherent. "Dear God, what have I created?"

"Mahth-ter!"

"Reg!"

"Don't you understand? I know Claudia suspected; that's why she made Galatea tell me her dreams."

"B-but they're only dirty dreams," Galatea wailed. "What could possibly be the harm?"

"Damn you and damn me! They were *not* dreams. They were reality in disguise. That's the harm. That's how your dreams lock in with my nightmares, which were reality, too. Christ! I've generated a monster!"

"Now calm yourself, Reg, and do try to make sense."

"I can't. There's no sense in it. There's nothing but that lunatic drop of acid I promised Valera."

"The mystery surprise in her?"

"You kept wondering what it was, Charles. Well, now you know, if you can interpret the evidence."

"What evidence?"

Manwright forced himself into a sort of thunderous control. "I dreamed I was pursued and caught by Red Indians, tied up, and ravished by a sexy squaw. I told you. Yes?"

"Yes. Interminably."

"Galatea dreams she's a Red Indian squaw, pursuing, capturing, and ravishing a paleface she desires. You heard her?"

"I heard her."

"Did she know about my dreams?"

"No."

"Did I know about hers?"

"No."

"Coincidence?"

"Possibly."

"Would you care to bet on that possibility?"

"No."

"And there you have it. Those 'dreams' were sleep versions or distortions of what was really happening; something which neither of us could face awake. Galatea's been coming into my bed every night, and we've been making love."

"Impossible!"

"Is she pregnant?"

"Yes."

"And *I'm* Valera's lover-boy, the stud responsible. My God! My God!"

"Reg, this is outlandish. Claudia, has Gally ever left her bed nights?"

NO

"There!"

❛His words were cut off, as if by a guillotine. In the ultralight from the glowing pool there was no mistaking the dark pregnancy band across Galatea's face. . . . He took a slow breath.❜

"Damn it, I'm not talking about a conventional, human woman. I didn't generate one. I'm talking about an otherworld creature whose psyche is as physically real as her body, can materialize out of it, accomplish its desires, and amalgamate again. An emotional double as real as the flesh. You've pestered me about the deliberate unexpected in my programming. Well, here's the $R = L \times \sqrt{N}$. Galatea's a succubus."

"A what?"

"A succubus. A sexy female demon. Perfectly human by day. Completely conformist. But with the spectral power to come, like a carnal cloud, to men in their sleep, nights, and seduce them."

"No!" Galatea cried in despair. "I'm not that. I can't be."

"And she doesn't even know it. She's an unconscious demon. The laugh's on me, Charles," Manwright said ruefully. "By God, when I do glitch it's a beauty. I knock myself out programming the Perfect Popsy with an engram for Valera, and she ruins everything by switching her passion to me."

"No surprise. You're very much alike."

"I'm in no mood for jokes. And then Galatea turns out to be a succubus who doesn't know it and has her will of me in our sleep every night."

"No, no! They were dreams. Dreams!"

"Were they? Were they?" Manwright was having difficulty controlling his impatience with her damned obtuseness. "How else did you get yourself pregnant, eh; *enceinte*, *gravida*, knocked up? Don't you dare argue with me, you impudent red saucebox! You know," he reflected, "there should have been a smidgen of Margaret Sanger in the programming. Never occurred to me."

He was back to his familiar impossible self, and everybody relaxed.

"What now, Reg?"

"Oh, I'll marry the snip, of course. Can't let a dangerous creature like Galatea out of the house."

"Out of your life, you mean."

"Never!" Galatea shouted. "Never! Marry you, you dreadful, impossible, conceited, bullying, know-it-all, wicked man? Never! If I'm a demon, what are you? Come, Claudia."

The two women went very quickly upstairs.

"Are you serious about marrying Gally, Reg?"

"Certainly, Charles. I'm no Valera. I don't want a relationship with a popsy, no matter how perfect."

"But do you love her?"

"I love all my creations."

"Answer the question. Do you love Gally, as a man loves a woman?"

"That sexy succubus? That naïve demon? Love her? Absurd! No, all I want is the legal right to tie *her* to a stake every night, when I'm awake. Ha!"

Corque laughed. "I see you do, and I'm very happy for you both. But, you know, you'll have to court her."

"What! Court? That impertinent red brat?"

"My dear Reg, can't you grasp that she isn't a child anymore? She's a grown young woman with character and pride."

"Yes, she's had you in thrall since the moment she was poured," Manwright growled. Then he sighed and accepted defeat. "But I suppose you're right. My dear Igor!"

"Here, mahth-ter."

"Please set up that table again. Fresh service, candles, flowers, and see if you can salvage the monsters you created for the dinner. White gloves."

"No brainth, mahth-ter?"

"Not this evening. I see the Mouton Rothschild's been smashed. Another bottle, please. And then my compliments to Ms. Galatea Galante, and will she have the forgiveness to dine, *à deux*, with a most contrite suitor. Present her with a corsage from me . . . something orchidy. This will be a fun necromance, Charles," he mused. "Parsley, sage, rosemary, and thyme, *alevai*. Man and Demon. Our boys will be devils, sorcery says, and the girls witches. But aren't they all?" ∞

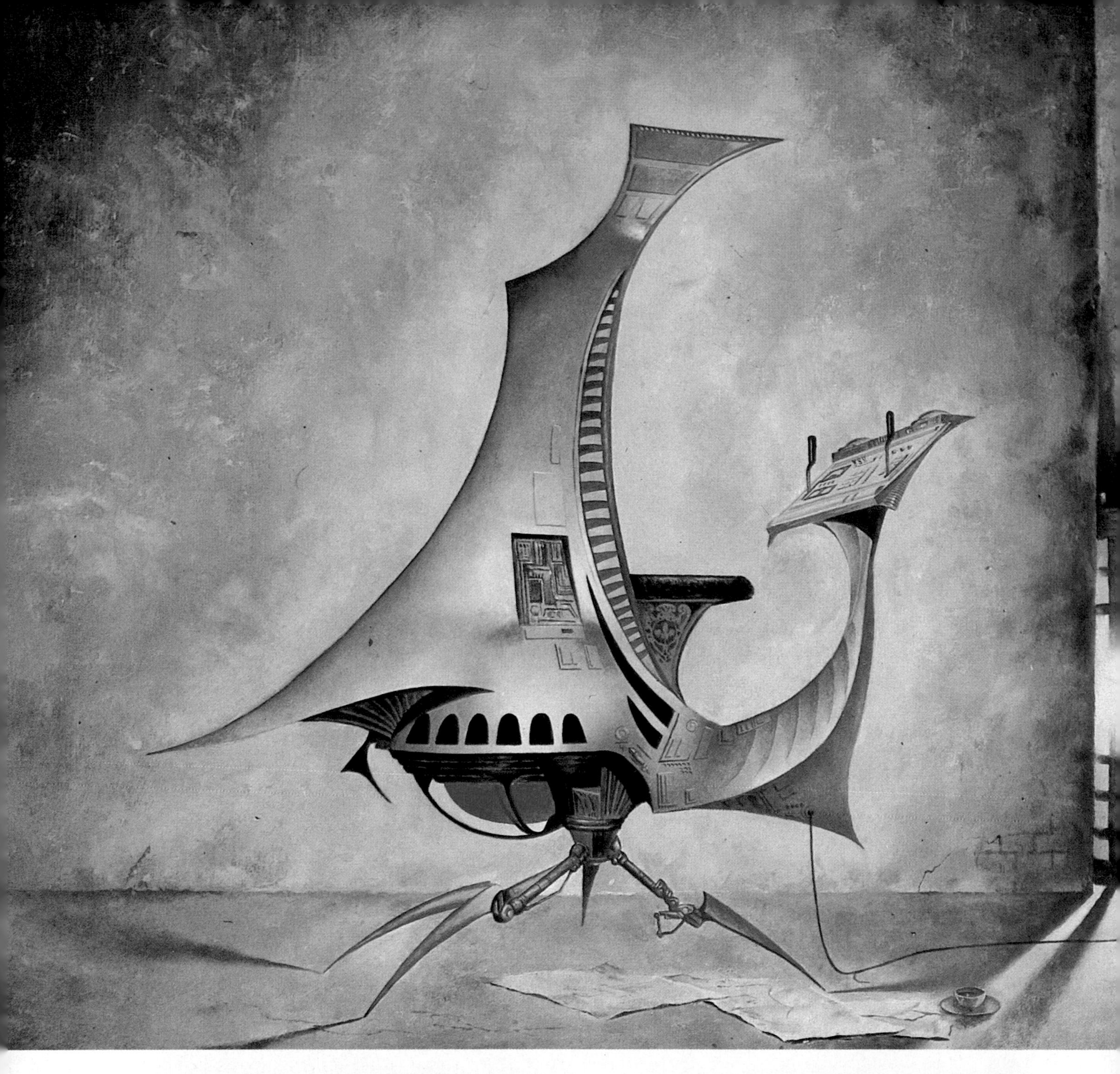

Illustrations by Les Edwards

ALIEN LANDSCAPES

Science-fiction classics, as envisioned by talented visual artists, show four worlds of imagination

THE TIME MACHINE

"The Time Traveler ... led the way down the long, draughty corridor to his laboratory.... We beheld a larger edition of the little mechanism we had seen vanish before our eyes.... Cut by the horizon lay the huge hull of the sun, red and motionless. The sky overhead was no longer blue.... I cannot convey the sense of abominable desolation that hung over the world."—*H. G. Wells*

"Paul looked down and saw sand spewing out of the metal and plastic beneath them . . . like a . . . tan and blue beetle."

Illustrations by Terry Oakes

DUNE

"Flecks of dust shadowed the sand around the crawler now. The big machine began to tip. . . . A gigantic sand whirlpool began forming. . . . Then they saw it! A wide hole emerged from the sand. Sunlight flashed from glistening white spokes within it. The hole's diameter was at least twice the length of the crawler. . . . 'Gods, what a monster!' muttered a man beside Paul. . . . The men crowded around him . . . staring fearfully." —*Frank Herbert*

Illustrations by Tony Roberts

MISSION OF GRAVITY

"The world [Mesklyn] is rather surprising in several ways. Its equatorial diameter is forty-eight thousand miles. From pole to pole . . . it measures nineteen thousand. . . . It rotates on its axis . . . making the day some seventeen and three quarter minutes long. At the equator I would weigh about four hundred eighty pounds . . . at the poles I'd be carrying something like sixty tons. . . . A large part of the southern hemisphere will receive no sunlight for fully three quarters of the year and should in consequence develop . . . frozen methane at the expense of the oceans. . . . Tremendous storms rage across the equator, carrying methane vapor . . . while the southern regions warm up . . . for creatures with liquid methane in their tissues."—*Hal Clement*

“The Earthman began to realize just what the winds of Mesklyn could do even in this gravity. . . .”

“From an embankment of the railroad, Chris sat silently watching the city of Scranton . . . preparing to take off.”

Illustrations by John Harris

CITIES IN FLIGHT

"There was no longer any reason why a vehicle to cross space needed to be small, cramped.... The most massive and awkward object could be lifted and hurled off the earth and carried almost any distance once antigravity was an engineering reality.... Whole cities could be moved."—*James Blish*

Illustrations from the book *Alien Landscapes*, by Robert Holdstock and Malcolm Edwards. Published in the U.S. by Mayflower Books (New York) and in the U.K. by Pierrot Publishing, Ltd.

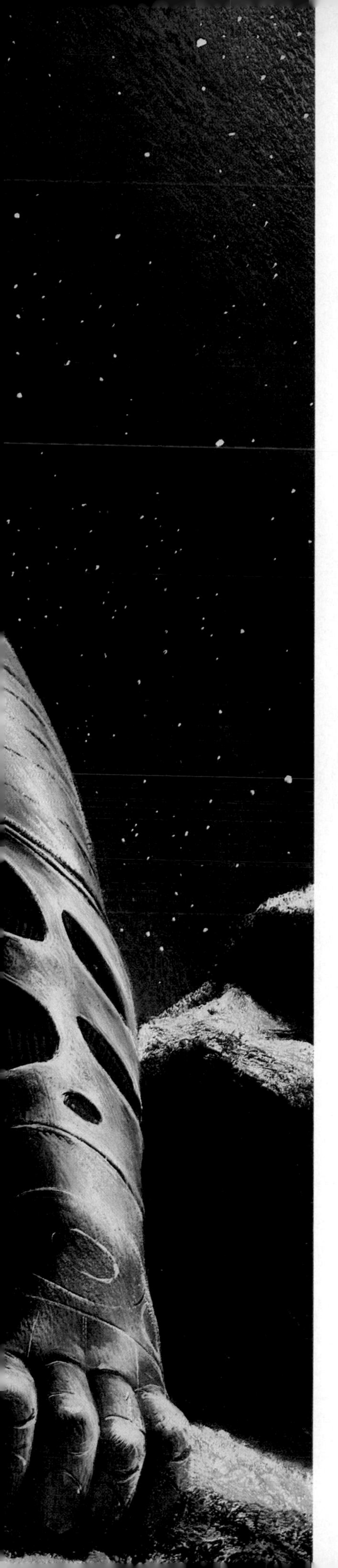

The astronaut trainees had to be taken down a peg— or so their officers thought

KINSMAN

BY BEN BOVA

Chet Kinsman is a young Air Force lieutenant, training to be an astronaut. His first mission in orbit, aboard a space shuttle, teams him with Lieutenant Frank Colt: black, brilliant, quick-tempered. Since Kinsman and Colt have scored highest among the astronaut trainees so far, the older officers in charge of the shuttle have decided to take them down a peg. Colt sees this as discrimination against him. And Kinsman realizes that his own chances to be an Air Force astronaut are inextricably linked with Colt's.

From the enthralling novel Kinsman, *published by Dial Press.*

When he finally slid out of his bunk, Kinsman felt too keyed up to be tired. Colt seemed tensed like a coiled spring, too, as they pulled on their pressure suits.

"So the Golddust Twins finally get their chance to go EVA," Smitty kidded them as he helped Kinsman with the zippers and seals of his suit.

"I thought they were gonna keep us after school," Colt said, "for being naughty yesterday."

"Pierce'll find a way to take you guys down a notch," Jill said. "He's got that kind of mind."

"Democracy in action," Kinsman said. "Reduce everybody to the same low level."

"Hey!" Art Douglas snapped, from across the compartment, where he was helping Colt into his suit. "Your scores weren't that much higher than ours, you know."

"Tell you what," Colt said. "A couple of you guys black your

PAINTING BY
JOHN SCHOENHERR

faces and see how you get treated."

They laughed, but there was a nervous undertone to it.

Kinsman raised his helmet over his head and slid it down into place. "Still fits okay," he said through the open visor. "Guess my head hasn't swollen too much."

Captain Howard slid down the ladder railing, already suited up, but with his helmet visor open. The pouches under his eyes looked darker than usual; his face had a gray prison pallor.

"You both checked out?"

Mr. Personality, thought Kinsman.

Howard wasn't satisfied with the trainees' check of their suits. He went over them personally. Finally, with a sour nod, he waved Colt to the airlock. The lock cycled, and then Howard himself went through, closing the metal hatch behind him.

Kinsman slid his visor down and sealed it, turned to wave a halfhearted "so long" to the others, then clumped into the airlock. The heavy hatch swung shut, and he could hear, faintly, the clatter of the pump sucking the air out of the phone booth–sized chamber. The red light went on, signaling vacuum. He opened the other hatch and stepped out into the payload bay.

Colt and Howard seemed to be deep in conversation, back beside the only remaining satellite in the bay. Kinsman shuffled toward them, keeping the lightly magnetized soles of his boots in contact with the steel strips set into the deck plates.

Colt tapped Howard on the shoulder and pointed to Kinsman. *Like scuba divers in an underwater movie*, Kinsman said to himself. Howard turned, tapped the keyboard on his left wrist, and held up four fingers.

Kinsman touched the button marked *Four* on his own wrist keyboard.

Howard's voice immediately came through his earphones. "We're using channel four for suit-to-suit chatter. Ship's frequency is three; don't use it unless you have to talk to the flight deck."

"Yes, sir," said Kinsman.

"Okay. Let's get to work."

Under Howard's direction, Colt and Kinsman peeled away the protective aluminized sheeting from the third and final satellite in the bay. It was a large, fat drum, tall as a man and so wide that Kinsman knew he and Colt could not girdle it with their outstretched arms. The outer surface of the satellite was covered with dead black solar cells.

"Kinsman, you come up top here with me to unfold the antennas," Howard ordered. "Colt, get back to the main bulkhead and open the doors."

Floating up to the top of the satellite with the captain beside him, Kinsman asked, "What kind of a satellite is this? Communications?"

"In a polar orbit?"

"Oh. No, I guess not. We've changed orbital planes so often that I didn't realize . . ."

"Start with that one." Howard pointed to the largest antenna, in the center of the drumhead.

Kinsman hung head-down over the satellite and read the assembly instruction printed on it by the light of his helmet lamp. The antenna support arms swung up easily and locked into place. Then he opened the parasol-folded parabolic dish that was the antenna itself.

"Now the waveguide," Howard commanded laconically.

"It's not an observation satellite," Kinsman said as he worked. "No ports for cameras or sensors."

"Keep your mind on your work."

"But what the hell's it for?" Kinsman blurted.

With an exasperated sigh, Howard said, "Strategic Command didn't bother to tell me, kid. So I don't know. Except that it's top secret and none of our damned business."

"Ohh . . . a ferret."

"A what?"

"Scuttlebutt that we heard back at the academy," Kinsman explained. "Satellites that gather electronic intelligence from other satellites. This bird's going into a high orbit, right?"

Howard hesitated before answering. "Yes," he replied.

Nodding inside his helmet, Kinsman went on: "She'll hang up there and listen on a wide band of frequencies, mostly the freaks the Soviets use. Maybe some Chinese and European bands, too. She just sits in orbit and passively collects all their chatter, recording it. Then when she passes over a command station in the States, they send up an order and she spits out everything she's recorded over the course of a day or a week. All data-compressed so they can get the whole wad of poop in a few seconds."

"Really." Howard's voice was as flat and cold as an ice tray.

"Yes, sir. The Russians have knocked a few of ours down, or so they told us at the academy."

Howard's response was unintelligible.

"Sir?" Kinsman asked.

"I *said*," he snapped, "that I never went to the academy. I came up the hard way. So I don't have as much inside information as you bright boys."

Touchy!

"Colt, when the hell are you going to get them doors open?"

"I'm ready anytime, sir," Colt's voice came through the earphones. "Been waiting for your order."

"Well, open 'em up, damn it, and get back here."

Soundlessly the big clamshell doors began to swing open. Kinsman started to return his attention to the satellite, but as the doors swung farther and farther back, he saw more and more stars staring at him: hard, unwinking points of light, not like

jewels set in black velvet, as he had expected, not like anything he had ever seen before in his life.

"Glory to God in the highest . . ." Kinsman heard himself whisper the words as he rose, work forgotten, drifting up toward the infinitely beautiful stars.

"Get your ass back here, Kinsman!" Howard shouted. It was like ice picks jabbing at his eardrums.

"But I never thought . . ." Kinsman found himself drifting halfway down the payload bay, high enough so that his head and shoulders were out in the open. He grabbed a hinge of the open door to steady himself.

Colt was beside him. "Fantastic!"

Kinsman realized his mouth was hanging open. But he didn't care. Inside the helmet, in the utter privacy of his impervious personal suit, he stared at the universe, seeing it for the first time. It was endless, shining, hypnotically beautiful.

"All right, all right." Howard's voice was softer, gentler. "Sometimes I forget how it hits some people the first time. You've got five minutes to see the show. Then we've got to get back to work or we'll miss the orbit-injection time. Here"—and Kinsman felt a hand on his shoulder—"don't go drifting loose. Use these for tethers."

He felt a line being hooked into one of the loops at the waist of his suit. Looking around, he saw Howard do the same thing for Colt.

"Go out and take a good look," Howard said. "Five minutes. Then we've got to count down the satellite."

Kinsman floated free, outside the confines of the ship, and let the full light of Earth shine on his face. It was dazzling, overpowering, an all-engulfing expanse of curving blue decked with brilliant white clouds. Hardly any land to be seen, just unbelievably blue seas and the pure white of the clouds.

It was *huge*, filling the sky, spreading as far as he could see: serene blue and sparkling white, warm, alive, glowing, a beckoning, beautiful world, the ancient mother of mankind. The earth looked untroubled from this distance. No divisions marred her face; not the slightest trace of the frantic works of her children soiled the eternal beauty of the planet. It took a wrenching effort of will for Kinsman to turn his face away from her.

By turning his body, Kinsman could see the sun shining so fiercely that even his heavily tinted photochromic visor wasn't enough protection. He squeezed his tearing eyes shut and spun away, angry yellow splotches flecking his vision.

"Can't see the moon," he heard Colt say.

"Must be on the other side of the earth," he answered.

"Look! That red star. I think it's Mars."

"No," Kinsman said. "It's Antares . . . in Scorpius."

"Christ, it's beautiful."

When I consider thy heavens, the work of thy fingers, the moon and the stars, which thou hast ordained . . .

"All right, all right," Howard's voice broke through to them. "Time to get back to work. You'll get plenty of chances to see more, soon enough. Come on. Hurry it up."

Reluctantly Kinsman turned away from the stars and back to the dark interior of the payload bay. Colt trailed behind him. Working with Captain Howard, they set the satellite on the shuttle's payload-deployment arm, a long metal boom that swung the squat drumlike mechanism up and completely outside the emptied cargo bay.

"Good work," Howard said. He touched his keyboard and reported back to the flight deck.

"Now we wait," he said to Colt and Kinsman. "You guys were so good, we finished eight minutes ahead of schedule."

Kinsman felt himself smiling at the captain. Not that they could see each other's faces through the tinted visors. But something had softened Howard. *He's just as wiped out by all this grandeur as we are.*

"As the boom swung back inside the payload bay and folded itself into place along the deck, Captain Howard said, "Now for the final chore. It's a big one; we've been saving it for you boys.""

Only he won't let his emotions show.

They switched their suit radios to the flight deck's frequency and listened to the final orbital maneuvering that placed the shuttle in the right spot for launching the satellite. Twice the control jets at the rear of the ship, near the root of the big tail fin, flared—such quick puffs of light that they were gone before they had truly registered on Kinsman's eyes. When the moment came to release the satellite, it was utterly unspectacular.

". . . three, two, one," said Major Jakes's heavy voice.

There was no sound, just a brief puff of escaping gas as the tiny thruster built into the bottom end of the satellite pushed the drum away from the boom arm. The satellite quickly dwindled into the distance and disappeared among the stars.

As the boom swung back inside the payload bay and folded itself into place along the deck, Captain Howard said, "Now for the final chore. It's a big one; we've been saving it for you boys."

Kinsman tried to glance over at Colt, but when he turned his head, all he saw was the inside lining of his helmet.

"You were too excited to notice," Howard was explaining, "but we haven't detached the booster fuel tank that we rode up on. It's still strapped to the orbiter's belly."

"Can't reenter with that thing hanging onto us," Colt said.

"Right. We have no intention of doing that. We're heading now for a rendezvous point where the last six missions have separated their booster tanks and left them in orbit. One of these days, when the Air Force gets enough astronauts and enough money, we're going to convert all those empty tanks into a permanent, full-sized space station."

"I'll be damned," Kinsman said, grinning to himself.

"Your mission," Howard went on, "is to separate our tank and attach it to the assembly that's already there."

"Simple enough," Colt said. "We did something like that at the neutral-buoyancy tank in Alabama."

"It sounds easy," Howard said. "But I won't be there to help you. You're going to be on your own with this one."

"Okay," Kinsman said. "We can handle it without any trouble."

Howard said nothing for a long moment. Kinsman saw him floating before them, his dark visor looking like the dead, empty eye of some deformed cyclops.

"All right," the captain said at last. "But listen to me. If something happens out there, don't panic. Do you hear me? Don't panic."

"We won't," Colt said.

What's he worried about? Kinsman wondered briefly.

But he put the thought aside as Howard began testing them on their proficiency with their suit-maneuvering units. They jetted themselves back and forth along the length of the empty payload bay, did pirouettes, planted their feet at precise spots that the captain called out to them—all on puffs of cold gas from the pistollike thruster units.

"There'll be no umbilicals or tethers on this task," Howard warned them. "Too much tankage hanging around to foul up your lines. You'll be operating independently. On your own. Do you understand?"

"Sure."

"No funny stuff and no sightseeing. You won't have time for stargazing. Now fill your propellant and air tanks. I'm going inside to check with the flight deck."

"Yes, sir."

"He's pretty edgy," Kinsman said on their suit-to-suit frequency after Howard had disappeared through the airlock.

"Just puttin' us on, man."

"I don't know. He said this is the most difficult task of the whole mission."

"That's why they saved it for us, huh?"

"Maybe."

He could sense Colt shaking his head, frowning. "Don't let 'em get to you. He had other jobs . . . like inspecting that Russian satellite. That was tougher than what we're gonna be doing."

"That was a one-man task," Kinsman said. "He didn't need a couple of rookies getting in his way. And the Reds probably have all sorts of alarm and detection systems on their birds."

"Yeah, maybe . . ."

"He's a strange little guy."

"You'd think he'd have made major by now," Colt said.

"Or light colonel. He's as old as Murdock. Maybe older."

"Yeah, but he's got no wings. Flunked out of flight training when he was a kid."

"Really?"

"That's what Art was telling me. He's nothing more than a glorified tech specialist. No academy. Lucky he made captain. He was almost passed over."

"No wonder he looks pissed off most of the time."

"*Most* of the time?"

Kinsman said, "I got the feeling he enjoyed watching us go bananas over the stars."

"Hey, yeah, I forgot all about that."

Kinsman turned and rose slightly off the deck plates so that he could look out at the sky again. *How quickly the miraculous becomes ordinary!*

"Sure is some sight," Colt said from beside him.

"Makes me want to just drift out of here and never come back," said Kinsman. "Just go on and on forever."

"You'd need a damned big air tank."

"Not a bad way to die, if you've got to go. Drifting alone, silent, going to sleep among the stars . . ."

"That's okay for you, maybe, but I intend to be shot by a jealous husband when I'm in my nineties," Colt said. "That's how I wanna go: bare-assed and humpin'."

"White or black?"

"The husband or the wife? Both of 'em . . . honkies, man. Screwin' white folks is the best part of life."

Kinsman could hear his partner's happy chuckling.

"Frank," he asked, "have you ever thought that by the time you're ninety there might not be any race problems anymore?"

Colt's laughter deepened. "Sure. Just like we won't have any wars and all God's chillun got shoes. That's just how it'll be."

"All right, there it is," Captain Howard told them.

The three men were hovering just above the open clamshell doors of the payload bay, looking out at what seemed to Kinsman to be a giant stack of beer bottles. *Except that they're aluminum, not glass.*

Six empty propellant tanks, each of them nearly twice the size of the orbiter itself, were arranged in two neat rows. From this distance they could not see the connecting rods that held the assembly together.

"You've got three hours," Howard told them. "The booster-tank linkages that hold it to the orbiter are built to come apart and reattach to the other tanks . . ."

"Yeah, yeah, we know," Colt said impatiently.

Kinsman was thinking, *This shouldn't take more than an hour. Why give us three?*

"Working in zero-g on a task like this ain't easy," Howard said, as if in answer to Kinsman's unspoken question. "It's different from the water tank. You'll be floating free—no resistance at all. Every move you make will make you *keep on* moving until you make a countermove to cancel the motion."

"We learned all that in training," Colt insisted. "And how we shouldn't overheat ourselves inside the suits."

"Yeah, sure you did. Pardon me. I should've remembered you guys know everything already." Howard's voice was acid again. "All right, you're on your own. Just don't panic if anything goes wrong."

Almost an hour later, as they were attaching the empty propellant tank to the six others, Colt asked, "How many times we practice this stunt in training?"

"This particular business?"

"Naw . . . just taking pieces apart and reassembling them."

Kinsman looked up from the bolt-

"Did you hear someone say, 'Eureka'?"

tightening job he was doing. Colt was floating some forty meters away, up at the nose end of the fat propellant tank. He looked tiny next to the huge stack of tanks, gleaming brightly in the strong sunlight. But his voice in Kinsman's earphones sounded as if he was inside the helmet with him.

"Hell," Kinsman answered, "we did so much of this monkey work I thought they were training us to open a garage."

"Yeah. That's what I was thinking. Then why was Howard so shaky about us doing this? You havin' any troubles?"

Kinsman shrugged inside his suit, and the motion made him drift slightly away from the strut he was working on. He reached out and grabbed it to steady himself.

"I've spun myself around a couple times," he admitted. "It gets a little confusing, with no up or down. Takes some getting used to."

Colt's answer was a soft grunt.

"The suit heats up, too," Kinsman went on. "I've had to stop and let it cool down a couple times."

"Yeah. Me, too. But no trouble."

"Maybe Howard's worried about us being so far from the ship without tethers."

"Maybe." But Colt didn't sound convinced.

"How's your end going?" Kinsman asked. "I'm almost finished here."

"I oughtta be done in another ten minutes. Three hours! This damned job's a piece of cake if ever . . . *Holy shit!*"

Kinsman's whole body jerked at the urgency in Colt's voice. "What? What is it?"

"Lookit the shuttle!"

Turning so rapidly that he bounced his shoulder into the tank, Kinsman peered out toward the spacecraft, some seventy-five meters away from them.

"They've closed the payload bay doors. Why the hell would they do that?"

Colt jetted down the length of the tank, stopping himself as neatly as an ice skater with a countering puff of cold gas from the thruster gun. Kinsman reached out and touched his arm.

"What the hell are they doing?" he asked, bewildered.

Colt said, "Whatever it is, I don't like it."

Suddenly a cloud of white gas jetted from the shuttle's nose. The spacecraft dipped down and away from them. Another soundless gasp from the reaction jets back near the tail and the shuttle slewed sideways.

"What the hell they doin'?" Colt shouted.

The shuttle was sliding away from them, scuttling crabwise farther from the propellant tanks where they were stranded.

"They got trouble! Somethin's wrong . . ."

Kinsman punched the stud on his wrist keyboard for the flight deck's radio frequency.

"Kinsman to flight deck. What's wrong? Why are you maneuvering?"

No answer. The shuttle was dwindling away from them rapidly now.

"Jesus Christ!" Colt yelled. "They're gonna leave us here!"

"Captain Howard!" Kinsman said into his helmet mike, trying to keep the tremble out of his voice. "Major Podolski, Major Pierce . . . come in! This is Kinsman. Colt and I are still outside the spacecraft! Answer, please!"

Nothing but the crackling hum of the radio's carrier wave.

"Those sons of bitches are stranding us!"

Kinsman watched the shuttle getting smaller and smaller. It seemed to be hurtling madly away from them, although the rational part of his mind told him that the spacecraft was only drifting; it hadn't fired its main engines at all. But the difference in relative velocities between the tankage assembly and the shuttle was enough to make the two fly apart from each other.

Colt was moving. Kinsman saw that he was aiming his thruster gun.

Grabbing Colt's arm to stop him, Kinsman snapped, "No!" Then he realized that his suit radio was still tuned to the flight deck's frequency.

Banging the stud on his wrist, Kinsman said, "Don't panic. Remember? That's what Howard warned us about."

"We gotta get back to the shuttle, man! We can't hang here!"

"You'll never reach the shuttle with the maneuvering gun," Kinsman said. "Not enough range."

"But something's gone wrong . . ."

Kinsman looked out toward the dwindling speck that was the shuttle. It was hard to see now against the glaring white of the earth. They were passing over the vast cloud-covered expanse of Antarctica. With a shudder, Kinsman felt the cold seeping into him.

"Listen. Maybe nothing's gone wrong. Maybe this is their idea of a joke."

"A joke?"

"Maybe that's what Howard was trying to tell us."

"That's crazy . . ."

"No. They've been sticking it to us all through the mission, haven't they? Pierce is a snotty bastard, and this looks like something he might dream up."

"You don't joke around with lives, man!"

"We're safe enough. We've got four hours' worth of air. As long as we don't panic, we'll be okay. That's what Howard was trying to tell us."

"But why the hell would they do something like this?" Colt's voice sounded calmer, as if he wanted to believe Kinsman, as if he needed to believe.

Your paranoia's deserted you just when you need it most, Kinsman thought. He answered, "How many times have they called us hotshots, the Golddust Twins? We're the top two men on the list. They just want to rub our noses in the dirt a little . . . just like the upperclassmen used to do at the academy."

"You think so?"

It's either that or we're dead. Kinsman glanced at the digital watch set into his wrist keyboard. "They allowed three hours for our task. They'll be back before that time is up. Less than two hours."

"And if they're not?"

"Then we can panic."

"Lotta good it'll do then."

"Won't do much good for us now, either. We're stranded here until they come back for us."

"Bastards," Colt muttered. Now he was convinced.

With a sudden grin, Kinsman said, "Yeah, but maybe we can turn the tables on them."

"How?"

"Follow me, my man."

Without using his thruster gun, Kinsman clambered up the side of "their" propellant tank and then drifted slowly into the nest created by the six other tanks.

Like a pair of skin divers floating in the midst of a pod of whales, Colt and Kinsman hung in emptiness, surrounded by the big, curving, hollow tanks.

"Now when they come back, they won't be able to see us on radar," Kinsman explained. "And the tanks ought to block our suit-to-suit chatter. So they won't hear us, either. That should throw a scare into them."

"They'll think we panicked and jetted away."

"Right."

"Maybe that's what they want."

"Maybe. But think of the explaining they'd have to do back at Vandenberg if they lost the two of us. Four officers' careers down the drain."

Colt giggled. "Almost worth dyin' for."

"We'll let them know we're here," Kinsman said, "after they've worked up enough of a sweat. I'm not dying for anyone's joke, not even my own."

They waited, while the immense panorama of the earth flowed beneath them and the stern stars watched silently. They waited and they talked.

"I thought she split because we were down in Houston and Huntsville and she couldn't take it," Colt was saying. "She was white, you know, and the pressure was on her a lot more than me."

"I didn't think Houston was that prejudiced. And Huntsville struck me as being pretty cosmopolitan . . ."

"How many times have they called us hotshots, the Golddust Twins? We're the top two men on the list. They just want to rub our noses in the dirt a little . . . just like the upperclassmen used to do at the academy."

"Yeah? Try it with my color, man. Try buying some flesh-colored Band-Aids if you wanna see how cosmopolitan everybody is."

"Guess I really don't know much about it," Kinsman admitted. "Must've been pretty rough on you."

"Yeah, but now that I think back on it, we were having our troubles in Colorado, too. I'm not an easy man to live with."

"Who the hell is?"

Colt chuckled. "You are, man. You're supercool. Never saw anybody so much in charge of himself. Like a big bucket of ice water."

Ice water? Me? "You're mistaking slow reflexes for self-control."

"Yeah, I bet. Is it true you're a Quaker?"

"Used to be," he said automatically, trying to shut out the image of his father. "When I was a kid." *Change the subject!* "I was when that damned shuttle started moving away from us. A real Quaker."

With a laugh, Colt asked, "How come you're not married? Good-looking, rich . . ."

"Too busy having fun. Flying, training for this. I've got no time for marriage. Besides, I like girls too much to marry one of them."

"You wanna get laid, but you don't wanna get screwed."

"Something like that. Like you said, there's lots of chicks in the world."

"Yeah. Can't concentrate on a career and a marriage at the same time. Leastways, I can't."

"Not if you want to be really good at either one," Kinsman agreed. *Oh, we are being so wise. And not looking at our watches. Cool, man. Supercool.* But out beyond the curving bulk of the propellant tanks the sky was empty except for the solemn stars.

They talked, so that the sound of their voices could steady their nerves, each of them staying calm and brave in the presence of the other.

Kinsman's mind drifted as he hung suspended in space, talking and listening with only the frontmost reflexive part of his mind. He watched the earth sliding by like some huge diorama, and his thoughts wandered back to Diane, to the first night he had met her, to that first lovemaking in the misty, dreaming light of earliest dawn back in her room in Berkeley.

He remembered coming out of the tiny bathroom later that morning, to see that she had set up toast and a jar of Smucker's grape jelly on the table by the window. The teakettle was on the two-burner stove, and a pair of chipped mugs and a jar of instant coffee stood alongside.

They sat facing each other, washing down the crunchy toast with hot, bitter coffee. Diane watched the people moving along the street below them. Kinsman stared at the clean, bright sky.

"How long can you stay?" she asked.

"I've got . . . I leave tonight."

"Oh."

"Got to report back to the Academy tomorrow morning."

"You have to."

He nodded.

"I was going to let you stay here . . . if you wanted to quit the Air Force."

He started to answer, but his mouth was suddenly dry. He thought of the Academy. The cold, gray mountains and ranks of uniforms marching mechanically across the frozen parade ground. The starkly functional classrooms, the remorselessly efficient architecture devoid of all individual expression.

And he thought of his father: cold, implacable. Was it pride and anger that moved him, or was it fear?

Then he turned back, looked past the woman across the table from him, and saw the sky once again. A pale ghost of a moon was grinning lopsidedly at him.

"I can't stay with you," he said quietly, finally.

That was probably the biggest mistake of your life, he said to himself.

Frank Colt's sharp-edged voice brought him back to reality, to the world he had chosen for himself.

"Switching back to the flight deck's frequency, the two lieutenants heard: "Pierce, goddammit, if those two kids have been lost, I'll put you up for a murder charge."

"I don't just wanna be good," Colt was saying. "I got to be the best. I got to show these honkies that a black man is better than they are."

"You're not going to win many friends that way."

"Don't give a shit. I'm gonna be a general someday. Then you'll see how many friends I get."

Kinsman shook his head, chuckling. "A general. Jeez, you've sure got some long-range plans in your head."

"Damn right! My brother, he's all hot and fired up to be a revolutionary. Goin' around the world looking for wars to fight against colonialists and injustice. Wanted me to join the underground here in the States and fight for justice against the Man."

"Why doesn't he stay in the States?" Kinsman asked.

"The FBI damn near grabbed him a year or so back, last time he came home."

"What for?"

"Hit a bank . . . to raise money for the People's Liberation Army."

"He's one of those?"

"Not anymore. There ain't no PLA anymore. Most of 'em are dead, the rest scattered. I watched my brother playin' cops and robbers. Didn't look like much fun to me. So I decided I ain't gonna fight the Man. I'm gonna *be* the Man."

"If you can't beat 'em . . ."

"Looks like I'm joinin' 'em, yeah," Colt said, with real passion building in his voice. "But I'm just workin' my way up the ladder to get to the top. Then *I'll* start givin' the orders. And there are others like me, too. We're gonna have a black president one of these days, you know."

"And you'll be his chief of staff."

"Could be."

"Where does that leave us?"

A small, sharp, beeping sound shrilled in Kinsman's earphones. *Emergency signal!* Automatically both he and Colt switched to the shuttle's flight-deck frequency.

"Kinsman! Colt! Can you hear me? This is Major Jakes. Do you read me?"

The major's voice sounded distant, distorted by ragged static, and very concerned.

Kinsman held up a hand to keep Colt silent. Then, switching to their suit-to-suit frequency, he whispered, "They can't see us in here among the tanks. And they haven't picked up our suit-to-suit talk. The tanks are blocking it."

"We're getting their freak scattered off the tanks?" It was a rhetorical question.

"Kinsman! Colt! Do you read me? This is Major Jakes."

Their two helmeted heads were close enough for Kinsman to see the grin glittering on Colt's dark face.

"Let 'em eat shit for a coupla minutes, huh?"

"Right."

The shuttle pulled into view and seemed to hover about a hundred meters away from the tanks. Switching back to the flight deck's frequency, the two lieutenants heard: "Pierce, goddammit, if those two kids have been lost, I'll put you up for a murder charge."

"Now, you were in on it, too, Harry."

Howard's voice cut in. "I'm suited up. Going out the airlock."

"Should we get one of the trainees out to help search for them?" Pierce's voice.

"You've got two of them missing now," Jakes snarled. "Isn't that enough? How about *you* getting your ass outside to help?"

"Me? But I'm . . ."

"I think it would be a good idea," said a new voice, with such weighty authority that Kinsman knew it had to be the mission commander, Major Podolski. Among the three majors he was the longest in Air Force service and therefore as senior as God.

"Eh, yes, sir," Pierce answered quickly.

"And you, too, Jakes. You were all in on this, and it hasn't turned out very funny."

Colt and Kinsman, holding on to one of the struts that connected the empty tanks, could barely suppress their laughter as they watched the shuttle's cargo doors swing slowly open and three spacesuited figures emerge.

"Maybe we oughtta play dead," Colt whispered.

"No. Enough is too much. Let's go out now and greet our rescuers."

They worked their way clear of the tanks and drifted into the open.

"There they are!" The voice sounded so jubilant in Kinsman's earphones that he couldn't tell who said it.

"Are you all right?"

"Is everything . . ."

"We're fine, sir," Kinsman said calmly. "But we were beginning to wonder if the spacecraft malfunctioned."

Dead silence for several moments.

"Uh, no . . ." Jakes said as he jetted up to Colt and Kinsman. "We . . . uh, well, we sort of played a little prank on you two fellas."

"Nothing personal," Pierce added.

Sure, Kinsman thought. *Nothing personal in getting bitten by a snake, either.*

They were great buddies now as they jetted back to the shuttle. Kinsman played it straight, keeping himself very formal and correct. Colt followed Kinsman's lead.

If we were a couple of hysterical, gibbering, scared tenderfeet, they'd be laughing their heads off at us. But now the shaft has turned.

Once through the airlock and into the passenger compartment, Colt and Kinsman were grabbed by the four trainees. Chattering, laughing with them, they helped the two lieutenants out of their helmets and suits. Pierce, Jakes, and Howard unsuited without help.

Finally, Kinsman turned to Major Pierce and said, tightlipped, "Sir, I must make a report to the commanding officer."

"Podolski knows all about . . ."

Looking Pierce in the eye, Kinsman said, "I don't mean Major Podolski, sir. I mean Colonel Murdock. Or, if necessary, the judge advocate general."

Everything stopped. Jill Meyers, who had somehow wound up with Kinsman's helmet, let it slip from her fingers. It simply hung there in midair as she watched, wide-eyed and open-mouthed. The only sound in the compartment was the faint hum of electrical equipment.

"The . . . judge advocate general?" Pierce looked slightly green.

"Yes, sir. Or I could telephone my uncle, the senior senator from Pennsylvania."

Now even the trainees looked scared.

"Now see here, Kinsman," Jakes started.

Turning to face the major, close enough to smell the fear on him, Kinsman said, "This may have seemed like a joke to you, sir, but it has the look of racial discrimination about it. And it was a damned dangerous stunt. *And* a waste of the taxpayers' money, too."

"You can't . . ." Pierce somehow lost his voice as Kinsman turned back toward him.

"The first thing I must do is see Major Podolski," Kinsman said evenly. "He's involved in this, too."

With a resigned shrug, Jakes pointed toward the ladder.

Kinsman glanced at Colt, and the two of them glided over to the ladder and swam up to the flight deck, leaving absolute silence behind them.

Major Podolski was a big, florid-faced man with an old-style RAF mustache. His bulk barely fitted into the commander's left-hand seat. He was half-turned in it, one heavy arm draped across the seat's back, as Kinsman rose through the hatch.

"I've been listening to what you had to say down there, Lieutenant, and if you think . . ."

But Kinsman put a finger to his lips.

Podolski frowned.

Sitting lightly on the payload specialist's chair, behind the commander, Kinsman let himself grin.

"Sir," he whispered, "I thought one good joke deserved another. My uncle was voted out of the Senate years ago."

He could see a struggle of emotions play across Podolski's face. Finally a curious smile won out. "I see . . . you want them to stew in their own juices, eh?"

Glancing up at Colt, Kinsman answered, "Not exactly, sir. I want reparations."

"Repa—What're you talking about, Mister?"

"This is the first time Frank and I have been allowed up on the flight deck."

"So?"

"So we want to sit up here while you fly her back through reentry and landing."

Podolski looked as if he had just swallowed a lemon, whole. "Oh, you do? And maybe you want to take over the controls, too."

Colt bobbed his head vigorously. "Yes, *sir!*"

"Don't make me laugh."

"Sir . . . I meant it about the judge advocate general. And I have another uncle . . ."

"Never mind!" Podolski snapped. "You can sit up here during reentry and landing. And that's all! You sit and watch and be quiet and forget this whole stupid incident. That's an order!"

"That's all we want, sir," Kinsman said. He turned toward Colt, who was beaming.

"You guys'll go far in the Air Force," Podolski grumbled. "A pair of smart asses with the guts of burglars. Just what the fuck this outfit needs." But there was a trace of a grin flitting around his mustache.

"Glad you think so, sir," said Kinsman.

"Okay . . . we're due to break orbit in two hours. You guys might as well sit up here through the whole routine and watch how it's done."

"Thank you, sir."

The major's expression sobered. "Only . . . who's going to tell Pierce and Howard that they've got to sit with the trainees?"

"Oh, I will," Colt said, with the biggest smile of all. "I'll be glad to!" ∞

The urban landscape of the future—fully automatic and utterly fantastic

SPACE CITIES

BY HARRY HARRISON

Science fiction has presented bigger, better, and more exciting cities than any others ever seen on the face of the Earth. Only recently have writers begun to see cities as places of oppression for mankind; after all, there have been more rural hells than urban ones in our history. Memory is fleeting, so we should keep reminding ourselves that right up to the end of the twentieth century, all the real action —intellectual, artistic, social, financial—took place in the cities. The creative people left their bucolic backgrounds and made their way to London or New York or the major city of their choice. Emily Dickinson wrote that she never saw a train, going anywhere, that she did not want to board. This is meaningless to a happily ensconced city dweller but elicits a depth of response from someone of intellectual ambitions who is buried in Booniesville.

So, writers who loved cities designed bigger and better ones for the future. Wells in *The Sleeper Awakes* had the sleeper wake up in a city full of gadgets and transportation and communication wonders. Almost all the book-length utopias have been citified utopias. Then, when the pulps began churning along, cities grew in complexity and design. Just as with the spaceship, a universal

From *Mechanismo* by Harry Harrison. Published in U.K. by Pierrot Publishing, in U.S. by Reed Books.

supercity came into existence, a concept shared by writers and illustrators. A writer could set a story in this city without going into too much background or detail. The reader accepted eagerly and read on. But city growth has its limits, reached in Asimov's *Foundation* series with the planet-wide city of Trantor (transformed to Helior and examined in some depth in Harrison's *Bill, the Galactic Hero*). There is a natural limit to this kind of growth; once you have the supercity built, you can either keep it running or destroy it. Or move it to a new dimension. Factories, power-generating satellites, spaceship

stations, war satellites—all of them have to be built in space, with the exception of James Blish's *Cities in Flight*. Here, great antigravity machines called spindizzies are put into position around Manhattan Island—and lift the entire heart of New York City into space. A dazzling concept indeed—New York followed by other cities that leave the tired economies of Earth for the excitement of the stars. For many years, the biggest city in space was in Clifford Simak's *Limiting Factor*, where the spacemen discover an artificial metal world that is so big that when they explore it, they can make no sense of it at all. However, this world, and all the others, are small-time when compared with the concept of physicist Freeman Dyson. He speculated that if all of the planets of the solar system were ground up and melted down, there would be enough material available to form a thin sphere about the sun, a giant shell that could be inhabited on its inner surface. This design was first used by Bob Shaw in *Orbitsville*, which, though written earlier, was not published until 1975. Here the Earth explorers zip into the sphere and must spend years getting back to the entrance they originally came in through. Dyson's design was also used by Larry Niven in *Ringworld* (1970), though he limited himself to a

single band in space rather than to a sphere. For every inhabited alien city we find in SF there must be a dozen ruined ones. Exploring them is fun—as well as being dangerous—and rarely so well done as by Beam Piper in *Omnilingual*, where our scientists learn to translate the records of a vanished alien race. Sounds impossible—until the author explains logically just how it can be accomplished. On a much larger scale is Arthur C. Clarke's wandering planet in *Rendezvous with Rama*, where an entire abandoned world-city comes whistling through our solar system. Now, inner-city violence seems to have put an end to the day of the

really "super" city. Authors are now returning to nature, the village, and the isolated house in the hills. The great cities are either dismembered or allowed to fall into ruins, warnings to the youth of the future of the error of their ancestors' ways.

SF is basically a literature of entertainment. The limitations are only those of the author. If you think big you write big. The open-minded philosophy of SF is a reflection of the best thinking in social and scientific man. ∞

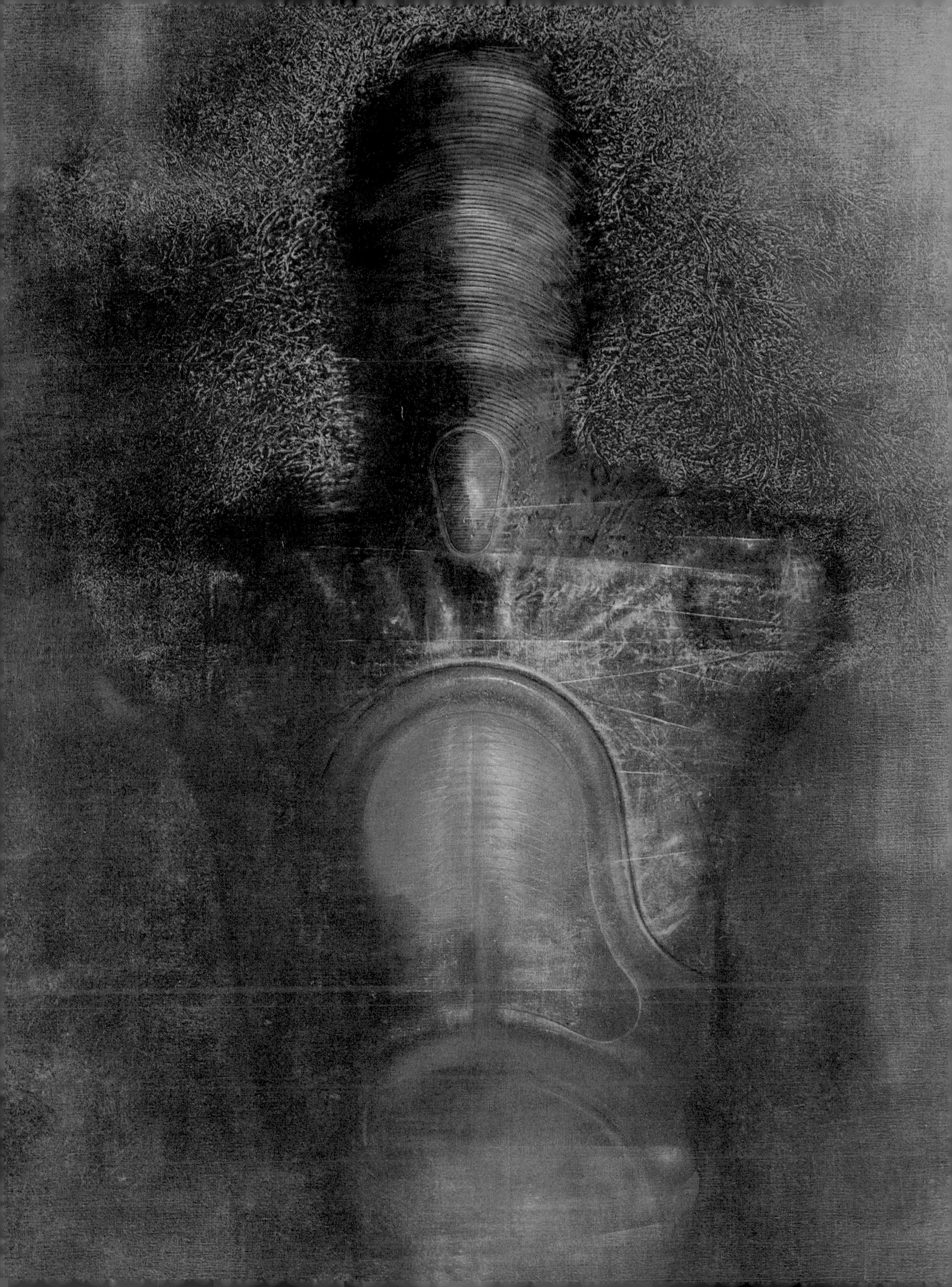

HALFJACK

Half-man, half-machine,
he roamed among the stars, seeking fulfillment

BY ROGER ZELAZNY

He walked barefoot along the beach. Above the city several of the brighter stars held for a few final moments against the wash of light from the east. He fingered a stone, then hurled it in the direction from which the sun would come. He watched for a long while until it had vanished from sight. Eventually it would begin skipping. Before then, he had turned and was headed back, to the city, the apartment, the girl.

Somewhere beyond the skyline a vehicle lifted, burning its way into the heavens. It took the remainder of the night with it as it faded. Walking on, he smelled the countryside as well as the ocean. It was a pleasant world, and this a pleasant city—spaceport as well as seaport—here in this backwater limb of the galaxy. A good place in which to rest and immerse the neglected portion of himself in the flow of humanity, the colors and sounds of the city, the constant tugging of gravity. But it had been three months now. He fingered the scar on his brow. He had let two offers pass him by, to linger. There was another pending his consideration.

As he walked up Kathi's street, he saw that her apartment was still dark. Good, she would not even have missed him, again. He pushed past the big front door, still not repaired since he had kicked it open the evening of the fire, two—no, three—nights ago. He used the stairs. He let himself in quietly.

He was in the kitchen preparing breakfast when he heard her stirring.

"Jack?"

"Yes. Good morning."

"Come back."

"All right."

He moved to the bedroom door and entered the room. She was lying there, smiling. She raised her arms slightly.

"I've thought of a wonderful way to begin the day."

He seated himself on the edge of the bed and embraced her. For a moment she was sleep-warm and sleep-soft against him, but only for a moment.

"You've got too much on," she said, unfastening his shirt.

He peeled it off and dropped it. He removed his trousers. Then he held her again.

"More," she said, tracing the long fine scar that ran down his forehead, alongside his nose, traversing his chin, his neck, the right side of his chest and abdomen, passing to one side of his groin, where it stopped.

"Come on."

"You didn't even know about it until a few nights ago."

She kissed him, brushing his cheek with her lips.

"It really does something for me."

"For almost three months—"

"Take it off. Please."

He sighed and gave a half-smile. He rose to his feet.

"All right."

He reached up and put a hand to his long, black hair. He

PAINTING BY MICHEL HENRICOT

took hold of it. He raised his other hand and spread his fingers along his scalp at the hairline. He pushed his fingers toward the back of his head and the entire hairpiece came free with a soft, crackling sound He dropped the hairpiece atop his shirt on the floor.

The right side of his head was completely bald; the left had a beginning growth of dark hair. The two areas were precisely divided by a continuation of the faint scar on his forehead.

He placed his fingertips together on the crown of his head, then drew his right hand to the side and down. His face opened vertically, splitting apart along the scar, padded synthetic flesh tearing free from electrostatic bonds. He drew it down over his right shoulder and biceps, rolling it as far as his wrist. He played with the flesh of his hand as with a tight glove, finally withdrawing the hand with a soft, sucking sound. He drew it away from his side, hip, and buttock, and separated it at his groin. Then, again seating himself on the edge of the bed, he rolled it down his leg, over the thigh, knee, calf, heel. He treated his foot as he had his hand, pinching each toe free separately before pulling off the bodyglove. He shook it out and placed it with his clothing.

Standing, he turned toward Kathi, whose eyes had not left him during all this time. Again, the half-smile. The uncovered portions of his face and body were dark metal and plastic, precision-machined, with various openings and protuberances, some gleaming, some dusky.

"Halfjack," she said as he came to her. "Now I know what that man in the café meant when he called you that."

"He was lucky you were with me. There are places where that's an unfriendly term."

"You're beautiful," she said.

"I once knew a girl whose body was almost entirely prosthetic. She wanted me to keep the glove on—at all times. It was the flesh and the semblance of flesh that she found attractive."

"What do you call that kind of operation?"

"Lateral hemicorporectomy."

After a time she said, "Could you be repaired? Can you replace it some way?"

He laughed.

"Either way," he said. "My genes could be fractioned, and the proper replacement parts could be grown. I could be made whole with grafts of my own flesh. Or I could have much of the rest removed and replaced with biomechanical analogues. But I need a stomach and balls and lungs, because I have to eat and screw and breathe to feel human."

She ran her hands down his back, one on metal, one on flesh.

"I don't understand," she said when they finally drew apart. "What sort of accident was it?"

"Accident? There was no accident," he said. "I paid a lot of money for this work, so that I could pilot a special sort of ship. I am a cyborg. I hook myself directly into each of the ship's systems."

He rose from the bed, went to the closet, drew out a duffel bag, pulled down an armful of garments, and stuffed them into it. He crossed to the dresser, opened a drawer, and emptied its contents into the bag.

"You're leaving?"

"Yes."

He entered the bathroom, emerged with two fistfuls of personal items, and dropped them into the bag.

"Why?"

He rounded the bed, picked up his bodyglove and hairpiece, rolled them into a parcel, and put them inside the bag.

"It's not what you may think," he said then, "or even what I thought until just a few moments ago."

She sat up.

"You think less of me," she said, "because I seem to like you more now that I know your secret. You think there's something pathological about it—"

"No," he said, pulling on his shirt, "that's not it at all. Yesterday I would have said so and used that for an excuse to storm out of here and leave you feeling bad. But I want to be honest with myself this time, and fair to you. That's not it."

❛Standing, he turned toward Kathi, whose eyes had not left him. . . . Again, the half-smile. The uncovered portions of his face and body were dark metal and plastic . . . machined. . . .❜

He drew on his trousers.

"What then?" she asked.

"It's just the wanderlust, or whatever you call it. I've stayed too long at the bottom of a gravity well. I'm restless. I've got to get going again. It's my nature, that's all. I realized this when I saw that I was looking to your feelings for an excuse to break us up and move on."

"You can wear the bodyglove. It's not that important. It's really *you* that I like."

"I believe you. I like you, too. Whether you believe me or not, your reactions to my better half don't matter. It's what I said, though. Nothing else. And now I've got this feeling I won't be much fun anymore. If you really like me, you'll let me go without a lot of fuss."

He finished dressing. She got out of the bed and faced him.

"If that's the way it has to be," she said. "Okay."

"I'd better just go, then. Now."

"Yes."

He turned and walked out of the room left the apartment, used the stair again and departed from the building. Some passersby gave him more than a casual look, cyborg pilots not being all that common in this sector. This did not bother him. His step lightened. He stopped in a paybooth and called the shipping company to tell them that he would haul the load they had in orbit; the sooner it was connected with his vessel, the better, he said.

Loading, the controller told him, would begin shortly and he could ship up that same afternoon from the local field. Jack said that he would be there and then broke the connection. He gave the world half a smile as he put the sea to his back and swung on through the city, westward.

Blue-and-pink world below him, black sky above, the stars a snapshot snowfall all about, he bade the shuttle pilot goodbye and keyed his airlock. Entering the *Morgana*, he sighed and set about stowing his gear. His cargo was already in place and the ground computers had transferred course information to the ship's brain. He hung his clothing in a locker and placed his bodyglove and hairpiece in compartments.

He hurried forward then and settled into the control web, which adjusted itself about him. A long, dark unit swung down from overhead and dropped into position at his right. It moved slowly, making contact with various points on that half of his body.

—Good to have you back. How was your vacation, Jack?

—Oh. Fine. Real fine.

—Meet any nice girls?

—A few.

—And here you are again. Did you miss things?

—You know it. How does this haul look to you?

—Easy, for us. I've already reviewed the course programs.

—Let's run over the systems.

—Check. Care for some coffee?

—That'd be nice.

A small unit descended on his left, stopping within easy reach of his mortal hand. He opened its door. A bulb of dark liquid rested in a rack.

—Timed your arrival. Had it ready.

—Just the way I like it, too. I almost forgot. Thanks.

Several hours later, when they left orbit, he had already switched off a number of his left-side systems. He was merged even more closely with the vessel, absorbing data at a frantic rate. Their expanded perceptions took in the near-ship vicinity and moved out to encompass the extrasolar panorama with greater than human clarity and precision. They reacted almost instantaneously to decisions great and small.

—It is good to be back together again, Jack.

—I'd say.

Morgana held him tightly. Their velocity built. ∞

"Charles has one of the first pacemakers ever built."

SANDKINGS

His interest piqued when told of the creatures' proficiency for warfare and worship

BY GEORGE R. R. MARTIN

Simon Kress lived alone in a sprawling manor house among dry, rocky hills fifty kilometers from the city. So, when he was called away unexpectedly on business, he had no neighbors he could conveniently impose on to take his pets. The carrion hawk was no problem; it roosted in the unused belfry and customarily fed itself anyway. The shambler Kress simply shooed outside and left to fend for itself; the little monster would gorge on slugs and birds and rockjocks. But the fish tank, stocked with genuine earth piranha, posed a difficulty. Finally Kress just threw a haunch of beef into the huge tank. The piranha could always eat one another if he were detained longer than expected. They'd done it before. It amused him.

Unfortunately, he was detained *much* longer than expected this time. When he finally returned, all the fish were dead. So was the carrion hawk. The shambler had climbed up to the belfry and eaten the hawk. Kress was vexed.

The next day he flew his skimmer to Asgard, a journey of some two hundred kilometers. Asgard was Baldur's largest city and boasted the oldest and largest starport as well. Kress liked to impress his friends with animals that were unusual, entertaining, and expensive; Asgard was the place to buy them.

This time, though, he had poor luck. Xenopets had closed its doors, t'Etherane the Petseller tried to foist another carrion hawk off on him, and Strange Waters offered nothing more exotic than piranha, glowsharks, and spider squids. Kress had had all those;

PAINTING BY ERNST FUCHS

he wanted something new, something that would stand out.

Near dusk he found himself walking down Rainbow Boulevard, looking for places he had not patronized before. So close to the starport, the street was lined by importers' marts. The big corporate emporiums had impressive long windows, in which rare and costly alien artifacts reposed on felt cushions against dark drapes that made the interiors of the stores a mystery. Between them were the junk shops—narrow, nasty little places whose display areas were crammed with all manner of offworld bric-a-brac. Kress tried both kinds of shops, with equal dissatisfaction.

Then he came across a store that was different.

It was very near the port. Kress had never been there before. The shop occupied a small, single-story building of moderate size, set between a euphoria bar and a temple brothel of the Secret Sisterhood. Down this far, Rainbow Boulevard grew tacky. The shop itself was unusual. Arresting.

The windows were full of mist—now a pale red, now the gray of true fog, now sparkling and golden. The mist swirled and eddied and glowed faintly from within. Kress glimpsed objects in the window—machines, pieces of art, other things he could not recognize—but he could not get a good look at any of them. The mists flowed sensuously around them, displaying a bit of first one thing and then another, then cloaking all. It was intriguing.

As he watched, the mist began to form letters. One word at a time. Kress stood and read.

WO. AND. SHADE. IMPORTERS. ARTIFACTS. ART. LIFEFORMS. AND. MISC.

The letters stopped. Through the fog Kress saw something moving. That was enough for him, that and the LIFEFORMS in their advertisement. He swept his walking cloak over his shoulder and entered the store.

Inside, Kress felt disoriented. The interior seemed vast, much larger than he would have guessed from the relatively modest frontage. It was dimly lit, peaceful. The ceiling was a starscape, complete with spiral nebulas, very dark and realistic, very nice. All the counters shone faintly, to better display the merchandise within. The aisles were carpeted with ground fog. It came almost to his knees in places and swirled about his feet as he walked.

"Can I help you?"

She almost seemed to have risen from the fog. Tall and gaunt and pale, she wore a practical gray jumpsuit and a strange little cap that rested well back on her head.

"Are you Wo or Shade?" Kress asked. "Or only sales help?"

"Jala Wo, ready to serve you," she replied. "Shade does not see customers. We have no sales help."

"You have quite a large establishment," Kress said. "Odd that I have never heard of you before."

"We have only just opened this shop on Baldur," the woman said. "We have franchises on a number of other worlds, however. What can I sell you? Art, perhaps? You have the look of a collector. We have some fine Nor T'alush crystal carvings."

"No," Kress said. "I own all the crystal carvings I desire. I came to see about a pet."

"A lifeform?"

"Yes."

"Alien?"

"Of course."

"We have a mimic in stock. From Celia's World. A clever little simian. Not only will it learn to speak, but eventually it will mimic your voice, inflections, gestures, even facial expressions."

"Cute," said Kress. "And common. I have no use for either, Wo. I want something exotic. Unusual. And not cute. I detest cute animals. At the moment I own a shambler. Imported from Cotho, at no mean expense. From time to time I feed him a litter of un-

wanted kittens. That is what I think of *cute*. Do I make myself understood?"

Wo smiled enigmatically. "Have you ever owned an animal that worshiped you?" she asked.

Kress grinned. "Oh, now and again. But I don't require worship, Wo. Just entertainment."

"You misunderstand me," Wo said, still wearing her strange smile. "I meant *worship* literally."

"What are you talking about?"

"I think I have just the thing for you," Wo said. "Follow me."

She led him between the radiant counters and down a long, fog-shrouded aisle beneath false starlight. They passed through a wall of mist into another section of the store, then stopped in front of a large plastic tank. An aquarium, Kress thought.

Wo beckoned. He stepped closer and saw that he was wrong. It was a terrarium. Within lay a miniature desert about two meters square. Pale sand tinted scarlet by wan red light. Rocks: basalt and quartz and granite. In each corner of the tank stood a castle.

Kress blinked and peered and corrected himself; actually, there were only three castles standing. The fourth leaned, a crumbled, broken ruin. The three others were crude but intact, carved of stone and sand. Over their battlements and through their rounded porticoes tiny creatures climbed and scrambled. Kress pressed his face against the plastic. "Insects?" he asked.

"No," Wo replied. "A much more complex lifeform. More intelligent as well. Smarter than your shambler by a considerable amount. They are called sandkings."

"Insects," Kress said, drawing back from the tank. "I don't care how complex they are." He frowned. "And kindly don't try to gull me with this talk of intelligence. These things are far too small to have anything but the most rudimentary brains."

"They share hiveminds," Wo said. "Castle minds, in this case. There are only three organisms in the tank, actually. The fourth died. You see how her castle has fallen."

Kress looked back at the tank. "Hiveminds, eh? Interesting." He frowned again. "Still, it is only an oversized ant farm. I'd hoped for something better."

"They fight wars."

"Wars? Hmmm." Kress looked again.

"Note the colors, if you will," Wo said. She pointed to the creatures that swarmed over the nearest castle. One was scrabbling at the tank wall. Kress studied it. To his eyes, it still looked like an insect. Barely as long as his fingernail, six-limbed, with six tiny eyes set all around its body. A wicked set of mandibles clacked visibly, while two long, fine antennae wove patterns in the air. Antennae, mandibles, eyes, and legs were sooty black, but the dominant color was the burnt orange of its armor plating. "It's an insect," Kress repeated.

"It is not an insect," Wo insisted calmly. "The armored exoskeleton is shed when the sandking grows larger. *If* it grows larger. In a tank this size, it won't." She took Kress by the elbow and led him around the tank to the next castle. "Look at the colors here."

He did. They were different. Here the sandkings had bright red armor; antennae, mandibles, eyes, and legs were yellow. Kress glanced across the tank. The denizens of the third live castle were off-white, with red trim. "Hmmm," he said.

"They war, as I said," Wo told him. "They even have truces and alliances. It was an alliance that destroyed the fourth castle in this tank. The blacks were becoming too numerous, and so the others joined forces to destroy them."

Kress remained unconvinced. "Amusing, no doubt. But insects fight wars, too."

"Insects do not worship," Wo said.

"Eh?"

Wo smiled and pointed at the castle. Kress stared. A face had been carved into the wall of the highest tower. He recognized it. It was Jala Wo's face. "How . . . ?"

"I projected a hologram of my face into the tank, then kept it there for a few days. The face of god, you see? I feed them. I am always close. The sandkings have a rudimentary psionic sense. Proximity telepathy. They sense me and worship me by using my face to decorate their buildings. All the castles have them, see." They did.

"The black castle was the first completed, followed by the white and red fortresses. Kress . . . sat on the couch, so he could watch. He expected . . . war to break out . . . now."

On the castle, the face of Jala Wo was serene, peaceful, and very lifelike. Kress marveled at the workmanship. "How do they do it?"

"The foremost legs double as arms. They even have fingers of a sort, three small, flexible tendrils. And they cooperate well, both in building and in battle. Remember, all the mobiles of one color share a single mind."

"Tell me more," Kress requested.

Wo smiled. "The maw lives in the castle. Maw is my name for her—a pun, if you will. The thing is mother and stomach both. Female, large as your fist, immobile. Actually, *sandking* is a bit of a misnomer. The mobiles are peasants and warriors. The real ruler is a queen. But that analogy is faulty as well. Considered as a whole, each castle is a single hermaphroditic creature."

"What do they eat?"

"The mobiles eat pap, predigested food obtained inside the castle. They get it from the maw after she has worked on it for several days. Their stomachs can't handle anything else. If the maw dies, they soon die as well. The maw . . . the maw eats anything. You'll have no special expense there. Table scraps will do excellently."

"Live food?" Kress asked.

Wo shrugged. "Each maw eats mobiles from the other castles, yes."

"I am intrigued," he admitted. "If only they weren't so small!"

"Yours can be larger. These sandkings are small because their tank is small. They seem to limit their growth to fit available space. If I moved these to a larger tank, they'd start growing again."

"Hmmm. My piranha tank is twice this size and vacant. It could be cleaned out, filled with sand . . . "

"Wo and Shade would take care of the installation. It would be our pleasure."

"Of course," Kress said, "I would expect four intact castles."

"Certainly," Wo said.

They began to haggle about the price.

Three days later Jala Wo arrived at Simon Kress's estate, with dormant sandkings and a work crew to take charge of the installation. Wo's assistants were aliens unlike any Kress was familiar with—squat, broad bipeds with four arms and bulging, multifaceted eyes. Their skin was thick and leathery and twisted into horns and spines and protrusions at odd places upon their bodies. But they were very strong, and good workers. Wo ordered them about in a musical tongue that Kress has never heard before.

In a day it was done. They moved his piranha tank to the center of his spacious living room, arranged couches on either side of it for better viewing, scrubbed it clean, and filled it two thirds of the way up with sand and rock. Then they installed a special lighting system, both to provide the dim red illumination the sandkings preferred and to project holographic images into the tank. On top they mounted a sturdy plastic cover, with a feeder mechanism built in. "This way you can feed your sandkings without removing the top of the tank," Wo explained. "You would not want to take any chances on the mobiles escaping."

The cover also included climate-control devices, to condense just the right amount of moisture from the air. "You want it dry, but not too dry," Wo said.

Finally one of the four-armed workers climbed into the tank and dug deep pits in the four corners. One of his companions handed the dormant maws over to him, removing them, one by one, from their frosted cryonic traveling cases.

They were nothing to look at. Kress decided they resembled nothing so much as mottled, half-spoiled chunks of raw meat. Each with a mouth.

The alien buried them, one in each corner of the tank. Then the work party sealed it all up and took their leave.

"The heat will bring the maws out of dormancy," Wo said. "In less than a week mobiles will begin to hatch and burrow up to the surface. Be certain to give them plenty of food. They will need all their strength until they are well established. I would estimate that you will have castles rising in about three weeks."

"And my face? When will they carve my face?"

"Turn on the hologram after about a month," she advised him, "and be patient. If you have any questions, please call. Wo and Shade are at your service." She bowed and left.

Kress wandered back to the tank and lit a joy stick. The desert was still and empty. He drummed his fingers impatiently against the plastic and frowned.

On the fourth day Kress thought he glimpsed motion beneath the sand—subtle subterranean stirrings.

On the fifth day he saw his first mobile, a lone white.

On the sixth day he counted a dozen of them, whites and reds and blacks. The oranges were tardy. He cycled through a bowl of half-decayed table scraps. The mobiles sensed it at once, rushed to it, and began to drag pieces back to their respective corners. Each color group was highly organized. They did not fight. Kress was a bit disappointed, but he decided to give them time.

The oranges made their appearance on the eighth day. By then the other sandkings had begun carrying small stones and erecting crude fortifications. They still did not war. At the moment they were only half the size of those he had seen at Wo and Shade's, but Kress thought they were growing rapidly.

The castles began to rise midway through the second week. Organized battalions of mobiles dragged heavy chunks of sandstone and granite back to their corners, where other mobiles were pushing sand into place with mandibles and tendrils. Kress had purchased a pair of magnifying goggles so that he could watch them work wherever they might go in the tank. He wandered around and around the tall plastic walls, observing. It was fascinating.

The castles were a bit plainer than Kress would have liked, but he had an idea about that. The next day he cycled through some obsidian and flakes of colored glass along with the food. Within hours they had been incorporated into the castle walls.

The black castle was the first completed, followed by the white and red fortresses. The oranges were last, as usual. Kress took his meals into the living room and ate, seated on the couch so he could watch. He expected the first war to break out any hour now.

He was disappointed. Days passed, the castles grew taller and more grand, and Kress seldom left the tank except to attend to his sanitary needs and to answer critical business calls. But the sandkings did not war. He was getting upset.

Finally he stopped feeding them.

Two days after the table scraps had ceased to fall from their desert sky, four black mobiles surrounded an orange and dragged it back to their maw. They maimed it first, ripping off its mandibles and antennae and limbs, and carried it through the shadowed main gate of their miniature castle. It never emerged. Within an hour more than forty orange mobiles marched across the sand and attacked the blacks' corner. They were outnumbered by the blacks that came rushing up from the depths. When the fighting was over, the attackers had been slaughtered. The dead and dying were taken down to feed the black maw.

Kress, delighted, congratulated himself on his genius.

When he put food into the tank the following day, a three-cornered battle broke out over its possession. The whites were the big winners.

After that, war followed war.

"The attacking sandkings washed over the spider. Mandibles snapped shut on legs and abdomen, and clung. One of them found an eye . . . ripped it loose. . . . Kress smiled and pointed."

Almost a month to the day after Jala Wo had delivered the sandkings, Kress turned on the holographic projector, and his face materialized in the tank. It turned, slowly, around and around, so that his gaze fell on all four castles equally. Kress thought it rather a good likeness; it had his impish grin, wide mouth, full cheeks. His blue eyes sparkled, his gray hair was carefully arrayed in a fashionable sidesweep, his eyebrows were thin and sophisticated.

Soon enough the sandkings set to work. Kress fed them lavishly while his image beamed down at them from their sky. Temporarily the wars stopped. All activity was directed toward worship.

His face emerged on the castle walls.

At first all four carvings looked alike to him, but as the work continued and Kress studied the reproductions, he began to detect subtle differences in technique and execution. The reds were the most creative, using tiny flakes of slate to put the gray in his hair. The white idol seemed young and mischievous to him, while the face shaped by the blacks—although virtually the same, line for line—struck him as wise and benevolent. The orange sandkings, as usual, were last and least. The wars had not gone well for them, and their castle was sad compared to those of the others. The image they carved was crude and cartoonish, and they seemed to intend to leave it this way. When they stopped work on the face, Kress grew quite piqued with them, but there really was nothing he could do.

When all of the sandkings had finished their Kress faces, he turned off the projector and decided that it was time to have a party. His friends would be impressed. He could even stage a war for them, he thought. Humming happily to himself, he began drawing up a guest list.

The party was a wild success.

Kress invited thirty people: a handful of close friends who shared his amusements, a few former lovers, and a collection of business and social rivals who could not afford to ignore his summons. He knew some of them would be discomfited and even offended by his sandkings. He counted on it. He customarily considered his parties a failure unless at least one guest walked out in high dudgeon.

On impulse he added Jala Wo's name to his list. "Bring Shade if you like," he added when he dictated the invitation to her.

Her acceptance surprised him just a bit: "Shade, alas, will be unable to attend. He does not go to social functions. As for myself, I look forward to the chance to see how your sandkings are doing."

Kress ordered a sumptuous meal. And when at last the conversation had died down and most of his guests had gotten silly on wine and joy sticks, he shocked them by personally scraping their table leavings into a large bowl. "Come, all of you," he commanded. "I want to introduce you to my newest pets." Carrying the bowl, he conducted them into his living room.

The sandkings lived up to his fondest expectations. He had starved them for two days in preparation, and they were in a fighting mood. While the guests ringed the tank, looking through the magnifying glasses that Kress had thoughtfully provided, the sandkings waged a glorious battle over the scraps. He counted almost sixty dead mobiles when the struggle was over. The reds and whites, which had recently formed an alliance, came off with most of the food.

"Kress, you're disgusting," Cath m'Lane told him. She had lived with him for a short time two years before, until her soppy sentimentality almost drove him mad. "I was a fool to come back here. I thought perhaps you'd changed and wanted to apologize." She had never forgiven him for the time his shambler had eaten an excessively cute puppy of which she had been fond. "Don't *ever* invite me here again, Simon." She strode out, accompanied by her current lover, to a chorus of laughter.

Kress's other guests were full of questions.

Where did the sandkings come from? they wanted to know. "From Wo and Shade, Importers," he replied, with a polite gesture toward Jala Wo, who had remained quiet and apart throughout most of the evening.

Why did they decorate their castles with his likeness? "Because I am the source of all good things. Surely you know that?" This retort brought a round of chuckles.

Will they fight again? "Of course, but not tonight. Don't worry. There will be other parties."

Jad Rakkis, who was an amateur xenologist, began talking about other social insects and the wars they fought. "These sandkings are amusing, but nothing really. You ought to read about Terran soldier ants, for instance."

"Sandkings are not insects," Jala Wo said sharply, but Jad was off and running, and no one paid her the slightest attention. Kress smiled at her and shrugged.

Malada Blane suggested they have a betting pool the next time they got together to watch a war, and everyone was taken with the idea. An animated discussion about rules and odds ensued. It lasted for almost an hour. Finally the guests began to take their leave.

Jala Wo was the last to depart. "So," Kress said to her when they were alone, "it appears my sandkings are a hit."

"They are doing well," Wo said. "Already they are larger than my own."

"Yes," Kress said, "except for the oranges."

"I had noticed that," Wo replied. "They seem few in number, and their castle is shabby."

"Well, someone must lose," Kress said. "The oranges were late to emerge and get established. They have suffered for it."

"Pardon," said Wo, "but might I ask if you are feeding your sandkings sufficiently?"

Kress shrugged. "They diet from time to time. It makes them fiercer."

She frowned. "There is no need to starve them. Let them war in their own time, for their own reasons. It is their nature, and you will witness conflicts that are delightfully subtle and complex. The constant war brought on by hunger is artless and degrading."

Kress repaid Wo's frown with interest. "You are in my house, Wo, and here I am the judge of what is degrading. I fed the sandkings as you advised, and they did not fight."

"You must have patience."

"No," Kress said. "I am their master and their god, after all. Why should I wait on their impulses? They did not war often enough to suit me. I have corrected the situation."

"I see," said Wo. "I will discuss the matter with Shade."

"It is none of your concern, or his," Kress snapped.

"I must bid you good-night, then," Wo said with resignation. But as she slipped into her coat to leave, she fixed him with a final, disapproving stare. "Look to your faces, Simon Kress," she warned him. "Look to your faces." And she departed.

Puzzled, he wandered back to the tank and stared at the castles. His faces were still there, as ever. Except—he snatched up his magnifying goggles and slipped them on. He studied the faces for long moments. Even then exactly what it was, was hard to make out. But it seemed to him that the expression on the faces had changed slightly, that his smile was somehow twisted so that it seemed a touch malicious. But it was a very subtle change—if it was a change at all. Kress finally put it down to his suggestibility, and he resolved not to invite Jala Wo to any more of his gatherings.

Over the next few months Kress and about a dozen of his favorites got together weekly for what he liked to call his "war games." Now that his initial fascination with the sandkings was past, Kress spent less time around his tank and more on his business affairs and his social life, but he still enjoyed having a few friends over for a war or two. He kept the combatants sharp on a constant edge of hunger. It had severe effects on the orange sandkings, which dwindled visibly until Kress began to wonder whether their maw was dead. But the others did well enough.

Sometimes at night when he could not sleep, Kress would take a bottle of wine into the living room, where the red gloom of his miniature desert provided the only light. He would drink and watch for hours, alone. There was usually a fight going on somewhere; when there was not, he could easily start one by dropping some small morsel of food into the tank.

Kress's companions began betting on the weekly battles, as Malada Blane had suggested. Kress won a goodly amount by betting on the whites, which had become the most powerful and most numerous colony in the tank and which had the grandest castle. One week he slid the corner of the tank top aside, and he dropped the food close to the white castle instead of on the central battleground, where he usually let food fall. So the others had to attack the whites in their stronghold to get any food at all. They tried. The whites were brilliant in defense. Kress won a hundred standards from Jad Rakkis.

Rakkis, in fact, lost heavily on the sandkings almost every week. He pretended to a vast knowledge of them and their ways, claiming that he had studied them after the first party, but he had no luck when it came to placing his bets. Kress suspected that Jad's claims were empty boasting. He had tried to study the sandkings a bit himself, in a moment of idle curiosity, tying in to the library to find out what world his pets originally came from. But the library had no listing for sandkings. He wanted to get in touch with Wo and ask her about it, but he

had other concerns, and the matter kept slipping his mind.

Finally, after a month in which his losses totaled more than a thousand standards, Rakkis arrived at the war games. He was carrying a small plastic case under his arm. Inside was a spiderlike thing covered with fine golden hair.

"A sand spider," Rakkis announced. "From Cathaday. I got it this afternoon from t'Etherane the Petseller. Usually they remove the poison sacs, but this one is intact. Are you game, Simon? I want my money back. I'll bet a thousand standards, sand spider against sandkings."

Kress studied the spider in its plastic prison. His sandkings had grown—they were twice as large as Wo's, as she'd predicted—but they were still dwarfed by this thing. It was venomed, and they were not. Still, there were an awful lot of them. Besides, the endless sandking wars lately had begun to grow tiresome. The novelty of the match intrigued him.

"Done," Kress said. "Jad, you are a fool. The sandkings will just keep coming until this ugly creature of yours is dead."

"You are the fool, Simon," Rakkis replied, smiling. "The Cathadayan sand spider customarily feeds on burrowers that hide in nooks and crevices, and—well, watch—it will go straight into those castles and eat the maws."

Kress scowled amid general laughter. He hadn't counted on that. "Get on with it," he said irritably. Then he went to freshen his drink.

The spider was too large to be cycled conveniently through the food chamber. Two other guests helped Rakkis slide the tank top slightly to one side, and Malada Blane handed his case up to him. He shook the spider out. It landed lightly on a miniature dune in front of the red castle and stood confused for a moment, mouth working, legs twitching menacingly.

"Come on," Rakkis urged. They all gathered around the tank. Kress found his magnifiers and slipped them on. If he was going to lose a thousand standards, at least he wanted a good view of the action.

The sandkings had seen the invader. All over the red castle activity had ceased. The small scarlet mobiles were frozen, watching.

The spider began to move toward the dark promise of the gate. From the tower above, Simon Kress's countenance stared down impassively.

At once there was a flurry of activity. The nearest red mobiles formed themselves into two wedges and streamed over the sand toward the spider. More warriors erupted from inside the castle and assembled in a triple line to guard the approach to the underground chamber where the maw lived. Scouts came scuttling over the dunes, recalled to fight.

Battle was joined.

The attacking sandkings washed over the spider. Mandibles snapped shut on legs and abdomen, and clung. Reds raced up the golden legs to the invader's back. They bit and tore. One of them found an eye and ripped it loose with tiny yellow tendrils. Kress smiled and pointed.

But they were *small*, and they had no venom, and the spider did not stop. Its legs flicked sandkings off to either side. Its dripping jaws found others and left them broken and stiffening. Already a dozen of the reds lay dying. The sand spider came on and on. It strode straight through the triple line of guardians before the castle. The lines closed around it, covered it, waging desperate battle. A team of sandkings had bitten off one of the spider's legs. Defenders leaped from atop the towers to land on the twitching, heaving mass.

Lost beneath the sandkings, the spider somehow lurched down into the darkness and vanished.

Rakkis let out a long breath. He looked pale. "Wonderful," someone else said. Malada Blane chuckled deep in her throat.

"Look," said Idi Noreddian, tugging Kress by the arm.

They had been so intent on the struggle in the corner that none of them had noticed the activity elsewhere in the tank. But now the castle was still, and the sands were empty save for dead red mobiles, and now they saw.

Three armies were drawn up before the red castle. They stood quite still, in perfect array, rank after rank of sandkings, orange and white and black—waiting to see what emerged from the depths.

Kress smiled. "A *cordon sanitaire*," he said. "And glance at the other castles, if you will, Jad."

Rakkis did, and he swore. Teams of mobiles were sealing up the gates with sand and stone. If the spider somehow survived this encounter, it would find no easy entrance at the other castles. "I should have brought four spiders," Rakkis said. "Still, I've won. My spider is down there right now, eating your damned maw."

Kress did not reply. He waited. There was motion in the shadows.

All at once red mobiles began pouring out of the gate. They took their positions on the castle and began repairing the damage that the spider had wrought. The other armies dissolved and began to retreat to their respective corners.

"Jad," Kress said, "I think you are a bit confused about who is eating whom."

The following week Rakkis brought four slim silver snakes. The sandkings dispatched them without much trouble.

Next he tried a large black bird. It ate more than thirty white mobiles, and its thrashing and blundering virtually destroyed that castle, but ultimately its wings grew tired, and the sandkings attacked in force wherever it landed.

After that it was a case of insects, armored beetles not too unlike the sandkings themselves. But stupid, stupid. An allied force of oranges and blacks broke their formation, divided them, and butchered them.

Rakkis began giving Kress promissory notes.

It was around that time that Kress met Cath m'Lane again, one evening when he was dining in Asgard at his favorite restaurant. He stopped at her table briefly and told her about the war games, inviting her to join them. She flushed, then regained control of herself and grew icy. "Someone has to put a stop to you, Simon. I guess it's going to be me," she said.

Kress shrugged and enjoyed a lovely meal and thought no more about her threat.

Until a week later, when a small, stout woman arrived at his door and showed him a police wristband. "We've had complaints," she said. "Do you keep a tank full of dangerous insects, Kress?"

"Not insects," he said, furious. "Come, I'll show you."

When she had seen the sandkings, she shook her head. "This will never do. What do you know about these creatures anyway? Do you know what world they're from? Have they been cleared by the Ecological Board? Do you have a license for these things? We have a report that they're carnivores and possibly dangerous. We also have a report that they are semisentient. Where did you get these creatures anyway?"

"From Wo and Shade," Kress replied.

"Never heard of them," the woman said. "Probably smuggled them in, knowing our ecologists would never approve them. No, Kress, this won't do. I'm going to confiscate this tank and have it destroyed. And you're going to have to expect a few fines as well."

Kress offered her a hundred standards to forget all about him and his sandkings.

She *tsked*. "Now I'll have to add attempted bribery to the charges against you."

Not until he raised the figure to two thousand standards was she willing to be persuaded. "It's not going to be easy, you know," she said. "There are forms to be altered, records to be wiped. And getting a forged license from the ecologists will be time-consuming. Not to mention dealing with the complainant. What if she calls again?"

"Leave her to me," Kress said. "Leave her to me."

He thought about it for a while. That night he made some calls.

First he got t'Etherane the Petseller. "I want to buy a dog," he said. "A puppy."

The round-faced merchant gawked at him. "A puppy? That is not like you, Simon. Why don't you come in? I have a lovely choice."

"I want a very specific *kind* of puppy," Kress said. "Take notes. I'll describe to you what it must look like."

Afterwards he punched for Idi Noreddian. "Idi," he said, "I want you out here tonight with your holo equipment. I have a notion to record a sandking battle. A present for one of my friends."

The night after they made the recording, Kress stayed up late. He absorbed a controversial new drama in his sensorium, fixed himself a small snack, smoked a couple of joy sticks, and broke out a bottle of wine. Feeling very happy with himself, he wandered into the living room, glass in hand.

The lights were out. The red glow of the terrarium made the shadows look flushed and feverish. Kress walked over to survey his domain, curious as to how the blacks were doing in the repairs on their castle. The puppy had left it in ruins.

The restoration went well. But as Kress inspected the work through his magnifiers, he chanced to glance closely at the face on the sand-castle wall. It startled him.

He drew back, blinked, took a healthy gulp of wine, and looked again.

The face on the wall was still his. But it was all wrong, all *twisted*. His cheeks were bloated and piggish; his smile was a crooked leer. He looked impossibly malevolent.

"He smiled and lowered his firing hand. "Cath was always hard to swallow," he said, delighted at his wit. "Especially for one your size. Here, let me give you some help. What are gods for, after all?""

Uneasy, he moved around the tank to inspect the other castles. They were each a bit different, but ultimately all the same.

The oranges had left out most of the fine detail, but the result still seemed monstrous, crude; a brutal mouth and mindless eyes.

The reds gave him a satanic, twitching sort of smile. His mouth did odd, unlovely things at its corners.

The whites, his favorites, had carved a cruel idiot god.

Kress flung his wine across the room in rage. "You *dare*," he said under his breath. "Now you won't eat for a week, you damned . . . " His voice was shrill. "I'll teach you."

He had an idea. He strode out of the room, then returned a moment later with an antique iron throwing sword in his hand. It was a meter long, and the point was still sharp. Kress smiled, climbed up, and moved the tank cover aside just enough to give him working room, exposing one corner of the desert. He leaned down and jabbed the sword at the white castle below him. He waved it back and forth, smashing towers and ramparts and walls. Sand and stone collapsed, burying the scrambling mobiles. A flick of his wrist obliterated the features of the insolent, insulting caricature that the sandkings had made of his face. Then he poised the point of the sword above the dark mouth that opened down into the maw's chamber; he thrust with all his strength, meeting with resistance. He heard a soft, squishing sound. All the mobiles trembled and collapsed. Satisfied, Kress pulled back.

He watched for a moment, wondering whether he had killed the maw. The point of the throwing sword was wet and slimy. But finally the white sandkings began to move again—feebly, slowly—but they moved.

He was preparing to slide the cover back into place and move on to a second castle when he felt something crawling on his hand.

He screamed, dropping the sword, and brushed the sandking from his flesh. It fell to the carpet, and he ground it beneath his heel, crushing it thoroughly long after it was dead. It had crunched when he stepped on it. After that, trembling, he hurriedly sealed the tank up again. He rushed off to shower and inspected himself carefully. He boiled his clothing.

Later, after drinking several glasses of wine, he returned to the living room. He was a bit ashamed of the way he had been terrified by the sandking. But he was not about to open the tank again. From then on, the cover would stay sealed permanently. Still, he had to punish the others.

He decided to lubricate his mental processes with another glass of wine. As he finished it, an inspiration came to him. He went to the tank and made a few adjustments to the humidity controls.

By the time he fell asleep on the couch, his wine glass still in his hand, the sand castles were melting in the rain.

Kress woke to angry pounding on his door.

He sat up, groggy, his head throbbing. Wine hangovers were always the worst, he thought. He lurched to the entry chamber.

Cath m'Lane was outside. "You monster," she said, her face swollen and puffy and streaked with tears. "I cried all night, damn you. But no more, Simon, no more."

"Easy," he said, holding his head. "I've got a hangover."

She swore and shoved him aside and pushed her way into his house. The shambler came peering round a corner to see what the noise was. She spat at it and stalked into the living room, Kress trailing ineffectually after her. "Hold on," he said, "where do you . . . you can't . . . " He stopped, suddenly horror-struck. She was carrying a heavy sledgehammer in her left hand. "No," he said.

She went directly to the sandkings' tank. "You like the little charmers so much, Simon? Then you can live with them."

"Cath!" he shrieked.

Gripping the hammer with both hands, she swung as hard as she could against the side of the tank. The sound of the impact set Kress's head to screaming, and he made a low, blubbering sound of despair. But the plastic held.

She swung again. This time there was a *crack*, and a network of thin lines appeared in the wall of the tank.

Kress threw himself at her as she drew back her hammer to take a third swing. They went down flailing and rolled over. She lost her grip on the hammer and tried to throttle him, but Kress wrenched free and bit her on the arm, drawing blood. They both staggered to their feet, panting.

"You should see yourself, Simon," she said grimly. "Blood dripping from your mouth. You look like one of your pets. How do you like the taste?"

"Get out," he said. He saw the throwing sword where it had fallen the night before, and he snatched it up. "Get out," he repeated, waving the sword for emphasis. "Don't go near that tank again."

She laughed at him. "You wouldn't dare," she said. She bent to pick up her hammer.

Kress shrieked at her and lunged. Before he quite knew what was happening, the iron blade had gone clear through her abdomen. Cath m'Lane looked at him wonderingly and down at the sword. Kress fell back, whimpering. "I didn't mean . . . I only wanted . . . "

She was transfixed, bleeding, nearly dead, but somehow she did not fall. "You monster," she managed to say, though her mouth was full of blood. And she whirled, impossibly, the sword in her, and swung with her last strength at the tank. The tortured wall shattered, and Cath m'Lane was buried beneath an avalanche of plastic and sand and mud.

Kress made small hysterical noises and scrambled up onto the couch.

Sandkings were emerging from the muck on his living-room floor. They were crawling across Cath's body. A few of them ventured tentatively out across the carpet. More followed.

He watched as a column took shape, a living, writhing square of sandkings, bearing something—something slimy and featureless, a piece of raw meat as big as a man's head. They began to carry it away from the tank. It pulsed.

That was when Kress broke and ran.

Before he found the courage to return home, he ran to his skimmer and flew to the nearest city, some fifty kilometers away, almost sick with fear. But, once safely away, he found a small restaurant, downed several mugs of coffee and two anti-hangover tabs, ate a full breakfast, and gradually regained his composure.

It had been a dreadful morning, but dwelling on that would solve nothing. He ordered more coffee and considered his situation with icy rationality.

Cath m'Lane was dead at his hand. Could he report it and plead that it had been an accident? Unlikely. He had run her through, after all, and he had already told that policer to leave her to him. He would have to get rid of the evidence and hope that Cath had not told anyone her plans for the day. It was very unlikely she had. She could only have gotten his gift late last night. She said that she had cried all night, and she was alone when she arrived. Very well, he had one body and one skimmer to dispose of.

That left the sandkings. They might prove more of a difficulty. No doubt they had all escaped by now. The thought of them around his house, in his bed and his clothes, infesting his food—it made his flesh crawl. He shuddered and overcame his revulsion. It really shouldn't be too hard to kill them, he reminded himself. He didn't have to account for every mobile. Just the four maws, that was all. He could do that. They were large, as he'd seen. He would find them and kill them. He was their god; now he would be their destroyer.

"When he shoved her, she looked briefly startled. She screamed as she tumbled down the stairs. "I'm hurt," she called . . . and shortly afterward . . . the screaming started."

He went shopping before he flew back to his home. He bought a set of skinthins that would cover him from head to foot, several bags of poison pellets for rockjock control, and a spray canister containing an illegally strong pesticide. He also bought a magnalock towing device.

When he landed late that afternoon, he went about things methodically. First he hooked Cath's skimmer to his own with the magnalock. Searching it, he had his first piece of luck. The crystal chip with Idi Noreddian's holo of the sandking fight was on the front seat. He had worried about that.

When the skimmers were ready, he slipped into his skinthins and went inside to get Cath's body.

It wasn't there.

He poked through the fast-drying sand carefully, and there was no doubt of it, the body was gone. Could she have dragged herself away? Unlikely, but Kress searched. A cursory inspection of his house turned up neither the body nor any sign of the sandkings. He did not have time for a more thorough investigation, not with the incriminating skimmer outside his front door. He resolved to try later.

Some seventy kilometers north of Kress's estate was a range of active volcanoes. He flew there, Cath's skimmer in tow. Above the glowering cone of the largest volcano he released the magnalock and watched the skimmer plummet down and vanish in the lava below.

It was dusk when he returned to his house. This gave him pause. Briefly he considered flying back to the city and spending the night there. He put the thought aside. There was work to do. He wasn't safe yet.

He scattered the poison pellets around the exterior of his house. No one would think this suspicious. He had always had a rockjock problem. When this task was completed, he primed the canister of pesticide and ventured back inside the house.

Kress went through the house, room by room, turning on lights everywhere he went until he was surrounded by a blaze of artificial illumination. He paused to clean up in the living room, shoveling sand and plastic fragments back into the broken tank. The sandkings were all gone, as he'd feared. The castles were shrunken and distorted, slagged by the watery bombardment Kress had visited upon them, and what little of them remained was crumbling as it dried.

He frowned and searched further, the canister of pest spray strapped across his shoulders.

Down in the wine cellar he could see Cath m'Lane's corpse.

It sprawled at the foot of a steep flight of stairs, the limbs twisted as if by a fall. White mobiles were swarming all over it, and as Kress watched, the body moved jerkily across the hard-packed dirt floor.

He laughed and twisted the illumination up to maximum. In the far corner a squat little earthen castle and a dark hole were visible between two wine racks. Kress could make out a rough outline of his face on the cellar wall.

The body shifted once again, moving a few centimeters toward the castle. Kress had a sudden vision of the white maw waiting hungrily. It might be able to get Cath's foot in its mouth, but no more. It was too absurd. He laughed again and started down into the cellar, finger poised on the trigger of the hose that snaked down his right arm. The sandkings—hundreds of them moving as one—deserted the body and assumed battle formation, a field of white between him and their maw.

Suddenly Kress had another inspiration. He smiled and lowered his firing hand. "Cath was always hard to swallow," he said, delighted at his wit. "Especially for one your size. Here, let me give you some help. What are gods for, after all?"

He retreated upstairs, returning shortly with a cleaver. The sandkings, patient, waited and watched while Kress chopped Cath m'Lane into small, easily digestible pieces.

Kress slept in his skinthins that night, the pesticide close at hand, but he did not need it. The whites, sated, remained in the cellar, and he saw no sign of the others.

In the morning he finished the cleanup of the living room. When he was through, no trace of the struggle remained except for the broken tank.

He ate a light lunch and resumed his hunt for the missing sandkings. In full daylight it was not too difficult. The blacks had located in his rock garden, where they built a castle heavy with obsidian and quartz. The reds he found at the bottom of his long-disused swimming pool, which had partially filled with wind-blown sand over the years. He saw mobiles of both colors ranging about his grounds, many of them carrying poison pellets back to their maws. Kress felt like laughing. He decided his pesticide was unnecessary. No use risking a fight when he could just let the poison do its work. Both maws should be dead by evening.

That left only the burnt-orange sandkings unaccounted for. Kress circled his estate several times, in an ever-widening spiral, but he found no trace of them. When he began to sweat in his skinthins—it was a hot, dry day—he decided it was not important. If they were out here, they were probably eating the poison pellets, as the reds and blacks were.

He crunched several sandkings underfoot, with a certain degree of satisfaction, as he walked back to the house. Inside, he removed his skinthins, settled down to a delicious meal, and finally began to relax. Everything was under control. Two of the maws would soon be defunct, the third was safely located where he could dispose of it after it had served his purposes, and he had no doubt that he would find the fourth. As for Cath, every trace of her visit had been obliterated.

His reverie was interrupted when his viewscreen began to blink at him. It was Jad Rakkis, calling to brag about some cannibal worms he would bring to the war games tonight.

Kress had forgotten about that, but he recovered quickly. "Oh, Jad, my pardons. I neglected to tell you. I grew bored with all that and got rid of the sandkings. Ugly little things. Sorry, but there'll be no party tonight."

Rakkis was indignant. "But what will I do with my worms?"

"Put them in a basket of fruit and send them to a loved one," Kress said, signing off. Quickly he began calling the others. He did not need anyone arriving at his doorstep now, with the sandkings alive and infesting the estate.

As he was calling Idi Noreddian, Kress became aware of an annoying oversight. The screen began to clear, indicating that someone had answered at the other end. Kress flicked off.

Idi arrived on schedule an hour later. She was surprised to find the party had been canceled but perfectly happy to share an evening alone with Kress. He delighted her with his story of Cath's reaction to the holo they had made together. While telling it, he managed to ascertain that she had not mentioned the prank to anyone. He nodded, satisfied, and refilled their wine glasses. Only a trickle was left. "I'll have to get a fresh bottle," he said. "Come with me to my wine cellar, and help me pick out a good vintage. You've always had a better palate than I."

She went along willingly enough but balked at the top of the stairs when Kress opened the door and gestured for her to precede him. "Where are the lights?" she asked. "And that smell—what's that peculiar smell, Simon?"

When he shoved her, she looked briefly startled. She screamed as she tumbled down the stairs. Kress closed the door and began to nail it shut with the boards and air hammer he had left for that purpose. As he was finishing, he heard Idi groan. "I'm hurt," she called. "Simon, what is this?" Suddenly she squealed, and shortly after that the screaming started.

It did not cease for hours. Kress went to his sensorium and dialed up a saucy comedy to blot it from his mind.

When he was sure she was dead, Kress flew her skimmer north to the volcanoes and discarded it. The magnalock was proving a good investment.

Odd scrabbling noises were coming from beyond the wine-cellar door the next morning when Kress went down to check things out. He listened for several uneasy moments, wondering whether Idi might possibly have survived and was scratching to get out. This seemed unlikely; it had to be the sandkings. Kress did not like the implications of this. He decided that he would keep the door sealed, at least for a while. He went outside with a shovel to bury the red and black maws in their own castles.

He found them very much alive.

The black castle was glittering with volcanic glass, and sandkings were all over it, repairing and improving. The highest tower was up to his waist, and on it was a hideous caricature of his face. When he approached, the blacks halted in their labors and formed up into two threatening phalanxes. Kress glanced behind him and saw others closing off his escape. Startled, he dropped his shovel and sprinted out of the trap, crushing several mobiles beneath his boots.

The red castle was creeping up the walls of the swimming pool. The maw was safely settled in a pit, surrounded by sand and concrete and battlements. The reds crept all over the bottom of the pool. Kress watched them carry a rockjock and a large lizard into the castle. Horrified, he stepped back from the poolside and felt something crunch. Looking down, he saw three mobiles climbing up his leg. He brushed

"Technical advisors."

them off and stamped them to death, but others were approaching rapidly. They were larger than he remembered. Some were almost as big as his thumb.

He ran.

By the time he reached the safety of the house, his heart was racing and he was short of breath. He closed the door behind him and hurried to lock it. His house was supposed to be pestproof. He'd be safe in here.

A stiff drink steadied his nerve. *So poison doesn't faze them*, he thought. He should have known. Jala Wo had warned him that the maw could eat anything. He would have to use the pesticide. He took another drink for good measure, donned his skinthins, and strapped the canister to his back. He unlocked the door.

Outside, the sandkings were waiting.

Two armies confronted him, allied against the common threat. More than he could have guessed. The damned maws must be breeding like rockjocks. Mobiles were everywhere, a creeping sea of them.

Kress brought up the hose and flicked the trigger. A gray mist washed over the nearest rank of sandkings. He moved his hand from side to side.

Where the mist fell, the sandkings twitched violently and died in sudden spasms. Kress smiled. They were no match for him. He sprayed in a wide arc before him and stepped forward confidently over a litter of black and red bodies. The armies fell back. Kress advanced, intent on cutting through them to their maws.

All at once the retreat stopped. A thousand sandkings surged toward him.

Kress had been expecting the counterattack. He stood his ground, sweeping his misty sword before him in great looping strokes. They came at him and died. A few got through; he could not spray everywhere at once. He felt them climbing up his legs, then sensed their mandibles biting futilely at the reinforced plastic of his skinthins. He ignored them and kept spraying.

Then he began to feel soft impacts on his head and shoulders.

Kress trembled and spun and looked up above him. The front of his house was alive with sandkings. Blacks and reds, hundreds of them. They were launching themselves into the air, raining down on him. They fell all around him. One landed on his faceplate, its mandibles scraping at his eyes for a terrible second before he plucked it away.

He swung up his hose and sprayed the air, sprayed the house, sprayed until the airborne sandkings were all dead or dying. The mist settled back on him, making him cough. But he kept spraying. Only when the front of the house was clean did Kress turn his attention back to the ground.

They were all around him, on him, dozens of them scurrying over his body, hundreds of others hurrying to join them. He turned the mist on them. The hose went dead. Kress heard a loud *hiss*, and the deadly fog rose in a great cloud from between his shoulders, cloaking him, choking him, making his eyes burn and blur. He felt for the hose, and his hand came away covered with dying sandkings. The hose was severed; they'd eaten it through. He was surrounded by a shroud of pesticide, blinded. He stumbled and screamed and began to run back to the house, pulling sandkings from his body as he went.

Inside, he sealed the door and collapsed on the carpet, rolling back and forth until he was sure he had crushed them all. The canister was empty by then, hissing feebly. Kress stripped off his skinthins and showered. The hot spray scalded him and left his skin reddened and sensitive, but it made his flesh stop crawling.

He dressed in his heaviest clothing, thick work pants and leathers, after shaking them out nervously. "Damn," he kept muttering, "damn." His throat was dry. After searching the entry hall thoroughly to make certain it was clean, he allowed himself to sit and pour a drink. "Damn," he repeated. His hand shook as he poured, slopping liquor on the carpet.

The alcohol settled him, but it did not wash away the fear. He had a second drink and went to the window furtively. Sandkings were moving across the thick plastic pane. He shuddered and retreated to his communications console. He had to get help, he thought wildly. He would punch through a call to the authorities, and policers would come out with flamethrowers, and . . .

Kress stopped in mid-call and groaned. He couldn't call in the police. He would have to tell them about the whites in his cellar, and they'd find the bodies there. Perhaps the maw might have finished Cath m'Lane by now, but certainly not Idi Noreddian. He hadn't even cut her up. Besides, there would be bones. No, the police could be called in only as a last resort.

He sat at the console, frowning. His communications equipment filled a whole wall. From here he could reach anyone on Baldur. He had plenty of money and his cunning; he had always prided himself on his cunning. He would handle this somehow.

Briefly he considered calling Wo, but he soon dismissed the idea. Wo knew too much, and she would ask questions, and he did not trust her. No, he needed someone who would do as he asked *without* questions.

His frown slowly turned into a smile. Kress had contacts. He put through a call to a number he had not used in a long time.

A woman's face took shape on his viewscreen—white-haired, blank of expression, with a long, hooked nose. Her voice was brisk and efficient. "Simon," she said. "How is business?"

"Business is fine, Lissandra," Kress replied. "I have a job for you."

"A removal? My price has gone up since last time, Simon. It has been ten years, after all."

"You will be well paid," Kress said. "You

"These continued rumors that I don't exist are making it very difficult for me to obtain credit!"

know I'm generous. I want you for a bit of pest control."

She smiled a thin smile. "No need to use euphemisms, Simon. The call is shielded."

"No, I'm serious. I have a pest problem. Dangerous pests. Take care of them for me. No questions. Understood?"

"Understood."

"Good. You'll need ... oh, three to four operatives. Wear heat-resistant skinthins, and equip them with flamethrowers, or lasers, something on that order. Come out to my place. You'll see the problem. Bugs, lots and lots of them. In my rock garden and the old swimming pool you'll find castles. Destroy them, kill everything inside them. Then knock on the door, and I'll show you what else needs to be done. Can you get out here quickly?"

Her face remained impassive. "We'll leave within the hour."

Lissandra was true to her word. She arrived in a lean, black skimmer with three operatives. Kress watched them from the safety of a second-story window. They were all faceless in dark plastic skinthins. Two of them wore portable flamethrowers; a third carried lasercannon and explosives. Lissandra carried nothing; Kress recognized her by the way she gave orders.

Their skimmer passed low overhead first, checking out the situation. The sandkings went mad. Scarlet and ebon mobiles ran everywhere, frenetic. Kress could see the castle in the rock garden from his vantage point. It stood tall as a man. Its ramparts were crawling with black defenders, and a steady stream of mobiles flowed down into its depths.

Lissandra's skimmer came down next to Kress's, and the operatives vaulted out and unlimbered their weapons. They looked inhuman, deadly.

The black army drew up between them and the castle. The reds—Kress suddenly realized that he could not see the reds. He blinked. Where had they gone?

Lissandra pointed and shouted, and her two flamethrowers spread out and opened up on the black sandkings. Their weapons coughed dully and began to roar, long tongues of blue-and-scarlet fire licking out before them. Sandkings crisped and shriveled and died. The operatives began to play the fire back and forth in an efficient, interlocking pattern. They advanced with careful, measured steps.

The black army burned and disintegrated, the mobiles fleeing in a thousand different directions, some back toward the castle, others toward the enemy. None reached the operatives with the flamethrowers. Lissandra's people were very professional.

Then one of them stumbled.

Or seemed to stumble. Kress looked again and saw that the ground had given way beneath the man. Tunnels, he thought with a tremor of fear; tunnels, pits, traps. The flamer was sunk in sand up to his waist, and suddenly the ground around him seemed to erupt, and he was covered with scarlet sandkings. He dropped the flamethrower and began to claw wildly at his own body. His screams were horrible to hear.

His companion hesitated, then swung and fired. A blast of flame swallowed human and sandkings both. The screaming stopped abruptly. Satisfied, the second flamer turned back to the castle, took another step forward, and recoiled as his foot broke through the ground and vanished up to the ankle. He tried to pull it back and retreat, and the sand all around him gave way. He lost his balance and stumbled, flailing, and the sandkings were everywhere, a boiling mass of them, covering him as he writhed and rolled. His flamethrower was useless and forgotten.

Kress pounded wildly on the window, shouting for attention. "The castle! Get the castle!"

Lissandra, standing back by her skimmer, heard and gestured. Her third operative sighted with the lasercannon and fired.

The heavy door was still nailed shut, as he had left it. But it bulged outward slightly, as if warped by some tremendous pressure. That made Kress uneasy, as did the silence. . . .

The beam throbbed across the grounds and sliced off the top of the castle. He brought the cannon down sharply, hacking at the sand and stone parapets. Towers fell. Kress's face disintegrated. The laser bit into the ground, searching round and about. The castle crumbled. Now it was only a heap of sand. But the black mobiles continued to move. The maw was buried too deeply. The beams hadn't touched it.

Lissandra gave another order. Her operative discarded the laser, primed an explosive, and darted forward. He leaped over the smoking corpse of the first flamer, landed on solid ground within Kress's rock garden, and heaved. The explosive ball landed square atop the ruins of the black castle. White-hot light seared Kress's eyes, and there was a tremendous gout of sand and rock and mobiles. For a moment dust obscured everything. It was raining sandkings and pieces of sandkings.

Kress saw that the black mobiles were dead and unmoving.

"The pool!" he shouted down through the window. "Get the castle in the pool!"

Lissandra understood quickly; the ground was littered with motionless blacks, but the reds were pulling back hurriedly and re-forming. Her operative stood uncertain, then reached down and pulled out another explosive ball. He took one step forward, but Lissandra called him, and he sprinted back in her direction.

It was all so simple then. He reached the skimmer, and Lissandra took him aloft. Kress rushed to another window in another room to watch. They came swooping in just over the pool, and the operative pitched his bombs down at the red castle from the safety of the skimmer. After the fourth run, the castle was unrecognizable, and the sandkings stopped moving.

Lissandra was thorough. She had him bomb each castle several additional times. Then he used the lasercannon, crisscrossing methodically until it was certain that nothing living could remain intact beneath those small patches of ground.

Finally they came knocking at his door. Kress was grinning maniacally when he let them in. "Lovely," he said, "lovely."

Lissandra pulled off the mask of her skinthins. "This will cost you, Simon. Two operatives gone, not to mention the danger to my own life."

"Of course," Kress blurted. "You'll be well paid, Lissandra. Whatever you ask, just so you finish the job."

"What remains to be done?"

"You have to clean out my wine cellar," Kress said. "There's another castle down there. And you'll have to do it without explosives. I don't want my house coming down around me."

Lissandra motioned to her operative. "Go outside and get Rajk's flamethrower. It should be intact."

He returned armed, ready, silent. Kress led them to the wine cellar.

The heavy door was still nailed shut, as he had left it. But it bulged outward slightly, as if warped by some tremendous pressure. That made Kress uneasy, as did the silence that reigned about them. He stood well away from the door while Lissandra's operative removed his nails and planks. "Is that safe in here?" he found himself muttering, pointing at the flamethrower. "I don't want a fire, either, you know."

"I have the laser," Lissandra said. "We'll use that for the kill. The flamethrower probably won't be needed. But I want it here just in case. There are worse things than fire, Simon."

He nodded.

The last plank came free of the cellar door. There was still no sound from below. Lissandra snapped an order, and her underling fell back, took up a position behind her, and leveled the flamethrower squarely at the door. She slipped her mask back on, hefted the laser, stepped forward, and pulled the door open.

No motion. No sound. It was dark down there.

"Is there a light?" Lissandra asked.

"Just inside the door," Kress said. "On the right-hand side. Mind the stairs. They're quite steep."

She stepped into the doorway, shifted the laser to her left hand, and reached up with her right, fumbling inside for the light panel. Nothing happened. "I feel it," Lissandra said, "but it doesn't seem to . . ."

Then she was screaming, and she stumbled backward. A great white sandking had clamped itself around her wrist. Blood welled through her skinthins where its mandibles had sunk in. It was fully as large as her hand.

Lissandra did a horrible little jig across the room and began to smash her hand against the nearest wall. Again and again and again. It landed with a heavy, meaty thud. Finally the sandking fell away. She whimpered and fell to her knees.

"I think my fingers are broken," she said softly. The blood was still flowing freely. She had dropped the laser near the cellar door.

"I'm not going down there," her operative announced in clear, firm tones.

Lissandra looked up at him. "No," she said. "Stand in the door and flame it all. Cinder it. Do you understand?"

He nodded.

Kress moaned. "My *house*," he said. His stomach churned. The white sandking had been so *large*. How many more were down there? "Don't," he continued. "Leave it alone. I've changed my mind."

Lissandra misunderstood. She held out her hand. It was covered with blood and greenish-black ichor. "Your little friend bit clean through my glove, and you saw what it took to get it off. I don't care about your house, Simon. Whatever is down there is going to die."

Kress hardly heard her. He thought he could see movement in the shadows beyond the cellar door. He imagined a white army bursting out, each soldier as big as the sandking that had attacked Lissandra. He saw himself being lifted by a hundred tiny arms and being dragged down into the darkness, where the maw waited hungrily. He was afraid. "Don't," he said.

They ignored him.

Kress darted forward, and his shoulder slammed into the back of Lissandra's operative just as the man was bracing to fire. The operative grunted, lost his balance, and pitched forward into the black. Kress listened to him fall down the stairs. Afterwards there were other noises—scuttlings and snaps and soft, squishing sounds.

Kress swung around to face Lissandra. He was drenched in cold sweat, but a sickly kind of excitement possessed him. It was almost sexual.

Lissandra's calm, cold eyes regarded him through her mask. "What are you doing?" she demanded as Kress picked up the laser she had dropped. "*Simon!*"

"Making a peace," he said, giggling. "They won't hurt god, no, not so long as god is good and generous. I was cruel. Starved them. I have to make up for it now, you see."

"You're insane," Lissandra said. It was the last thing she said. Kress burned a hole in her chest big enough to put his arm through. He dragged the body across the floor and rolled it down the cellar stairs. The noises were louder—chitinous clackings and scrapings and echoes that were thick and liquid. Kress nailed up the door once again.

As he fled, he was filled with a deep sense of contentment that coated his fear like a layer of syrup. He suspected it was not his own.

He planned to leave his home, to fly to the city and take a room for a night, or perhaps for a year. Instead he started drinking. He was not quite sure why. He drank steadily for hours and retched it all up violently on his living-room carpet. At some point he fell asleep. When he woke, it was pitch-dark in the house.

He cowered against the couch. He could hear *noises*. Things were moving in the walls. They were all around him. His hearing was extraordinarily acute. Every little creak was the footstep of a sandking. He closed his eyes and waited, expecting to feel their terrible touch, afraid to move lest he brush against one.

"Something moved from shadow into light. A pale shape on the seat. . . . It was as long as his forearm. Its mandibles clacked together softly. . . . Kress slowly backed away."

Kress sobbed and then was very still.

Time passed, but nothing happened.

He opened his eyes again. He trembled. Slowly the shadows began to soften and dissolve. Moonlight was filtering through the high windows. His eyes adjusted.

The living room was empty. Nothing there, nothing, nothing. Only his drunken fears.

Kress steeled himself and rose and went to a light.

Nothing there. The room was deserted.

He listened. Nothing. No sound. Nothing in the walls. It had all been his imagination, his fear.

The memories of Lissandra and the thing in the cellar returned to him unbidden. Shame and anger washed over him. Why had he done that? He could have helped her burn it out, kill it. *Why* . . . he knew why. The maw had done it to him, had put fear in him. Wo had said it was psionic, even when it was small. And now it was large, so large. It had feasted on Cath and Idi, and now it had two more bodies down there. It would keep growing. And it had learned to like the taste of human flesh, he thought.

He began to shake, but he took control of himself again and stopped. It wouldn't hurt him; he was god; the whites had always been his favorites.

He remembered how he had stabbed it with his throwing sword. That was before Cath came. Damn her, anyway.

He couldn't stay here. The maw would grow hungry again. Large as it was, it wouldn't take long. Its appetite would be terrible. What would it do then? He had to get away, back to the safety of the city while the maw was still contained in his wine cellar. It was only plaster and hard-packed earth down there, and the mobiles could dig and tunnel. When they got free . . . Kress didn't want to think about it.

He went to his bedroom and packed. He took three bags. Just a single change of clothing, that was all he needed; the rest of the space he filled with his valuables, with jewelry and art and other things he could not bear to lose. He did not expect to return to this place ever again.

His shambler followed him down the stairs, staring at him from its baleful, glowing eyes. It was gaunt. Kress realized that it had been ages since he had fed it. Normally it could take care of itself, but no doubt the pickings had grown lean of late. When it tried to clutch at his leg, he snarled at it and kicked it away, and it scurried off, obviously hurt and offended.

Carrying his bags awkwardly, Kress slipped outside and shut the door behind him.

For a moment he stood pressed against the house, his heart thudding in his chest. Only a few meters between him and his skimmer. He was afraid to take those few steps. The moonlight was bright, and the grounds in front of his house were a scene of carnage. The bodies of Lissandra's two flamers lay where they had fallen, one twisted and burned, the other swollen beneath a mass of dead sandkings. And the mobiles, the black and red mobiles, they were all around him. It took an effort to remember that they were dead. It was almost as if they were simply waiting, as they had waited so often before.

Nonsense, Kress told himself. More drunken fears. He had seen the castles blown apart. They were dead, and the white maw was trapped in his cellar. He took several deep and deliberate breaths and stepped forward onto the sandkings. They crunched. He ground them into the sand savagely. They did not move.

Kress smiled and walked slowly across the battleground, listening to the sounds, the sounds of safety.

Crunch, crackle, crunch.

He lowered his bags to the ground and opened the door to his skimmer.

Something moved from shadow into light. A pale shape on the seat of his skimmer. It was as long as his forearm. Its mandibles clacked together softly, and it looked up at him from six small eyes set all around its body.

Kress wet his pants and backed away slowly.

There was more motion from inside the skimmer. He had left the door open. The sandking emerged and came toward him, cautiously. Others followed. They had been hiding beneath his seats, burrowed into the upholstery. But now they emerged. They formed a ragged ring around the skimmer.

Kress licked his lips, turned, and moved quickly to Lissandra's skimmer.

He stopped before he was halfway there. Things were moving inside that one, too. Great maggoty things half-seen by the light of the moon.

Kress whimpered and retreated back toward the house. Near the front door, he looked up.

He counted a dozen long, white shapes creeping back and forth across the walls of the building. Four of them were clustered close together near the top of the unused belfry, where the carrion hawk had once roosted. They were carving something. A face. A very recognizable face.

Kress shrieked and ran back inside. He headed for his liquor cabinet.

A sufficient quantity of drink brought him the easy oblivion he sought. But he woke. Despite everything, he woke. He had a terrific headache, and he stank, and he was hungry. Oh, so very hungry! He had never been so hungry.

Kress knew it was not his *own* stomach hurting.

A white sandking watched him from atop the dresser in his bedroom, its antennae moving faintly. It was as big as the one in the skimmer the night before. He tried not to shrink away. "I'll . . . I'll feed you," he said to it. "I'll feed you." His mouth was horribly dry, sandpaper-dry. He licked his lips and fled from the room.

The house was full of sandkings, he had to be careful where he put his feet. They all seemed busy on errands of their own. They were making modifications in his house, burrowing into or out of his walls, carving things. Twice he saw his own likeness staring out at him from unexpected places. The faces were warped, twisted, livid with fear.

He went outside to get the bodies that had been rotting in the yard, hoping to appease the white maw's hunger. They were gone, both of them. Kress remembered how easily the mobiles could carry things many times their own weight.

It was terrible to think that the maw was *still* hungry after all of that.

When Kress reentered the house, a column of sandkings was wending its way down the stairs. Each carried a piece of his shambler. The head seemed to look at him reproachfully as it went by.

Kress emptied his freezers, his cabinets, everything, piling all the food in the house in the center of his kitchen floor. A dozen whites waited to take it away. They avoided the frozen food, leaving it to thaw in a great puddle, but carried off everything else.

When all the food was gone, Kress felt his own hunger pangs abate just a bit, though he had not eaten a thing. But he knew the respite would be short-lived. Soon the maw would be hungry again. He had to feed it.

Kress knew what to do. He went to his communicator. "Malada," he began casually when the first of his friends answered, "I'm having a small party tonight. I realize this is terribly short notice, but I hope you can make it. I really do."

He called Jad Rakkis next, and then the others. By the time he had finished, five of them had accepted his invitation. Kress hoped that would be enough.

Kress met his guests outside—the mobiles had cleaned up remarkably quickly, and the grounds looked almost as they had before the battle—and walked them to his front door. He let them enter first. He did not follow.

When four of them had gone through, Kress finally worked up his courage. He closed the door behind his latest guest, ignoring the startled exclamations that soon turned into shrill gibbering, and sprinted for the skimmer the man had arrived in. He slid in safely, thumbed the startplate, and swore. It was programmed to lift only in response to its owner's thumbprint, of course.

Rakkis was the next to arrive. Kress ran to his skimmer as it set down and seized Rakkis by the arm as he was climbing out. "Get back in, quickly," he said, pushing. "Take me to the city. Hurry, Jad. *Get out of here!*"

But Rakkis only stared at him and would not move. "Why, what's wrong, Simon? I don't understand. What about your party?"

And then it was too late, because the loose sand all around them was stirring, and the red eyes were staring at them, and the mandibles were clacking. Rakkis made a choking sound and moved to get back in his skimmer, but a pair of mandibles snapped shut about his ankle, and suddenly he was on his knees. The sand seemed to boil with subterranean activity. Rakkis thrashed and cried terribly as they tore him apart. Kress could hardly bear to watch.

After that, he did not try to escape again. When it was all over, he cleaned out what remained in his liquor cabinet and got extremely drunk. It would be the last time he would enjoy that luxury, he knew. The only alcohol remaining in the house was stored down in the wine cellar.

Kress did not touch a bite of food the entire day, but he fell asleep feeling bloated, sated at last, the awful hunger vanquished. His last thoughts before the nightmares took him were about whom he could ask out tomorrow.

Morning was hot and dry. Kress opened his eyes to see the white sandking on his dresser again. He shut his eyes again quickly, hoping the dream would leave him. It did not, and he could not go back to

sleep, and soon he found himself staring at the thing.

He stared for almost five minutes before the strangeness of it dawned on him; the sandking was not moving.

The mobiles could be preternaturally still, to be sure. He had seen them wait and watch a thousand times. But always there was some motion about them: The mandibles clacked, the legs twitched, the long, fine antennae stirred and swayed.

But the sandking on his dresser was completely still.

Kress rose, holding his breath, not daring to hope. Could it be dead? Could something have killed it? He walked across the room.

The eyes were glassy and black. The creature seemed swollen, somehow, as if it were soft and rotting inside, filling up with gas that pushed outward at the plates of white armor.

Kress reached out a trembling hand and touched it.

It was warm; hot even, and growing hotter. But it did not move.

He pulled his hand back, and as he did, a segment of the sandking's white exoskeleton fell away from it. The flesh beneath was the same color, but softer-looking, swollen and feverish. And it almost seemed to throb.

Kress backed away and ran to the door.

Three more white mobiles lay in his hall. They were all like the one in his bedroom.

He ran down the stairs, jumping over sandkings. None of them moved. The house was full of them, all dead, dying, comatose, whatever. Kress did not care what was wrong with them. Just so they could not move.

He found four of them inside his skimmer. He picked them up, one by one, and threw them as far as he could. Damned monsters. He slid back in, on the ruined half-eaten seats, and thumbed the startplate.

Nothing happened.

Kress tried again and again. Nothing. It wasn't fair. This was *his* skimmer. It ought to start. Why wouldn't it lift? He didn't understand.

Finally he got out and checked, expecting the worst. He found it. The sandkings had torn apart his gravity grid. He was trapped. He was still trapped.

Grimly Kress marched back into the house. He went to his gallery and found the antique ax that had hung next to the throwing sword he had used on Cath m'Lane. He set to work. The sandkings did not stir even as he chopped them to pieces. But they splattered when he made the first cut, the bodies almost bursting. Inside was awful; strange half-formed organs, a viscous reddish ooze that looked almost like human blood, and the yellow ichor.

Kress destroyed twenty of them before he realized the futility of what he was doing. The mobiles were nothing, really. Besides, there were so *many* of them. He could work for a day and night and still not kill them all.

He had to go down into the wine cellar and use the ax on the maw.

Resolute, he started toward the cellar. He got within sight of the door, then stopped.

It was not a door anymore. The walls had been eaten away, so that the hole was twice the size it had been, and round. A pit, that was all. There was no sign that there had ever been a door nailed shut over that black abyss.

A ghastly, choking, fetid odor seemed to come from below.

And the walls were wet and bloody and covered with patches of white fungus.

And worst, it was *breathing*.

Kress stood across the room and felt the warm wind wash over him as it exhaled, and he tried not to choke, and when the wind reversed direction, he fled.

Back in the living room he destroyed three more mobiles and collapsed. What was *happening*? He didn't understand.

Then he remembered the only person who might understand. Kress went to his

communicator again, stepped on a sandking in his haste, and prayed fervently that the device still worked.

When Jala Wo answered, he broke down and told her everything.

She let him talk without interruption, no expression save for a slight frown on her gaunt, pale face. When Kress had finished, she said only, "I ought to leave you there."

Kress began to blubber. "You can't. Help me, I'll pay—"

"I ought to," Wo repeated, "but I won't."

"Thank you," Kress said. "Oh, thank—"

"Quiet," said Wo. "Listen to me. This is your own doing. Keep your sandkings well, and they are courtly ritual warriors. You turned yours into something else, with starvation and torture. You were their god. You made them what they are. That maw in your cellar is sick, still suffering from the wound you gave it. It is probably insane. Its behavior is . . . unusual.

"You have to get out of there quickly. The mobiles are not dead, Kress. They are dormant. I told you the exoskeleton falls off when they grow larger. Normally, in fact, it falls off much earlier. I have never heard of sandkings growing as large as yours while still in the insectoid stage. It is another result of crippling the white maw, I would say. That does not matter.

"What matters is the metamorphosis your sandkings are now undergoing. As the maw grows, you see, it gets progressively more intelligent. Its psionic powers strengthen, and its mind becomes more sophisticated, more ambitious. The armored mobiles are useful enough when the maw is tiny and only semisentient, but now it needs better servants, bodies with more capabilities. Do you understand? The mobiles are all going to give birth to a new breed of sandking. I can't say exactly what it will look like. Each maw designs its own, to fit its perceived needs and desires. But it will be biped, with four arms and opposable thumbs. It will be able to construct and operate advanced machinery. The individual sandkings will not be sentient. But the maw will be very sentient indeed."

Kress was gaping at Wo's image on the viewscreen. "Your workers," he said, with an effort. "The ones who came out here . . . who installed the tank . . . "

Wo managed a faint smile. "Shade," she said.

"Shade is a sandking," Kress repeated numbly. "And you sold me a tank of . . . of . . . infants, ah . . . "

"Do not be absurd," Wo said. "A first-stage sandking is more like a sperm than like an infant. The wars temper and control them in nature. Only one in a hundred reaches the second stage. Only one in a thousand achieves the third and final plateau and becomes like Shade. Adult sandkings are not sentimental about the small maws. There are too many of them, and their mobiles are pests." She sighed.

"And all this talk wastes time. That white sandking is going to waken to full sentience soon. It is not going to need you any longer, and it hates you, and it will be very hungry. The transformation is taxing. The maw must eat enormous amounts both before and after. So you have to get out of there. Do you understand?"

"I *can't*," Kress said. "My skimmer is destroyed, and I can't get any of the others to start. I don't know how to reprogram them. Can you come out for me?"

"Yes," said Wo. "Shade and I will leave at once, but it is more than two hundred kilometers from Asgard to you, and there is equipment that we will need to deal with the deranged sandking you've created. You cannot wait there. You have two feet. Walk. Go due east, as near as you can determine, as quickly as you can. The land out there is pretty desolate. We can find you easily with an aerial search, and you'll be safely away from the sandkings. Do you understand?"

"Yes," Kress said. "Yes, oh, yes."

They signed off, and he walked quickly toward the door. He was halfway there when he heard the noise, a sound halfway between a pop and a crack.

“Kress stopped suddenly. "No," he said, "oh, no. Oh, no." He backpedaled, slipped on the sand, got up, and tried to run again. They were ghastly little things with bulging eyes and dusky orange skin.”

One of the sandkings had split open. Four tiny hands covered with pinkish-yellow blood came up out of the gap and began to push the dead skin aside.

Kress began to run.

He had not counted on the heat.

The hills were dry and rocky. Kress ran from the house as quickly as he could, ran until his ribs ached and his breath was coming in gasps. Then he walked, but as soon as he had recovered, he began to run again. For almost an hour he ran and walked, ran and walked, beneath the fierce, hot sun. He sweated freely and wished that he had thought to bring some water, and he watched the sky in hopes of seeing Wo and Shade.

He was not made for this. It was too hot and too dry, and he was in no condition. But he kept himself going with the memory of the way the maw had breathed and the thought of the wriggling little things that by now were surely crawling all over his house. He hoped Wo and Shade would know how to deal with them.

He had his own plans for Wo and Shade. It was all their fault, Kress had decided, and they would suffer for it. Lissandra was dead, but he knew others in her profession. He would have his revenge. This he promised himself a hundred times as he struggled and sweated his way eastward.

At least he hoped it was east. He was not that good at directions, and he wasn't certain which way he had run in his initial panic, but since then he had made an effort to bear due east, as Wo had suggested.

When he had been running for several hours, with no sign of rescue, Kress began to grow certain that he had miscalculated his direction.

When several more hours passed, he began to grow afraid. What if Wo and Shade could not find him? He would die out here. He hadn't eaten in two days, he was weak and frightened, his throat was raw for want of water. He couldn't keep going. The sun was sinking now, and he'd be completely lost in the dark. What was wrong? Had the sandkings eaten Wo and Shade? The fear was on him again, filling him, and with it a great thirst and a terrible hunger. But Kress kept going. He stumbled now when he tried to run, and twice he fell. The second time he scraped his hand on a rock, and it came away bloody. He sucked at it as he walked, and he worried about infection.

The sun was on the horizon behind him. The ground grew a little cooler, for which Kress was grateful. He decided to walk until last light and settle down for the night. Surely he was far enough from the sandkings to be safe, and Wo and Shade would find him come morning.

When he topped the next rise, he saw the outline of a house in front of him.

It wasn't as big as his own house, but it was big enough. It was habitation, safety. Kress shouted and began to run toward it. Food and drink, he had to have nourishment, he could taste the meal already. He was aching with hunger. He ran down the hill toward the house, waving his arms and shouting to the inhabitants. The light was almost gone now, but he could still make out a half-dozen children playing in the twilight. "Hey there," he shouted. "Help, help."

They came running toward him.

Kress stopped suddenly. "No," he said, "oh, no. Oh, no." He backpedaled, slipped on the sand, got up, and tried to run again. They caught him easily. They were ghastly little things with bulging eyes and dusky orange skin. He struggled, but it was useless. Small as they were, each of them had four arms, and Kress had only two.

They carried him toward the house. It was a sad, shabby house, built of crumbling sand, but the door was quite large, and dark, and it breathed. That was terrible, but it was not the thing that set Simon Kress to screaming. He screamed because of the others, the little orange children who came crawling out of the castle, and watched impassively as he passed.

All of them had his face. ∞

PLANET STORY

How an army of lizards missed the train

A new pictorial novel by Harry Harrison and Jim Burns dramatizes the sense of experimentation publishers are now bringing to science fiction.

Planet Story opens with an eccentric space commander who decides that the fragile planet Sabinus is an ideal spot to pursue his hobby: driving antique locomotives. A monstrous machine is dispatched to lay track indiscriminately over the tiny planet's surface.

The mothership descends on Sabinus to off-load a gold-plated locomotive. The commander's entourage boards the train and roars off down computer-built tracks. It becomes immediately clear to everyone on board that Sabinus is not uninhabited. Lizardlike aliens appear everywhere. Their outrage at the earthling assault is a call to battle, but their puny spears are no match for the speeding train.

Having leveled one alien enclave, the train stops on the far side of a simulated London Bridge. The commander asserts that no manner of lizardoid "greenie" will disrupt his penchant for rodding and railing.

Illustrations from the book *Planet Story*, by Jim Burns and Harry Harrison. Published in the U.S. by A&W Publishers, Inc., and in the U.K. by Pierrot Publishing, Ltd.

❛Lasers burned to the accompaniment of shrill alien screams. Depressed by their newest failure, the lizards withdrew.❜

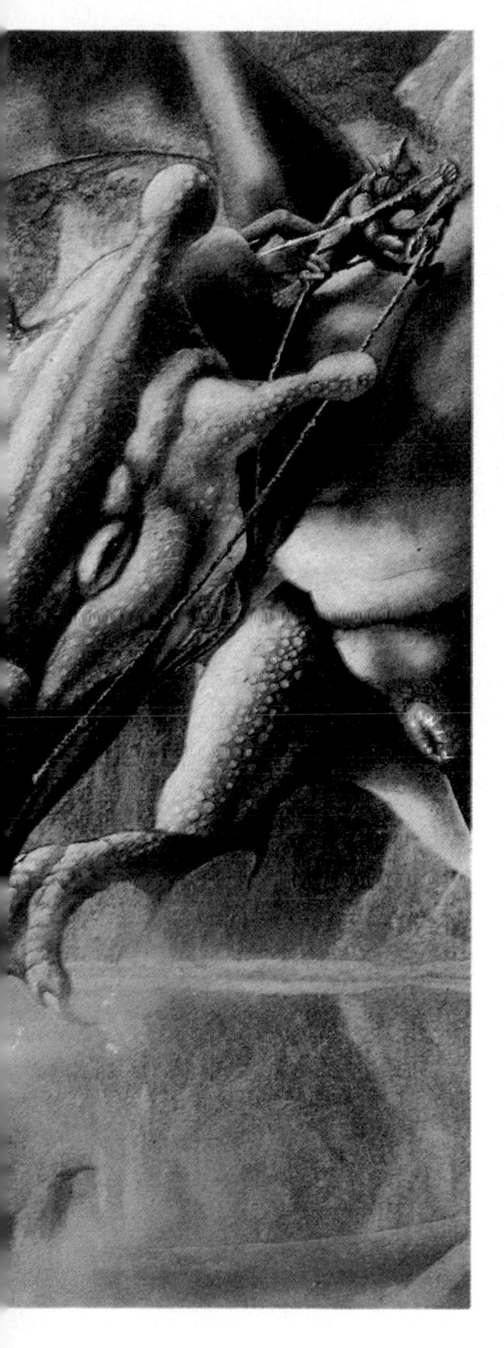

The commander's ruminations are rudely interrupted by a squadron of lizardoids straddling pterodactyllike beasts. Their armament, to everyone's astonishment, is feces. "They're divecrapping us!" yells the commander, confident that the aliens are harmless. The train lurches toward the next obstacle — a wall built across the tracks. From behind it the lizardoids pelt the locomotive with boulders. Short, powerful bursts of laser are the train's response. The aliens are gone long before their wall is.

"Supertrack cut the lizardoid city exactly in two, which is why the aliens had prepared a pointed welcome."

The train rolls on to the outskirts of what appears to be the capital of lizardoidom. Awaiting the locomotive is a giant spike set on the tracks, there to impale the oncoming earthlings. The time has come to parley with these aliens. Talking through a translator, the two sides reach an agreement: The train will go free if the humans help the lizardoids defeat the latter's mortal enemy, a gaggle of crustaceans. The lizardoids prepare to scout enemy lines in a spy balloon. Several humans go along.

As soon as those lizardoids grab us, they'll nationalize your railroad and you'll follow us through the kitchen.

The balloon veers too close to crustacean AA batteries and is shot down. In the melee that follows, our human heroine is captured and carried away to the lobster king. Far too smart for the crusty monarch, she quickly takes him prisoner. He offers to deal. His "people" are in trouble. The lizardoids want to eat them. Humans, he assures the commander, will be next. Convinced, the commander agrees to dupe the lizardoids into following his train away from the defenseless lobsters. Aware only at the last minute of this trickery, the lizard hordes charge after the train—but the locomotive is safe. It chugs off into the final episode of Planet Story, *brought to you by A&W Publishers (New York).*

"There's a tremendous amount of space travel going on around the universe. When a vehicle arrives here, we'll know about it"

INTERVIEW

ARTHUR C. CLARKE

In 1945, a young English technical officer who had spent World War II helping to develop radar systems for the Royal Air Force published a remarkably prescient article in the British journal *Wireless World*. The article showed in detail how artificial satellites could be used to relay electronic communications around the world. The writer was Arthur C. Clarke.

Thus began the most remarkable marriage of far-flung imagination and realistic scientific fact in the history of English letters, for, as much as anyone, Clarke has been a founder of the Space Age. In his writings, both fiction and nonfiction, Clarke has been the Space Age's prophet and one of its chief movers.

His books are world renowned, and his writing has earned international awards. Less well known is the fact that he helped to push a doubting scientific community into serious consideration of space flight, back in the days when "shooting for the moon" was synonymous with attempting the impossible.

As chairman of the British Interplanetary Society, Clarke encouraged scientists and engineers to look at the real possibilities of space travel. His invention of the communications satellite was a natural outgrowth of his ceaseless search for the practical realities that would bring the dream of space flight into useful life.

In his science-fiction stories and novels, he painted future scenarios in which space travel was an integral and irreplaceable part of human life in the very near future. In his nonfiction articles and books, he presented powerful arguments for exploring space—and the inner depths of Earth's oceans.

His nonfiction works include such classics as *Interplanetary Flight*, *The Exploration of Space*, *Profiles of the Future*, *Voices from the Sky*, and *The Promise of Space*. His science-fiction novels are, if anything, even better-known around the world. Perhaps Clarke's most stunning contribution was his screenplay (with Stanley Kubrick) and novel, *2001: A Space Odyssey*.

Clarke now resides in Sri Lanka, where he was interviewed exclusively for *Omni* by journalist-photographer Malcolm Kirk.

Photograph by Malcolm S. Kirk

SRI LANKA, MARCH 1979

Omni: I understand you have given up writing for good. About any subject whatsoever, or simply about science fiction?

Clarke: I won't even write a one-sentence blurb for the jackets of books for my best friends. I mean, I have to be absolutely firm, because once you've made exceptions, you know, you can't stop. I've said all I want to say in both fiction and nonfiction, at least at this point. But that doesn't mean in five years or so I won't recharge my batteries and start writing again. I may get involved in controversy from time to time. In fact, in the local papers I'm having a controversy with some astrological people who think that the planets are going to be lined up at Christmas 1982 and all hell will break loose. And I had fun pointing out that this is utter nonsense, the planets aren't lined up in '82. So occasionally things like this will trigger me off, but I don't expect to do any writing.

In *The View from Serendip* I have put all my recent nonfiction essays, and particularly Sri Lanka articles, and sort of wrapped that all up. On the fiction side, I'm sure I'll never do anything as good as *The Phantoms of Paradise* [Harcourt Brace Jovanovich]. Everything came together in it—the locale, the theme. I got the biggest theme I've ever tackled: a serious, real theme which may involve the large-scale exploitation of space on a scale never dreamed of, even by people like Gerard O'Neill with his space colonies. And yet, this is real hard engineering. All sorts of things have come together—religion, philosophy—in this one book.

Also, I want to enjoy my declining years and have some time for skin diving. I've learned to play the piano, a secret ambition I've had all my life and never dreamed I'd have the chance of realizing. I've got a library of videotapes I'm building up.

Omni: On what subjects?

Clarke: Mostly science. It started with a commercial I did for the Bell Telephone System when they made a two-hour version of *The Man in the Iron Mask*, a fine performance with Louis Jourdan, Ralph Richardson, and the star Richard Chamberlain, a very fine actor. Then the Bell System flew a team out here to film me in Sri Lanka, and they gave me a video system so I could see the result. So now I'm building up a library with a lot of science programs, and also, I've got a 16mm library that I'm building up.

Omni: Do you film much yourself?

Clarke: We used to do quite a bit of filming. A partner of mine and I made a film called *Beneath the Seas of Ceylon* for the Ceylon tourist board. A thirteen-minute 16mm film. Then we did a two-hour Ceylonese epic that was a smash hit and is still one of the best films ever made on the local market—in color, original sound, original music, a really first-rate film. We reissued it after more than ten years, and it is packing them in.

And the next thing I did was *2001*.

Omni: Have you ever intended, after *2001*, to get involved in anything else major?

Clarke: No, because when one starts at the top like that, where do you go from there?

Omni: Was there at one point any talk of doing a film version of *Childhood's End*?

Clarke: There's always talk of doing a film version of *Childhood's End*. I started the movie more than twenty years ago, and at the moment there's a cease-and-desist order out from my agent to Universal Studios, who claim they're making a tv version of it. I don't know what's going on. About five of my books have been sold to the movies.

Omni: Bob Guccione was very interested in working on some film with you, if you showed any interest at all. Do you think you would be interested or not?

Clarke: Well, I've spread the word around that if anyone wants to film any of my books, I'm willing to talk to them for a few days, here in Sri Lanka, or on the telephone, if they call at a reasonable hour. And I'll even look at scripts, although I hate scripts; movie scripts are terrible, they're meaningless, except to directors. But I'm quite willing to cooperate within limits. What I won't do is sit down at the typewriter for long periods of time when the sun is shining and the waves are sparkling at the reef.

But I'm willing to talk to anybody in general terms about projects and discuss things. I've got a stunning new opening for *Childhood's End* if anybody does want to film it.

Omni: Are there any other kinds of projects that you might be interested in working on—underwater or anything like that?

Clarke: On the underwater side, my partner, Hector Ekanayake, and his fiancée, Valerie Fuller, are taking divers out from all over the world. In fact, our most distinguished clients were the *Apollo 12* team when they came back from the moon. We took them diving in Trincomalee. So I'm surrounded by diving activities, and I hope to spend some time underwater. I have a bungalow on the south coast of the island in the most beautiful bay you can imagine and a lovely reef outside it.

Omni: What brought you to Sri Lanka in the first place? For how long are you here, and what keeps you here?

Clarke: Space brought me to Sri Lanka, I suppose, if you go back to the beginning. I became interested in underwater exploring and diving simply because I realized that it was the only way of reproducing the condition of weightlessness, which is characteristic of space flight. You aren't quite weightless, strictly speaking, underwater, but it's the nearest approximation you can get for any length of time. So that's why I learned diving.

Omni: How long ago was that?

Clarke: This was in the late forties. I went to the Great Barrier Reef in Australia, and on the way I passed through Sri Lanka and went out by the old *Himalaya* one afternoon and met some local divers and . . .

Omni: Excuse me, what's the *Himalaya*? Is that an old P. and O. [Pacific and Orient] ship?

Clarke: Yes; she's broken up now. And during the course of this I got more and more interested in the country. I met many friends and kept coming back and eventually settled down here. I just hate being anywhere else.

Omni: It seems an odd place to find a science-fiction writer. One would imagine you to be in Cambridge or Palo Alto, London or New York, and instead you've chosen a sort of chaotic situation here.

Clarke: I've been to all those places. I have friends in all. But because it is quiet here I have time to read all the material that's been sent me. I have at least twenty journals of various kinds and a vast correspondence, and everybody passes through Sri Lanka eventually. My friends come here. Bucky Fuller was here a few months ago, and we flew him around and showed him the locales of my new novel.

And there are also emotional, inner reasons for being here. It is a very nice way of living, as you can see. I finally got everything organized in this house, which I moved into four years ago. The only nightmare I've had is about leaving Sri Lanka.

Omni: Are you here all year at this point?

Clarke: I haven't been out of the country for a year. I don't plan to go out for another year, and then it will only be for a brief visit to England. And if I never leave again, that's fine with me. I know in fact I shall be going. Something very important may come up that I can't possibly turn down. But I've said half-jokingly, or maybe quarter-jokingly, that as much as I love America—and I have a great many friends there—the only thing that will get me back is when there's a seat in a space shuttle for me. I told the NASA administrator that.

Omni: How do you occupy yourself in a typical day here?

Clarke: Oh, my goodness. I've often tried to answer this question, and I found there's no such thing as a typical day. But I get tea at six-thirty and hear the Voice of America news; then at seven have breakfast and hear the BBC. Then my day starts about eight. My working day starts about eight o'clock. I've always got about twenty books waiting to be read. I count that I have about thirty-six hours of reading for every twenty-four hours. The mail bombs me out. And then I try to get in at least an hour on the piano. I have anything up to ten visitors a day.

Omni: What are they usually here to see you about?

Clarke: Sometimes they just come for autographs. A lot of diving people, of course. I normally never leave the house at all, except at four o'clock in the afternoon, when I go to the local swimming club and play a vicious game of table tennis for a couple of hours. That's my only recreation. I am a table-tennis addict. I can still beat most of the amateurs there. Then I come back and may have a film show, may listen to some music and get to bed quite early, around nine o'clock. I never go to receptions, cocktail parties, dinners, simply because they're so time-consuming.

Omni: No more bashing away at the typewriter?

Clarke: No; I haven't used a typewriter since January, I suppose. I'm thinking of taking the typewriter down to the reef and photographing it surrounded by fish.

Omni: You're not active in the scuba diving or the school?

Clarke: I haven't been active in that way for a long time. I became totally paralyzed in 1962 as a result of a spinal injury, and I was a basket case for many months. I'm lucky to be alive, let alone to be able to move around. And I never recovered my strength, so I've got to take things rather carefully. But I still enjoy snorkeling when I have a chance of doing it. I can still stay underwater for a minute by my own power if I have to. I used to be able to stay underwater for nearly four minutes, even though I didn't take up diving until I was nearly thirty.

Omni: Hyperventilating?

Clarke: Yes, which is dangerous, a stupid thing to do.

Omni: Are you actively involved in any programs connected with the ocean?

Clarke: Yes; I am fighting to save the reefs here. The coral reefs have been smashed up to make lime, and around the tourist centers you'll see hundreds of people smashing up the beautiful reefs, right beside the hotels. It's incredible. It's against the law, but there's such an economic pressure to do it that no one is able to stop it. I'm also trying to set up marine sanctuaries.

Omni: Do you see exciting developments in the future of oceanographic exploration, work with dolphins—things along those lines?

Clarke: Well, I've always been fascinated by dolphins, and I have written a couple of books about them. *Dolphin Island*, I mentioned, is being filmed by Radnitz Productions. I've tried to get them to come here, although the story takes place on the Great Barrier Reef. Of course, the ocean is the other great frontier, as everybody says. I mean, this is a cliché now. The most important thing in the ocean at the moment is probably oil and deep-sea mining, which is now held up with the problem of getting international agreement. The other thing I'm interested in, which is rather speculative, is ocean thermal power. That's the use of the temperature differential in the tropical oceans, where it is always about eighty degrees [F] or more on the surface and thirty-five or so a mile down. I wrote "The Shining Ones" on this theme. It was set in Trincomalee, in Sri Lanka—there was a deep canyon coming right in close to land, so you had deep water very close to land, and this is an ideal place for it.

I wrote this story partly to alert people to the possibilities. I've done that several times, although as a rule I'm very much against writing fiction to teach people. According to Sam Goldwyn, "If you got a message, use Western Union." But that is one story that I did do for that purpose, to make people think of ocean thermal power. But the classic case is my story "I Remember Babylon." That was about the possibility of communication satellites, before there were any communication satellites. Although that story is, I hope, worth reading as a story, it was a deliberate attempt to say communication satellites are possible—they can make a big difference to your world.

Omni: Someone mentioned that you have the only tv set in Sri Lanka. Is that true? You can't receive any image, can you?

Clarke: This video system here is, of course, closed, and when we do get tv here, which will be next year, it will be a different system anyway. But I did have in fact the only television receiver in the country two years ago and, as far as I know, the only privately owned Earth-satellite station in the world.

In 1976, the Indians had this very important experiment, broadcasting educational programs from a satellite loaned by NASA.

❛Space brought me to Sri Lanka. I was interested in diving here simply because it is the only way of reproducing the condition of weightlessness, which is characteristic of space flight.❜

It was called the Satellite Instructional Television Experiment. And to my delight and surprise, the Indian Space Research Organization flew in a complete ground station, set it up on my roof, and gave it to me so I could see the programs. For one year, I had the only set on the island. And everybody, from the president down, came to see the television programs.

Omni: Is there going to be any follow-up on this? Have they stopped it altogether?

Clarke: Well, the satellite was only on loan for one year, and now it's gone back and is doing much the same thing for the Eskimos and over the western United States. The Indians will have to follow on fairly quickly with their own satellite.

Omni: Do you think the current interest in science fiction is a passing fad? Or do you think it indicates a wider interest among the population at large in the near future?

Clarke: There's always been a background of interest in science fiction. It's always been popular, whether it's been called science fiction or not. Right back to Verne and Wells and then to the modern era with the science-fiction magazines. Almost any number of well-known writers have tried their hand at science fiction at some time or another, some with disastrous results, some with good results. H. Bruce Franklin wrote a book, *Future Perfect*, claiming that every major American writer had written some science fiction, and his anthology, which is an interesting one, tries to prove his point. The first robot language in English fiction was written by Herman Melville, for instance, something not generally realized. I'm afraid the pulp magazines tended to degrade science fiction in many ways and ghettoize it. And now it's becoming slowly recognized and respected, and people are not turned off by it. Obviously, judging by *Star Wars* and *Close Encounters of the Third Kind*, which I haven't yet seen.

Omni: I was just going to ask you about that.

Clarke: I am dying to see *Close Encounters*. I've seen *Star Wars* twice and thoroughly liked it, like everybody except a few tough-nosed characters. I think it's a marvelous film. At its level, I don't see how it could be improved. I do appreciate George Lucas's saying that *2001* is better. Well, you can't really compare the two. It's like comparing steak-and-kidney pudding with strawberries and cream. *Close Encounters* I've not yet seen. Obviously this is a new phenomenon. There's a great deal of interest in the universe and great possibilities, and of course I'm very happy about this.

Omni: How do you think *Omni* fits into this, by the way?

Clarke: I was really very impressed. The contents were uniformly interesting. There was none or very little of the nonsense I'd rather feared. I mean, you can't keep the UFO people out. The treatment of that sort of thing in the fringe sections was very sensible. I felt in many ways that it was the sort of magazine I'd like to have designed for myself.

Omni: What else would you like to see in *Omni*?

Clarke: I would like to see a hard-nosed treatment of some of the cranks who are littering the scene and fringes of science. Some of my friends, like Martin Gardner and James Randi, are trying to put some sense into the public about Uri Geller, who I think is now more or less discredited. Although I like Uri. I think he's a real charmer. And the Bermuda Triangle, which is, of course, utter nonsense.

I think it would be a pity if there weren't some people like that around to liven up the world, but what does annoy me are the Von Dänikens and the ancient-astronaut people, because I do take this very seriously. Because of their activities it's now almost impossible to get an important subject taken as seriously as it should be. I hope *Omni* can do something about this. Of course, there's nothing you can do about the complete nuts, the religious maniacs who believe in flying saucers landing all the time. I mean, they're just mad, and that's all there is to it.

Omni: What are your feelings about things like telepathy and UFOs and faith healing?
Clarke: Well, you've put a bunch of different things together. In general, I've always been interested in ESP, and, of course, *Childhood's End* was about that. But I've grown disillusioned, partly because after all this time they're still arguing about whether these things happen. I suspect that telepathy does happen, partly because the evidence seems so overwhelming. On the other hand, you have to have a much higher level of evidence for this kind of thing than for anything else. Something strange is going on.

Obviously, we don't know all about the universe. As far as psychokinesis, metal bending, and that sort of thing . . . I've stood beside Geller when he bent my door key, and I think I know how he did it. People like Randi are quite sure they know how he did it.
Omni: How do you think he did it?
Clarke: First of all, there's always chaos around Uri, and several things are happening at once. No one is quite sure what went on at any given time. You'd have to have three video cameras, X, Y, and Z, watching him. I've seen good conjurers do the same sort of thing that he does. And I've seen some conjurers do some things that I still, to this day, don't know how they possibly could have done. Unless you're a professional conjurer, it's utterly useless for a layman to even comment on this. And it's amazing how few scientists seem to realize this.
Omni: You do have an open mind, to a certain extent?
Clarke: It's getting less and less open. I suspect that telepathy occurs, and I suspect that some kind of precognition occurs, partly because I had some experience myself, but it's very hard to rule out coincidence.
Omni: We've talked on this trip to someone who said he's never suffered from headaches, and yet one particular morning he had the most splitting headache that he'd ever had in his life. Later that morning he found out his son had died.
Clarke: There are so many examples of this. Yet, it's hard to get a statistical correlation. You forget the misses and remember the hits. So how can one prove that even the hits are significant, because anything, no matter how fantastic, can happen by pure coincidence. And it's difficult to quantify this.

One person you might get on to is Professor Louis Alvares, the Nobel Laureate in physics at Berkeley. Louis is a man who invented ground-control-approach radar. Louis then assembled the first atomic bomb. Then he got the Nobel Prize for physics a few years ago, and he's perhaps one of the most distinguished American physicists. Well, he's tackled this problem of coincidences and the paranormal and has written a number of interesting letters to science about it.
Omni: What's your own opinion about UFOs?
Clarke: When I'm asked this question, which I have been asked approximately a hundred thousand times, of course, I say when you've seen as many UFOs as I have, you won't believe in them. And this is not entirely a flip answer. I've seen maybe ten now, and every one of them would have convinced the layman.

Having been through the mill, I'm totally uninterested in UFOs now. I'm as convinced as one can be that they're unimportant. But I can't be sure. I had an absolute beauty the other night in back of my house, one of the best I've ever seen. It turned out to be the local net balloon caught by the sunlight, and I was able to prove this by getting the position of the MET balloon. But in other cases, of course, one can never find out what it is one saw, and so the mystery remains. The only UFOs I'm interested in now are ones where people see and approach an artifact and forget all about lights in the sky, mystery things. We should only be concerned with close encounters. Either they exist or they don't exist. Forget all the others and let's just concentrate on the reports of close encounters. They're the only ones that matter, if they do exist. If anyone reports that there's a *Tyrannosaurus rex* loose in Central Park, I'd be skeptical. But I'm quite certain that we'd know for sure very shortly. The same with flying saucers.

❛We should only be concerned with close encounters. Either they exist or they don't. If anyone reported a Tyrannosaurus rex loose in Central Park I'd verify it quite quickly; same with flying saucers.❜

Omni: Then you're skeptical, but you don't dismiss them out of hand?
Clarke: I take it for granted there's a tremendous amount of space traffic going on around the universe, and I'm quite sure that when one vehicle arrives here, we'll know about it. That's why I can't believe it's been going on in recent times. I think it's more probable that in the remote past, maybe even historic times, there may have been visitors, but the universe is so huge, it's hard to believe that there can be all that amount of traffic in this local area.
Omni: Do you think that everything that's reported now has to be explicable in terms of current scientific understanding?
Clarke: Obviously there's a vast amount that we don't know. In fact, I'm very fond of quoting Haldane's "The universe is not only queerer than we imagine; it's queerer than we can imagine."
Omni: Have you personally seen any unusual phenomena besides the experiences you've just recounted?
Clarke: No, they all turn out to be sort of explicable in the long run, even though I'm sure that many of the astronomical and atmospherical phenomena I've seen would have fooled the average layman who didn't know what they were. I'm really fond of pointing out Venus in the daylight. Venus is shining up there at the moment, and I could show it to you if it were clearer. People don't realize you can see a bright star in the daytime. And they see Venus—it's easy to see, but once you've lost it, it's very hard to find it again, so they think it's sort of shot off at an enormous speed. That's such a big old example.
Omni: Looking back on it, how accurate do you think you were in *Profiles of the Future* and *Prelude to Space*?
Clarke: Well, of course, *Prelude to Space* was written in 1948, and in detail it wasn't accurate. I had a horizontally launched, atomic-fueled spacecraft. But we're coming toward that sort of concept. The shuttle would look rather like my lunar spacecraft, even though the shuttle isn't atomically powered. I'm quite happy with my record as a whole, particularly with the communication satellite. Also, some of my other early ideas are now coming to the fore. The lunar-based electromagnetic launcher which Gerry O'Neill has made the basis of his scheme is one. He calls it the mass driver. This was worked out by me in 1950 or '51. It is the key to all these space-colonization plans.
Omni: If you were to update either of those books, would there be any changes that you would make?
Clarke: What I have done, in fact, is to write a new preface to *Prelude to Space*. I wouldn't dream of updating in the sense of changing the text of the book, any more than I'd dream of updating H. G. Wells's *War of the Worlds*. They're period pieces and must be left untouched in their own time stream. But what I have done is to set them in a modern perspective by comparing the reality of the Apollo program with my ideas of almost twenty years before. *Profiles of the Future*, again, I've updated with a new preface and footnotes, pointing out where things have diverged. In fact, I wrote *Profiles of the Future* with an eye to the pretty long-distance future, because I was fairly sure there'd be no major changes. And this has proved to be the case.
Omni: So the future doesn't appear to you any different now than it did at the time that you wrote those?
Clarke: Not in general. Of course, a lot of things have turned out different. The biggest surprise of all was the speed at which we got to the moon. Second-biggest

surprise was the speed at which we left the moon. No one would ever have dreamed that we'd have got to the moon by early 1969 and would have left it again by the early seventies, probably not be back again until the end of the century.

Omni: In *Rendezvous with Rama*, you described an elaborate space settlement. Do you think human beings are ready psychologically and socially for such a break with nature?

Clarke: When you talk about a break with nature, I mean just look at New York City. A lot of people live there perfectly happily. My friend Isaac Asimov is a city boy. He won't travel at all. Certainly not by air. But people like Isaac seem perfectly happy totally out of their natural environment. Isaac's *The Cage of Steel* is a perfect example of this. The human being is incredibly adaptable. Look at Hong Kong.

Omni: Yes, but there's this need to listen to water or to expose your body to the sun or smells. Even in that kind of artificial environment, we still need to get back to nature, don't we? We can't break that link.

Clarke: Yes. And I get the best of both worlds. In fact, I'm surrounded by trees, you see, and now some of these colonies they've been talking about are more back to nature than any of the cities. In fact, they're rather ridiculous. Parks transported into space ... which is feasible, I'm sure, but I think we'll do it different ways.

Omni: What do you think of the possibility of placing our industry out in space and keeping Earth as a natural wilderness?

Clarke: I think that perhaps many of the heavy industries and production systems may go to space, or I suggest the planet Mercury, where you have all the power you need from the sun and probably all the heavy metals as well. I don't want to mess up the moon. I want to preserve the lunar wilderness.

Omni: But you think that human beings can make that psychological break with Earth and live in those kinds of artificial environments?

Clarke: I'm sure that human beings can go anywhere and do anything as long as they know what they're doing and perhaps have some means of relaxation—if they need it. But, incredibly, some people don't seem to need it.

Omni: What ideas do you have about trying to communicate with extraterrestrial civilizations? Do you think we're setting about it the right way?

Clarke: Well, there isn't any other way we can do it at the moment except listen to the radio, and I'm appalled that Senator Proxmire has succeeded in destroying the first attempts to set up a listening system. He sort of got the SETI project thrown out of Congress, and in fact has even awarded it the Golden Fleece, which is his sarcastic term for the project which he thinks is least worthwhile. He doesn't seem to realize that with long-term imaginative projects you can never guarantee success. But unless you do have some of them, you'll never get anywhere. I'm sure Proxmire isn't such a fool as some of his statements suggest. I don't envy the congressmen who have the problem of selecting different budgets for different things, especially in view of the fiscal stringencies. You see what's happened today. Jimmy Carter has put out all these projects for improving the economy and ending inflation, and the dollar drops to the lowest level ever.

Omni: How do you think we ought to communicate with possible civilizations out in space? I was reading an interesting little book called *Lives of a Cell* that suggested music be our form of communication.

Clarke: That was the idea in *Close Encounters*, wasn't it?

Omni: That's right.

Clarke: I think that's wrong, because I don't think music is the form of communication. You don't know how difficult it is to make any sense of Eastern music for Western ears. So I think music may turn out to be a very restricted thing.

> *"The biggest surprise was the speed at which we got to the moon. Second-biggest surprise was the speed at which we left the moon, probably not to be back until the end of the century."*

Omni: How would you do it, yourself?

Clarke: By logic and mathematics, which must be universal.

Omni: What kind of information do you think we ought to send out?

Clarke: Well, it's too late. We've sent out so much now that that's all been settled years ago. Unfortunately, think of all the super-civilizations looking at *I Love Lucy*.

Omni: What sort of repercussions do you think there would be if we were to learn we are alone in the universe?

Clarke: Well, we can never learn that, of course, because the universe is so enormous that if we go on for the next hundred million years exploring it and finding nobody, we can't be quite sure that over the next hill there isn't someone. I admit that after the next hundred million years or so it will look more and more like there's nobody there. Just as at the moment on Mars, even though we've only looked at two landing sights, we found no trace of anything, and so it seems probable that there's no life on Mars. But we can't be sure, by any means.

Omni: What do you see as the most interesting developments in the near future, technology oriented—social change?

Clarke: Hmmm ... I don't think anything unexpected. Well, obviously if it was unexpected I wouldn't be thinking of it. Usually it is the unexpected things which are the most important. But as far as one can see on the horizon at the moment: the coming computers and the communications revelations. Maybe home computers. Not only home computers, but the computer revolution. Microprocessors are getting into everything. We won't be able to pick up a single piece of equipment in the near future, except maybe a broom, that hasn't got a microprocessor in it.

Omni: How will they affect our lives, in a very general sense?

Clarke: They'll take over much of the routine thought. Now what this is going to do to culture, to education, to art, is the big problem. A lot of people are very worried. Let's take a case that everybody knows about now—the hand calculator. No one's going to learn arithmetic, but does this mean they'll go on to learn more real mathematics? It could well be. Because one of the beauties of the hand calculator is that it encourages you to do all sorts of calculations that you would never dream of doing if you had to do them by pencil and paper, because they would be too tedious. It can act as a wonderful toy and interest children in mathematics. On the other hand it may produce a generation of—what's the equivalent of illiterates?—enumerates who can't add up a grocery bill. So you have these two possibilities. And that's why we have a real challenge.

Omni: I seem to remember Huxley saying in *Brave New World* that the most decisive changes in the future would be biological changes rather than technological ones. Do you agree with that or not?

Clarke: I don't think biological changes in the sense of human biology. Obviously, biology is going to be very important, and genetic engineering too. That's already starting. It's going to have a revolutionary impact on society. Now they've got the first patent for a new organism issued by the patent office. That would have been incredible a few years ago. We can produce insulin now from purely biological, microbiological methods, and if anyone can succeed in getting a nitrogen-fixing organism, that will remove one of the main fertilizer problems. The impact on the Third World will be enormous. All sorts of terrific possibilities. Also some negative ones. People are worried about this recombinant-DNA work. I think that fear is greatly exaggerated, though I'm not an expert in this area.

Omni: Are you gloomy or optimistic about the future in terms of the way we're going to utilize information that we're receiving? Do you think we're going too far, too fast? Do you think it's time to pause?

Clarke: No, we can never pause. You fall flat on your face if you do. I'm an optimist. We have a 51 percent chance of survival. ∞